HE TOUCHED HER . . . AND SHE WAS ONE BURNING FEVER OF DESIRE

Justin lay down beside her, gathered her into his arms, and Caroline could feel the flame of his body against her own as she arched beneath him, inviting, demanding. She could hear his gasping breath, she could feel his leashed-in passion—and sensation, such as she had never known, shot through her like a ribbon of fire. She was burning, mad with longing.

He began kissing her, his lips exploring, his tongue teasing, teasing. And even as she moaned in weak protest, Caroline knew that before Justin had entered her life she had been but a poor imitation of a woman. She had been born for this joy, for these tearing explosions of delight. . . .

SAVAGE EDEN

Big Bestsellers from SIGNET

SAVAGE EDEN

— by —

Constance Gluyas

A SIGNET BOOK from
NEW AMERICAN LIBRARY
TIMES MIRROR
PUBLISHED BY
THE NEW AMERICAN LIBRARY
OF CANADA LIMITED

To My Husband, Don, Always with Love.
And to My Mother, Who Has Found Her Own Eden.
And My Aunt Violet,
My Very Dear and Peculiar Aunt.

*NAL Books are also available at discounts in bulk quantity
for industrial or sales-promotional use. For details, write to
Premium Marketing Division, New American Library, Inc.,
1301 Avenue of the Americas, New York, New York 10019.*

First Signet Printing, October, 1976

1 2 3 4 5 6 7 8 9

 SIGNET TRADEMARK REG. U.S. PAT. OFF. AND FOREIGN COUNTRIES
REGISTERED TRADEMARK — MARCA REGISTRADA
HECHO EN WINNIPEG, CANADA

SIGNET, SIGNET CLASSICS, MENTOR, PLUME AND
MERIDIAN BOOKS are published in Canada by The New
American Library of Canada Limited, Scarborough, Ontario

PRINTED IN CANADA
COVER PRINTED IN U.S.A.

Part I
London, 1700

❧

Chapter 1

The people were jammed tightly together on either side of long and narrow Bellrood Street. They had been gathering since the early hours of the morning to witness the flogging and the public humiliation of Caroline Fane, the convicted murderess, adulteress, and thief.

Caroline Fane gave no sign that she was aware of her audience. Already, although the procession to advertise her shame had started off from Newgate Prison a scant fifteen minutes ago, she was a pitiful sight. To make her humiliation the more complete, her bodice had been torn from her shoulders. Even for the month of June, the sunshine beating down on her half-naked body had a fierce and unusual intensity that was an added torture. The delicate skin of her wrists was rubbed raw from the thin leather thongs that bound her tightly to the tail of the cart. Her back was marked by a crisscross pattern of red lines that, as yet, oozed only small beads of blood, showing that the full savagery of her punishment had not yet begun. Drawn along by the slow-moving cart, she stumbled over the rough raised cobbles, her bare feet cut and bleeding.

"Shame!" a voice cried. The crowd, given a lead, took fire from this, and various epithets were hurled. "Whore! Filthy trollop! Murdering cow!"

Caroline Fane heard. She was innocent, but they cried out against her. Let them! Let them all do their worst! She had done with pleading innocence to ears that would not hear. The lash whistled through the air, landing on her back and bringing with it an explosion of pain. She stumbled, almost falling. Recovering herself, she clamped her lips tightly together to stifle her scream. She continued to stare straight ahead, trying to pretend indifference to the barrage of jeers and insults, but feeling—the feeling that she had fought so hard to stifle—was trying to break through her assumed indifference. With a tremendous effort of will she raised her head in the haughty and arrogant way she had been noted and condemned for throughout her trial.

The trial! A shudder went through Caroline. Standing there in the hot, stuffy courtroom, bewildered, frightened, that defiant gesture had been her only defense against those who sought to prosecute her for a crime she had not committed. It was her defense now against all the staring and hating eyes. Caroline bit down hard on her lower lip as the lash seared her back again. In that courtroom, her fevered thoughts roved on, she had made her plea of innocence not once but several times. On each occasion it had been swept aside. The matter was ended. Her accusers had made up their minds that she was guilty, and no words from her would sway their conviction. She thought of the fate that awaited her, and her heart began an agitated thumping. In a few days' time she would mount the scaffold. The rope would be placed about her neck! O God! Merciful God! Give me the courage to die bravely. Allow me that much pride!

The cart turned a corner and made its lumbering way down Wychmore Street. There was a mad scramble as the people, fighting to retain favorable positions of viewing, went with it. The driver of the cart, his face surly, his feelings disgruntled by the turn of events, hawked loudly and spat a gob of phlegm over the side of the cart. This whipping at the cart tail, coming as it did on the same day as the Monday hangings at Tyburn, was forcing him to miss some rare sport, the hanging of Justin Lawrence, the "Smiling Rogue," as he was known. The driver hawked and spat again. Aye, the Smiling Rogue had led the law a merry chase before he had finally been captured. With a sudden spurt of pure malice, the driver urged his flagging horse to a slightly brisker pace. Caroline Fane! Bah! What cared he for that murdering bitch! Let her lose her footing. Maybe she would fall on her face. That ought to spoil her pretty looks!

Unlike the driver, who had a single desire, the crowd keeping pace with the cart and urging the flogger on was torn between the two: the hangings at Tyburn, always a popular event, and an almost equal desire to see the Fane creature soundly flogged for her crimes. The eyes fixed on Caroline Fane showed a variety of emotions—hatred, shocked horror, indignation, simple curiosity, and the bright feverish gleam of those who enjoyed cruelty for its own sake and lusted for blood.

The story of the prisoner's infamy went whispering through their ranks. Caroline Fane looked to be no older than nineteen years, twenty at the most, and yet she had first cuckolded her elderly merchant husband with a number of lovers, and then, not content with this betrayal of a good man, she had finally ended his life by administering to him a poison that had brought on a horrible and painful death. But even that had not been enough for the trollop! She had barely waited for the merchant to draw his last gasping breath before she had calmly set about the task of ransacking his house of everything of value she could find. Nothing was too bad for such an evil creature. No punishment too severe. It was right that they, as public-spirited citizens, should witness her well-deserved punishment. As long as the flogger managed to keep her alive so that she would not cheat the hangman, honor and public indignation would be satisfied.

Those of the crowd who had decided to see the flogging through to the end began to hurl angry comments at the driver of the cart. It was feared that his increased speed would rob them too soon of their full enjoyment. Glaring truculently, grunting, the man unwillingly slowed the animal's pace.

Full attention was once more focused upon the prisoner. It was generally felt that Caroline Fane, as a target for their scorn and horror, was unsatisfactory. They wanted to see her break down under the punishing blows, to hear her scream aloud, to beg for mercy. That she did none of these things roused them to a frenzy, causing their hatred to reach out to her. They looked at her torn feet and her lacerated back, and they wondered how she could continue so proud and so stubbornly silent. They stared at the slender figure, at the small, shapely head, the matted and sweat-darkened blond hair. To their bewildered anger, they noticed that her large, soft, dark-brown eyes, which now and again turned to them briefly, seemed to hold an expression that was almost contempt. That whore! How dared she look at them as if they were dirt? "Murderess! Thief! Dirty slut!"

One man, his hand rubbing at his crotch, his lustful eyes fixed on the prisoner's bare breasts, exclaimed in a hoarse, excited voice, "Will you jus' look at them tits o' hers. It do seem a shame to bury 'em in the ground, don't it? Might never have been caught, that bitch, if it hadn't been for old Bill."

"Old who?" his companion queried.

The first man, continuing with his furtive exercise, his eyes still fixed on the bobbing breasts, was nonetheless eager to show off his knowledge of the case against Caroline Fane. He told of how Bill, an old man who hawked lavender from a pitch on the corner of Parchfield Street, where the Fanes had lived, had seen Caroline Fane hurriedly emerging from the house of death. Old Bill had not known then that murder had been committed; rather, it was the distraught expression on Mistress Fane's usually calm face that had aroused his curiosity and had caused him, on a whim, to follow her. It later transpired that he had followed her to the very house where she had intended to hide herself until the hue and cry should be over. It was when Bill heard of the cold-blooded murder of the kindly merchant Thomas Fane that he thought it to be his duty to come forward with his story. So, when commanded to do so, he had led the law to Caroline Fane's hiding place.

"And she was still there?"

Regretfully, the other man abandoned his rubbing. "Aye, she was there, all right. Took her off to Newgate Prison right away, they did. Didn't take 'em long to bring her to justice, neither."

"Did she plead innocent?"

"O' course she did. Don't they all?"

"How d'you know she's not innocent?"

"How do a bird know how to fly! 'Course she's guilty, you gudgeon! There jus' ain't no getting aroun' that."

"What about them things she stole? The law find 'em?"

"No. Never did. Bill said, when he followed her, that she wasn't carryin' nothin' wi' her."

"Then what do you think she did with them valuables?"

"How'd I know? Maybe she's got some kind o' hiding place in her old home. Likely she was hoping to get back there an' recover the stuff. But if you was to ask me, I think . . ." The man broke off with a startled gasp as a woman, pushing past him, ran toward the prisoner.

The woman, her face purple with the heat and distorted with passion, lifted her hand with two fingers stiffly extended in the sign to ward off evil. "Witch!" she shrieked in a high, hysterical voice. "Murderess! Witch! Hanging's too good for the likes of you. You should be burned at the stake. If I had my way, I'd be the one to pile the fagots around your feet!"

Emboldened by this outburst, another woman broke from the crowd. Her eyes blazing, her mouth ugly with hatred, she caught at the remnants of the gown hanging about Caroline Fane's hips. "Come on," she shouted in a loud, challenging voice, "let's strip the bleedin' harlot naked!"

The flogger, who had been momentarily taken aback, raised his whip menacingly. "Get back, the lot o' you. You ain't getting your 'ands on 'er. She's got to be brung in safe an' sound so's the 'angman can 'ave 'er."

Still gripping the gown, the woman gave him a defiant look. "Whyn't you let us have her? Look at her. She don't show no proper feelings, she don't. Know what that means? It means that she ain't got no shame, that she ain't human!"

"Don' matter none about that. I said for you to get back."

The woman capitulated with bad grace. "All right, I'll get back. But first I got to do this." Releasing her grip on the ragged skirt, the woman screwed up her mouth and spat in the prisoner's face. "That's what I think of you, murdering trollop that you are!"

There was no response from Caroline Fane, yet her eyes had taken on a curiously blank look. It was as though she walked in her sleep, removed from them. Unseeing, unhearing, unfeeling.

"Cut her!" a man yelled. "Go on, cut her. Let's see blood! Let's see bone!"

The flogger looked fearfully from side to side. It was not unknown for an angry crowd to take things into their own hands. He must lay it on a bit harder, and chance the girl dying. As he lifted the heavy whip with its weighted tip, a small shower of stones struck him. His arm dropped. "What you bloody people want o' me?" he bawled. "I ain't supposed to kill 'er, see. Me orders is to save 'er for the 'angman's rope."

"Lay it on harder, then. Cut her! Ribbon the witch up!"

Again the flogger's eyes shifted uneasily. No matter what his orders were, it might be wiser to play up to them. He had no fancy to have them turn on him and rend him. His brawny arms emerging from his sleeveless leather jerkin

bulged as he flexed his muscles, the skin about them glistening as though it had been oiled. Grinning, he postured for
them. Then, sensing their impatience, he lifted his right arm
high, flourishing the whip. A breathless silence fell as they
waited for the blow to descend upon Caroline Fane's narrow
back. In the stillness, the voice of the priest, who, in accord-
ance with the rules, followed four paces behind the flogger,
could be clearly heard. Both hands holding aloft a large
golden crucifix, he chanted, "Repent ye, O miserable sinner.
Repent ye, lest ye be cast into everlasting darkness. Blessed
Lord, look well upon this sinner." The priest saw that the
blow was about to descend, and, determined to be heard, he
raised his voice to a shout. "Repent ye, sinner! The hour of
repentance is now!"

Caroline was felled by the monstrous and shocking force
of the blow. Lights seemed to explode in her brain, glaring
first white, then changing to bloodred. Dear God! The blows
that had gone before were as nothing to this one that had
bludgeoned her to her knees. This was an agony she had
never known, had never thought to know. Pain! Sweet Christ,
help me! In all the world there was only pain! A scream tore
from her throat, a raw, spiraling sound, like a tortured animal's. She screamed again and again as her writhing body
was dragged over the rough cobbles.

At this first sign of human feeling, the crowd went wild.
They watched without pity as her helpless body was dragged
over the cobbles. They exclaimed with all the glee of malicious children as they pointed out to each other the painful
upward-straining position of her arms, caused by wrists still
firmly bound to the cart tail, her contorted face, her wide-
open screaming mouth, and her long blond hair, fouled by
the filth and rubbish that lay in the untended street. Blood
welled from the great wound the lash had torn in her flesh,
dyeing her upper body red. Now primitive feelings overwhelmed the crowd. Stamping, whistling, cheering, they urged
the flogger on. A voice screamed out in trembling and uncon-
trolled excitement. "More! More! Lash her again!" The
crowd took up the cry, a piercing scream torn from many
throats. "Again! More!"

Carried away by the raw emotion on all sides, his face a
bright red from exertion, the flogger continued to rain blows
on the rolling figure. He had forgotten that his orders were to

keep the prisoner alive. For the moment he was the hero of the crowd.

The priest looked on, petrified, the crucifix held limply in his right hand. He found himself unable to move. Then, as common sense and a strong feeling of self-preservation came rushing back, he flinched inwardly. His was an extremely delicate position. He knew that later, when order was restored and the people had calmed down sufficiently to think, he would be blamed for this ghastly scene. Their blood lust dwindling and dying, they would tell themselves, those smug and righteous hypocrites, that it was not fitting for a man of the cloth to stand by and watch the savaging of a woman, even such a one as Caroline Fane. They would remember he had spoken no word of protest, and they would hold this against him. He, the man of God, sworn to carry out His precious word, had let them plunge into sin, and had not put out a hand to stay them.

The priest's thin lips twisted cynically. People! The more he dealt with them, listened to their confessions, their greed, the often petty motives that drove them, the more he distrusted them. It had been his experience that most people would generally list to the prevailing wind and take, as always, the most expedient way. Just as he knew that they must always look for a scapegoat upon whom to hang their guilts and their cowardly fears, those fears caused by their deliberate sinning and the prompting of uneasy consciences. If he did not act now, he would become that scapegoat. They would choose not to remember that theirs had been the voices that cried aloud for more blood, for a greater suffering.

"Stop!" The priest lunged forward and caught the flogger's arm in his hot, moist grip. Finding his voice lost in the babble all about him, he raised it to a bellow, at the same time holding the crucifix aloft. "Stop! In the name of merciful God, I command you to stop!"

Annoyed by the priest's interference, the flogger glared at him belligerently. But the raised crucifix, flashing brightly in the sun, awed the crowd and brought to the fore their fears of punishment for this day's work. The crucifix, like a flaming sword thrown into their midst, had become an impassable division between the will of the mob and the helpless girl.

The priest turned cold pale-blue eyes on the flogger. "Assist the maiden to her feet," he commanded in a clear, carrying voice. "God will punish her, and likewise the law of this land. It is not for such as you or I to usurp the rights of God and of justice." He glanced at Caroline Fane's crumpled and bloody form, then quickly averted his eyes. "There will be no more flogging today. You will cut her free and place her in the cart."

The flogger's eyes glittered with rage. Was he going to allow this long-nosed, pasty-faced priest to interfere with his duty? "Now, you look 'ere, Father," he snarled, "you ain't got no right to interfere wi' the law. I got me orders, and the law says she's got to be flogged."

The priest held the angry gaze steadily. "Flogged, yes. But where in your orders does it tell you that Mistress Fane is to be murdered at your hands?"

The briefly kindled fire died slowly from the flogger's eyes. "All right," he agreed in a sullen voice, "I won't flog 'er no more. But for all that, I ain't cutting 'er free. She'll 'ave to walk, same as all the prisoners do."

"Very well." The priest inclined his shaven head. "I must leave that to your conscience. If you feel the maiden has the strength to walk, then so be it."

"She's conscious, ain't she? Don't you fret yourself none about 'er, Father. She'll find the strength. They always do."

Caroline felt rough hands lifting her to her feet. Dimly, through the mist clouding her brain, it seemed to her that she heard the confused babble of many voices. People? So many of them. Where had they come from? And where was she? She whimpered with pain as something tugged hard at her wrists, forcing her feet to move forward. The whimper turned into a scream. She could not stand the pain! Her body felt as though it were wrapped about in a sheet of flame. It was agony to draw her breath. The scream died to a strangled sound of pure terror, and she flinched as the face of her husband loomed large and terrifying on her inner vision. Pain! It was associated with him. Thomas! Why had he done this to her? Why had he hurt her so cruelly? Was he punishing her because he was dead, because she had not stayed to weep over his cold, stiff body? But she had been so terribly afraid. Didn't he understand that? Wanting to be done with old ghosts, with the black and dragging memory of unhappiness, she said to the looming face, "Thomas, I did not know what else to do. I had to run away. Had to, had to!"

"Whore! Filthy wanton bitch!" Thomas struck her hard in the face. Her chest heaved as she fought to suck in air. Go away! she wanted to scream. Stay dead! But Thomas would not stay dead, for there he was again, looming larger than ever, his eyes slitted, hating her! She could see his scanty gray beard moving up and down as he spat out his venomous words. Watching him, she was sickened with loathing. Dear Christ, how she loathed and despised him!

She tried to turn away, but he was tugging at her wrists again, holding her captive to his will, forcing her to look at him. Staring into his hate-filled eyes, she was remembering that at first she had been very grateful to Thomas, for it had been his timely intervention that had saved her father from ruin. Oh, but even for gratitude she had not wanted to marry him! She would not have done so had not her father, her beloved but frighteningly weak father, made her see that it was the only way. Thomas Fane, he told her, would not lift a hand to help him, not if she refused to marry him. In the face of that, adoring her father despite all his faults, she had done what she must do to save him from debtors' prison.

At first, in the early days of the marriage, she had been timid and effacing, but for all that, she had tried very hard to please Thomas. But it seemed that she could do nothing right. Often, when he ranted at her, she would ask herself in despair why he had married her. Whore! Thomas called her. She was a whore who used his hard-earned money to scent her body and to clothe it in silk to tempt her lovers, her many lovers. He was insane! She had no lovers. And how could she scent her body, or buy silk to clothe it, on the paltry pittance Thomas allowed her?

She shuddered. When had she first begun to fear that narrow and suspicious mind of his, that mind that saw only evil in those about him? What chance of happiness had the marriage, when everything about him outraged and offended her fastidiousness? As if his eternal and chronic suspicion was not enough, there were other things too. His stale breath, his damp, thin hands, his pale, flabby body, and his penny-pinching ways. He was a wealthy middle-class merchant, but it seemed to bring him physical pain when he was forced to spend money for the necessities of life. Sometimes, though, as in her case, he realized that money could be used to good effect to buy something greatly desired. And in those early

days, he had greatly desired her, the Lady Caroline Flaxwell.
He had used his money shrewdly to buy her for his bride. After the marriage, the coffers had been tightly closed, lest she
make too many demands upon him.

A laugh shook her, causing the pain to leap to new fury.
Gasping for breath, she considered the Lady Caroline
Flaxwell. How pitifully ignorant of life, how naïve she had
been, that Caroline who had lived so peacefully and happily
in a manor house denuded of all its treasures. In vain attempts to pay off her father's vast gambling debts, she had
watched the treasures go one by one. And that same Caroline, watching her father sink deeper and deeper, day after
day, into an alcoholic haze, had at last become aware of the
clouding-up of her life. Desperate for a way to help him, she
had prayed with youthful intensity for a miracle. Her prayers
had been answered. The miracle, in the form of elderly
Thomas Fane, came walking through the front door of the
manor house. Her father owed Thomas a great deal of
money. But Thomas, whom she remembered seeing once or
twice, was willing to cancel her father's debt. Not only that,
he would pay off all the other creditors. She had been ready
to love him for his generosity, and for the relieved smile he
had set on her father's face, for she had not known then that
a price had been set upon it. The price was herself. Suddenly,
with bewildering rapidity, Lady Caroline Flaxwell, scarce out
of the schoolroom, had become Mistress Caroline Fane. The
nightmare had begun! The irony of it was that it had all been
in vain. A month after the marriage of his sixteen-year-old
daughter to her sixty-eight-year-old bridegroom, her father
had died of a seizure of the heart. Roger Flaxwell was no
more, but she was caught fast in the horror her life had become.

Caroline's thoughts scattered, and her eyes dilated in horror.
The heavy iron poker was in Thomas' hand, its tip glowing
white-hot. He was coming toward her! She tugged desperately
at her tightly bound hands, but she could not free herself.
He was coming toward her. Thomas, Thomas, don't hurt
me any more, don't! His voice roaring and booming in her
ears. "What must I do to keep you from your whoring ways?
Must I ruin that deceitful and lovely face of yours before I
can finally know peace? I'll do it, if I must! I'll do it, whore,
I will!"

Why did he always call her by that ugly name? There was no sense or reason in it. She hated him—she could not deny that to herself—but for all that, she had been faithful. How could he smear the few innocent friendships left over from the carefree days of her childhood with his vile, suspicious mind? There was William Thomas, her old playmate. But William was not only happily married, he was the proud and happy father of three children. There was Rupert Baxter, of course, who loved her for her father's sake and perhaps a little for her own. Surely Thomas could not suspect Rupert, that gentle, reserved, and scholarly man? But it seemed that he did. Then what must she do? Must she warn old friends to keep away, never on any account to visit her at the house?

God have mercy! While she had been thinking, Thomas had moved yet nearer. She could feel the heat of the poker on her face. "I'll do it!" He snarled the words at her. "I will, I will!"

"No! No!" her voice, yet sounding strangely unlike her own, screamed out in terror.

He was nearer still! Please God, stop him! Was it a direct answer to her prayer that made her pain dwindle so suddenly to nothing? She was free! Her body was weightless. And now she was running swiftly, leaving Thomas far behind. She ran on, her arms outstretched in love and longing, speeding back to that cool and green and peaceful past where Thomas had no voice, no name, no place.

It was no use. Thomas Fane's name, though only a shrinking whisper in her mind, was pushing the green peace and the happiness away. It was dwindling, vanishing. She could not hold on to it. The nightmare held her fast again. She was back in the house on Parchfield Street. The late-afternoon sunshine was pressing against the latticed windowpanes. She had been sleeping, for her cheek was still hot from its contact with the pillow. Something had awakened her. A noise. A dull thud.

She got up from the bed and made her way from the room. Creeping quietly and slowly down the stairs, she found that, for no reason she could think of, she was very frightened. No, she did not know what she feared. But the dark, narrow house seemed to brood about her, closing in, stifling her. Everything was so deathly still. Even the sounds of the busy life beyond the four walls of the house had a

muted and curiously unreal quality. She stopped for a moment, listening for Thomas' brisk footsteps, the clearing of his
throat, the sound of his short, dry cough. Nothing! She swallowed hard, fighting the unreasonable fear. Arriving at the
bottom of the flight of stairs, she hesitated in the hall, staring
at the open door of Thomas' office. It was unlike him to
leave it open, especially when he was working on his accounts.

Standing there, the misery that her life had become seemed
to settle upon her like a crushing burden. She could not go
on like this! Perhaps if she called to Thomas now, spoke to
him softly, smiled, perhaps they might manage to build some
sort of peace and understanding between them.

She did not call to him, finding herself unable to master
the surge of loathing that his name on her lips always
brought. On silent feet she approached the office and looked
through the door. Her heart gave one hard, terrible thump,
then seemed to hesitate in its beating. Thomas! Oh, my God!
She pressed a shaking hand to her mouth, her dilated eyes
staring at him. He lay on the floor, unmoving, his head in a
pool of blood. His face! It was twisted and blue. He had been
poisoned, she was sure of it. Would Thomas take his own life?
Mean and narrow though he had made it, he loved life. So he
had to have been murdered. But by whom?

She went reluctantly into the room and knelt down beside
him. Touching the blood with a shrinking finger, she found it
to be still warm. Shuddering, fighting nausea, she wiped her
finger on her white bodice, leaving a rusty smear. The sound
she had heard had been Thomas falling. He must have struck
his head on the corner of the desk. Thomas? Dead! There
was horror in the thought, but she could feel no grief. She
was free!

But she must do something. Call someone. Tell them what
had happened. She made to rise, and then froze. Sinking
back, she tilted her head, listening. The house was no longer
silent. Above her head she could hear soft, stealthy footsteps.
The footsteps were followed by a dragging sound, as though
something heavy were being pulled across the floor. Someone
was in the house! Not a servant, for they had none. Then,
who upstairs walked with such stealth? Was it someone
Thomas had admitted, believing that he let in a friend? She
looked at the silver beaker that lay just beyond his hand.

Bright-red drops of wine still dribbled from it. The intruder had put poison in Thomas' wine. He had murdered him, and he was even now engaged in robbing the house!

She clamped her lips tightly to suppress the scream that rose in her throat. She must not scream; she must not alert the murderer to her presence. To her straining ears, it seemed to her that the soft footsteps were much nearer. They seemed to be approaching the stairs. She must not be seen! Gasping, almost blind with terror, she scrambled to her feet and rushed from the room. Reaching the front door, she wrenched it open. She heard a shout behind her, but now she no longer cared. She was outside in the safety of the blurred gold of the afternoon.

At the corner of Parchfield Street she hesitated. She must find some quiet place where she could think out sanely and calmly what she must do next. But Thomas dead? It was unbelievable! A new terror struck her. Perhaps it would be thought that she had killed him. She hastened her footsteps until she was almost running. She would go to Rupert Baxter, her father's friend and hers. He would tell her what to do.

She was with Rupert Baxter when the law came for her. Frantic with fear, she clung to Rupert. He had persuaded her that innocence would stand out from the circumstantial evidence against her, that she must tell her story without fear. Rupert had been wrong. She had told her story in the courtroom, and had not been believed. They called her murderess, thief, adulteress.

Newgate Prison, the dreadful stench of the place! The degradation and the misery all about her. They had told her, her accusers, that she was to be whipped at the cart tail. Later she was to be hanged by the neck until she was dead. But she had done nothing wrong. She had not killed Thomas. She was innocent! They must believe her, they must!

Someone was thrusting something large and golden beneath her nose. Her dulled senses registered its shape. A crucifix. Now she could hear a voice droning words. "Repent ye, woman! Repent ye of your sins. The hour of judgment draws nigh!"

Fretfully, wanting only to be left in peace, she turned her head away. "I have done nothing. Leave me alone!" Was that her voice, that slurred, thick, mumbled sound?

The man was speaking again, his voice buzzing in her ear,

as tormenting as a circling wasp. "I fear I cannot understand your words, child. But if you think to deny your crimes, it would be further sin. God sees all, He knows all. I do pray that the whipping has driven the evil from you!"

The priest had another job that day. He had to move on. He returned to the flogger. "I'm off to Tyburn," he said to the man. "I must join my brothers at the hanging of Justin Lawrence. He will have need of my prayers."

"Him!" The flogger looked at him as though he were a dim-witted child. "I can tell you don't know much about the Rogue."

The priest gave him an austere look. "A man approaching death will often change."

The flogger shrugged. "It ain't likely with the Rogue. Still, you can 'ave a try at it. You've still got time. Just before I started off with the prisoner, I 'eard that the condemned procession was going to be late."

"Why is there to be a delay?"

"Don't know. It might be because the Rogue's loved as well as hated. He's got a lot of friends. Could be that the law didn't want no disturbance. Might be some folks who'd 'ave a try at rescuing him." He glanced at the drooping prisoner. "If I 'urry that wench up, maybe I'll be in time to see the Rogue turned off. I'd like that, I would. The Rogue's an interfering swine at times, and he's 'ad his nose in my affairs many a time."

"Has he? In what way?"

"The Rogue don't like cruelty, see. He reckons I lay the whip too 'ard on the prisoners." He gave a croak of laughter. "That's funny, that is. I 'eard he can be bleedin' cruel 'imself."

The priest ignored the remark. He looked back at the prisoner, and then said in a solemn voice, "I would not advise you to hurry the prisoner for the sake of your own enjoyment. If you do, it is quite possible that she will die."

A man who had been standing nearby and listening intently to the conversation between the two raised his voice in an excited shout. "Come on, everybody! I just heard that they're going to be late hanging the Rogue. If we hurry, we can see it all!"

The ripple of excitement caused by his shouted words

widened and caught them all up in a general eagerness to be on to the next entertainment. As the man started off at a run, the people, deserting the whipping procession, went rushing after him.

Chapter 2

The driver of the lead cart turned startled eyes on the people streaming toward the condemned procession. They seemed to be coming from all directions. Pouring from Bellrood Street, Wychmore Street, Lilac Lane, and Barleycorn Street. Dismayed and more than a little alarmed, he swore beneath his breath. The procession had been deliberately held up in order that there might be no demonstrations on behalf of Justin Lawrence, the jewel thief. He was to be hanged today. The Rogue, as he was known, because of his audacious charm, his daring, his suave manner, and his brilliant smile, was not only popular, he had also become something of a public hero. Because of this knowledge, the authorities thought that attempts might be made to rescue him. Always before, the Rogue had managed to slither out of the traps set for him. This time, it had been determined, they would take no chances on his getting away. A general silence had been preserved on the exact time the condemned procession, bearing this very important prisoner, would start out.

The driver scowled, pondering on the uncanny way things got out. They had started off from Newgate Street, reached Holborn Hill, and slid easily down into Holborn, and he thought that the secret had been well kept. But evidently there had been a leaking of information. Those in the know had apparently passed it on to others, gathering a larger audience as they went.

He tightened his hands on the reins, taking a quick look at his whip. Should trouble start, he was quite prepared to snatch the whip from the holder and use it on those around him. They still had to traverse Oxford Street before they reached Tyburn Road. Already the people who had erupted from the surrounding streets were calling out to the Rogue. Some of them were running along beside the cart, even at-

18

tempting to clamber up the sides. But for all that, all was still reasonably serene, and the guards at the back of the procession were on the alert. He took a quick look over his shoulder, frowning as he saw that some of the enthusiastic audience were jumping up and trying to touch the Rogue's hand. That slender, aristocratic-looking hand, the thin fingers laden with flashing rings. No doubt, the driver thought sourly, the Rogue had stolen those rings. In fact, he would go further and say that there was not the slightest doubt of it.

The driver's scowl deepened. Listening to the crowd, who would think that the Rogue was just a common thief? Well, perhaps "common" was not quite the right word, the driver conceded grudgingly. The Rogue's victims were usually women, and he robbed them with such easy charm, such exquisite courtesy, that he almost made them like it. Or perhaps it was the Rogue himself that they liked. Had he been an ordinary man, the women would doubtless have howled "Thief!" to high heaven. But Rogue Lawrence was no ordinary man either in looks or disposition. Few of the Rogue's victims could be persuaded to come forward and give evidence against him. In fact, while the Rogue was incarcerated in Newgate Prison, many of these women, braving the stench and horror of the prison, had paid out sums of money to ensure that they could visit him every day. They even brought him gifts of fruit, wine, and many other delicacies. Some of the more bold and shameless of these females had actually bribed the turnkey to allow them to stay the night with him. And the Rogue had availed himself of the freely offered gift of their bodies.

The driver clicked his tongue at his horse. The animal's ears twitched in automatic response, but it made no appreciable increase in its speed. He stole another look over his shoulder. The Rogue was really holding court. You could count on him to do the different and the unusual, and in this particular case, the macabre. The condemned could either be seated in the cart, or, if they preferred, they could stand up and take a good look at the world they were shortly to leave. The prisoners took their coffins with them, and the Rogue, the sun shining on his thick, unruly, curling black hair, the laces at his throat and wrists fluttering in the slight breeze, had chosen to sit on his coffin.

The driver turned his head away quickly. He was annoyed

to find that against his will he had responded to the smile the Rogue had sent in his direction. Ah, he thought grimly, those cheering people were far from knowing the real Rogue Lawrence. Beneath all that charm, he could be ruthless. The driver himself had seen evidence of that in the prison. Always determined to have his own way, was the Rogue. And when he was finished with a woman, he was really finished. If they kept on pestering him after being given their dismissal, he treated them with cold courtesy that held no hope or encouragement. And yet still the fools, unable to believe it, kept coming back for more of the same treatment. The Rogue was no saint, and to do him justice, he did not pretend to be. Except when he was angry or offended, the brilliant smile and the charm came naturally to him. But the driver had seen the Rogue angry. No smiles then. Those eyes of his, eyes almost as black as his hair, had looked frighteningly cold and bleak, the craggy, handsome lines of his face taut with rage, the expression forbidding.

An elderly woman clad in a too-youthful bright pink gown, a scarf of the same color tied over her white hair, ran past the driver. With determined energy she kept pace, calling out in a loud voice, "Rogue, Rogue! Gi' us a smile, lad."

Justin Lawrence regarded the woman with smiling dark eyes. Rising from the coffin, he reached down and grasped her arms, pulling her up until her face was level with his. "Dear madam," he said in his low, pleasant voice, "I will give you more than a smile. I will give you a kiss to remember me by."

Blushing like a young girl, the woman shrieked with delight as his lips touched her cheek. "Never you fear, Rogue, it ain't likely that a woman could forget you."

"Even you?" he said, laughing.

"And why not me? Inside, I'd have you know, I'm none so old." Her smile vanished, and she looked at him with mournful eyes. "Oh, lad, it's a dirty shame! You're too bonny to die."

"Ah! But then the same might be said of everybody. Come, now, no tears for me. Will you tell me your name, please?"

"Betsy. Betsy Field, that's me name."

"Betsy?" He put his head on one side, pretending to consider. "Ah, Betsy, love, my most exciting mistress had the same name."

She laughed. "Go on wi' you, wicked lad!"

"I am certainly that, Betsy." He kissed her cheek again. "Down you go." He held her until her feet touched the ground. Straightening again, he called to her in a light voice, "Betsy, sweetheart, you have left something with me. I would like to return it to you." He held up a round object. "This is yours, I believe."

The woman clapped a hand to her bodice. "Why, that's my brooch!" Laughing, she looked up at him. "You bad lad! You stole it right off my gown, and I never even felt it go."

Justin pulled his face into an expression of mock sadness. "I fear that I am incorrigible. But stealing, madam, if you remember, is my particular art." He tossed her the brooch. "You must be more careful with whom you associate. Are you not aware that there are thieves and rogues about?"

Responding to the general laughter that greeted this sally, Justin waved a nonchalant hand and resumed his seat. To the people staring at him and calling out their cheerful and often ribald comments, he seemed not to have a care in the world. But behind the smiling eyes, air of calm assurance, and easy, affable manner, he was afraid. He feared death at the rope end. Dreaded that moment when he would go spinning out into space. In imagination he could feel the rope cutting off his air, killing him in a slow strangling, inch by inch. How long? How long would it take him to die?

Justin glanced at the other two men who were to be hanged. One, staring dull-eyed into space, apparently saw or heard nothing about him. His name was Herbert Dudfield. He had been a soldier in the king's army. A happy and contented man, he had returned to his home one day, intending to give his wife a pleasant surprise. It was he who had received the surprise. He had found his wife in bed with a lover. He had shot the man down and had then strangled his faithless wife to death.

The other man, who looked to be even younger than Justin's own twenty-nine years, was Peter Cook. Peter Cook was a bigamist and a forger, and, finally, a murderer. He was small and slight, with large, innocent-looking blue eyes and a snub nose set in a round pink-cheeked face. Openly sobbing, he was twisting a spotted silk kerchief between his trembling hands.

Justin averted his eyes from the broken and tear-blubbered

face. Nodding and waving to his audience, he found his mind
drifting back to the start of this fatal journey.

The prisoners in the condemned hold had been awakened
at first light by the ringing of a handbell, and the turnkey's
voice calling loudly, "Awake! Awake, all ye condemned to
die! The time has come when you must face your Maker.
And may He have mercy on your black and heathen souls!"

In actual fact, the time had not yet come. There had been
a long and unexplained delay. Nerves, already taut, tightened
still more as the great bell of St. Sepulchre's kept up a
mournful tolling, telling them, as if they needed to be reminded, of their approaching death. When, finally, the
turnkey came for them, the sun had climbed high in a sky of
cloudless blue.

Watched by a group of young ladies clad in bright, thin
summer gowns with saucy little bonnets perched provoca-
tively on prettily curled hair, Justin and his companions had
taken their places in the first cart. With the deep sound of the
tolling bell following them, the cart had started off on its
journey to Tyburn. The other carts, containing yet more
wretched prisoners, rumbled noisily behind.

Justin frowned uneasily as Peter Cook's sobbing became
louder. Soon now they would arrive at their destination. He
thought of the number of times he had seen the hanging tree
at Tyburn. The "fatal tree," as it was called. In all those
times he had passed by, he had given little or no thought to
the victims. Certainly he had never expected to hang there,
his body making a feast for the crows and other scavenging
birds. He had always told himself he was too smart, much
too clever and wily to be caught.

It was a woman who had trapped him. A woman he had rejected. He should have remembered that a rejected woman
makes a dangerous enemy. But because Mary Mallison had
seemed willing to accept friendship in place of love, he had
been off guard. Smiling brightly, nodding her head in agreement to each suggestion, his erstwhile mistress had listened to
their plan, his and his brother's, for robbing Grange Hall, in
Surrey. When they had finished talking, the hour had grown
late. Bidding them good night, Mary Mallison went quietly
away. Her calm expression and her unruffled air had given
not the slightest indication of what they might expect from a
woman as jealous and as madly possessive as Mary.

On the day of the robbery, Justin had found himself neatly caught in the trap laid for him by the law and Mary Mallison. Fortunately, Paul, his brother, and the other two men working with them had managed to get away. The law officers made only a token gesture of pursuing the men. It was the Rogue thay were interested in. The wily Rogue, long sought, whom they had despaired of catching.

He had been in Newgate Prison for only two days before Paul, disguised and disregarding the danger to himself, had visited him. He had hoped, seeing his young brother's white, strained expression, that Paul would do nothing rash. Paul was hotheaded at times, acting first and thinking later. He must not be allowed to do anything that would send him to the gallows.

Paul, however, for all his troubling expression, was docile enough to Justin's every command. He was used to obeying him without question. He had done all that had been asked of him. Even, at Justin's request, bringing the new suit of red velvet. "My hanging suit," Justin had jested.

"Don't!" Paul said in a thick voice. He turned his head away, his shoulders heaving as he wept quietly and bitterly for the brother he worshiped. Later, when he rose to go, he had regained his self-possession. Speaking of Mary Mallison, he said in a voice made the more chilling by its very lack of emotion, "Mary is hiding. But I will find her, and then I will kill her."

"No! You will do nothing of the sort!" Justin's normally lazy voice was sharp and commanding. "You will think, Paul. You will use your head. One Lawrence is enough to give to the fatal tree." Smiling then, he put his hand on Paul's shoulder and squeezed gently. "I have no wish for this particular Lawrence to end up as crow bait. I would far rather he grew old and venerable."

"Justin! Don't make light of this thing!"

Justin's smile faded. "Ah, but I was never more serious. Paul, lad, listen to me. I want you to leave Mary Mallison alone. You are not to search for her. She is not worth putting your head into a noose for. Do you understand?"

Paul, drawing himself up to his full height, spoke with whatever strength he could muster. "I think you are forgetting, Justin, that I have outrun the law before. If need be, be sure that I can do so again."

Justin frowned and waved his hand in an impatient gesture. "I do not question that. Nonetheless, you will leave Mary Mallison alone. Hear me well, Paul. I intend to be obeyed."

Paul looked at him steadily. It was on the tip of his tongue to remind Justin that he was not now in a position to enforce obedience. But one look at that dark, hawklike face, the lips grim, the usually smiling eyes without light, caused him to change his mind. Covering his misery with a sullen expression, he inclined his head as if in agreement. Shortly after that, with a mumbled word or two, he terminated his visit.

Justin sat down slowly. Staring at his clasped hands, he felt reasonably sure that Paul, if only from a long habit of unquestioning obedience, would abandon his planned revenge. But it was the other things that might be brewing in his head, things that he had not mentioned, perhaps some foolhardy plan to rescue him, that concerned him now. Justin pushed the half-formed worry from him, his mouth softening as he continued to think of his brother. Young Paul, with his rumpled honey-blond hair that always looked in need of a good brushing, his shy smile, his deep-blue eyes, and his light, thickly freckled skin, a heritage from their dead mother, was the only being for whom he had ever felt love and concern. So different in looks were he and Paul that they might not have been brothers. He himself, dark, swarthy of complexion, took after their father, who had died soon after his wife. But for all the difference in looks, their blood was the same. Paul was studious, yet the strong streak of recklessness in his own nature was apparent at times in Paul too. It was simply that his thinking was a little slower, and though he had not let Paul see this, he worried about him constantly.

It was on one of Paul's subsequent visits to the prison that Justin had felt compelled to question him closely. It was unlike his careless nature to press, and Paul's surprised expression showed that he had noticed this. He did not, however, allow Justin the smallest glimpse into his mind. Surprisingly, his open, eager manner was gone; that was surprising in so young a boy a reticence had taken its place, and a new dignity. Even while it irritated, Justin found it oddly touching. He noticed, too, that Paul, parrying the questions and putting them lightly but firmly to one side, seemed to have grown up overnight far beyond his mere nineteen years.

Yet, on the night before the hanging, Paul seemed to be his old self. He no longer seemed unhappy which confused and even hurt Justin. Right up until the time of departure, when he must take his last farewell, his face was bright with smiles, and his manner so gay and lighthearted that Justin, despite himself, could not help feeling offended and ill-used. Conquering an unusual impulse to give in to self-pity, he smiled his brilliant smile and held out his hand. "Well, Paul, we'll not be meeting again. Say good-bye quickly, youngster, and then get on your way."

From the way Paul regarded the proffered hand, it might well have been a snake. The color draining slowly from his face, he had said in a loud, almost belligerent voice, "No! I will not shake hands with you."

"You will not?" Justin's brows rose in interrogation. "Do you tell me that you refuse to say good-bye?"

The freckles, dark blotches against the pallor of Paul's skin, stood out startlingly. "We must never say good-bye. Never! Do you hear me? Why should I say it? We will be together soon."

"Paul!"

Paul had backed swiftly to the door. "Save your breath, Justin. I am in command, not you. Aye, just for this once, I have the command."

Paul, you young fool! You cursed dunderhead! What the devil do you think you are about? What are you planning?"

"Ask me no questions. You will rest easier." He wrenched open the heavy door.

"Come back here, Paul!" Justin thundered. "At once! Do you hear me!"

It had been too late. Paul was already outside. Just before the door closed finally behind him, Justin had heard him in amicable conversation with the turnkey.

Coming back to the present, Justin dismissed his sense of foreboding. There was nothing Paul could do now. His dark brows drew together in irritation as he looked once more at the sobbing Peter Cook. There was no way out for them, and that being so, it would be better if the youth ceased his lamenting and showed some backbone. Besides, Justin was tired of that cursed wailing sounding in his ears.

Justin hesitated; then, making up his mind, he rose from the coffin and seated himself beside Cook. "Have done," he said, placing his hand upon the shaking shoulder. "Would you have these gawkers think of you as less than a man?"

Cook shrank away from his hand. Huddling lower, he seemed to be trying to make himself as small and inconspicuous as possible. "It's all right for you," he said in a broken voice. "You're a cool devil, you are. Seems like you don't fear nothin'."

"Nonsense!" Justin said in a voice that was meant to be bracing. "Whatever my reputation might be, never think I do not fear death. Aye, I fear it. Make no mistake about that."

Cook turned his drowned, guileless-looking blue eyes on Justin. "You do?"

"Naturally. I am only human, you know."

Fresh tears welled into Cook's eyes and ran down his cheeks. "All very well for you to say that, but you don't seem 'uman to me. I seen the way what you been a-bowing and a-smiling at them swine out there. It's a 'oliday for them, it is, to see men 'anging. So don't you expect me to go a-smiling at 'em. I'm afraid, I am. I keep on a-thinking 'bout 'ow I'm going to die, an' I can't stand it! What I got to die for, when I ain't even reached me nineteenth birthday?"

So he was not yet nineteen. Almost of an age with Paul. Justin felt a sudden surge of compassion for the miserable youth. He had always thought of this compassion he had for the young as a weakness, but there seemed to be nothing he could do about it. For children he had a special tenderness. He liked to think he was in full control of himself, and rarely did he allow his hot temper to master him. But on those occasions when he had come across an abused child, his rage had been such, and the punishment he meted out to the offenders so severe and so completely outside of the law, that the advent into their lives of what they could only think of as an avenging fury was long remembered by them with horror and fear. Because of this fear, many a child had been spared further suffering.

Justin's hand tightened on Cook's shoulder. "Try for some courage, Peter lad," he said in a gentle voice. "We will see this thing through, eh? We will show them how to die. Do exactly as I do, and you and I together will give them a grand show."

At that moment the cart turned into Tyburn Road. As it approached the fatal tree, Justin felt his heart lurch uncomfortably. Cook took one horrified look and then burst into renewed wailing. His voice rose hysterically as he began to plead, "Jesus, dear Jesus, have mercy on me! Save me!"

Herbert Dudfield turned his dead eyes on the youth and spoke for the first time. "Shut up that row!" he said. His voice once started, words began to pour from him, words that should have been passionate but were instead so utterly devoid of all emotion as to make what he had to say a simple statement of fact. "Why the hell should Jesus listen to you, Cook? Listen, eh? That's bloody funny, that is! He never listened to me when I was off fighting for the king. Nay, not He!" Dudfield glared at Cook, his face twisting at the memory of unbearable pain, but his voice as he went on was still emotionless. "I tell you, fool, He never listened. I used to pray to Him every night to keep my woman and my home safe. Know what He did about that? Laughed at me, that's what He did. Aye, and stood by and let my woman turn herself into a whore with every man she met. Laughed and looked on and let her destroy my home, with her whoring ways. But I had my revenge, I did. I killed her and her lover. Let Him, that bloody Jesus of yours, laugh that one off!"

Cook stared at him. Even the stubborn pink in his cheeks was not proof against the stark terror Dudfield's words had inspired in him. He turned a drained face to Justin. "You tell me if that's true what Dudfield said. You're a gent, an' you ought to know. Ain't Christ gentle an' loving like what we've always been taught? Ain't we got nothing to 'ope for?" In his desperation, he put his hand on Justin's arm and shook it. "Tell me! Ain't there nothing?"

Justin was not a religious man, but Cook's expression moved him to pity. It was the expression of a child who pleads to be reassured. "Take heart, lad," he answered firmly. "We may have to pay a little price for our sins on this earth, but it is all there waiting for you. Love and comfort and understanding. All you can want of it."

At that moment the cart came to a halt. Voices rose in excitement, and there was a bustle of movement as the crowd began to fight among themselves for the best viewing positions. Only when order was finally restored were the prisoners allowed to dismount. The guards, their duty done, wheeled their mounts about and headed back the way they had come.

It was only a few steps to the wide execution cart, but to

Justin, trying so hard to put on the bold front expected of
him, while at the same time by a glance and a comforting
pressure endeavoring to soothe Cook's terror, it seemed like a
mile—a mile that saw all his misdeeds appear before him like
boldly painted signposts. Even now, the fact of the matter
was that he could not be as properly penitent as, he imagined, was expected of him. It was more than possible that, in
the unlikely event that he be suddenly freed, he would do the
same things all over again.

Feeling Cook falter, Justin took his arm and drew him on.
The safe and respectable life as lived by many of his friends
was not for him, he thought. Were he to let himself be
hemmed in by conventions, the right thing to do, he would
not be able to breathe, and he would go mad with boredom.
To his credit, there was the fact that he had never taken a
human life. But on the debit side, he had not taken to a life
of crime because he was poor and desperate and needed the
money. He had been born of wealthy parents, and he had
never known privation. He had long faced the fact that he
was the rotten limb on the otherwise upright Lawrence family
tree.

Justin sighed. If he could be said to have any regret at all,
it was that his brother, loving him, had elected to follow after
him in his lawless career. Crime did not come naturally to
young Paul, who was of a quite different turn of mind. He
could have stopped Paul, but he had not. Another black
mark against him. No, he had not begun a life of crime for
gain, but for the sheer thrill of it. Yet he had never really
thought he would be caught. He had always had great confidence in his luck. Luck, he would tell himself, was a lady,
and when had he failed to soften a feminine heart? He should
have remembered that most women were capricious. He
should have been prepared for that time when Lady Luck,
tiring of the game, would turn her face from him. But since
she had turned from him, it behooved him not to whine about
his fate. For the benefit of the people gathered here to watch
him die, he would be bold and confident to the end. This was
expected of him. For that matter, it was what he expected
of himself.

For the first time, perhaps because he was only a few steps
away from death, Justin consciously allowed himself to wonder about God. Did such a being really exist? If so, he hoped

that He had a sense of humor. Enough of it, at least, to understand and appreciate that to Justin Lawrence, one of His less admirable creations, life was not meant to be lived grimly and earnestly and in trembling fear of the Lord's vengeance. Life, he felt, was to be lived in the way he had always seen it, as a jest, a glorious and rib-tickling jest.

Justin cursed beneath his breath as he was forced to urge Cook on again. His faults were undoubtedly numerous, Justin's thoughts roved on, but at least the Lord could never accuse him of being a hypocrite. He was not a good and worthy man, and he had never pretended to be. He could be brutal when the occasion warranted, and completely ruthless. He was, as he was called, a rogue. But he had found that if you combined with your roguery a certain charm, you seemed to be more beloved of people than the God-fearing, clean-living, worthy man. Another of life's little ironic jests. In regard to the women in his life, he could claim that he had never deceived them. He had taken their bodies, but only if they were willing. From the very first, he never had failed to warn his partner of the moment that he was not a marrying man. If their desire was to hear wedding bells ringing out a merry peal for them, then he was most certainly not their man. It might well be in bemoaning their lost virginity, as was the habit of some females after the deed was done, that they would think of him with some bitterness. But he hoped that the mutual pleasure they had enjoyed at the time would outweigh the gall.

Justin smiled wryly. When the score was tallied, there was not much to recommend him. But it might be that the good Lord, whose eyes must surely look deeper than the eyes of mere men, would find some small virtue in him. If nothing at all be found to his credit, he would be fairly in the soup. But perhaps, before his potful of sins began to bubble too violently, he might, with a little luck, be fished out and allowed to dry off in the benevolent sunshine of the Deity's forgiveness.

Justin turned his head and smiled slightly as Cook's trembling hand took a firmer grip on his arm. "Courage, lad," he said softly. "It will soon be over."

The boards of the execution cart creaked as the executioner came forward with a heavy and deliberate tread. He stood on the edge of the cart looking down at the prisoners.

He looked briefly at Dudfield and Cook, but his interest was centered on Justin. His smile was without malice as he said in a booming voice, "Never thought to see you here, Rogue, bloody crafty fox that you are! I thought you'd outrun us to the end."

Justin smiled. "But you must remember that even the fox is not proof against the vixen."

The executioner stared. Then, evidently seeing humor in the situation, his big belly began to jerk with laughter. "So a woman done it to you? Got you nobbled, eh, Rogue?"

"She did indeed." Justin looked at Cook's drawn face, his wild eyes, and his jerking hands. "But while I appreciate, my dear executioner, that the occasion that brings us together is a cause for much mirth," he went on in his carelessly drawling voice, "I would much appreciate it if you would get on with your job."

"Can't wait, eh?"

Justin looked meaningfully at Cook. "Some of us cannot. The suspense is perhaps a little too much for nerves already overstrained. So may I again suggest that you get on with it?"

"Right. As you know, Rogue, it's you what's the big attraction. So you'll get turned off last." He nodded at Cook and Dudfield. "Them two go first. They get hanged together. But you'll dangle all on your own, nice and private like."

"I am gratified."

"Thought you might be." The executioner crouched down and extended a large hand to Cook. "Up you come, then, lad. We're all ready for you."

Ignoring the hand, Cook turned blindly to Justin. "Please 'elp me, guv! Oh, Jesus, somebody's got to 'elp me!"

Dudfield brushed past them. Without looking at the other two, he took the executioner's hand and mounted the cart.

The executioner grinned at Justin. "Now, there's a lad what's right willing." Again he extended his hand to Cook. "Come on, lad. Don't be wasting my time. We've not got all day now, have we? There's another lot to be turned off after you."

"A moment, if you please," Justin said, giving him a coldly quelling glance. "If you have no objection, I have something I would say to my friend."

"It's all right with me, Rogue. Just don't be too long-winded about it."

Turning his back on the executioner, Justin took Cook by the shoulders. "Listen to me, young Peter"—his voice could be heard only by the trembling and terrified man—"I want you to answer a question for me. If you show everybody how afraid you are, will it stop you from hanging?"

Tears jetted from Cook's eyes as he shook his head violently. "What sort o' question is that, guv? You know it won't."

"Then tell me this. If you mount the cart with dignity and as much courage and calm as you can possibly muster, will that stop you from hanging?"

Cook stared.

Justin looked deeply into the lad's frightened eyes. "So be courageous, Peter. It is all that is left to us—pride, dignity in the face of death."

Cook stared at him in bewilderment, his terror for a fleeting moment forgotten. This man with his gentle eyes and his softly coaxing voice was very different from the Rogue Lawrence about whom so many tales were told. Never once had Cook heard that Rogue Lawrence could be sympathetic and kind. Somehow one did not associate such qualities with the kind of man he was reputed to be. Cook blinked his moist eyes, while he fumbled in his mind to understand.

Justin in that moment was an enigma to himself. He was well aware that Cook could not be classed as a child; and yet, inexplicably, he saw him as such. Perhaps it was his rounded and pink-cheeked face, so boyish-looking, that heightened the illusion and brought forth his compassion and that tenderness of which, on rare occasions, he was capable. And so, in Justin's mind, he was not talking to a man who had murdered without a second's thought. He was talking to a frightened child, and this was reflected in his eyes and his voice.

"Mount the cart bravely, Peter, there's a good lad," Justin urged him. "Do it for your loved ones, if there be any, and perhaps a little for me."

Cook made up his mind. "I'll try, Rogue. Maybe I can do it for me mum and for you." He held out his hand. "Will you shake wi' me?"

Justin gripped his hand for a brief moment, and then released it. "I'm proud of you, lad! Up you go. You'll show them what kind of stuff Peter Cook is made of, eh?"

Cook nodded. Trying to smile, he took the executioner's

hand and was helped aboard. Standing near Dudfield, he kept his eyes on Justin as the rope was passed about his neck and Dudfield's and the end securely fastened to the gibbet. Like one in a dream, he heard the laughter of the onlookers, their high, excited voices, the laughter of children, who, unimpressed by the drama of the moment, were romping in play. Babies wailed, some hungry, some made irritable by the heat. Hawkers added to the uproar. With their trays slung about their necks by leather straps, they moved among the crowd loudly extolling their various wares. "I got nice 'ot pies what'll 'earten you a treat." . . . " 'Ere's cold drinks to quench your thirst. Who's for a cold drink?" . . . "Try me nice scented cloths. 'Ere, lady, take a niff o' this. Ain't that lovely? It'll cool you orf, an' the smell'll make your gent all romantic." . . . " 'Ere's a fan, lady. Look 'ere at this del'cate work what's in it. Come on, guv, don't be mean. Buy your lovely lady one o' me fans."

Cook stiffened as the chaplain came forward to request that prayers be heard for the souls of the condemned, but still he did not remove his eyes from Justin's face. It was as though the sight of Justin was a rock of strength to which he clung. He had the trembling inner feeling that if he once took his eyes from that encouraging face, he would crumble into his former condition of abject terror. His lips moved without sound. "God bless you, Rogue Lawrence! Looks like God sent you to 'elp me."

Dudfield stood erect, his hands at his sides, his shoulders squared, like the soldier he had once been, but his face was remote and his eyes without life. He remained stubbornly silent, refusing to join in the prayers, refusing to respond in any way.

Cook's lips moved in mechanical response to the prayers, but he was not aware of the words he uttered. Only of Rogue Lawrence. The Rogue was his strength. Through him he could draw on the needed courage to see him through to eternity. For the first time in his life someone believed in him.

"Peter Cook," the executioner's voice, suitably grave now, said. "By the law of this land, you are to be hanged by the neck until you are dead. Before you face your Maker, you have anything you wish to say?"

Cook saw Justin's faint nod. "Yes," he whispered. "I got somethin' to say."

"Speak, then. Look at the people whose laws you have outraged, Peter Cook, and say what you have to say."

Cook found it impossible to obey this last request. His desperate eyes continued to cling to Justin's face. "It . . . it ain't much . . . what I . . . I got to say." He faltered. "It's jus' that I'm sorry for what I done. If I 'ad me another chance, I wouldn't do it no more."

Justin smiled and raised his clasped hands in a gesture of approval. Something triumphant glowed inside Cook, lighting his face to a faint radiance.

The executioner then turned to Dudfield and repeated his set speech.

As though the man's words were the spark that ignited him, Dudfield came to a sudden blazing life. His eyes fiery and dangerous-looking, he began to shout, "Don't you expect to see no sorrow from me! I'm glad I killed the bitch and her whoreson of a lover. You hear me? I'm glad! She was my wife, but that didn't stop her from turning herself into a thing what opened her legs for every swine that came along. I hope she rots in hell! I hope she burns forever! Damn her! Damn you all!"

Eyeing the throbbing veins in Dudfield's forehead, the angry roar of the crowd in his ears, the executioner shifted his feet uneasily. It was his opinion that the guards should have stayed behind to help restrain this dangerous prisoner if it proved necessary.

Dudfield, however, his brief spurt of life over, had subsided into his former condition. He did not seem to notice when the executioner held up the black caps that would cover the faces of the prisoners. Without a protest or any sign of emotion, he stood very still as his wrists and ankles were lashed tightly together and the black cap, the front pulled down like a curtain to hide his face, was placed upon his head.

Submitting to the binding, Cook found his previous terror struggling to awaken. With a strength of will he had not known he possessed, he fought to subdue it, and won. Only the bright glitter in his eyes showed as the aftermath of the struggle, but his face was calm. Beyond a heavy, wrenching sigh, he said nothing as the cap was placed upon his head and the front pulled down. Justin's face was hidden from him now, but he could still picture it in his mind.

"Peter Cook, Herbert Dudfield," the chaplain intoned in a solemn voice, "may the Lord have mercy on your souls!"

The executioner turned away and made his way to the driver's seat. For the benefit of the people, he posed for a moment, holding his heavy whip above his head with both hands. Then, settling himself comfortably in the seat, he brought the whip down across the backs of the two docile horses. "Get up!" he shouted. "Get up!"

Docility fled abruptly with the sting of the whip. Neighing, the animals plunged forward. They galloped forward for a few yards, only to be brought up short by the sawing on their reins. They stood very still, their muscles quivering with reaction.

A cheer arose as Cook and Dudfield dangled into space. Still clapping their approval, the people stared avidly at the hanging men. Something happened then that Justin had heard of but had never seen. As if a signal had been passed among the crowd, men left their places and rushed across the small space that divided them from the victims. Their faces grim with purpose, they grasped at the dangling legs and began to swing upon them. Those women who had had the forethought to provide themselves with billets of wood ran after the men. They began to beat savagely at the bodies, trying to aim the wooden billets in the general direction of the heart.

Watching them, Justin felt his stomach knot painfully. He swallowed hard, pressing his kerchief tightly to his lips until the urgent impulse to bend over and vomit had passed, leaving him cold and trembling. He began to reason with himself. The actions of the people would naturally seem callous and brutal to one who had never witnessed such a scene before, and especially one in his present unfortunate position. But their intentions were meant to be kindly. This method of swinging and beating upon the bodies was generally thought to be an aid that would enable the men to die quickly.

Justin closed his eyes for a moment, then opened them quickly. The sight of those men, their faces red with exertion, swinging like monkeys upon the legs of the dying men, and the women, hair loosened and wisping untidily about sweating faces as they kept up their hammering, was a sight he could not watch for too long. Out of respect for his still-queasy stomach, he averted his eyes quickly.

Fifteen minutes, he thought, or so he had heard, before the

men would be pronounced legally dead. After that, his turn
to hang. The dead men, if they were fortunate enough to
have a little money, would then be cut down and given over
to the hovering men who waited to bury them. Though at best,
it would probably be a pauper's graveyard for them. Those
that had no money at all were usually strung to another tree
to await the scavenging birds, who would rapidly pick them
clean. The rich could avoid the common burial. Their money
would ensure them rest in the parklike grounds of the rich. So
even under these circumstances, wealth could still guarantee
you preferential treatment.

A memory of Cook's drawn face and haunted eyes came
to him. Whatever the lad had been, whatever he had done, he
deserved better than being strung up again to make a feast
for the birds, or to be shoveled like offal into a nameless
grave. Both Cook and Dudfield deserved better. He would
speak to the executioner before he made his final disposal of
the bodies. He would pay him well to plant the two men in
decent surroundings. That much, at least, he could do for
them. His mind reverted again. Fifteen minutes! Did it really
take that long to die?

The people were streaming back to their places. Justin
started as he realized that the fifteen minutes allowed were
up. Time had sped by so swiftly that he, immersed in his
thoughts, had not noticed it. His hands clenched. Damn! His
nausea seemed to have returned. He felt as sick as a dog.
Disliking such weakness in himself, he tried to blame it on
the indigestible prison food, and not on the careless way the
bodies of the two men were first cut down and then wrapped
in indifferent fashion in dingy tattered blankets taken from the
cart. He watched as they were laid on the trampled grass to
await the executioner's decision as to their ultimate fate. The
chaplain, looking harried, mumbled a final flustered prayer
over them before hurrying to join the executioner, who had
already taken up the reins, preparatory to backing the cart
into its former position.

As the cart reached him and came to a halt, Justin raised
his voice above the babble about him. "A word with you," he
shouted.

The man heard. Nodding, he climbed down from his high
perch and came leisurely toward him. "I've not forgot you,
Rogue," he said, grinning, "so don't you go getting yourself

into a fret. Well, what can I do for you, other than hanging you up all neat and tidy?"

"Those two men, Cook and Dudfield." Justin's voice was without its customary drawl. "I wish them to be buried in Manor Oaks Churchyard. You will arrange it, please."

"I will, will I?" The executioner's eyes were suddenly narrowed and greedy. "If you want 'em planted in Manor Oaks, along o' the swells, you must have money to burn. You got the boodle, have you, Rogue?"

Justin held up his ringed hands. "I have these."

The executioner's small brown eyes blinked as he eyed the flashing rings. "Aye," he said at last. "Reckon they'd pay for the burial, all right."

Justin's dark brows rose in cynical amusement. "My good man, I may be about to die, but I assure you that the dismal prospect of death has not robbed me of my wits. One ring alone, this emerald for instance, would be more than adequate. There would also be a goodly sum left over for yourself, you cursed pirate!"

Unoffended by this plain speech, the executioner rasped at his stubbled chin with callused fingers. "You gi' me the ruby as well as the emerald, and I'll even see the poor perishers get flowers."

"Naturally, I don't believe you for a moment. But then, you didn't expect me to do so, did you?"

" 'Course not." The executioner winked at him. "Knowed you wouldn't. Ain't never been no flies on you, eh, Rogue?"

"Very true." Shrugging, Justin slipped off the two rings and placed them in the executioner's quickly extended palm. "You may have them both. Where I am going, they will be of little use to me."

The executioner closed his fingers about them. "Where you're going, Rogue, the heat'd melt 'em. I didn't have to bargain wi' you, you know. After I laid you out all stiff and cold, I could've took 'em off your fingers."

"So you could," Justin said thoughtfully. "Can it be that there is a grain of honesty in that gross body of yours?"

"Might be." The man's cheerful good humor was unabated. "I have me moments." He laughed. "A fine one you are to be talking about honesty, ain't you?"

Justin smiled. "A shrewd hit, but under the circumstances,

unworthy of you. But perhaps you still intend to remove the other rings? Could it be so, executioner?"

"Never know, will you?" He glanced about him. Meeting the concentrated stare of many eyes, he said, "I don't like to be hurrying you none, lad. But it's time for you to be giving them people the show what they been waiting for. You want to come up now?"

"Do I have a choice?"

"Nary a one, lad."

"A pity. Your hand, man."

Unlike the previous execution, an almost complete silence descended as Rogue Lawrence mounted the cart. Even the hawkers momentarily ceased to cry their wares. He was immaculate in rich red velvet, against which the ruffles at his throat and wrists stood out white and crisp. They gaped at him with open curiosity, and, in some cases, speculation. For this man with the laughing eyes and the ready wit, whose love affairs were scandalous, remained, despite all the tales they had heard about him, many of them conflicting, surrounded in glamour and mystery. It was rumored that he had stolen simply for the thrill of it, and now he was about to die. He stood before them very erect, the sun picking out blue-black lights in his thick hair and making a bright dazzle of his red-velvet garments. He looked back at them sober-faced, his eyes grave; and then, suddenly, he smiled.

A woman's voice broke the silence. "You got a smile like a burst of sunshine, damned if you ain't! Speak to us, Rogue."

Justin's eyes had found the speaker. He looked at her trim figure clad in a gown of soft pink. She had a pretty, rather doll-like face surmounted by a cloud of fluffy blond hair upon which was perched a beflowered and beribboned straw bonnet. Justin leaned his elbows on the side of the cart. "You know, mistress," he called to her, " 'tis not fair to parade your charms before me. You make me regret that I am about to die. Together, snug and close in a bed, we could do wonderful things together."

Laughter rose up in a wave. "Ain't it marvelous?" a man shouted. "You're about to swing, Rogue, and here you are thinking about tumbling a wench."

"You wouldn't 'ave to coax this wench, Rogue," another man called. "This 'ere is Emmie Barnes. Does it for money, she do. Me an' me pals've all 'ad 'er."

The woman gave an indignant toss of her bonneted head. "Don't pay no attention to 'em," she cried in a shrill voice. "Anyway, Rogue, I'd give it to you for nothin'."

Justin looked at her thoughtfully as an idea came to him. He waited until the laughter and chatter had once more subsided; then he called in a clear voice, "Come here to me, Emmie."

The executioner stepped forward, his eyes uneasy. "What you up to, Rogue? I can't let you go inviting people up here. Serious business, this is."

With a pang, Justin thought of Paul. He had half-expected to see his brother's face in the crowd, but evidently Paul had decided against making an appearance. It would be too harrowing an occasion for him. His sudden emotion did not show as he answered in a calm voice, "It is the privilege of a condemned man, as you know, to have his friends and relatives beside him to take one last fond farewell."

"Laughing at me, I can see that by your eyes," the executioner said roughly. "Aye, Rogue, it's your privilege, but that wench ain't no relation of yours. She's nothing but a whore."

"Ah! You are fond of me. You fear she will contaminate me, is that it?"

"Laughing again!" the executioner said in a wrathful voice. "All right, have her up, if you like. But it ain't the thing."

Justin smiled. "But we will not consider the conventions at a time like this, will we? So I create Mistress Barnes my closest and most loved relative."

"What you up to, Rogue?"

"Nothing, I assure you." Justin looked at Emily again. "Come here," he repeated.

With a squeal of delight, Emily Barnes ran to the cart. With a flurry of pink skirts, white petticoats threaded with pink ribbon, and small pink-and-white laced shoes, she was hoisted up to stand beside Justin. Meeting his eyes, she blushed vividly. "What you want of me, Rogue?" she blurted, placing her faintly trembling hands in Justin's. "Whatever it is, you can have it." She paused, then added significantly, "Aye, Rogue, whatever it is!"

Justin's eyes crinkled in laughter. "What, here, Emily? For shame!"

"Go on! You an' me don't need to have no shame." She broke off, giggling, her eyelashes fluttering nervously.

Studying her, Justin saw that close up she was not as young as he had thought her. There were lines grooved beneath the large blue eyes, and her face, with the fading of the blush, had a white, starved look. The gown she was wearing was of a cheap material, and shoddily made. The flimsy bodice that exposed her breasts almost entirely was already showing signs of wear. She looked what she was. A woman past her first youth, who sold her body to anybody who had a copper or two to spare. Did she like her way of life? Justin wondered. Did she sell herself from necessity or choice? He rather thought it would be from necessity. "Emmie," he said abruptly, "if you had sufficient money for your every need, what kind of life would you choose to lead?"

Emily stared at him in bewilderment. She opened her mouth to give the pert answer she believed was expected of her, but changed her mind as she saw his serious expression. "Why," she said in a small voice, "if I had money, I'd get me a nice cottage in the country." Her smile flashed, showing unexpected dimples. "Aye, that's what I'd do." Emmie looked down at her feet. She had grown suddenly and inexplicably shy of this handsome stranger who was holding her hands in a firm, warm clasp. She looked up at him again and added wistfully, "And I'd never have to have a man in my bed unless I wanted one. It would be my choice, see?"

"Yes, Emmie, I do see." Justin dropped her hands and drew the last two rings from his fingers. "Give me your hand again."

Wonderingly, she obeyed. She gasped aloud as Justin dropped the rings into her hand and closed her fingers about them. "Now you have money, Emmie. Sell the rings. They are worth a great deal. More than enough for your cottage in the country." He tweaked a lock of her hair. "And they were come by honestly. Is it not an amazing confession?"

"Why, Rogue?" Tears crowded her eyes, and she began to tremble. "Why you giving them to me? I ain't nothing to you."

"Nonsense. I have created you my relative, have I not?"

Emmie's mouth quivered. "They say you're a bad man. But you ain't, Rogue. You're good and kind."

"Nay, Mistress Barnes," Justin exclaimed in mock horror, "for God's sake do not take my reputation away from me. It is all I have left. I am a bad man. Aye, every bit as black as I have been painted, I assure you."

Overcome, Emmie burst into tears. "No, you ain't! You ain't!" She flung her arms about his neck and clung to him.

Laughter mixed with ribald comments was coming from the spectators. Listening, Justin knew that he had delayed long enough. It was time for the interlude to end. He would make his last speech. And afterward would come the darkness. Firmly but gently he released himself from Emmie's clinging arms. "I honestly cannot live up to such a saintly reputation, wench. If it will make you feel better, I will tell you that I would not have parted with my treasures had I the least expectancy of life. So I am not as good as you think me."

Emmie shook her head. "Yes, you are. You are good. I'll always th-think so!"

Justin smiled widely as he met the executioner's angry eyes. "I know how you feel, man. You had plans for those baubles, didn't you? My heart bleeds for your disappointment."

"You was going to give 'em away all along," the man accused in a sullen voice.

"Nay, my lad, you wrong me. It was a spur-of-the-moment decision. But since you have the ruby and the emerald, which are worth a fortune, you surely cannot feel too ill-used. And as I told Mistress Emmie, you have the additional assurance that they are honestly come by."

With those laughing eyes upon him, the executioner's lips relaxed into a reluctant smile. "Honestly come by!" he growled. "Bloody likely story, that is."

"Yes, isn't it? I rather liked it myself."

"You win, Rogue. Like you said, I got my share." He looked at Emmie. "The wench'll have to go now."

Justin nodded. Taking Emmie into his arms, he kissed her firmly on her trembling mouth. "Sweets to take with me into eternity," he teased. "Good-bye, my pretty darling. Remember me."

Emmie could not speak for the tears that were choking her voice, but she looked at him with such passionate gratitude that he felt himself flushing.

Clutching the rings, Emmie allowed herself to be swung

down to the ground. A moment longer she stood there looking up at Justin; then, lowering her head, she stumbled blindly away to hide herself in the crowd.

Justin heard her sobbing. Even after she was lost to sight,
he imagined he still heard it. With a touch of cynicism, he reflected that it took but one small act of charity, performed, as
he had said, on impulse, and to one person his crimes were
wiped out as completely as if they had never been. To Emmie Barnes, enjoying her newfound comfort and peace, he
would remain half-saint and wholly hero. He smiled, finding the thought oddly pleasing. One small candle to grace,
and Emmie Barnes the keeper of the tiny flame. It was better
than nothing.

"Rogue," the executioner called. "Come over here and
stand in front o' me and the chaplain."

Justin moved to obey. He was feeling the nausea again.
Strangely, his only thought as he stood in front of the two
men was: Let me not vomit and disgrace myself. Nothing of
this showed in his face. It was an effort to smile, but he
achieved it.

The chaplain frowned. It was indecent, he felt, for the man
to be smiling in that carefree way. He was facing death, and
shortly he would be standing before his God. But looking at
him, one would think he was about to attend a ball. The
chaplain began the prayer for the soul of the condemned
man, and the prayerbook shook in his hand as his anger
grew. Justin Lawrence, who should be humble and abject,
was ignoring the responses to the prayer. Instead, he was
waving at the assembled people, turning that smile on them
and kissing his hands in their direction. Disgraceful! He
would answer to God for this last irreverence.

The prayer came to an end. The chaplain closed his book
with a little snap and stepped back. If only the man would
show one small touch of regret! Surely that was not asking
too much?

"Justin Anthony Lawrence," the executioner began, "by
the law of this land, you are—"

"Yes, yes, I know," Justin interrupted. "Let us dispense
with the formalities."

The executioner turned away to hide a smile. Meeting the
chaplain's pained eyes, he pulled himself together and said in

a brisk, businesslike voice, "You got anything you want to say?"

Justin nodded. To those watching him, he appeared perfectly cool and calm. "I send my love to the ladies, and my good wishes to the gentlemen. One boon only do I ask of you all. It is that you leave my body untouched. I do not care to act as a swing for agile gentlemen, nor yet a drum for the ladies to pound upon. Is it agreed?"

A concerted roar of agreement came from all sides. Satisfied, Justin bowed to them.

Scratching his head, the executioner said in a puzzled voice, "That's a funny thing to ask 'em. Don't you want to die quickly, Rogue?"

"I prefer to die in my own way. With a little dignity. I am sure you understand."

"Ain't much dignity dangling at the end of a rope."

"But even less dignity when one is pounded and swung upon. Humor me."

The executioner went over to a corner of the cart and picked up a coil of rope. Coming back to Justin, he said in an apologetic voice, "I got to bind you, lad."

"So you have. Do your duty, then."

Justin had no more words. He stood very still while his wrists and ankles were tightly lashed. He was going to die! It was incredible, terrifying! He thought of Cook, whose outward terror had been a faithful copy of his own inner turmoil. But Cook, more honest than he, had not been able to hide it. Not, that was, until the end. He had died bravely, that young lad. Could he do less? Despising himself, hating the nausea that struggled to claim him, the fear-induced perspiration that clustered thickly on his brow and ran in little streams down his neck, he struggled to find words sufficiently glib to disguise his terror. They came. As the executioner got to his feet, he said lightly, "Now that you have me trussed up like a cursed fowl, I presume it is time for my ride into thin air?"

"It is indeed, lad." The executioner looked at him with admiration. "You're a one, you are! I reckon you don't know the meaning of fear, Rogue."

Half-suspecting sarcasm, Justin gave him a sharp look. He decided that the man was sincere. But was he really so blind? Could he not see the shameful, craven fear looking from his eyes? "What's to fear, executioner?" he said in the same light voice. "Death is something we must all face."

The executioner slid the noose over the prisoner's head. It was strange, Justin thought, but the rough rope felt cool, almost silky against his hot flesh. Paul! The boy's face came clearly into his mind, and he experienced an agonizing dart of renunciation mixed with self-reproach. Are you out there, Paul? Are you somewhere in the crowd, my brother? Don't look, lad, don't look! Why did I not play the stern elder brother to you? Why was I so careless of your young life? I should have forbidden you to follow after me. But I saw your admiration, I basked in the glow of your hero worship, and I did not want to do without it. Vanity? Aye, lad, my vanity and my foolishness. I knew even then that had I forbidden you to follow, you would have obeyed. You might have been resentful, for you saw much glamour in my way of life, but you would have been safe. It is my fault, all mine! Paul, I have changed my mind. If you are out there, it will be better if you watch your brother choke his life away. Afterward, it would be my wish that you go home and think on what you have seen. Think to good purpose, and I know you will endeavor to do differently. We are brothers, but there is a world of difference between us, and you are the better of the two. So go home. Study. Marry a nice little wench who will love you and give you children. But if one of your children should show any signs of inheriting Rogue Lawrence's wild blood, then you must try to beat it out of him or her. You would not have a child of yours dangle at the rope end, as I am about to do. Forgive me my neglect, lad. And if you must remember me, then remember only the quiet and happy times we spent together before our parents died.

"It's time, Rogue."

Justin started at the sound of the executioner's voice, his face flushing. "Aye," he said, "I know it." He was pleasantly surprised to hear his voice come out cool and assured.

"You got anything more you want to say to them out there?"

With Paul foremost in his mind, Justin looked out at the sea of upturned faces. If Paul was there, would he understand and believe what he now must say, or would he know it for the lie it was? He must take his chance on that, for speak he would. He nodded to the executioner.

"All right," the man said, surprised. "Don't make it too long."

Justin stepped forward. For a moment he was silent, his eyes searching the crowd. Then he raised his voice to a shout. "Listen to me. If you would not end like Rogue Lawrence, with a rope about your neck, then go home and pursue your peaceful ways. I repent of my deeds! I am truly sorry! If I had it to do over again, I would do very differently. That is all I have to say, but I beg you to think on it, and to think well."

"I never thought to hear you say you were sorry, Rogue," the executioner exclaimed. " 'Twas the last thing I expected. It don't somehow seem like you."

"For a lie, it went over very well, I thought."

"Ah, then, you never meant it. Why'd you say it?"

"It was for the benefit of someone I know. If he is there, I hope he has taken my words to heart. And now, executioner, enough of talk. You may do your worst."

"Good-bye, Rogue. I'm sorry I got to do this to you."

"I believe you. But you are no sorrier than I." Justin smiled. "Come, man, cheer up, or you will have me believing you have a tender heart."

"Good-bye, Rogue, good-bye!" It was a scream from the people. Somebody began a loud sobbing, and a woman's voice shouted clearly, "God bless you, Rogue!"

The executioner forgot to posture for the crowd. Scowling, he seated himself on his high perch. His hand trembling, he lifted his whip and brought it down on the animals. Full of pain and fury, whinnying their resentment, they bolted forward.

Justin felt himself jerked upward and outward. Sweet Christ! The fearful weight of his body trying to drag him downward. The iron fingers about his throat, pressing, gouging, cutting off life and breath! Bursting lights before his eyes, the colors lurid and evil. Head bursting, pounding with the frenzied gathering of interrupted blood flow. The pain! The unbelievable pain! He heard a sound in his ears like a high, demented screaming. "Stop it!" he tried to say. "In the name of Christ, stop that screaming!" But he had no words, no voice! A flickering edge of blood-streaked darkness was trying to quench the blazing lights. Trying, trying, almost overcoming! The last face he saw was Paul's. Paul, with his blue eyes shining and his lips parted in a smile. The last voice he heard, rising like a clap of thunder above the screaming: " 'Ot pies!" the voice boomed. "Try me nice 'ot pies!"

Chapter 3

The people had gathered around the hanging tree to gape with awe and curiosity at the dangling body of Justin Lawrence. Mary Mallison, swept unwillingly along with the excited crowd, found that she could not look away. Her eyes wide and feverishly bright, she continued to stare like one hypnotized. She put a shaking hand to her mouth, her fingers digging into her flesh. This was her handiwork, this tragic result that her jealousy and spite had brought about. She had done this to him, her love! She had murdered Rogue!

Mary gasped as a stout woman, suddenly surging forward, elbowed her to one side. Horrified, she watched the woman reach up a hand and rip the ruffles from Rogue's wrist. In bitter anguish a voice inside her cried out: Don't! Leave him alone. Oh, please don't touch him!

"Keepsake!" the stout woman shouted. Triumphantly she stuffed the delicate muslin into her bodice.

Keepsake! Mary shuddered. Soon they would all be wanting some memory of Rogue Lawrence. They would strip his body of everything they could get. They would leave him naked. And so he would be robbed not only of his life but of his dignity too. Dignity. It had always meant a great deal to him. How often had she heard him say: "No matter what life or circumstances may do to you, Mary, try to hold on to your dignity. It is a valuable possession."

With an inarticulate cry, Rogue's voice still sounding in her ears, Mary turned and began to fight her way through the press of people. Some of them, momentarily distracted by the violence of her pushing, looked with open curiosity at the white-faced girl with the tumbled black hair and the big burning blue eyes. She had a demented look.

Emerging at last into an open space, Mary Mallison leaned against the gnarled trunk of a tree. Her breast rose and fell quickly with her agitated breathing, and she was trembling so violently that she looked like one in the throes of some seizure. You killed him! The words roared in her head. You killed Rogue!

A moan broke from her lips. She loved him so! And yet she had brought about his death. Pictures flashed before her eyes. Rogue holding her, kissing her, teasing her unmercifully until, against her will, she was helpless with laughter. A rumpled bed, and herself lying naked beneath him. His lips on her breasts, the ecstasy she had felt as he thrust into her. Rogue, her lover! He could be gentle or violent. She had always wanted the violence, wanted to be hurt as they made love. Thinking of it now, she felt her limbs go weak and fluid. Almost she could feel again his rough penetration, the battering of his body against her own. Unconsciously her fingers began to stroke at her body as her own moans of pleasure sounded in memory. Dear Rogue! Always after the act he would look at her with faintly worried eyes. "Did I hurt you, Mary? Was I too rough this time?"

Her voice answering him. "No, no, you could never be too rough for me. I want you to hurt me, Rogue. I want it!"

"Punishing yourself, Mary?"

"Punishing myself? Oh, no. It is my nature. I like you to hurt me."

She remembered the time when she had drawn Rogue's head down to her breast. Her body jerking spasmodically beneath his, had burned for his entry, but there was something else she wanted first. "Rogue," her hoarse voice had whispered, "bite my nipples. Bite them so hard that they bleed!"

That was the first time she had seen him disgusted with her. As cold as ice, frighteningly formal, he had said, "I'll kiss your breasts, I'll savage and abuse your body all you desire, within limits, of course, but that I will not do."

She had been afraid then that he would leave her. She flung her arms about him, clinging tenaciously. "Then you need not, Rogue. Don't look at me like that! Love me!"

When he had made no movement of response, she had thrust him from her and begun to kiss his body. Her lips had traveled lower and lower until his hard, burning erection quivered and jumped beneath her caressing lips.

He had taken her then, as brutally as ever she could desire.

The next morning, with sunlight streaming across the bed, she had lovingly touched the bruises on her body. The slight pain, the remembrance of when and how they had been inflicted, roused her to a fresh frenzy of desire. She had flung herself upon Rogue. Moaning, clawing at him, pressing hungry kisses upon him, she had awakened him. That occasion stood out from all the others. The sweet thrusting of him inside her, the bruises, the delicious pain, all combined! She exploded into one furious orgasm after another.

It was after that time that Rogue had seemed to change toward her. He was cool but polite. She had always known that he could not for too long be faithful to any one woman. She told herself that this was simply because he had never been in love. Deluding herself, she had expected him to be faithful to her. She could not conceive of ever losing him. Had she not been his mistress for two years? Had he not been faithful to her for far longer than he had been to any other woman? It was true, she told herself. He could not have tired of her. He loved her.

When, finally, he had spoken his mind, the words rejecting her, she had been half out of her mind. In that light and laughing way of his, he had offered her friendship. Friendship instead of love! She could not endure it! It was then that the vindicative and avenging fury began to consume her. She swore to herself that if she could not have him—she alone— she would see him in hell before he took another woman to his bed! And so she had sent him to hell. Because of her betrayal he hung there, a feast for the eyes of the curious.

She stole another look at him. It seemed long hours ago to her since he had been hanged, and yet it was really hardly any time at all.

Mary pushed herself away from the tree. A sudden shouting and a thunder of hooves penetrated her grief. She felt weak. The will to move left her, and she fell back against the tree. The barking sound of firing muskets came to her. She heard the screaming and shouting of the people around the tree; she saw them almost trampling each other in their haste to get out of the way of the rapidly approaching riders.

Mary tried to move then, but she found that she could not; the strength had gone out of her. She stopped her small struggle. Why move? Nothing mattered anymore. There was a high, whining sound, like a swarm of angry insects, and then something struck her hard just above the heart. She put a hand to the pain, staring stupidly at the blood that came oozing through her fingers. Shot! She had been shot!

The horsemen were much nearer now. There were three of them. Mary's dazed eyes widened. Paul! One of the horsemen was Paul Lawrence, Rogue's brother. With him were John Fletcher and Billy Stone. She had a flashing glimpse of Paul's grim young face. He was colorless, his freckles standing out darkly, and in his eyes was a blaze that she had never seen before. He, Fletcher, and Stone all held leveled muskets.

There was a swirling before Mary's eyes, and she blinked hard to clear it. Suddenly everything began to happen at once. Seemingly from nowhere, two guards appeared and began firing on the horsemen. The sound of shot crashed in her ears, and it seemed to her that she stood in a ring of fire. Fletcher and Stone were firing back, but Paul seemed oblivious of everything but his brother. He thrust the musket into his belt and snatched out his knife. The blade glittered in the sunlight as he sliced through the rope that held his brother. Then Rogue Lawrence's limp and helpless body was slung across his saddle.

Shuddering, Mary saw a guard fall. The hangman ran forward to snatch up the musket that had fallen from his hand. Straightening up, he leveled the weapon straight at Paul. Mary saw the swift rising of Paul's hand, the bright arcing of his knife as it flew through the air to bury itself in the hangman's shoulder. Cursing, the man dropped the weapon and clapped a hand to his wounded shoulder.

"Ride!" Paul shouted in a harsh, commanding voice. "Let's get out of here!"

Mary saw Stone and Fletcher crouch low, and then they were away. Paul wheeled his horse about just as Mary moved forward. The animal reared in fright, one front hoof striking her a glancing blow. Paul noticed nothing as he went galloping after the other two men.

Lying on her back, her glazed eyes staring up at the sky, her arms flung outward, Mary Mallison was unaware of the people who came to surround her. She did not hear their exclamations of horror as they stared at the bright blood staining the bodice of her yellow gown. She was aware of nothing but her own thoughts. She was dying, and she was glad! Without Rogue, she did not want to go on living in the world.

Life was slipping away from her, and she was no longer part of it. She never would be again, please God! Had it been Paul's bullet that had buried itself in her body? she wondered. It would be fitting. She began to laugh, and blood appeared at the side of her mouth. Her lips moved. "Paul, my executioner!" she said clearly. Choking, she retched on a gush of blood. The onlookers saw her stiffen as her head fell heavily to one side.

A woman crouching down by the motionless figure looked up and said in a dismayed voice, "Poor lass! She's dead."

The hangman, still clutching his bleeding shoulder, stared down at the body. "It was the freckled lad who done it," he said in a fierce voice. "Wheeled his horse about and deliberately run her down, the murdering young swine! Flung his knife into me, too, he did."

"But she's been shot," the woman said.

"Well, maybe he shot her, too. How'd I know, with all that uproar going on?"

"I don't think he run her down deliberate," another woman spoke up. "I don't think he even seen her. I don't think he seen nothing but that body across his saddle."

The hangman's eyes narrowed. "Paul?" he said musingly. "The lass said Paul, didn't she?"

"Aye, that was the name."

"I wonder now if she could have been meaning Paul Lawrence, the Rogue's brother?"

"Maybe she did," a redheaded man put in, "and then again, maybe she didn't. Anyway, it don't matter much, do it? Law's had its way. The Rogue's dead."

The hangman stared at him. "What about his brother murdering this lass?"

The redheaded man shrugged. "Seems to me there were bullets flying all over the place. Could have been an accident. Besides, I saw the freckled lad. Didn't look much like Rogue to me."

Unimpressed by this argument, the hangman continued to scowl thoughtfully. After a moment of brooding silence he said in a loud, commanding voice, "Two o' you men carry the lass to the cart. Can't do it meself, I'm hurt."

"What about the guard?"

"He ain't hurt too bad. He'll be all right."

"I wonder who the lass is," the redheaded man said.

The hangman shrugged. "Don't suppose we'll ever know."

Urging his horse forward, John Fletcher thought that they were lucky to be alive. He frowned, wondering why he and Stone had allowed themselves to become mixed up in this business. Taking orders from a boy! He and Stone must have been out of their heads. But Paul had been so insistent that he would rescue his brother from under the very nose of the hangman that somehow they had become infected with all his eagerness. Listening to him, Fletcher had thought it all seemed possible. But they had been too late to save the Rogue. He was dead. Poor Paul, poor lad! He had had such dreams of rescuing him. How would he go on now?

Fletcher's frown deepened. And that melee about the hanging tree. He had seen the guard fall. Was he dead? If so, it was likely that the law would soon be posting after them. And there was another thing to worry him. Paul's choice of a hideout. Badger Street was all but on the doorstep of Tyburn Road. To his and Billy Stone's vehement protests, Paul had argued that nobody would think of searching for them in their own backyard. It would be natural that they would be thought to have gone much farther afield. That, he assured them, was the cunning of his choice.

Fletcher's hands tightened on the reins. The only merit in it, as far as he was concerned, was that they would soon be at their destination and out of sight. On a hanging day, the streets were all but empty, thanks be! No one, if they could possibly help it, liked to miss the hangings. As for the people who lived on Badger Street, curiosity was not encouraged. Few questions were asked by the occupants of the crumbling, seedy-looking houses, for most of them were hiding out from the law themselves. All the same, if a substantial reward should be offered for information, there would be some willing, he was sure, to point a finger at them.

Paul turned into Richthorpe Street. Fletcher and Stone saw him rein in his horse. Damning the delay, the two men came to a halt beside him.

Fletcher took one look at the cause of the holdup. "Bloody cart-tail procession!" he fumed.

"Not much of it, though," the more placid Stone answered. "They'll soon he out of our way." He whistled on an incredulous note. "By Christ, Paul, look at that wench! The bastards have ribboned her up some, ain't they?"

Paul's horse pranced nervously as he clenched his hands on the reins. The miserable little procession that was slowly passing by was attended by only a few onlookers. Most of the people, he guessed, had deserted the smaller excitement for the more popular hanging day at Tyburn. Tears came into Paul's eyes, but he blinked them angrily away. Rogue! I was too late to save you. How can I ever forgive myself? How do I go on without you?

Feeling Fletcher's and Stone's eyes upon his face, Paul flushed. He must pull himself together. He'd not disgrace Rogue by bawling like a child. What was done was done. Somehow he would take up his life again, as he felt sure Rogue would have him do. He concentrated his eyes on the procession.

The driver of the cart, a sour expression on his face, his eyes half-closed, was crouched low in his seat. Behind the cart came the flogger, a tall, burly man clad in a sleeveless leather jerkin and rough brown breeches, his heavy whip clutched in his hand. It was the girl who engaged Paul's full attention. Her wrists were lashed tightly to the cart tail. Her long blond hair had spilled forward, hiding her face, and she was stumbling drunkenly along on feet that were torn and bleeding. At the sight of her back, Paul drew in his breath sharply. It reminded him sickeningly of a lump of raw meat. Blood still dripped from the ugly lacerations, spotting the ground in fat, sluggish drops. A cloud of green flies buzzed about her and constantly settled on her tortured flesh. A sudden blazing anger awoke in him. Like Rogue, he had always hated cruelty, and here before him was another victim of the same law that had killed Rogue. Whatever the wench might have done, she did not deserve such savage punishment. It was degrading to the human spirit! It was bestial!

Fletcher saw the expression on Paul's face, and he was immediately uneasy. The line of the boy's tightly set lips reminded him suddenly and strongly of Rogue Lawrence. Just so had the Rogue looked when he was planning something daring and outrageous and was determined to have his way. Fletcher's worst fears were realized when Paul spoke abruptly. "Fletcher, Stone, I want that girl cut free. We will take her with us."

That hard, commanding voice that brooked no opposition, thought Fletcher in reluctant admiration. It might have been Rogue himself speaking. "Take her with us?" he exploded. "Damn, Paul, we can't do that! We've already piked off with one body, and now you want to lumber us with another."

Again that uncanny echo of Rogue. With or without their help, he said, he would have his way. He glanced at Stone and was annoyed to find him grinning. "Here's a fine young cockerel in command, Fletcher," Stone said. "Let's do it, eh? Truth is, I'm sorry for that little wench."

Paul pulled his musket from the holder. "Cover you or come with you?" he asked. "Take your choice."

Stone looked at the body in front of Paul. "Nay, stay here. Hang on tight to Rogue."

Paul nodded. He put his hand into his pocket, then immediately withdrew it. "I left my knife behind," he said in an expressionless voice. "Do you have your knife on you, Stone?"

"Aye, lad, leave it to us."

The flogger, who had glanced only casually at the three mounted men, and didn't notice the body, had dismissed them contemptuously as the usual gawkers. He was still brooding upon his disappointment that he had not after all been able to attend the hangings. Reluctant though he had been to heed it, his common sense had told him that if Caroline Fane was to be returned alive to Newgate Prison, then he must make no further attempts to hurry her on. Angered, afraid to use his whip on her again, he had been forced to proceed at a snail's pace.

A yell from the driver of the cart scattered his thoughts. The flogger's eyes widened in alarm as he saw two of the horsemen bearing down upon him, their muskets at the ready. The third horseman was covering the cowering driver. All three of them looked dangerous, he thought, raising his whip menacingly. " 'Ere!" he bellowed. "What do you think you're doing?"

Fletcher pulled up beside him. "If I were you," he said calmly, looking down into the flogger's mottled face, "I'd drop that whip. Unless, of course, you'd like me to blast a nice neat hole in that thick skull of yours."

Almost dancing with rage, the flogger flung the whip to the ground. "I don't know what the 'ell you think you're up to, but you'll pay for this! This 'ere is a lawful parade, and you ain't got no right to interfere. You could get your bleedin' neck stretched for this, and so I tell you!"

Fletcher made no reply. The fuming flogger was forced to watch as the other man quickly sliced through the cords that bound the girl and gently lifted her into his arms. "You wait, you bleeders!" he shouted. "You'll be sorry for this!"

Fletcher laughed. "Aye, I daresay we will, if we're caught. But it's more likely you'll be the one to pay. I'd not like to be in your shoes when you report that your prisoner escaped." His expression grew grim. "After seeing what you've done to that wench, I'd come singing and cheering to your hanging."

"That so? That wench what you're so sorry for is Caroline Fane. Murderess, she is, and more. Done 'er 'usband in wi' poison. That's who you gone an' set free. Serve you right if she goes an' slips a dose o' poison in your ale, then we'd see who'd be laughin'. But maybe I ain't telling you nothin' you don't already know. You one o' 'er fancy lads, are you?"

Fletcher experienced a sense of shock. He had heard of Caroline Fane, as who had not. Like many who were familiar with the case, he had unhesitatingly condemned her as a cold-blooded murderess. He wondered if Paul would have been so eager to take the girl with them had he known her identity. He looked down at the flogger, his calm expression disappointing the man. "Stow the questions. I'll still be there to cheer when you're hung up."

The flogger stood there, watching with hot and angry eyes as he rode over to his two accomplices. He looked about him. The onlookers, unwilling to be involved, had scattered to a safe distance. The driver sat like a stone on his seat, apparently paralyzed with fright; there was nothing that he alone could do about it. Cursing vilely, he sent a stream of spittle after the departing horsemen.

Something had changed, Caroline Fane thought. She tried to think what it might be, but her tired brain would not allow coherent thought. Something settled about her shoulders. What was it? A cloak? It must be, she decided. She tried, but she could not restrain her moan of protest as the soft cloth touched her flesh. It hung on her like an intolerable weight and caused her pain to take on a new savagery. She wanted to push it away, but she had not the required strength. There was a swift jogging movement beneath her that brought nausea to mingle with her agony. Where was she being taken? Who was holding her? "Hanged by the neck until you are dead!" Someone had said that to her, but who? Terror awoke. Was she even now on her way to be hanged? Half-fainting, she struggled to find words, but they would not come. It was a man's voice, loud, excited, almost hysterical, that brought her back from the edge of darkness.

"Fletcher! Stone!" the voice cried. "He's alive. I felt him move!"

"No, Paul. You know that is not possible."

"Don't you tell me that, Stone! I tell you that Justin is alive! My hand was resting on his back. I felt his muscles quiver."

The jogging motion beneath Caroline ceased. Leather creaked as somebody brushed past her, bringing her another flaring of pain. Then she was sliding downward, to be held in a pair of arms. It was the same man, the one with the chest-rumbling voice, who was holding her. "I'll take the wench up," he said. "Fletcher, you help Paul with Rogue. And, Paul, lad, for God's sake stop that laughing. Damned if you're not hysterical! If you are right about Rogue, you are going to need all your wits and strength to pull him through this. But don't hope too much. You might be mistaken."

"No! I know I am not."

Caroline felt the man's shrug. Then they were moving. She was being carried up a flight of stairs that creaked loudly. There was the smell of stale food, dirt, and mice in her nostrils. Quite suddenly she was overwhelmed with a new terror. Behind her, following closely, they were bringing the man who had so miraculously come back to life. Was that man Thomas, her husband? A whimpering built in her throat. It must not be Thomas! She was too weak and too full of pain to face him now. She must try to remember what had happened. If only the pain in her head would go away, she would be able to think clearly. Wait! She did remember. She had run away from Thomas. She had deserted him, left him alone with the enemy who had struck him down. Poison! Thomas' face all twisted and blue, his head bleeding. Blood! His blood smearing her bodice. Footsteps, stealthy, terrifying! Wine draining from a silver beaker, the red drops like rubies. And Thomas? He was dead! And above her head his mur-

derer stalked, coming nearer, nearer! And now Thomas had
come back to life. They were carrying him up the stairs. But
he would punish her for her desertion. He would slap her
face, as he had so often done before. He would punch her
body and twist her flesh cruelly in his hard, pinching fingers.
She would smell his stale breath in her nostrils, and hear his
voice rising shrill and ugly as he called her whore! Oh, God!
They must not bring him back to life! Her swollen lips
formed words. "Hide me from him, please! Don't let Thomas
find me!"

"Hush, lass, hush!" the man carrying her said. She knew
then with a sense of despair that he had not understood her.
They had stopped climbing. The man had entered a room.
Walking across a floor that creaked as loudly as the stairs, he
laid her down very carefully on her stomach. There was a
softness beneath her. She put out an exploring hand, testing
the softness, as wary as an animal with the scent of danger in
its nostrils. It was a bed! A bed, when for so long she had
been in such discomfort! Tears brimmed into her eyes, and
she opened her mouth to thank him for his kindness. But he
had already left her side. He had gone to join those others
who were so carefully carrying the man who had returned to
life. Now there was movement and bustle all about her. She
was forgotten. She could hear footsteps, people passing by,
the wind of their hasty passages blowing against her hot face.

"By Christ, Paul," Caroline heard a raised voice say, "you
were right! The Rogue is alive!"

"Justin! Justin!" It was the young voice again.

Rogue? Justin? It was not Thomas, then. Cautiously, Caroline raised her head and peered through the bars of the bed.
She saw somebody lying on the floor. Three other men knelt
beside him. The prone figure was clad in red velvet. She tried
to make out the faces of the men, but there was a mist before
her eyes. Wearily she dropped her head. She was so tired!
But she must not sleep, dare not. She must keep her ears alert
in case Thomas should return, after all. The voices went on
and on. If only they were not so loud.

"His chest rose, Stone! Look! It is faint, but he is breathing."

"I see it, Paul. We both see it, don't we, Fletcher?" Stone's
voice was low and soothing, the voice of one speaking to an
overexcited child. "Pull yourself together, lad, for you must

help him. Put your hands on either side of his chest. Yes, that's right, like that. Now, press down, release, press down again. Keep on doing it. It's helping him, I can see. Rhythm, slow and easy rhythm, that's the ticket. Nay, lad, don't lose your head and hurry it. Slow and easy, slow and easy. Ah! Now you've got it."

After a long while, Caroline heard an odd sound. It was like a long, loud snore. The triumphant shout that followed this odd sound made her jump and flinch.

"He doesn't need help to breathe anymore. Look, Stone, look, Fletcher! His breathing is quite strong now."

"Aye, lad, we're looking!"

There was shared laughter. Then a gasp, followed by a burst of sobbing. Caroline heard the young voice again. It was broken with tears, yet at the same time exultant. "S-sorry. I didn't meant to m-make a bloody fool of myself. I just can't get over Justin being alive, when I . . . I . . ."

"We know, lad, don't you worry. We understand how you feel. But now you must get a hold on yourself. He is still going to need you, you know."

"Paul!" Stone's calm voice was suddenly shaken. "His eyes are opening."

"By God, so they are!" Paul bent over Justin. "Can you hear me, Justin? It's me, Paul. I don't want you to worry about anything. You're safe!"

Justin's eyes stared vaguely, then began to clear very slightly. His throat worked, and an expression of intense pain crossed his face.

Paul caught his hand in his and held it in a tight, desperate grip, trying to impart some of his own living warmth. "You must not talk, Justin. Don't even try." He turned his head and looked up at Stone. "Will you help me to get him on the bed, please?"

Suddenly remembering the girl, Stone frowned. "What shall we do about the wench?"

"The wench? Oh, damn! I had forgotten all about her. I know, spread out a blanket, and we'll settle her on the floor."

Stone shook his head. "She's too badly cut up. It's best, I think, that she stay where she is. The bed's wide enough to take them both."

"Anything you say," Paul said impatiently. "Let's get Justin settled."

Caroline felt hands lifting her and moving her from the center of the bed. She was settled to one side, but so gently that her pain was hardly increased. The mattress sagged as the man in the red-velvet suit was placed beside her. She knew that it was not Thomas who lay there so still, so why did she fear? Her heart was beating in such thick, heavy strokes that she could scarcely breathe. She opened her mouth to drag in air. Justin, the young voice had called him. Justin, not Thomas. She must remember that.

Caroline jumped as the young voice, torn with sharp anxiety, sounded loudly in her ears. "Fletcher, look! His eyes have closed again. Something is wrong!"

Caroline felt rather than saw the man stooping over the bed. "Calm yourself, Paul. You're as hysterical as a girl. He's fallen into a natural sleep, that's all."

"You are sure?"

"I am." There was a suggestion of laughter in Fletcher's voice. "Look for yourself. See how easily and regularly he is breathing? Don't disturb him, let him sleep all he can. Believe me, he needs it."

Caroline heard a scraping sound. A chair being pulled across the floor, she guessed. "I'll sit here beside him, then." The anxiety was gone from the voice. "Where are you going, Stone?"

"To get some hot water. That wench needs attention. If her wounds are not attended to, they might become poisoned. There's an old woman on the floor below. I daresay she'll have some kind of a salve I can smear on those lacerations. I'll ask her."

"All right. But say nothing to her about Justin or the girl. Say the salve is for me."

"No need to tell her anything. By now, I have no doubt, she knows all there is to know. Badger Street people are wary of strangers, but they can't afford to be ill-informed."

"Then that means we must move on as soon as possible."

"No one on this street will betray you. To do so might mean betraying themselves. In any case, they can't be moved for a while. By the way, do you know who that girl is?"

"How could I?"

"She is Caroline Fane."

"What! I don't believe you!"

"You can believe it. That's who she is, all right. Why the

long face, lad? She's as weak as a kitten. I doubt she can do any harm."

"I'm concerned for Justin."

"No need," Stone answered impatiently. "Try remembering, Paul, that you're his brother, not his mother."

"Yes, but—"

"Stow it, Paul. What do you expect the wench to do? Go after Rogue with a hatchet?"

Paul flushed. "Sorry," he said in embarrassed apology. "It was just the thought of Justin lying next to that . . . that . . ."

" 'Murderess' is the word you're seeking, Paul. Yes, it is horrifying to think of Saint Rogue being exposed to such evil."

Paul laughed. "All right, Stone, and to hell with you. You've put me in my place."

"See you stay in it, you young cub," Stone answered him in a light voice. "I'll be back soon."

"I'll come with you," Fletcher said.

Caroline heard the door close behind them. She lay rigidly in the bed, silent tears coursing down her cheeks. Once again she had been judged and condemned. Was innocence to have no voice? She closed her eyes tightly. Why should she care what people thought? She wouldn't let herself be hurt anymore! Damn all the upright and moral people who judged without thought!

It was some hours later before Caroline Fane opened her eyes again. Darkness pressed against the small windows, and the room was lit by the flickering light of candles. How long had she been lying in this bed? She seemed to have lost all track of time. She lay very still, feeling almost at peace with herself. She could remember the man Stone returning. Had that been hours or days ago? She had been full of panic when he had come to the bed and stooped over her. He knew who she was, and she had thought that he might deliberately hurt her. She had misjudged him. His tending hands had been very gentle and his touch light. Even so, the agony she had endured beneath his ministrations had sent the perspiration streaming down her body. She had been forced to clamp her teeth in her lower lip to prevent herself screaming out. After that, nothing. She was thankful for the unconsciousness that had spared her further agony. The pain was still there. It would spring up again at her first incautious movement. But for the moment it was surprisingly quiescent. She put a hand to her lips. Much of the swelling had gone down. They, at least, felt almost normal.

A soft sigh, the warmth of the expelled breath fanning her ear, drew her surprised attention. The man in the red-velvet suit! How could she have forgotten about him? She felt the nervous jump of his body, the spasmodic twitch of his fingers that touched her with a brief fluttering movement. His body jumped again, and she wondered what thoughts troubled his sleep. Slowly and carefully Caroline turned her head on the pillow. She looked first at the sleeping youth who was slumped in a chair by the bed. As she stared at the nodding head with its bright crest of rumpled blond hair, her brain suddenly cleared. She had heard the youth's name. It was Paul. His had been the young and wildly excited voice she had heard through the fog of her pain. He was the brother of this man who lay beside her. Beyond Paul, stretched out on the dusty wooden floor with rolled-up blankets beneath their heads, were the other two men.

She turned her eyes to the man beside her. He was as dark as a gypsy. A flush stained the swarthy complexion, as though he might be suffering from a fever. Thickly curling hair fell over his forehead, and his lashes were thick black crescents against his cheeks. His features were regular and well-cut. Altogether, it was a strong, decidedly handsome, almost arrogant face. His lips were sensitive, but his cleft chin had a firm line that spoke of a strong and stubborn will.

As though her concentrated gaze had disturbed him, Justin's brows drew together in a frown. Moving restlessly, coughing, he put a groping hand to his throat. The choking sounds he made, the way his fingers were pressing deeply into his flesh, alarmed Caroline. She looked quickly at Paul, expecting him to awaken, but he was still deep in sleep. Painfully, she moved her arm until her hand was touching his face. "Don't," she whispered urgently to Justin. "Take your fingers away. Don't do that!"

Her voice, though still slurred, must have reached him, for the fingers stopped pressing into his flesh. His breathing was harsh and labored, but the terrible choking sounds gradually ceased. Wondering if she should awaken Paul, Caroline saw Justin's lids lift. Just for a moment, before they drooped again, she found herself staring into his dark and unfocused eyes. She gasped, biting back a cry of pain as he edged closer to her and rested his head against her shoulder. After a moment, to her intense relief, he moved again, and his head found his pillow.

When the first severity of her renewed pain had begun to abate, Caroline found herself wondering who he might be. Justin, Paul had called him. But the other two men had referred to him as Rogue. Justin? Rogue? Both names seemed oddly familiar to her. She drew in her breath sharply. He was Justin Lawrence, of course. The Smiling Rogue! But she had heard that he was to hang. They had hanged him. Then, as she stared at the sleeping face, everything fell suddenly into place. The wild excitement in Paul's voice. "He's alive! Justin is alive?" They must have cut down Rogue Lawrence before he could strangle to death! She was suddenly very frightened. Paul and his followers had rescued her, and for the moment she was protected from those who would destroy her. But when the Rogue recovered, what would he do with her? Would he, because of his own former plight, have sympathy with hers? It was hard to tell. She had heard it said that he could be cold and ruthless.

Muttering something unintelligible, Rogue Lawrence moved again. And, with the movement, Caroline's fear dissolved into amusement. The situation in which she now found herself was a good joke on the law that had condemned them both to death. Murderess, they had branded her. And now that same murderess lay beside Justin Lawrence, thief and rogue, the man that should be dead.

Caroline looked at Paul Lawrence, her eyes softening. He and his men had rescued her, and for the time being she was safe. It was true that she could live only from moment to moment, always wondering when the hand of authority would fall again on her shoulder. But she owed Paul something for her reprieve. She owed all three men. She lay very still, pricklingly conscious of Rogue Lawrence beside her, pain fading as her senses began to haze. Her last thought was: I am here. It is enough for the moment. Let the future take care of itself.

When Caroline awakened again, it was to a scene of pandemonium. Sunlight streamed through the tightly closed dusty windows and fell slantingly across the bed. Justin Lawrence, his eyes wild, his mouth sagging as he fought to draw in breath, was struggling madly to escape the tight hold Paul had on him. The cords in his throat strained. The high, tortured whine of his breathing, followed by a harsh rattling sound, filled the room. Caroline's mouth went dry with fear. It was a terrible sound, and she knew that at any moment the struggle to breathe would cease. He could not go on like that. It was too much of a strain on his heart. She looked at Paul. His face was white and terrified. Except for themselves, the room was empty. She owed Paul something. He had helped her, and now she must forget her own pain and help him.

"Paul!" Caroline's voice was sharp with command. "I want you to open both of those windows wide. He must have air. Hurry!"

She had half-feared that Paul would not understand her thick voice, but evidently it was clearer now, for he nodded. With a last distracted look at Justin, he rushed to obey.

Caroline managed to raise herself. For a moment she thought she might faint with the agony. The moment passed. "Be still!" She touched Justin's arm. "Don't struggle. I will help you!"

She had had no hope that her voice would reach him, and she was surprised when his head turned in her direction. His eyes were still wild, and she knew that he did not see her. The movement of his head toward her had been a blindly seeking and silent cry for help. His hands went to his throat, clawing downward, leaving bloody furrows. "R-r-rope!" His fingers made plucking movements, as though he tried to tear something away. "H-help m-m-me!"

Paul came dashing back to the bed. "I heard him speak! What did he say?" Without waiting for an answer, he touched Justin's heaving shoulders with a trembling hand. "I've opened the windows, Justin. You'll be all right now."

"No, Paul," Caroline said. "He will not be all right until you take off the rope that is choking him."

"But ..." Paul stared at her, his jaw dropping. "How can ... ?"

"You must!" Inwardly praying that she was right, she said urgently, "The rope about his neck is choking him. Do you understand, Paul? Take it off. Now!"

To her relief, she saw understanding dawn in Paul's eyes.

She watched him as he made the necessary movements. His fingers touched Justin's throat, fumbled there very gently, then traveled upward. She had no idea of how much Justin could hear or understand, or if he knew anything at all, but he must not know he was being humored. That would be fatal. Obviously, to him there was a rope about his neck still. It was very real to him, and it must be treated as a reality.

"The rope has gone, Justin," Paul said in a clear voice. "It's gone. Do you hear me? You are free."

Again Caroline's hand touched Justin's arm. "You heard what Paul said, Justin. He has taken off the rope. He has thrown it away. There is no need to struggle anymore. Breathe deeply and easily, for all is well. Do you understand?"

From the great distance to which he had retreated, it was evident even to Paul's anxious eyes that Justin had not only heard, he had understood. With awed amazement and gratitude, Paul saw something that was almost a smile touch the blue-tinged lips. "You knew!" Paul said to Caroline. "How did you know?"

She put a finger to her lips, giving him a warning look. With a long, sighing sound, Justin collapsed back against the pillow. His throat still strained, but the distressing struggle to breathe was rapidly easing. "Get me a cloth, Paul," she said.

Paul looked about him, and then fumbled in his pocket. He handed her a crumpled but clean kerchief. "Will this do?"

Caroline nodded. Taking it, she dabbed gently at the great drops of perspiration that were still trickling down Justin's face. "His mind is at rest now, Paul," she said, smiling at him.

"You knew!" Paul said again in a low voice. "How?"

"Common sense, and the few words he managed to·say." She lowered her voice to a whisper. "In his mind, the rope was there. I feel sure of that. If you had not removed it, he would have died."

"Will it . . . will it happen again?"

"I don't know. It might, and you must be prepared for it. But we know now what we must do."

Color flooded Paul's face, and his eyes had a sudden bright sheen. He rubbed an impatient hand across his eyes. "M-my brother means a great deal to me. I don't k-know how to thank you!"

"No thanks is needed, Paul. You helped me, and I helped you."

"Aye. Thank God I did. It must have been meant." The flush in Paul's face deepened. "I know who you are, Mistress Fane. I am ashamed of the thoughts I had about you. I . . . I believed you guilty."

"How do you know that I am not?"

"You could not have been so kind and understanding if you were . . . were . . ." Unable to go on, he looked at her helplessly.

Caroline averted her eyes. She was barely twenty years old, and she imagined that she and Paul were much of an age, and yet she felt infinitely older than he. She had helped his brother, and for Paul, any doubts he might have had of her innocence were immediately swept away. She saw his troubled eyes upon her, and she said in a soft voice, "I am innocent. Thank you for believing that. It means a lot to me."

Paul was about to say something more when he saw her sudden wince of pain. He started guiltily. "Your back! You must be in agony."

"It was just a twinge. To tell the truth, it feels numb at the moment."

"Is there anything I can do for you? You have only to say."

Caroline did not answer. Her attention was on Justin again. His breathing was all but normal now, but something was still troubling him. He was frowning and moving restlessly. Because of her own discomfort, which had begun some time ago, she thought she knew what was troubling him. She had been brought up to be modest and reserved, but she was also country-bred and practical. "I believe your brother has need of the chamber pot," she said calmly.

Color flooded Paul's face. "I should have thought of that for myself." He looked at her, and Caroline, smiling a little at his patent embarrassment, obligingly turned her head away.

She could hear him groping under the bed, the clink of china, and then Justin's faint moan as he was hoisted to his feet. "Hold on to him tightly, Paul," she said. "Don't let him fall."

She heard Justin urinating, and the sound increased her own urgent need. It seemed a long time to her before the mattress sagged again with the weight of his body. She heard the hoarse, painful mumble of his voice, and she turned her head to look at him. His eyes were closed. He looked peaceful, but he was still too flushed. She felt a small spasm of irritation. It was evident that Paul did not think too clearly when he was worried. Justin should not be lying in the bed in his heavy velvet garments. After her own need was satisfied, she would speak to Paul about it.

Holding the chamber pot, Paul crossed over to the window. He was grateful to Mistress Fane for her matter-of-fact manner, but he felt miserably embarrassed for the girl in the bed. Apart from his mother and a small cousin, he knew little about females. He liked them, and he hoped one day to have a girl of his own, but he was cursed with a shy nature, and he always felt clumsy and tongue-tied in their presence. He should have known Justin's need without having to be told. What a fool she must think him! Sighing, Paul emptied the pot out of the window. He was startled by an anguished howl from below.

"Bleedin' sod!" a voice bellowed. "Look what you done to me, you bastard!"

Paul put his head out of the window and looked apologetically at the enraged little man below. "Sorry," was all he could find to say.

Shaking his fist, the man glared up at him. "Wait'll I get me 'ands on you, you'll be sorry all right!" He took off his sodden cap and brushed at the trickles of moisture running down his face. Shaking the cap, he jammed it back on his head again. "Nice thing it is when a person can't go walking wi'out 'aving pots emptied over 'is bleedin' 'ead."

"I am sorry," Paul said again, "but you should have been looking."

"I 'ope you're looking when you go strolling under my winder, that's all I got to say to you, you perisher!"

Paul drew in his head hastily. He wished that he could be more like Justin, who would undoubtedly have found the incident highly diverting. He took things too seriously, he knew. He could not laugh at life as Justin did. Going back to the bed, Paul looked down at his sleeping brother. There were dark shadows beneath Justin's eyes, and the hollows beneath his high cheekbones were more pronounced. Had it all been for nothing? he wondered. Had he cut Justin down in time to save him, only to lose him now? He could not help thinking that death still stood stubbornly at his elbow.

"Paul"—Caroline's voice cut in on his troubled thoughts—"I have the same need as your brother, but I can't get out of bed without assistance. Will you help me?"

There was the barest pause before he answered in a carefully casual voice, "Of course, Mistress Fane. It will pleasure me."

Without looking at her, he came around to the side of the bed and placed the chamber pot on the floor. Poor lad, she thought pityingly. How easily that fair skin of his flushed. He no doubt thought he was hiding it well, but his embarrassment was painfully obvious. Well, she was embarrassed too. There was nothing to be done about it.

Paul lifted her as gently as possible from the bed, but his touch awoke demons of pain that clawed at her with burning talons. The pain became so excruciating that she could not hold back a scream. The room dipped and wavered about her, and her feet did not seem to belong to her. Her control over herself broke. Frightened, she began to sob brokenly as her long-held urine flooded down her legs, splattering Paul and pooling about her bare feet. It was too much! Her voice rose on a note of hysteria as she cried out to him, "I'm sorry! It was too long a wait!"

Her anguished outcry touched his heart, banishing his embarrassment. He smiled at her, hoping to convey reassurance. "Please don't cry, Mistress Fane," he said huskily. "Come, let me put you back in the bed."

Caroline looked quickly at Justin. The commotion had not disturbed him, for he still slept. She could at least be thankful that her humiliation had not been observed by those gypsy-dark eyes. Despair rose again as Paul's last words penetrated. "How can I lie in the bed like this?" she cried out wildly. "My body stinks! My hair is fouled! And if that were not enough, I have managed to foul my person still further. Oh, God, I wish I were dead!"

"No! You must never wish that."

"But I do. Look at me! I wonder you do not vomit when you stand so near to me. I am offensive, filthy! I have not bathed since they came for me and took me to the prison. They would not let me bathe. I cannot bear it, I tell you! The stench of Newgate has penetrated my very skin. I ... I will never be rid of it!"

As he listened to her, an idea came to Paul. He said earnestly, "You will be clean and comfortable, Mistress Fane. I am going to see to it. Will you trust me?"

Clean and comfortable. If only she could be! She nodded. "I do trust you, Paul."

Without another word, careful not to hurt her more than necessary, Paul lifted her into his arms and strode over to the door. It was standing slightly ajar, and he kicked it open and carried her out. The landing was dingy and dark, the walls damp from the constant seeping of water that had collected in the rotting timbers. A candle in a black iron sconce burned at the head of the stairs, but the frail flame did little to alleviate the gloom. Looking about him, Paul felt a sudden longing for his home. If he waited another two weeks, would Justin be sufficiently recovered to travel? He would surely recover his strength quickly in the familiar and beautiful surroundings of Bewley Grange.

Caroline stiffened in Paul's arms. She had said she trusted him, and she had. Now she was no longer sure. Why was he hesitating at the top of the stairs? What was he thinking about? Perhaps he had asked her to trust him in order to allay any suspicion she might have. She was an encumbrance to him and whatever plans he might have for his brother, and she was suddenly sure that he meant to abandon her. "What are you going to do with me?" she said in a faint voice. "W-where are you taking me?"

Paul looked down at her. He was shocked by the terror in her brown eyes. "What is it, Mistress Fane?" he said gently. "Why do you look so frightened? Do you think I mean you harm?"

His gentle tone caused some of her fear to fade, but she was still suspicious. "I would know where you are taking me."

"That is easily answered," Paul said, smiling. "Mistress Benson, who lives just below, makes her living by taking in washing, and she always has plenty of hot water. Stone told me, for he is a great one at making friends. I thought if I paid her, she would help you to bathe. And maybe, if you think you can endure it, she will even wash your hair."

"Oh, Paul!" Ashamed of her suspicion, she smiled at him

radiantly. "I can bear the pain. If only I can be clean again, I can bear anything!"

He was touched by her pleasure, and he felt a wish to add to it. "She might have a gown you can wear," he said shyly. "Even if it be old, it will at least be clean."

She was looking at him as if he had offered her heaven. "It will be so wonderful to be clean again! So wonderful!"

"It means that much to you?"

"Oh, yes, yes!"

Wondering if she would be able to endure the pain of such attention, he began to descend the stairs slowly and carefully. "I will tell Mistress Benson that she must be as gentle as possible," he soothed. "I will say that she is on no account to touch your back."

"Dear Paul! Thank you."

On the landing below, Paul paused before an ill-fitting door. The sound of somebody singing in a cracked voice came to them. Paul grinned. "Mistress Benson, I would imagine," he said.

Before he could knock at the door, Caroline halted him. It was becoming more and more of an effort to speak, but she wanted to do something for him. It was not much she had to offer, just a few words of advice. "Paul, Justin is too hot in those heavy garments he is wearing. Take them off. Get some warm water and sponge his body. If he is cool and comfortable, it will help his recovery."

Paul's smile was rueful. "Something else I should have thought of for myself. I'm an idiot!"

"No, Paul. Justin is here. I am here. Two escapes in one day. An idiot could not have done it." She gasped as pain stabbed deeply. Fearful that he would change his mind and take her back, she managed a wavering smile. "You will find that Justin w-will be better off without clothes."

"Naked? But he will be in the same bed with you!"

His look of profound shock amused and touched her, and she felt a rush of affection for the shy and gentle boy. He was so ingenuous! How came he to have a brother so different in nature? From all she had heard of him, Rogue Lawrence was hard and bold, daring and ruthless. Everything, she was sure, that Paul was not. They were as different as night and day. But since Paul was so obviously devoted to the Rogue, there might be more to him. Something, perhaps, that inspired such devotion. A quality that Rogue Lawrence kept hidden from a stranger's eyes. Paul was looking at her, expecting an answer. She said quickly, "You will think me immodest, Paul, but it will not matter to me."

"No?"

"No. Do you think me immodest?"

"Oh, no. The . . . the circumstances are unusual."

"Who's that talkin' out there?" a sharp voice challenged. The door was pulled open abruptly. The woman who stood in the doorway seemed at first sight to be very old, so wizened was she, but the faded blue eyes in the thin, wrinkled face were remarkably alert. The eyes rested first on Paul, then flicked briefly over the girl in his arms. "What you doin' whispering outside me door?" she demanded in a voice that bristled with suspicion. "What you doin' out 'ere, eh?"

Paul hastened to soften her hostile attitude. "You know me," he said, smiling at her. "You've seen me before."

She did not return the smile. "I seen you, but don't know you. And don't know as I want to. What you want?"

Paul launched into an explanation. The woman heard him out without a perceptible change in her expression. When his voice died, she stood to one side. "You'd better bring the wench in," she said grudgingly. "Folks like you—gentry folks, from the sound o' your voices—is all the same. They think nobody ain't got nothin' better to do than wait on 'em. What makes you think I want to waste me time cleanin' up any stray what you like to bring to me door?" Seeing the flash in Caroline's eyes, she added sharply, "No temper, gal, or out you go!"

Sniffing her displeasure, she waited until Paul had deposited Caroline carefully on a chair; then she turned her disconcerting eyes on him. "I'll do what I can. Can't say fairer than that. But you'll 'ave to pay me. I ain't doing it for nothing. An' if you was thinking so, then you're all wrong in your 'ead!"

Chapter 4

Caroline sat in a chair by the uncurtained window, her restless hands folded tightly in her lap. The view of Badger Street, seen through the dusty panes of glass, was more depressing than usual. Afraid to let her mind wander, she concentrated firmly on a woman in a tattered brown coat who was weaving her way unsteadily along the street. The woman stopped and peered into the overflowing gutter, her eyes searching for something that might be of use to her.

A movement came from the bed behind her. Caroline stiffened. It was an effort not to turn her head and steal a look at Justin Lawrence, but she resisted the impulse. Was he awake? Was he looking at her with those disturbing dark eyes of his? That look he sometimes gave her that made her flesh tingle and burn—was it turned on her now? She pressed her lips tightly together. Only yesterday, when his hand had accidentally brushed hers, she had begun to tremble like a fool. The trouble was that she was too much aware of him. He roused feelings in her she had never known before. She wondered if he knew it and was amused by her reactions to him.

The movement came again, and still she would not turn. "Carrie," Justin called her, knowing full well that the abbreviation of her name annoyed her. "Carrie." That strange whispering, husky voice of his almost made the little name into a caress. Paul worried because Justin had not regained his natural tones and did not seem likely to do so. But she, never having heard his voice before the hanging had altered it, found the whispering, husky voice quite fascinating. Sometimes she even carried the echo of it into her dreams.

Frowning, Caroline glanced quickly toward the door. If only Paul would come soon. Perhaps then she would stop thinking about Justin. She would not keep remembering the vulnerable look on his face when he was sleeping, the restless

way he had of encroaching on her side of the bed, and the
way his head always seemed to find its way to her shoulder.
She hated him! He mixed her up, made her feel strange. She
was suddenly quite sure that she must be going insane. She
hated men; Thomas had taught her to hate them. Then why,
last night, when his head had snuggled against her shoulder,
had she had the impulse to put her arms about him and hold
him tightly to her? Insanity! It was the only answer. She
didn't want Justin. She didn't want any man.

She looked at the door again. Why did Paul leave her
alone so often with Justin? It was true that Justin was much
better. But he was still weak, and the nightmares, though less
frequent, still troubled him. Now that Fletcher and Stone had
departed, both men being too restless to stay long in one
place, there were just the three of them. Paul was always ab-
senting himself, and Justin's care devolved upon her. He must
go out, Paul had explained to her. Not only to purchase food;
by mingling with the people, he might be able to gain information that would tell him the way the wind blew in regard to Caroline Fane.

Caroline moved restlessly in the chair. It had been three
weeks since she had been snatched away from the flogging
parade. It was more than possible, she told Paul, that the hue
and cry had died down. He agreed with her, but he was still
cautious. Before they could move on, he told her, he must
make quite sure that the patrols had abandoned the search.
The discovery of Caroline Fane would inevitably lead to the
discovery of Rogue Lawrence, and that would mean another
hanging party.

In that three weeks, her back had all but healed. She could
even lie on it without experiencing too much discomfort. She
had Mistress Benson to thank for that rapid healing. She had
coated the wounds with her special salve. A proven recipe,
she had told Caroline, handed down to her by her grandmother. Caroline smiled. Mistress Benson was not the dragon
she had at first appeared to be. She had been kindness itself.
Caroline's body, from the frequent baths taken in the dingy
room downstairs, was always fresh, her hair shining and
fragrant with Mistress Benson's special herb rinse, another
recipe of her grandmother's. Even the old print gown she
wore, the back carefully cut out so that it would not irritate

her healing wounds, she owed to the woman's thoughtful kindness.

Caroline frowned as she found her thoughts once more turning to Justin. It would not do! She must not keep thinking of him. She would think instead of Bewley Grange, Paul's much-loved home. He had told her much of Bewley Grange. They would be going there when Paul thought it safe to make the move.

Caroline's stiff posture relaxed, and her eyes took on a dreaming look. Bewley Grange was in Yorkshire. And Paul, touchingly grateful for her care of his brother, had insisted that she come with them. She must make the Grange her home for as long as she pleased. At first she demurred, but he would not take no for an answer. Now she had grown used to the idea, and she counted the days until they would be gone from this place. She was eager to leave London far behind. She wanted to fill her lungs with the crisp, tangy, scented breath of the moors.

Paul loved his home with a passion. He had talked of it so much that he had built a picture in her mind. She could see the tall, graceful building set upon a slight hill. The ever-changing sea at its back, the wild moorland at its front. The moors, where blew purple heather, and sturdy wild ponies roamed. She saw clearly the sun-faded red-brick walls of the house and the vines that climbed those walls. In the summer, the vines were burdened with small starry white flowers whose subtle fragrance permeated every room. Birds nested under the eaves of the house. Pigeons were everywhere, fluttering among the ancient surrounding trees and filling the air with their mournful calling.

Yorkshire, Paul told her, was wild and rugged country. But that wildness ended at the great iron gates that bore the family crest of the Lawrences. Inside those gates it was all peace and tranquillity. A little world set apart.

Most of all in these talks between them, Caroline cherished the knowledge of Paul's friendship and trust. At first she had thought his attitude to be prompted only by gratitude for her care of his brother, but as their talks went on, she had realized that he genuinely liked her for herself, and his trust in her was complete. So complete, indeed, that, through his vivid description, which held nothing back, she felt that she knew Margaret Lawrence, their mother, and the two small boys, as Justin and Paul had been then.

It was under the elm tree nearest to the house that Margaret Lawrence had sat and worked on her embroidery. What thoughts had been hers? Caroline wondered. Had she perhaps pondered on the difference in her two sons? Had it worried Margaret Lawrence, the fervent admiration and apparently unbreakable attachment the quiet, studious Paul had for the headstrong Justin? She did not know of the folly into which Justin had plunged, for this was carefully kept from her. But loving him as she did, she might have guessed at the disastrous direction in which her elder son was headed. This inner knowledge, if indeed she had it, added to the further knowledge that Paul, her quiet son, would always put aside those things that were important to him to follow wherever Justin beckoned, must have been especially bitter and heartbreaking for her.

Then death came. It invaded that little world that was set apart. Within scant days of being struck down, Margaret Lawrence was dead of the smallpox. A short time afterward her husband, Jonathan Lawrence, followed her. When the sad finalities of death were over, Bewley Grange was, for a time, abandoned. The house waited for the return of Justin and Paul Lawrence, as serene and as unchanging as ever, its trees alive with birdsong. When they finally were able to return, the house absorbed them as if their absence had never been. Justin, Paul told Caroline, did not love the house with his own single-minded passion, but Bewley Grange meant something to him for all that. It was solid and secure, an anchor, this place that was unchanging in a rapidly changing world.

Caroline leaned back, her fingers tapping the arm of the chair. Having come so near to death, would Justin abandon his old ways and settle down to the life of a country gentleman? Paul hoped for this. He even believed it would come to pass. But she, who knew Justin only from hearsay and from mumbled words in the night, could not imagine him ever changing. Yet it might be that Justin would never be the same again. In those first days, when the nightmare came to him so frequently, it was to her, the stranger in their midst, that Justin had clung, seeming, in some way known only to himself, to derive strength from her. She knew that weak, helpless as a child, he was not aware of her as a woman. She was a quiet voice that managed to reach him. She was a pair of soothing hands. Sometimes he fought those hands, but more often he allowed them to comfort.

Caroline shuddered as she thought back to those terrible days and nights. Justin struggling, trying to breathe, his chest heaving, his fingers endlessly trying to remove the rope from about his neck. When she tried to get him to swallow something that would sustain life, she winced for the pain that must be his. His wild eyes did not see her, but he heard her voice. That voice bade him swallow, and like an obedient child, he did his best to obey. The result was always the same. He would manage to get down a little, then his throat seemed to close. The choking would begin, and she would hold on to him with careful, gentle hands. Afterward the pain and the fever would increase. She had worried that he might die, and she had seen that same worry in Paul's eyes. The change, when it came, had come suddenly. In this last week it was as though he had turned a dangerous corner and left it far behind. Now his eyes were clear and intelligent, always following her. To celebrate that first victory over death, she had fed him crumbled bread in a bowl of sweetened milk. She had been half-afraid that his stomach would reject the food. But though his face had darkened, he had managed to get it down without too much effort. He had even smiled at her. Since then his progress had been little short of remarkable. He grew stronger every day. In his elation, Paul spoke more and more of Bewley Grange. He was convinced that only the familiar surroundings and the crisp, strong, healthgiving Yorkshire air were needed to complete the cure.

Justin lay quietly, watching the girl by the window. He could remember everything now. They had hanged him. Paul had saved him before he could strangle to death. How he had saved him was not yet clear to him. He had not been aware of Paul. For a long time he had been detached from his brother. He had been wandering in some dark and terrible place where Paul might not enter. Even now, with his mind clear and able to reason again, the memory of it could still make him shudder and sweat. He had been all alone in his own private hell. A place where the stifling darkness was sometimes shot through with bolts of searing flame, where fiery and unbearable pain consumed him. Rope nooses had dangled from twisted trees, waiting to trap him. He was run-

ning, always running! He knew, if he stopped, that the noose
would fall about his neck and tighten. Once or twice in his
headlong flight, he had tripped, and then that dangling black
snake of a rope had caught him. But before the rope could
tighten and cut off his breath altogether, he would hear someone calling to him, quietly, insistently, saying his name, re-
peating it over and over again. It was that voice that had
saved him. But there were other things that the voice could
not save him from. It was powerless to silence the demented
screaming that went on endlessly, splitting his eardrums with
the incredible and awful din. It could not save him from the
booming nightmare voice that bellowed above the screaming.
" 'Ot pies," the voice that had followed him into hell would
cry out. "Try me nice 'ot pies!"

Justin pushed memory aside and concentrated instead on
the girl. Caroline Fane! What the devil was she doing here?
From the moment he had opened his eyes to sanity, he had
recognized her. He had first heard her story whispered in the
streets. It had interested him. He could understand the many
things that motivated people to murder. But Caroline Fane,
he understood, was a young and delicate girl. A lady. What
was it that had motivated her? Driven by curiosity and that
penchant he had for ignoring danger, he had decided to attend the trial of Caroline Fane. Under the very eyes of those
men who had planned so many times to capture Rogue
Lawrence, wigged, dressed in carefully chosen sober clothing,
he had watched Caroline Fane almost with fascination. That
stony face of hers had remained imprinted on his memory.
She had stood there in the dock, so rigidly unmoving, so apparently uncaring and contemptuous of those around her.
What thoughts, he had wondered, went on behind her blank
brown eyes?

He moved restlessly in the bed. And now he no longer
questioned her presence; he felt too tired for sustained
thought. He accepted it instead as one of life's little ironic
jests, the coming together in this dingy room of the thief and
the murderess. A man who should be dead, and a woman
who was seemingly without conscience or morals. No, how it
had come about need not concern him now. Later, when he
questioned Paul, he had no doubt that the puzzle would be
explained. Once again he thought of the soft and gentle
hands that had reached out through his nightmare to touch

him reassuringly, of the quiet voice that had soothed his terror and comforted him and brought him back from the
darkness. Had those hands, that voice, belonged to Caroline
Fane, the girl he had seen in the dock on trial for her life? It
could not be! Gentleness did not seem to go with the hard
and uncaring impression he had had of her. Caroline Fane
looked after him, it was true. She fed him and did many
things that added to his comfort. But it seemed to him that
she did them unwillingly. And when she looked at him
directly, it was always with hostility. So it might be that he
had only imagined the gentle hands and the quiet voice. In
the face of her hostility, it must be so.

The sun striking through the window laid bright fingers on
Caroline's hair, turning it to a silvery sheen. Staring at her,
Justin was gripped by that same unwilling fascination he had
felt in the courtroom. Something stirred in his groin as he
looked at her breasts beneath the faded blue gown. They
were pointed and provocative and distinctly tempting. He
smiled to himself. He had certainly come a long way along
the road to recovery if he now found himself wanting a
woman. How would Caroline Fane be? His hunger grew as
he thought of her lying naked beneath him. Her long, slim
legs twining about his body and gripping him fast. Her body
flooded with passion and jerking spasmodically beneath his
own. It was said that Caroline Fane had had many lovers.
Was it true? True or false, it mattered little; he only knew
that he wanted her. He thought of her lying beside him, and
his heart began to beat faster. But there was that cursed hostility of hers. Damned if he'd take an unwilling woman. He
never had, and he would not start now. He was not used to
waiting for a woman to turn his way; usually they came
willingly. Now, perversely, because he felt she would resist
him, he wanted her more than he had ever wanted any other
woman. Well, he told himself, he could wait. But for now he
would have her near him. For some reason, he was nervous.
Annoyed, he tightened his fingers on the sheet and called to
her softly. "Carrie."

At the sound of the husky voice, Caroline started violently.
"So you are awake," she said, rising to her feet. "I had hoped
you were sleeping."

"No. I think I have slept too much, and I am becoming

tired of lying in bed. I have been awake for some time. I have been watching you, Mistress Caroline Fane."

Color scorched her face. "When Paul told you my name," she said stiffly, "it did not seem to mean anything to you at that time. Why do you say my name now in such a tone?"

"I merely said your name. I was not aware that I imbued it with any particular meaning." He smiled. "The girl who nursed me was called Caroline, but it was easier and pleasanter to say Carrie. Even a little amusing when the abbreviation seemed to cause my nurse some annoyance. But I was not quite in my right mind at the time, you understand? It was not until my mind began to clear that I connected my Carrie with the notorious Caroline Fane."

"I am not your Carrie!" she flared. "And do not call me notorious!" Her hands clenched tightly at her sides. "And now that you have made the connection, what now? Should I be terrified that you will give me up to the Watch?"

He looked at her in genuine surprise. "Terrified? Of me? What nonsense is this? I have been aware of your true identity for this last week."

"Then why have you not questioned me or Paul?"

"I have been too tired. But I will. I am interested to know how you come to be here."

"I will tell you."

"No, later." He smiled at her lazily. "Come over here. Sit beside me."

She hesitated. She was uncomfortably aware of the heat in her body and the racing of her pulses. She was suddenly terribly afraid of the violent emotions that his mere glance and the sound of his voice could arouse in her. She saw his slight smile and the half-mocking lift of his eyebrows, and it seemed to her that he could read her thoughts. Pride overcame her fear. Slowly and unwillingly she went toward him. She did not look at him as she seated herself on the chair by the bed.

"That's better, Carrie. Now I can see you clearly."

She lifted her eyes to his face. "My . . . my name is Caroline. I dislike it when you call me Carrie."

"You will always be Carrie to me." He reached out and took her hand in his. His eyes softened as he felt the nervous twitch of her fingers. "You have such soft and pretty hands, my Carrie." He raised her hand to his lips and kissed it softly. "Are these the hands that touched me so gently when I was ill?" His eyes on her face were suddenly intent. "Was it your voice that called to me, Carrie?"

If only he would not touch her! Caroline had the sudden wild feeling that he must surely hear the thumping of her heart. Oh, why did he look at her in that disturbing way? His eyes were so dark, so deep, so intense! Above that mad beating of her heart, she heard her voice say coldly, "I have no notion of your meaning. I helped Paul look after you. That is all."

He felt a curious sense of disappointment. No, it could not have been this girl with her wooden face and her blank and lightless eyes. Masking his disappointment, he said lightly, "Then it must have been something I dreamed." Compelled to have her yet nearer to him, and half-annoyed by the excitement she aroused in him, he tugged gently on her hand. "You are too far away from me, Carrie. Sit on the bed, please."

"No!" Her voice was sharp, almost shrill. "I am near enough."

"But I have said you are too far away, Carrie. Come."

His smiling eyes were on her face. She wanted to run, and yet at the same time she wanted to be as near to him as she could possibly get. But he must not know. He must not laugh at her! She rose to her feet and seated herself stiffly on the bed. "Well?" she demanded, her eyes avoiding his. "Am I now near enough to suit you?"

"Look at me, Carrie." His hand touched her chin and tilted her face upward.

She stared into his eyes. He was so close that she could feel his breath fanning her lips. "Don't!" she said faintly. "Don't!"

"Don't what, Carrie?" He took her face in his hands, holding it gently. "What is it I must not do?"

His husky, fascinating voice was intimate, almost tender. "I . . . I don't know," she stammered. "I don't know what I m-meant."

"Do you mean I must not do this?" His lips touched her brow. "Or this, Carrie?" His mouth covered hers.

His kiss was so gentle, so very sweet, that she found herself wanting to cry, to cling to him in search of some comfort that she could not give a name to. Then, as his kiss became deeper, fiercely demanding, she felt the fire racing through her veins. Her body no longer seemed to belong to her; it was throbbing, incandescent. She had never felt like this before. She was a stranger to herself, wild, pagan. She moaned softly against his lips, and her arms wound themselves tightly about his neck. Justin! Justin!

She drew back as his head lifted. "Carrie!" He looked at her searchingly. He saw the soft, trembling mouth, the glow in her eyes. His arms went around her, his lips kissed her hair, her face, her mouth, the hollow in her throat. "I want you, Carrie! I want you!"

His fingers touched her bodice, began to undo the tiny buttons, and still she was powerless to resist him. He pulled the bodice down over her shoulders and helped her to free her arms from the sleeves. Then his face was buried between her breasts. Madness! she thought. But such sweet madness! Tears gathered in her eyes and spilled down her cheeks as she pressed the dark head closer. Her hands stroked his hair. It was when his lips touched her nipple, moving gently, that Thomas Fane's face arose in her mental vision. Fear awoke, clawing at her like an infuriated animal, and with the fear came a wave of distaste so intense that she was nauseated by its strength. "Don't!" With all her strength she pushed him away from her. "Oh, God! Don't touch me. Never put your hands on me again!"

The look of shock occasioned by her outburst left his face. He watched with puzzled eyes as she thrust her arms into the sleeves of her bodice, dragged it up, and buttoned it securely. "Carrie, what is it? I did not mean to frighten you. Perhaps I was mistaken, but I thought you wanted me as much as I wanted you."

"You . . . you were mistaken. I don't want you. I don't want any man. Filthy animals, all of them!"

Ignoring her flinching, he took her face between his hands again. "No, don't fight me. I only want to talk to you. Listen to me, Carrie, you must not fear me." Very gently he kissed both of the tear-wet cheeks. "You are a child, a frightened child. My poor Carrie! Who has done this to you? Who in your life has made you believe that all men are animals?"

"They are! Thomas . . ."

"Thomas?" He waited for her to answer. When she did not, he went on. "No, Carrie, you had the wrong teacher.

Love and passion, when shared between the right man and woman, can be very sweet. It is a beautiful experience. Don't you know that?"

Her lips tightened obstinately. Why must he look at her so gently? That strange voice of his was so very tender. She said sullenly, "You do not live up to your reputation. I had heard you were wild and violent."

His laugh broke the tension between them. "So I might be, Carrie." His hands released her face, and he wiped her tears away with his fingers. "Aye, I know my reputation all to well. But Rogue Lawrence has one virtue, and only one. He is never wild and violent with children."

"I am not a child!"

"Yes, you are. But I will tell you something. When you begin to grow away from your fear, you will discover that an extremely passionate woman has taken the place of the child."

"I will never let another man put his hands on me!" She shuddered.

Smiling, he lay back against the pillows. "Caroline Fane, I know not how you gained your reputation for promiscuity. A mistake has been made somewhere. By God it has!"

"It is all a mistake. I am not what they say. I am innocent. Do you believe me?"

"In all truth, Carrie, I am bewildered. I thought you guilty. I even attended you at your trial, and watching you in that courtroom, your indifference, your contempt, aye, I did think you guilty. But now I know not what to believe."

She was surprised to hear he had been at the trial, but shrugged it off. "Then you must think whatever you please. I care naught!" Anxious to be out of his reach, afraid that he might touch her again and bring back the fire and the yearning, she rose quickly to her feet and ran back to the chair by the window.

Watching her, Justin wondered what Caroline Fane was really like. He himself was no saint, and it mattered little to him whether she be innocent or guilty. But she bewildered and disturbed him, made him uncertain. She was an enigma to him, and he was uncertain in all things save one. He wanted her. He had wanted many women, but never as he wanted this one. There was something about her, her touch, that set his heart pounding like a schoolboy in love. He frowned. In love? His illness must have softened his brain. Love was for other men, but never for him. Love tied you down, made you weak and vulnerable to hurt. And in any case, it was not in him to love. He had proved that quite satisfactorily to himself. But what in the plague was it about Caroline Fane that stirred him so? She was beautiful, although at this moment, sitting there with that sullen expression on her face, she looked quite plain. But it could not be that alone, for he had known many beautiful women. It was something else, something that pulled at his senses. She gave out a sexual aura. Sexual? He almost laughed aloud. That frightened little girl? No, damned if he could put a label on it. He only knew that she did something to him that other women did not do. He would have her, he vowed to himself. But only when she turned to him willingly. He was surprised at the anger that stirred him as he thought of the various titles bestowed upon her by those who had followed her trial: "the Fane vixen," "Stone-hearted bawd," "Legs-apart Caroline," "Pretty Poison," to name but a few. Quickly he dismissed the anger. She attracted him; he would not deny it. But she was nothing to him, so why the anger?

Caroline closed her eyes. It seemed to her that she could still feel Rogue Lawrence's gently caressing hands, the weight of his head against her breast. Shuddering, she thought of Thomas Fane, the only man her body had ever known. Rogue Lawrence's words echoed in her ears—"Love and passion can be very sweet." No, no, she did not believe him, she could not! The act was the same with all men. She could not go through that again, never, never again!

Wedding night! Her hands clenched into tight fists as the words leaped into her mind and lingered there. Wedding night! A sixteen-year-old bride and an old man for a husband. Once more she felt Thomas' overwarm and trembling flesh against her own. His shaking fingers prying her legs apart, abusing her body, biting savagely at her breasts, doing things to her with those fingers that so disgusted and repelled her that she had screamed aloud. He had silenced her with a hard blow, setting her head reeling with the force of it. The full horror of it overcame her then. This old man—he even smelled old—was her husband! She felt his wet kisses slobbering over her body. She heard his hoarse voice crying out her name. "Caroline! I am not a young man. You will have to help me." His hand had taken hers and guided it downward. "You help me like this, Caroline, see. Like this."

"No, Thomas, no!" She had snatched her hand away. He had disgusted, sickened her. "Please don't make me. I cannot do it!"

Snarling with rage, he had hit her again. And then he had forced her to take hold of that piece of inert flesh. After an unbearably long time, in which he grunted and whimpered with frustration, it had grown beneath her shrinking touch. Then he was upon her, hammering into her body like a man gone mad. There had been no tenderness in him, no concern for her pain and her fear; he had been intent only upon his own satisfaction. He was afraid to withdraw even for a moment, lest his penis become shriveled and useless.

When it was over, he had rolled off her. Lying on his back, his thin limbs carelessly sprawled, he had been an unlovely and almost grotesque sight, his snores echoing through the small room. She had lain awake for what seemed to her to be hours, fighting revulsion, her tears spotting the pillowcase, but at last she had slept. When she awakened, Thomas was gone. She stared at her blood staining the sheet; then she rose. Pouring water into a white china bowl, she slowly and carefully washed every part of her body.

But however much she washed herself, she could not wash away the feel of Thomas, the sour, old smell of him. Night after night the same degrading performance must be repeated, and each time it took longer. No matter how long she lived, she would always hear his voice begging her help to arouse that part of him that always failed at the crucial moment. But he did not always beg; he demanded. Perhaps it was because she looked at him with such loathing and horror that he always accompanied his commands with such vicious blows. But he need not have hit her, for she was afraid to disobey him. So, at his request or command, she touched, grasped, fondled, did all the things he asked of her, until at last he was able to fling himself upon her body and penetrate. Still as a log, she lay there and let him take his frenzied will. He had been vile; the things he asked of her, degrading.

She looked across at Rogue Lawrence. She was relieved to find that he was not looking at her. Would he be like Thomas? She would never find out. He must never touch her again. She hated him! She hated all men!

Justin stared at the stain on the wall just beyond his bed. It had a strange shape. It looked like a bent old woman who was carrying a load of wood on her back. He concentrated on it fiercely, trying to ignore the ominous thickening in his throat that presaged one of his fits of choking. He had not had one for quite a while, and he had thought himself to be over them. When they came, he was as helpless as a child, but at least, since he had regained full consciousness, Paul had been here to aid him. Caroline Fane would aid him; he had no doubt of that. But did he want her sullen and reluctant help? His throat tightened, closed. He was choking! Fighting for air!

At the first tortured sound he made, Caroline was out of her chair and running to his side. "It's all right!" She took his flailing hands and gripped them tightly. "Don't struggle, my darling! Let me help you!" Her hands rubbed at his back, his chest, massaged his throat, and all the time she spoke to him in a low, soothing voice.

Dimly, Justin's mind registered her words. His nostrils flared, his chest heaved, his hands clung tightly to her—like those of the frightened child he had previously named her. The spasm ended, but it had taken the last of his strength away. Exhausted, he lay against her, comforted by the feel of her arms about him. Wonderingly, he heard her voice. "There, my love, my darling, it is all over now. All over!" Her hand stroked his hair tenderly.

She spoke to him as she would to a babe, and he found himself touched by her tenderness, the endearments she uttered, and the gentle, soothing, stroking hand on his hair. Did she realize what she was saying? Did she think him insensible to her touch, deaf to her voice? This was quite another Caroline Fane. This was the Caroline who had brought him back from the nightmare. "Carrie," he said hoarsely. "It was you I heard. Don't try to deny it."

The arms holding him dropped away. She rose, helped lower him on the pillows, and then turned her face from him. "I helped Paul," she said in a colorless voice. "I told you that."

"Carrie, sit down. No, I promise not to touch you. Please, Carrie!"

She sat down on the edge of the bed, looking at him with eyes full of suspicion. "Well?"

He smiled at her. "I think you must like me just a little, or else you could not have spoken to me as you did. True?"

"No! I spoke to you as I would to any sick and suffering creature."

"Is that all I am to you, a sick and suffering creature?"

"That is all." Her eyes challenged him. "Do you wish to be more?"

"Yes, Carrie, much, much more."

She rose abruptly. "Go to sleep. Your attacks grow fewer, but sleep is still needed to restore you."

He did not attempt to detain her. Later, Mistress Caroline Fane, his mind said. Later you and I will have this out. A sick and suffering creature? Bah! You are as aware of me as I am of you. I will break down your fear and your resistance. I will make you flame in my arms. You will become the wild and passionate woman you were surely meant to be. His heavy eyes closed. A few moments later he slept.

Some two hours later, Justin was abruptly awakened by Paul's tempestuous entrance into the room. Paul's fair hair was in its usual state of disarray, his eyes were shining, and he looked pleased and excited.

"Caroline," Paul said, nodding to her. Passing her, he strode over to the bed. "How are you, Justin? Are you feeling all right?"

Justin threw Caroline a quick glance that warned her to say nothing about his recent attack. "Never better," he said, smiling. "You are looking very pleased with yourself, Paul. Do you have news?"

"I most certainly do."

"Then sit yourself down, youngster, and tell me all about it."

Paul dragged up a chair to the bed and sat down. "It is time for us to move on. You do feel strong enough for a journey, don't you?"

"Of course," Justin said lightly. "I'm fighting fit."

"Then we will go home tomorrow. Think of it, Justin, we will be going home to Bewley Grange!"

"Then you have decided that it is safe to travel?"

"There is still a risk, of course, but it is safer than it might be at any other time." Paul leaned forward eagerly. "Interest is centered elsewhere at the moment. Have you heard of Andrew Wilson?"

Justin nodded. "Aye, who has not? The last I heard of him, he was cooling his heels in Newgate."

Paul laughed. "He is out of prison and back at his old game."

"Do you tell me that he is leading yet another rebellion against the king?"

"He is. And very convenient it is for us. They do not know at what point Wilson will strike, and the soldiers have been put on the alert. The news is being whispered through the streets that this time Wilson will succeed in bringing down King William. Turmoil in the nation, as you know, will always turn eyes and thoughts in a different direction. This is the time for us to take the risk, Justin. Don't you agree?"

Grinning, Justin nodded. "What with the threat of Wilson, and the supporters of Princess Anne yapping at his heels, it would seem that our little Dutch king is having a stormy time of it."

"He has never been popular. And Queen Mary's callous indifference to her father's troubles has scarcely endeared her to the people."

Justin's eyes were momentarily grave as he thought of the deposed King James II, who had been forced to flee England with his wife, Mary of Modena. Neither Anne nor Mary, his two daughters, had made a move to help their father. And now James was exiled, and his eldest daughter, Mary, and her husband, William of Orange, ruled England. "He is certainly having a time of it," Justin said again.

Paul's shrug dismissed the many troubles of King William III. His mind was centered on Bewley Grange, his home. "Well, it need not concern us, Justin," he said cheerfully. "We are going home."

Paul was full of his plans for easing out of London as unobtrusively as possible. Justin, whose mind was on Caroline, was only half-listening. What was to become of Caroline Fane? Where would she go? What would she do? Then, as something Paul said caught at his attention, he sat up in the bed and listened intently. Mistress Caroline Fane, Paul said, was to accompany them to Bewely Grange.

Feeling oddly relieved, and unable to account for the feeling, Justin smiled warmly at Caroline. "I am glad you come with us, Carrie," he said softly.

Caroline gave him a faint smile in return, and then quickly

averted her eyes. She felt a wave of relief at his reception of the news, for she had anticipated his displeasure. But would they get there? Her brow creased as worry nibbled at her mind. They had far to go before they reached their destination. It was hard to believe that all the road patrols about the city would be withdrawn and sent back to London itself. And yet, if Paul's story was correct, that rabble-rouser Andrew Wilson now had a formidable army to march with him against the king. Under those conditions, with every man needed, it might well be that the patrols would be withdrawn. But what if someone should recognize them? What if they were captured and taken back to the death they had escaped?

Part II
Bewley Grange

Chapter 5

Caroline was aware of the eyes watching her from the various windows of the house in Badger Street. But although her heart was beating fast with excitement and fear, her step did not falter as she took her place beside Justin in the old carriage that Paul had somehow managed to purchase. Wrapped in an old cloak of Mistress Benson's, the hood drawn well forward to hide her face, she prayed inwardly for the success of this journey they were about to take to Bewley Grange.

Her hands tightly clasped in an unconscious attitude of prayer, she looked about her. The carriage was the best that Paul, with his limited funds, had been able to afford. He had first seen the vehicle in the mews just beyond Badger Street. The owner, a man who was himself in hiding from the law, never used the carriage, and he had been only to eager to sell. The carriage had obviously seen better days. It was very shabby now. The leather of its upholstery was ripped in several places and showed tufts of gray and black flocking. Throughout its disuse, the leather curtains had been kept rolled down, and the air that managed to penetrate had not been able to disperse the smell of stale sweat, unwashed bodies, and the ghost of the perfume of its many previous occupants.

Caroline saw Justin's nose wrinkle in distaste at the odor that permeated the carriage. It did not matter to her, she thought. She would gladly have endured, had the odor been a thousand times worse. In the knoweldge that they were at last on their way, she would have stepped as lightheartedly into a sewage cart. She became aware that her fear had, for the moment, left her. No doubt, as the miles rolled away, it would return, but for now she felt not only lighthearted but also safe and full of confidence and hope. She was grateful too to Justin and Paul, who were opening their home to her. But she would not, she determined, be an encumbrance on them. There must be some way she could find to repay them for their ungrudging hospitality. But only time could show her the way.

Caroline frowned, then smiled wryly at the sudden flash of self-honesty that had come to her. Of course she was grateful, and of course she wanted to serve, if she could, but in the main her motives were purely selfish. Why not admit it? It was herself she wanted to serve. In her very eagerness, she reminded herself uncomfortably of a stray cat who, having been given a home, was fearful that her new owners would change their minds and turn her out again into the cold uncertainty of a homeless life.

She glanced at Justin. He had not spoken since they had entered the carriage, and he showed no disposition to do so. He appeared to be deep in thought. She had a wish that the vehicle was not quite so cramped for space. It would have been better for her peace of mind had it been Paul who sat beside her, and Justin who was driving so skillfully over the rutted roads. The carriage, styled in an earlier age, had been built to accommodate only two passengers. The builder had quite obviously believed in intimacy, for the space between herself and Justin was infinitesimal. Although she sat in the other corner, her skirt brushed against his legs. With each lurch of the carriage, her shoulder came into contact with his. She flushed vividly as a sudden lurch all but threw her into his lap. Mumbling an apology, she pressed her back against the tattered upholstery and sat there rigidly. "You may remove your hand," she said coldly.

Justin took his hand from her waist. "I regret, Carrie, the enforced intimacy of our cramped quarters." He flashed her a brilliant smile. "Had I not caught you when I did, you would have no doubt ended in my arms. A delightful arrangement for me. How would you have felt about it?"

She met the laughing dark eyes. "I would have loathed it."

"That is what I thought." Smiling, Justin returned to his thoughtful silence.

But you don't believe it, Rogue Lawrence, she thought angrily. You cannot conceive of any woman not wanting to be in your arms.

Pulling her hood farther forward, Caroline found herself troubled by yet another flash of self-honesty. Rogue

Lawrence was many things, but he was not conceited. No, it was not conceit so much as a sure knowledge of his power over women. This, she imagined, from the stories told her by Paul, had been brought about by the attentions and the freely granted favors of almost every woman who came into contact with him. Caroline's lips folded grimly. If she were too tinglingly aware of him, she was nonetheless determined to be the exception to the rule. There was nothing Justin could say or do that would bring her into his arms. Gradually, as Justin continued to keep his silence and as much distance as was possible between them, her grim mood faded, and a sense of humor came to her aid. What a fuss she was making about accidental contact with this man with whom she had shared a bed. She had lain by his side, she had fed and washed him, she had even held him tightly in her arms and soothed as best she could the horror of his nightmares. She was a fool. And if the truth be told, it might be she rather than Rogue Lawrence who was indulging in conceit. It was true that he had kissed and caressed her once, and had wooed her with that husky and oddly attractive voice of his, and she, to her shame, had allowed him to do so. But that might have been the normal reaction of any man who found himself alone with a reasonably pretty woman. Yes, she might be called reasonably pretty. But she must not allow herself to think that she was outstanding, because she was not. Or that Justin was so attracted to her that he would try the same thing again. He probably thought of her as a nurse, and beyond that, was not interested in her. After all, he must have known many women who were far more beautiful and attractive than she could ever hope to be. Having come to this sensible conclusion, she felt a gust of unreasonable annoyance and a deep and resentful dislike of these unknown women.

Paul drove along the roads, a deep frown between his brows. His eyes searched constantly, and he gripped the reins tightly in tense hands. Some of his tension must have communicated itself to the animals, for they were inclined to behave skittishly, and they had a tendency to shy at the least little thing. He relaxed his grip and called to them soothingly, but as the worry once more invaded his mind, his grip tightened again. They had not yet passed a road patroller, but could their luck possibly last? He understood that patrols had been withdrawn for the defense of King William, it being that monarch's contention that every man possible must be rallied to march against Andrew Wilson and his rabble army.

The left horse shied, bringing Paul's mind back to the problems of the moment. Controlling the horse and bringing it back to the easy gait of its teammate, he wondered if all the patrols had been withdrawn, or if they would run into some farther along the way. Of course, the greater the distance between themselves and London, the less chance there was of recognition, but this was little consolation to him at the moment. If it came down to it, he and Justin would make a fight for freedom, but it would doubtless end in either their death or their imprisonment, which was much the same thing, since it had death at the end of it.

Paul's uneasy thoughts drifted to the stops they would be forced to make at the various inns along the way. But they would be on the road for several days, and they had no choice. The horses must be fed and watered and bedded down comfortably, if they were to go on the next day with any degree of spirit. And they themselves must eat and rest. Especially he, for he must do all the driving. Justin had several times offered to take over the reins, but Paul had refused. Justin was too well-known and too easily recognizable. To have Justin on the box tooling the horses would be the greatest piece of folly.

Paul could not help the trembling of his hands and the leaping of his heart as, some hours later, they drew up at their first stop, the Goose and Grapes Inn.

Chiding himself for a coward, Paul jumped down from the box. Handing the reins to a hostler, he issued his instructions for the welfare of his animals in a strained voice that was quite unlike his own. Then, having assisted Caroline to alight, he nodded to her and his brother and strode toward the cheerfully candlelit door of the inn.

Following, Caroline sensed Paul's uneasiness, and although she fought it, she could not help being infected by it. When they entered the inn parlor, she was trembling so much that it was only Justin's arm that upheld her. The eyes resting upon them seemed to her to be hostile. The eyes of potential enemies.

"Be calm, Carrie," Justin's voice murmured in her ear. "Calm and poise are everything."

She looked at him. There was a careless ease to his manner, an air of being utterly unperturbed. Did nothing move him? "It is all very well for you," she answered in a low, furious voice. "You are simply not human!"

Smiling at Paul, who had chosen a table in the darkest corner of the room, Justin drew out a chair for her. "I assure you that I am very human," he answered her. "It is simply that I have never believed in showing all the cards in my hand." He seated himself beside her.

"And I do, I suppose?" she retorted.

"If you persist in glaring so truculently at the peaceful patrons of this inn," he answered her calmly, "it might well be that you will arouse suspicion in their otherwise unsuspicious breasts. That would be called, I believe, showing all the cards in your hand."

He was infuriating. She would not speak to him. All the same, she had taken his words to heart. When the cheerful landlord came bustling up to take their order, she did not look at him. Neither did she allow her eyes to stray from the platter before her. Her mood was not improved when Justin's drawling voice informed her that this new attitude of hers was, if possible, worse than her previous belligerent stares.

The same thing happened at every inn at which they stopped. With Paul showing his uneasiness, she perforce shared his mood. She had several times tried to emulate Justin's easy attitude, but she found it quite impossible. The food seemed to clog in her throat, the wine failed to warm her, and lying in the unfamiliar beds of this inn or that, she would stare wide-eyed into the darkness, unable to sleep. The only rest she got was when they were once more on the road. Then her eyes would close and her head would nod. Awakening with a start, she would look suspiciously at Justin. Once or twice she caught him looking at her, but more often than not his head was turned away.

When they left the Green Cock, the last inn on their way, and she knew they would not have to stop again until they reached Bewley Grange, she blessed the angel of good fortune who had ridden with them. She smiled as the sound of Paul's cheerful whistling came to her. She turned to Justin, wanting to share her mood of thankfulness with him, and found that he had fallen asleep.

Her eyes softened as she saw his uncomfortably nodding

head. Perhaps she had misjudged him, she thought. Perhaps, after all, he was simply more adept than either Paul or she at hiding his feelings. She found herself remembering how ill he had been. Regretting the sharp things she had said to him, she closed the tiny space between them and drew his head to her shoulder. The sharp, sweet thrill this contact with him gave her startled her, but she did not let him go. Instead, with a little sigh she put both her arms about him and rested her chin against his hair.

"Why the sigh, Carrie?" Justin's husky voice caused her to start violently.

Confused, she blurted out, "I ... I thought you were asleep."

"I was. But you awakened me when you took me so passionately into your arms." She stiffened at the undercurrent of laughter she thought she detected in his voice. "My dear Carrie," he went on, and the note of laughter was plain now, "you really must control this compulsion you have to attack an innocent sleeping man."

"Don't!" she said in a choked voice. Then she realized she was still holding him tightly, and her arms dropped away. "Don't!" she said again, her face flaming with her embarrassment. "Please don't!"

"Carrie?" Justin sat up and looked at her inquiringly. "Do you tell me that my little jest has upset you? Come, now! Where is your sense of humor?"

"I see nothing humorous in it. You have no right to laugh at me when I ... when I was only trying to make you comfortable!"

"My apologies. But I had thought we would laugh together."

He was looking at her with genuine concern, but she chose not to heed it. "I know you were laughing at me. You always do!"

At the sharp note in her voice, his mood veered. Once more she heard that undercurrent of laughter as he said lazily, "If it comes right down to it, Carrie, why should you try to make me comfortable, when, as you are always at great pains to make apparent to me, you detest me? But perhaps you had forgotten that I am no longer a sick and suffering creature?"

"You are!" She glared at him. "You are still far from well."

"I am well enough." He considered her for a moment. "Keep on telling yourself that you hate me, Carrie, if it pleases you to do so. But do you know something? I think that the reverse is true."

"Oh! How can you say such a thing? You ... you are conceited and arrogant!"

"Not I." Smiling, he shook his head. "I am just stating a truth."

"It is not a truth! I do hate you!"

"Do you?" He leaned toward her. "Tell me," he pursued in an interested voice, "is it just me you hate? Or is it all men?"

"All men!" she answered, drawing back. "But I told you that before."

"So you did. I remember now. Then Paul, I imagine, must be included in your general indictment of men?"

"Paul?" She stared at him. "Of course not! Who could hate Paul?"

With a gesture of impatience, he thrust his fingers through his thick hair, disordering it. "Lucky Paul," he said, leaning back against the seat, "to have achieved such an honor. Why, one might almost believe that he did not belong to the despised sex."

"He is a boy!"

"Don't shout, Carrie. It makes my ears ring." He smiled at her. "Paul is nineteen. On the threshold of manhood, you might say. Tell me, if you are still with us when he gains his majority, will your affection for him then turn to hatred?"

"No, damn you, no! You are laughing at me again!"

"Temper! Yes, Carrie, I admit it. I was laughing a little. You are such a cursed bundle of contradictions. When I am conscious, you look at me with hostility. But when I am sleeping, you take me in your arms and hold me close."

"Be quiet!"

He shook his head. "Do you think I do not remember the little endearments you uttered when I was sick and helpless? There, perhaps I have hit upon the truth. Can you hold a man only when he is helpless, Carrie? Can you love him only then?"

"Stop it!" In a fury, she launched herself at him, trying to strike him with her clenched fists. "How dare you say such a thing to me! How dare you!"

He caught her hands and held them tightly. "Why such fire and fury, Carrie? Have my words struck at an exposed nerve?"

"You beast!"

"A sick or sleeping man cannot hurt you, can he?" His eyes on her white face, Justin went on relentlessly. "He cannot force his loathsome attentions on you. That is the way you think, isn't it?"

"No!"

"I think it is. And yet, there is passion in you, Carrie. I know that, too. But what a weak way to expend it! A few endearments, your arms about a helpless man. Will that really serve to quench the fire in your body?"

She went suddenly limp. Her lips trembled, and the tears that had gathered in her eyes spilled over. "How can you be so unkind?" she whispered.

"It is the other way around. You are unkind to yourself. Wake up, Carrie. Live. Be the woman you were meant to be."

"I can't! You don't understand."

"But I want to understand." Releasing her hands, he put his arms about her. "No," he said quickly, "don't poker up. Tell me what has happened in your life to hurt you so."

She shook her head. "No, please don't persist."

"I will persist," he said calmly. "And you will tell me now, Carrie."

And she did tell him. Without quite knowing why, she capitulated. Shaking, the tears still pouring down her cheeks, she sobbed out her story. Somehow, in the telling, her head found its way to Justin's shoulder.

"You poor little wench!" Justin said, his hand softly stroking her tumbled hair. "Now I begin to understand. Other women, of course, have entered into distasteful marriages, and they have survived them. But you were little more than a child. I can well imagine the profound effect it would have upon you. But all men are not like Thomas Fane, little one."

Little one! She had not known he could sound so tender. Something in her wanted to receive the endearment and cherish it, but she could not. "Don't tell me that. They are all the same. I know it!"

"Do you think I am cut from the same cloth as Thomas Fane? By God, then the women I have loved have deceived me into believing myself strong and virile. When, in reality, if you are right, I must have been weak and impotent."

She felt another wave of antagonism toward those women he had loved. "Have ... have you loved many women, Justin?"

He laughed. "I have not lived like a monk. But why do you ask? Does it matter to you?"

"Certainly not! Why should it?"

"Look at me, Carrie."

"No!"

"Why not? Are you afraid to look at me?"

"Afraid of you, Rogue Lawrence? You will never see that day!"

"Then look at me."

Slowly, reluctantly, she raised her head and looked into his eyes. They seemed to her bemused senses to be even more brilliant, darker and more intense than before. She could not look away. "Yes?" she whispered.

"Let me take the bad memory away. Let me release you, Carrie."

"H-how?"

"Let me love you as you should be loved."

She started. "After all I have told you, you can ask that of me?" she cried out in wild accusation. "Never! Do you hear me? Never!"

"Hush! Stop lying to yourself, Carrie. You want me as much as I want you. The truth is plain in your eyes, no matter what your tongue may say to the contrary."

"No!" She tried to struggle out of his arms. "You know it is not true!"

"But it is true. You know it." His arms tightened about her. "Be still. I am not going to hurt you or take you against your will. But I am going to kiss you." He saw the widening of her eyes, and he felt her shrinking, and he added gently, "A kiss is not a rape of your body, Carrie."

Not a rape of her body? Just to see him, to have him look at her, to hear him speak her name was a rape of more than her body, it was a rape of all her senses! There in his arms, something strange was happening to her, something she did not understand. She actually wanted him to kiss her. She

craved the feel of his lips against her own. Stunned, she
heard her own voice speak the incredible words. "Yes, kiss
me, kiss me!" Her eyes closed, and her lips parted in invitation.

For a moment he hesitated; then he put his mouth to hers.
Her arms came up, her fingers caressed him, and her clinging
lips seemed to flame beneath his. He crushed her tightly to
him, his heart pounding. By God, he thought, but here is a
tigress! Here is fire and flame and fury! When, finally, they
drew apart, he was shaking, and there was perspiration on his
forehead. "Carrie!" he said in an unsteady voice. "Let me
come to you tonight. Let me love you!"

Even as he spoke, he sensed her retreat. Once more the terrified child peered from her eyes. "Don't ask that of me yet,
Justin. I am . . . am not ready!"

He smiled, trying to soothe and reassure her. "But you are,
love, you are."

"No!" She clung to him frantically. "Not yet. You must
give me time."

He sighed. "All right. If that is what you want, I will give
you time." He tried to release himself from her clinging arms,
but she would not let him go. "Damn, Carrie!" he exploded.
"Will you take your arms away? What the devil do you think
I am made of?" He tugged at her arms. "I warn you," he said
in an ominous voice, "I can endure only so much!"

"But I want you to hold me. Please, please!"

"No!" He put her roughly from him. "I am not a man to
play games with. When you make up your mind that you
want me to love you, then you must come to me and tell me
so."

Brought rudely out of her dream, she stared at him in
outrage. His black brows were drawn together in a formidable frown. His expression was cold, giving her a fleeting
glimpse of that other Rogue Lawrence who dwelled beneath
the tender and understanding front he had shown to her. He
seemed now to be very calm, remote, unapproachable. But
when he lifted his hand to straighten his neckcloth, she saw
the trembling of his hand. So he was not then as calm as she
had believed. She found her voice. "I must come to you! I
must tell you that I want you! Oh, how can you ask that of
me?"

He gave her an impatient glance. "What, then, do you

want of me, Carrie? I have asked you to let me love you, but I'll not beg you. I will not beg any woman. I will not continue to play out this game of advance and retreat. Either you want me, or you do not. It is as simple as that. Make your mind up. But in the name of Christ, make it up soon. Much more of this dithering, and you might find that I am no longer interested."

"You dare to speak to me like that!" She tore her wrists from his grasp. She smacked him sharply across the face. "The devil fly away with you, you conceited popinjay!"

The sound of the blow seemed to linger in the throbbing silence that followed. She felt a quiver of fear as she saw the blaze of anger in his eyes. "You asked for it!" she said in a high, defiant voice. "And I hope it stung."

"You bloody little bitch!" He grabbed her and pulled her roughly into his arms. "If you think I'll put up with your cursed tantrums, you had best think again!" He put his face close to hers. "What are you, a spoiled child or a woman?"

"Let go of me!" she shouted, trying to mask her fear with a display of anger. "I'll hit you again. I will!"

"I promise you it will be the last thing you ever do, for I'll break your damned neck!" He crushed her closer. "I'll let you go when I'm ready." His mouth came down on hers, stifling the words she was about to utter, scattering her senses. His kiss was hard, savage, and when he released her, she was trembling like someone in the grip of an ague. "Well, Carrie?" His smile was taunting. "Are you child or woman?" He kissed her briefly. "Is it blood you have in your veins, or water?"

It was certainly not water, she thought. She felt on fire, and the thundering of her heart produced a sense of suffocation. "You'll ... you'll never find out!" She gasped out the words with some difficulty.

"No?" His arms, which had loosened, tightened again.

"No!" Speech came easier now. "There, I have said it. Now you know where you stand with me!"

"That is your final word?"

"It is."

"A pity. But if it is not to be, it is not to be." Casually he thrust her from him. "You may now retire into your virginal isolation."

"You! I wish you were dead!"

"Ah!" He winked at her. "Then you should not have worked so hard to save me."

Without deigning to reply, she presented her back to him. A silence fell between them, which was broken at last by his laughter. She turned to look at him, giving him a burning glance. But this had the effect of increasing his amusement. She was even more annoyed when she found that her own lips were beginning to twitch in response. She met his eyes, and it was her undoing. She could not stifle the laughter that bubbled to her lips. "B-brute!" she gasped. "D-d-damned great conceited f-f-fool!"

"I . . . I know. I am everything you s-s-say." His shoulders shook, and tears of laughter gathered in his eyes. "But your face, Carrie! If you c-could only have seen your face!"

Suddenly, as if those last violent moments had never been, they were clinging helplessly to each other. It was only when Bewley Grange came into view that they managed to sober a little.

Unconsciously groping for Justin's hand, Caroline held on to it tightly while she stared with fascinated eyes at the graceful and majestic house.

Justin drew her close to his side, and she did not protest. "You like it?" he asked.

"Oh, yes! It is so beautiful. It has such an air!"

"Then you should know a little of its history. Bewley Grange first came into the possession of the Lawrences in the reign of Henry VII." He laughed. "Simon Lawrence, a buccaneering ancestor of mine, who, like myself, was a little on the disreputable side, had rendered services to the king which might be described by the respectable as somewhat lawless. The king had a reputation for being mean and grasping, but even he had his moments. So, in grateful recognition, he gifted Simon with Bewley Grange."

"Fascinating!"

"Do you really think so?"

He sounded faintly bored, and Caroline stole a quick sideways glance at him. It was not so much boredom, she decided, as tension. If he could have avoided this return to Bewley Grange, he would have done so. The house, set like a jewel in its beautiful surroundings, was, to Justin, something to escape from as quickly as possible. It spelled peace and order and monotony to him, and it was the last thing he wanted. But quite suddenly she found herself longing for those very things he apparently despised. She wanted that peace and order and monotony; she wanted to live at Bewley Grange, aloof from the world, safe.

Justin seemed to be reading her thoughts, for he said softly in her ear, "No, Carrie, the peaceful life is not for you, either. You think so now, because you have been badly frightened. But I will give you six months, perhaps less. After that time, you will begin dying of boredom, of the placid sameness of everything, of day following day without event."

"No!" She turned on him almost violently. "You do not know me, Justin."

"Bah! The facade you present is not the real Carrie Fane. I know, because like always recognizes like. You are more like me than you know. You crave excitement, adventure, change. You have never been allowed to be yourself, that is the trouble. Strip yourself of all pretense, and you will find that you are as lawless and as rebellious as I am."

She wanted to protest, but she could not. Something in her had quivered in response to his words. Was he right? Was that why her life had always seemed so dimly colored, lacking something essential? She thought of her trembling excitement and the flame that seemed to engulf her whenever she was in Justin's presence, and she was utterly dismayed. Had she, without knowing it, been shaped in the same wild and lawless mold as he? No! She was being foolish to allow his carelessly spoken words to disturb her. Of course he was not right. Until the catastrophe had overtaken her, had she not been a model of what every young lady should be? Had she not been quiet and soft-spoken, modest and demure? She was shaken with doubt again as she thought of the secret rebellion of that model young lady. She had rebelled; she could not deny it. Beneath her demure exterior had been the urge to shock and to do the exact opposite of what convention and society demanded of her. There had been her most unladylike thoughts, and that wish that so often visited her to laugh outright at the primness and hypocrisy of polite society. Yes, granted. But it did not mean that she was like Justin. Of course it did not!

Caroline found her anxiety fading as she followed Justin and Paul into the house. The wide, paneled hall was bright with firelight and redolent with the pleasantly pungent scent

of burning apple logs. Tall candles in silver sconces cast a
flickering patina of golden light over the highly polished floor
that was broken here and there with brilliantly colored rugs.
The furniture looked soft and comfortable and inviting, and
the fabrics that covered it were as brilliant and as fresh as the
rugs. Vases of flowers were set upon each of the wide window seats, and a round table near the fire held a silver bowl
of crimson flowers which gave off a delicious perfume, but
whose species Caroline could not identify.

She took a deep breath, and it seemed to her that she drew
in the atmosphere of the house. She had the feeling that it
was enfolding them, welcoming them. So did the bent and
balding old man who came hurrying forward with both hands
outstretched. Tears shone in his faded blue eyes, and a delighted smile creased his gnomelike face. "Master Justin!
Master Paul! This is a grand, grand day!"

The old man's name was Henry Chobham. In those days
when the family had been all together at the Grange, he had
been the butler. When the family had disintegrated, he had
become the custodian. Quite by accident, Paul had told her,
Chobham had found out about Justin's other and secret life.
No word of it had ever passed his lips, and so he had also become the custodian of a secret. Chobham had been able to
keep the truth about her elder son from Margaret Lawrence,
for not once had the law or anybody else who came into contact with him connected the Rogue with the distinguished
Lawrence family of Bewley Grange. Justin himself, by the
spreading of various misleading stories, had worked hard to
prevent this connection being made. He had no wish to hurt
his mother or to bring disgrace on his family. It had not been
hard. Lawrence was a common enough name.

Chobham's knowledge of Justin's double life had not
caused his love for the young man to deviate one whit; that
was obvious to Caroline. She found herself touched by the af-
fectionate greeting he gave to both men. But to her, the
stranger, Chobham's faded eyes were slightly wary. His bow,
however, was polite. He repeated her name after Justin as if
to make sure he had heard it aright. Her name, Caroline
could see, meant nothing at all to him. It was not surprising;
news would be slow in traveling to this quiet corner of England.

The greetings over, Henry Chobham fluttered anxiously

about them. He was delighted that his beloved lads were once more in residence, but he was also considerably agitated because he had been caught unprepared. "Let me go into the village, Master Justin," he pleaded in his thin, rather high voice. "For I tell ye that there's lasses aplenty who'll be only too happy to work at the Grange. Aye, and there's a many of the old Grange servants who'll be happy to bide here again and look to ye young masters."

"No, Chob." Justin shook his head firmly. "The hour is late. They will all be in their beds, as you should be." Smiling, he put a friendly hand on the frail, bent shoulders.

Justin could be very kind, Caroline thought, trying to harden herself against him. But she knew well that he was a man with two faces, and neither one to be trusted.

"But, Master Justin," Chobham exclaimed, his old face shocked. "The linen for the beds has not been aired. Ye'll be taking a chill." He glanced at Caroline and added as an afterthought, "The young lady, too."

Justin laughed. "The young lady has slept under worse conditions, Chob. We'll not use the bedchambers tonight. We will draw up the two settles and a comfortable chair to the fire. We are all tired. We'll have no difficulty in sleeping."

Disapproval was now added to Chobham's shock. He sniffed. "Don't seem right for the young lady to be sleeping so rough. Nor it don't seem right for her to be sleeping in the same room with ye young masters. 'Tain't the thing!"

"I know, Chob, I know." Justin grinned at him. "But don't you have a worry in the world. I give you my word that I won't tear her clothes off or attempt to rape her."

"Well! Think shame of yourself, Master Justin!"

Paul stifled a laugh. "Don't tell me we have been away so long, Chob, that you have forgotten my brother's rather peculiar sense of humor?"

"Not likely, Master Paul," Chobham said somewhat stiffly. "But 'tis not fitting to say such things in front of a young lady."

"I'm sorry, Chob," Justin said meekly. "Am I forgiven?"

Chobham could not restrain his smile. "Oh, aye, don't I always forgive ye, bad lad that ye are? I even forgave ye when ye chased my niece into the orchard and put yer hand up her—"

Paul's quick cough interrupted. "You are shocking Mistress Fane, Chob."

Chobham colored. "I forgot myself, miss," he said hastily. "I'm right sorry."

"It's all right, Chobham," Caroline said in a cool voice. "Association with your Master Justin has rendered me quite unshockable." She met Justin's smiling eyes. "Has it not, dear Justin?"

"You think so, dearest Carrie?" he replied lightly. "But you are only just beginning to know me. You do not as yet know what it is to be really shocked. But you will, love. I promise."

"Enough, Master Justin!" Chobham's severe voice reminded Caroline of a stern father rebuking a small boy. "Ye know that nicely brought-up young gentlemen do not talk to a young lady in such a disrespectful fashion. Do ye not, now?"

Caroline swallowed her amazement. Chobham might know him for Rogue Lawrence, but that knowledge made no difference to him. To him, Justin was the small boy, grown now to man size, whom he had always loved, and had quite often had occasion to rebuke, as he was doing now.

Justin was not in the least discomfited by Paul's laughter and the wide smile Caroline now directed at him. "Yes, Chob, I do know," he said in that misleadingly meek voice. "I won't do it again."

"I know ye, Master Justin, and I doubt ye'll remember my words." Relenting, he smiled. "Help the young lady nicely to a chair. I'll be bringing ye food and wine."

"Just bring the wine, Chob," Justin said, obediently settling Caroline into a chair. "We'll help ourselves to anything else we need. It's time for you to get yourself to your bed."

Chobham hesitated. "Then I'll bring the wine, Master Justin. For the truth is, I'd not be saying no to my bed."

Some minutes later, Chobham returned with a crystal decanter of wine and matching goblets. Setting them down on the table, he continued to hover, a look of distress on his face. "Are ye sure that there is nothing more I can do, Master Justin?"

"Yes. You can go to bed." Justin took him by the arm and led him over to the door. "Good night, Chob."

Chobham gave a dignified bow. "Good night, Master Justin. Miss. Master Paul." He hesitated, then added, "Ye'll be seeing to it, Master Paul, that Master Justin is not getting himself into mischief?"

"I will, Chob. Don't worry."

Chobham bowed again. "Then good night, all."

Laughing, Justin closed the door behind him. "That old man still thinks I am six years old, I swear."

"He'll never see either of us any differently," Paul said. "So resign yourself. But you are Chobham's special pet, Justin. He always did worry more over you."

"And not without reason," Caroline said with sweet-toned malice. She looked at Paul. "Isn't it strange that the black sheep is often the most loved?"

"Wine for the lady," Justin said, handing her a goblet half-filled with ruby-red wine. He bent over her, his eyes glinting wickedly. "Lady by birth," he whispered, "but for all that, you're not really a lady, my love. I'd hate it if you were. A prim, well-brought-up young lady without any vices would be insufferably boring."

Refusing to rise to his taunt, Caroline sipped her wine. "Being so full of vice yourself," she replied in an unmoved voice, "you would naturally feel that way."

He prodded her cheek with his finger. "Do you sit there barefaced and tell me you are a lady, Carrie?"

"Certainly I do."

"But not in the sense usually meant?"

"Exactly in that sense."

He laughed. "You delude yourself. You are too much like me."

"I am not!" she said sharply. "Don't hang over me. Go away."

"Do you really want me to go away, Carrie?" He stroked her cheek caressingly.

She refused to answer him. But her face flushed as she saw his eyes rest briefly on her trembling hands.

"What are you two whispering about?" Paul called.

"The lady is telling me that she will miss me in her bed this night," Justin answered, turning to Paul.

Paul heard Caroline's indignant gasp, and he saw the twinkle in Justin's eyes, and his faint look of shock faded. "Don't worry, Caroline. I know it is only Justin's nonsense."

"Nevertheless," Justin insisted, "just in case she should miss me, I intend to sleep at her feet."

Justin was as good as his word. With Paul resting on one settle and Caroline on the other, he stretched himself out on the floor, a cushion beneath his head. Paul went to sleep quickly. Listening to his deepened breathing, Caroline envied him, for she could not sleep or even relax. She lay stiffly, her eyes on Justin. He was right, she admitted to herself. She did wish that he lay beside her. She missed his warmth, the small restless movements he made, the way he had of edging closer until his head rested heavily against her shoulder.

Justin turned over on his back and met her eyes. "Can't sleep, Carrie?" he whispered, sitting up.

"No. I'm too restless."

"Miss me?"

She shook her head firmly. "Well, I miss you," Justin went on in a wistful voice. "It is hard on the floor, Carrie."

"Then sleep beside Paul. The settle is wide enough for two."

He reached up and touched her hand. "So is yours. If I lie beside you and hold you in my arms, perhaps then we will manage to get some sleep."

At the picture his words conjured up, her face flamed. As if she could sleep with Justin holding her close against his body! Without pausing to think, she said swiftly, "But then I would not wish to sleep."

"Carrie, Carrie!" He managed to sound both reproving and virtuous. "A true lady would not say that."

"I . . . I did not mean it that way," she stammered. She saw the dancing mockery in his eyes, and she cursed the bright firelight that allowed him to see her confusion and embarrassment. "You . . . you mix me up. You make me say things I do not mean."

"If you did not mean it, then I am disappointed."

"Go to the devil!" she snapped.

"A fine thing to say! Surely you will not refuse to allow a sick man to lie beside you?"

"I am sorry you're not feeling well," she answered him coldly. "Go and share Paul's settle. He has as much room as I."

He looked at her reproachfully. "But I cannot take Paul in my arms. He would not like it. He is odd that way."

"Will you stop!"

"But I only want to lie beside you and hold you in my arms. I am feeling very weak, and it will comfort me."

Comfort him indeed! The man should have been an actor, so easily did he slip from one role to another. She would not laugh. She would not! To prevent it, she bit down hard on her lip. After a moment, she said in a muffled voice, "Go away."

He seemed not to have heard her. She stiffened as he pulled the blanket to one side and slipped in beside her. "I will only hold you. I promise," he said, drawing the blanket over them. Taking her into his arms, he tucked her head casually beneath his chin. "This is much better," he murmured. "Good night, Carrie, love."

For a moment she could not move. She had a longing to yield, to lie there cradled in the comfort of his arms. Because of this guilty longing, her outrage was the greater. She struggled free from him and struck out with both clenched fists. "How dare you! Get out!"

He warded off her blows easily. "Don't shout, love. You will wake Paul."

"I'll scream," she threatened. "I'll scream so loudly that I will awaken Chobham as well as Paul!"

"Don't hiss at me, Carrie," he complained. "You sound like a gander. Very well, I will leave you. But before I do, I would like you to know that you have offended and hurt me to the very core." He raised himself and looked down at her. "To the very core," he repeated.

She saw the look in his eyes, and suddenly everything was clear to her. He had said that she must ask him to love her, and he was trying to force her to do so. Damn him to hell! Quivering with rage, she sat up. "Get out, you wicked swine! Go!" She pushed at him violently. Taken unawares, he rolled over the side and fell heavily to the floor. At the look on his face, she began to laugh on a helpless hysterical note.

"Laugh, will you!" Jumping to his feet, he flung himself across her, holding her pinioned with his weight. "Ask me, you bloody wildcat!" He twined his fingers in her hair and jerked her face up to his. "Ask me to love you, damn you! Ask me!"

"I won't! How like you to think of making love to me, and Paul in the same room!"

Her eyes were so wide and horrified that he could not help

smiling. "You wrong me, love. I had no intention of outraging Paul. I will take you to a place where we may have a decent privacy."

"If you think you have won, Rogue Lawrence, you are mistaken. I will never ask you!"

"You will." He kissed her hard and bruisingly. "Ask me now!"

"No!" She saw that his face had darkened; there was a glint of anger in his eyes. She stopped struggling. She lay there passive, enjoying the feel of his body against her own.

As though he sensed this, he rolled away from her and rose abruptly to his feet. "Then good night, Carrie. Sleep well."

She watched him make his way to Paul. Paul muttered a sleepy protest as Justin moved him gently to one side. He settled himself comfortably and closed his eyes. "Good night," he said again.

She did not answer him. She lay there stiffly, uncomfortably aware of the torment of her awakened body, and she hoped passionately that he would not be able to sleep. She resented the way he made her feel. She did not want to feel this way for any man, and especially not for Rogue Lawrence. She was furious when, in a surprisingly short time, she heard the little catch in Justin's breathing that told her he was genuinely asleep.

She turned over on her side, frowning fiercely. She hated him, and yet she loved him. She fought him violently, and yet she longed to give in. But give in to what? To further repellent and degrading behavior such as Thomas had forced her into? Justin had said that it would not be like that. But how could she know? She was afraid to take the step that would give her the answer. When, finally, she fell into a fitful sleep, Justin's laughing, faintly mocking face was still in her mind.

They awakened to a day of brilliant sunshine, a beaming and satisfied Chobham, and a fully staffed house. The conscientious Chobham took his duties seriously. His love for as well as his sense of obligation to his young masters had so weighed on his mind that he had found himself unable to sleep. At first light he had slipped out of the house and made his way to the village. As he had predicted, there were old servants who were eager to return to the Grange, and new girls who had never worked before but were anxious to gain the undoubted distinction conferred on one who became a Grange servant. With a full complement of servants, he had returned in triumph to the Grange.

Caroline watched Justin greeting the old servants and smiling upon the new. He lingered just a little longer than was strictly necessary before one dark-haired young girl with piquant pretty features, Caroline thought with a stab of jealous anger. The women smiled shyly upon both of the Lawrence brothers, but Caroline noticed that their eyes lingered longest upon Justin. That damnable charm of his, she thought angrily. The way that some of them were staring at him was positively indecent.

Justin spoke to them a few moments longer, and then nodded a pleasant dismissal. "Did you notice the dark wench, Paul?" he said, when the door had closed behind them. "The one with the enormous blue eyes?"

Paul grinned. "Trust you to notice her! Chobham tells me that she's Amos Dale's daughter."

"Is she, by God! I never would have believed that that skinny little girl I used to see about the village could grow up into such a beauty."

Paul shrugged. "Cassie Dale is well enough, I suppose, but she is too dark for me."

"You prefer a blond beauty, do you?"

"I do. I have never cared too much for brunettes."

"Well, well, my young brother is beginning to grow up fast." Justin turned thoughtful eyes to Caroline, smiling as he noted her sullen expression. "Our darling Carrie is a blond, Paul. Tell me, do you admire her looks?"

Paul's fair skin flushed vividly, and he did not look at Caroline as he answered. "Yes, you might say that Caroline has the type of looks I most admire." He hesitated, flashed his quick, shy smile, and then made his way hurriedly from the room.

"Are you satisfied now that you have managed to embarrass Paul?" Caroline said in a low, furious voice.

"You do not know Paul as well as you think you do, Carrie. He was not in the least embarrassed. It was that cursed shyness of his that caused his hasty retreat." Justin thrust his hands into the pockets of his black-velvet jacket and strolled toward Caroline, his head on one side, his smiling eyes inspecting her. "So Paul admires your looks," he said at last. "I wonder why? Certainly you are not at your best when you are scowling."

He wondered why! How dare he say that! Her eyes showing her resentment, she turned away from him and walked over to the door.

He caught up with her. "Where are you going, love?"

"If you have no objection, I am going to the bedchamber Paul has assigned to me."

"My, how stiff and proper we are." He leaned toward her, his eyes twinkling. "Did you know that the bedchamber Paul has . . . er . . . assigned to you is right next to mine?"

"Is it? That will not trouble me. I shall keep my door locked at all times."

"Ah, but there are two keys to every door."

Her face hot, she escaped from him. She could hear his laughter as she fled up the stairs.

As she entered the bedchamber, her anger left her. She looked about her, feeling the same wonder she had felt earlier when Paul had conducted her to this room and told her that it should be hers as long as she cared to stay. As long as she cared to stay! At this moment she felt that she would never want to leave. She would like to stay at Bewley Grange for the rest of her life. She walked over to the wide, comfortable bed and touched the embroidered red-velvet canopy with caressing fingers. Colored lights from the stained glass of the windows made a rainbow dazzle across the smooth white coverlet. Moving slowly about the large, luxurious room, she was touched with the same radiance. She stood still for a moment; then she returned to the bed and touched the canopy again. And in her touching, there was the need to convince herself that she was actually here at Bewley Grange. In that moment it seemed to her to be a haven of safety wherein she might hide forever.

Chapter 6

Caroline smoothed the skirts of her rustling green-silk gown with a careful and loving hand. The gown was embroidered at the low square neckline and at the hem of the skirt with a design of pink-and-white clover flowers. The skirt, belling out like a giant exotic flower, made her waist seem incredibly small. Her matching green slippers were laced about her slender ankles with twined pink and white silken cords. And, as a finishing touch, a cameo fastened to a dark-green-velvet ribbon circled her throat. She could not help knowing that she looked well in the gown, for this particular shade of sea green had always suited her.

Since she had come to the Grange, Caroline's appearance had certainly improved. She had Justin to thank for that. He had made her a gift of Margaret Lawrence's clothes. Since her death, they had been carefully packed away in a large chest and preserved with sweet-smelling herbs. Caroline's delight in his gift, her profuse thanks, had startled Justin. For the first time since she had known him, she had seen him at a loss, almost embarrassed. In the three weeks they had been at the Grange, he had grown used to her sullen air and her belligerent attitude whenever he approached her or sought to draw her into conversation. It was not to be wondered at, in view of this, that he should become cool and indifferent toward her. No, she could not blame him, since it was she herself who had made this rift between them by her fear of the surge of passion and longing she experienced whenever he was near. How could she give in to it? How could she relent? The memory of Thomas Fane still haunted her. She was afraid to smile at Justin, to soften in any way, lest she find herself shackled to that same degradation. And yet, though she knew it to be unreasonable on her part, Justin's attitude hurt her. His remark when he had presented her with the

clothes had hurt too. Quickly recovering from his temporary
confusion, he had eyed her glowing face with cynical eyes.
"It would seem, then, that I should have plied you with gifts
before making my approach to you, Carrie," he had said in a
dry voice. "Apparently it makes quite a difference."

Stung, she had cried out. "You are wrong, Justin. I am
grateful to you, and I was trying to express my gratitude.
Don't you understand?"

"Understand? No, Carrie, I have given up trying to understand you, so let us not discuss understanding. You are much
the same size as my mother," he had continued with an obvious wish to change the subject. "I imagine that her shoes will
fit you too. I think she would like you to have her things."
With an inclination of his head, he had closed the lid of the
chest and walked away.

He had been right. Margaret Lawrence's clothes, even her
shoes, fitted her as though they had been made for her. As
was to be expected in the rapidly changing world of fashion,
the garments were a little old-fashioned. But they were well
made, and the materials were jewel-toned and quite beautiful.

Caroline began playing idly with a small ivory-and-green
fan. Her pleasure in her appearance had been spoiled, for
Justin had once again absented himself from the dinner table.
Paul, too, had paid her scant attention. He had had little to
say, and his usually pleasant expression had given way to a
frown. Once or twice she had caught him watching her cov-
ertly, but when she smiled at him, he looked away. His
frowning silence, relieved only by a remark here and there,
had lasted all through dinner. Was he worrying about Justin?
she wondered. These days Justin rarely smiled. It was apparent to her that he was bored and spoiling for excitement.
It might be that Paul was reluctantly beginning to recognize
the impossibility of caging up the tiger for too long. And yet
they had been only three weeks at the Grange. If three weeks
could produce such a change in Justin, what would three
months do?

Frowning, Caroline put a hand to her head, her fingers
touching the gleaming waterfall of curls that Amy, the little
maid who served her needs, had arranged so beautifully.
Looking at herself in the mirror after Amy had finished with
her, she had wondered if Justin would notice her hair and her
gown, and perhaps think she was not ill-looking. But he had

not been there to notice. Why had he not come to the dinner table? Where was he?

Laying aside the fan, she rose to her feet and prowled restlessly about the room. What was it she really wanted? she asked herself. The answer, as if it had been lurking in her brain waiting for her attention, came to her immediately. It was Justin she wanted! She loved him, needed him! Could she go to him and tell him how she felt? But perhaps it was already too late, for had he not warned her that he was not a man to play with? And Justin himself? She sighed, her eyes turning brooding and unhappy. He did not love her—she knew that; but she did interest him. Or she had, before she had earned his indifference. Could she break through that indifference? Thomas Fane's face rose up before her, and she asked herself despairingly if she would ever find the courage to try.

She stopped her prowling. She would go outside for a while; she needed air. She took her cloak from the clothes press, placing it about her shoulders and tying the strings beneath her chin. The thought came to her that she, too, was being slowly stifled by the luxury all about her, and the unending monotony of the days. She realized with a start that she was bored and in need of a change.

Walking through the cool night air toward her favorite place, the little summerhouse at the end of the winding path, she castigated herself. Bored, was she? What she really was, was a monster of ingratitude! She had been saved from death. She was safe and secure in a beautiful home. She had lovely clothes to wear, a maid to attend her. She had everything, in fact, that she could possibly need to make life pleasant. What more could she ask or want? She was not even required to work. She had pleaded with both Paul and Justin to let her do something to earn her keep, even if it was only arranging flowers, but neither would hear of it.

In the face of such generosity, surely she should feel a proper sense of gratitude? Well, she did, of course, she began belatedly to defend herself. Who would not be grateful? It was just that she was so terribly, terribly bored with the sameness of things. If she could only go back and undo her conduct. Had she not treated Justin so curtly and so rudely, boredom would have been far from her thoughts.

Caroline stopped short as she saw that someone was standing before the entrance to the summerhouse. She studied the dark blur, wondering who it might be. Was it Paul? One of the servants? Or—her heart quickened in sudden excitement—was it Justin? She walked on, her feet in their soft silk slippers noiseless on the path. Now she could make out a tall cloaked form. It was Justin!

"Good evening, Justin." Her voice shook nervously.

He turned slowly to face her. "I did not hear you coming."

"No. You seemed to be lost in thought."

"I was," he admitted. "In view of the news, it is hardly to be wondered at, is it? I imagine you have been entertaining similar thoughts to mine. Do we run for it? Or do we stay here?"

"What?" She stared at him in bewilderment. "What do you mean?"

"You mean that Paul didn't tell you?"

She shook her head. "Tell me what?"

"Damn!" he said impatiently. "He promised me that he would tell you."

"Justin, please! Tell me what?"

"That the hunt has been resumed for you and Paul."

"What!" She put her hand to her throat and stared at him with stricken eyes. "I . . . I didn't know."

"It was to be expected, wasn't it?" he said in a gentler voice. "Because of Wilson's march on London and the danger to the king's person, it died down for a time. But now that Wilson has been recaptured, the hunt is on again."

She swayed. "How do you know?"

"Chobham. We had to have someone scouting for us. That was why he went to London, to find out what he could."

"He knows about me?"

"He knows everything. Exactly what happened on that day, that I am supposed to be dead, everything. But don't worry. You can trust Chobham with your life."

"But, Justin, what shall we do?"

"I think our best plan would be to do nothing. We will stay right here."

"Yes, but—"

"My true identity is not known," he interrupted, "and neither is Paul's. Lawrence? What kind of a clue is that? Paul could belong to any one of a million or more Lawrence families. It is known by now, of course, that Paul Lawrence rescued not only his dead brother but Caroline Fane also, yet he left no trail behind him. Where will the law look? Whom will they question? Will they bring in all the Lawrences for miles around and subject them to examination?"

Caroline shook her head helplessly. "I don't know what to think."

"We will stay here," Justin said firmly. "Rogue Lawrence is dead. He was seen to die, remember that. So where is the connection between a dead man and Justin Lawrence of Bewley Grange?"

She felt there was a flaw in his argument somewhere, but for all that, she felt weak with relief. Justin was right, she told herself. She would not think about how well-known were Rogue Lawrence's features, or of the many people who had seen him. She did not want to think about it. If the hunt came nearer, he would think for her. In the meantime, she would put worry from her. She was deceiving herself. She knew it, and she did not care.

"Are you all right, Caroline?"

She nodded. At that moment the fact that he had called her Caroline meant more to her than the news he had just given her. He had rarely called her Caroline before, she thought with a sharp stab of regret. It showed how far he had removed himself from her. With a passionate wish to bring him near again, she walked into the summerhouse and sat down upon the padded bench. "Sit here beside me, Justin," she said in a low voice.

He hesitated. She had the sudden desolate feeling that he was about to walk away. Then, with evident reluctance, he seated himself beside her. "An invitation from Mistress Fane," he said coldly. "Are you playing some new game, perhaps?"

"I know I deserve that, Justin. But please don't!"

He made no answer. She wanted to tell him that she was sorry and to ask him if they could not go back to the old relationship, but she had not the words. She would even welcome the anger he could so easily stir in her, she thought. Love and hate. The two feelings she had for him were so inextricably mixed that she did not know from one moment to the next which emotion would be the stronger.

A full moon came out from behind the clouds. Its bright silvery glow penetrated the widely spaced latticework of the summerhouse and flooded the ground about them. In its light she saw that Justin's hair was wildly ruffled, as if he had repeatedly thrust impatient fingers through it. It was a habit of his when he was angry or uncertain. He was looking grim and unhappy, but perhaps that was because he knew he did not belong in this quiet and peaceful place. He was a fish out of water, just as she was. As for herself, if she belonged anywhere at all, it would be wherever Justin chose to go.

"What is it?" She started as his hand covered hers. It was a purely involuntary gesture, she knew, for his inquiry was coldly polite. "You are trembling. Come, now, we will be long gone before the law raids Bewley Grange. I have ways and means of getting information, and I will know all their moves ahead of time."

He took his hand away, and she clasped both of hers tightly together. "I was not thinking about that. There is something I have to say to you, and I was trying to find the right words. I . . . I do not find it easy to apologize, but that is what I am trying to do. Will you please forgive me, Justin, for my rudeness and my unfriendly attitude?"

"Of course," he said indifferently. "But what has come over you? You sound humble, and that is not like you."

"I am not being humble!" she snapped.

"Now, that sounds more like you."

So he did not intend to make it easy for her. He moved, and his arm brushed hers. Indignation was drowned in a wave of longing. She opened her mouth to say the words he had demanded from her—"Please love me, Justin"—but she could not bring them out. Frightened, she rose quickly. "It . . . it is late. I must go in now."

He rose too. "Wait, Carrie." His voice was gentle now. "There seems to me to be something different about you tonight. Something softer. For the first time, you appear to be more woman than frightened child." His hand touched her shoulder. "Am I wrong?"

"No, you are right." She could say no more. Wrenching herself free, she fled.

Once inside the candlelit hall, she found that her trembling legs could not quite manage the stairs. She turned instead into a small anteroom to the right of the hall. A bright fire burned in the large grate, and several vases of late-blooming roses filtered their delicate perfume through the room. She sat down. Her hands felt cold and cramped, and she held them out to the fire to warm them.

"Carrie." She turned her head without surprise as Justin came into the room. She had been expecting him. She said nothing as he approached. He did not sit down in the chair next to hers. Instead, he knelt down beside her and took her hand in his. "Carrie?" It was a question.

Unanswered, it hung between them. She stared into his eyes. They held a bright gleam. Gone was his stiff coldness. He was the hunter again and she the hunted. The difference was that she was his willing quarry. "Yes, Justin," she said softly. "Yes."

Doubt clouded his eyes, and the hand holding hers was rigid. She was filled with fear that he meant to punish her, to reject her. "Why?" he said at last. "Tell me why, Carrie."

Her heart was thudding. She would not draw back now if she could. She felt gloriously free as the words tumbled from her lips. "Because I love you, Justin. I want you." She knew a moment of wonder. Her fear seemed to have vanished as though it had never been.

She heard his expelled breath. "You are quite sure?"

"Yes, Justin. I am sure."

"And what has happened to your fear?"

"I . . . I don't know. Justin, do you still want me?"

He rose to his feet, drawing her up with him. "I want you, Carrie," he said simply. He put both arms about her and lifted her from her feet. "Yes, love, I do."

Going up the stairs, she saw their elongated shadows upon the wall. Watching them, she laughed like a joyous child. Lifting her arms, she clasped them tightly about his neck. "Justin!" Her lips touched his deeply clefted chin. She strained upward, trying to reach his mouth.

He laughed softly. "Have a care, Carrie, my wench, or you will have us both tumbling down the stairs."

Subsiding reluctantly, she rested her head against his shoulder. Only a small return of fear came as he entered his bedchamber and placed her gently on the wide, curtained bed. He stood over her, and in the light of the candles she saw his serious eyes. "I will ask you only once more, Carrie. Are you quite sure?"

She half-rose, as though even now she would run from

him. Then, with a little sigh, she sank back again. "Yes, I am
sure," she whispered. "Teach me passion, Justin."

He smiled, his serious look disappearing. "I think, love,
there will be little need to teach you. It is there, dammed up
inside you, waiting to flame up."

Dreamily she watched him disrobe. As he came toward
her, she closed her eyes tightly, waiting for the trembling, the
sickness, and the revulsion inspired by Thomas Fane to begin.
When she opened them again, she saw that Justin was
watching her closely.

"Carrie?" He sat down on the side of the bed. "Are you all
right?"

"Yes." There was no sickness or revulsion, only a shyness
engendered by the look in his eyes. She put out an uncertain
hand and touched his naked body lightly. "Why," she
breathed, "you are not in the least like Thomas. You are . . .
you are beautiful!"

"Beautiful?" His laughter rang through the room. "That is
a strange thing to say to a man." His voice softened. "Carrie,
will you let me undress you?"

She smiled at him radiantly. Taking his hand, she guided it
to the small buttons that fastened her bodice. "Yes, Justin.
Undress me."

His fingers were cool and competent, and she guessed he
had done this many times before. She shut the thought out,
refusing to be roused to jealousy. She heard her own high
laughter as he moved her about, grumbling at the number of
petticoats she wore. At last she was lying naked before him.
"Carrie!" His hands caressed her breasts, trailed over her
stomach, her thighs. He lay down beside her and gathered
her into his arms. She could feel the burn of his body
against her own. "Carrie, love!" His voice was shaken. "Beautiful, beautiful Carrie!"

She quivered when his hands guided her. Then she was lying on her back and his body was covering hers. She could
feel the hard throbbing bulge of him against her. Not like
Thomas! Never like Thomas! This was no inert piece of
shriveled flesh that touched her now. This was a demanding
battering ram. Feeling, sensation such as she had never
known, shot through her like a ribbon of fire. She moaned in
protest when he lifted himself slightly, thinking he meant to
leave her. He began kissing her body, his lips exploring every

part of her, a fiery trail that was driving her mad with long-ing. Now his lips were against her breasts, caressing first one nipple and then the other, his tongue teasing, teasing. She was burning up! In some dim part of her mind she laughed at her folly in believing this man would be like Thomas. That she had expected that he, like Thomas, ignoring her pain and her fear, would thrust into her at once. There was no compari-son. She could feel Justin's leashed-in passion, but he was putting her needs before his own. He was being gentle and tender and thoughtful. But he was ready, she knew, just as she was. She wanted so badly to feel him inside her! Her body arched beneath his, inviting, demanding. "Justin! Please, love! Please, darling!"

She was one burning fever of desire as his hands touched her legs and parted them gently. Impatient to accommodate him, she moved them wider herself. He entered her. She could feel him deep, deep inside her. Crying his name, she reared up, her legs clasping his body. Why had she ever feared? She could laugh now at that other Caroline Fane, that poor frightened imitation of a woman. She had been born for this joy, for these tearing explosions of delight.

Justin was moving slowly and rhythmically, and her hoarse cries, the drumming of her heels against his body, incited him on. She heard his gasping ragged breathing as he began to move faster and faster. And then she knew that until this mo-ment she had but touched on the border of delight. His gentleness was gone now. He was violent, dominant, and she, in her response, matched his violence. She was all fevered sensation. His perspiration splashed down on her face, and his driving force shook her body. He met and matched her at the same moment, as, with one last hard thrust, he spilled himself inside her.

Lying across her body, he was silent for a moment; then his husky voice said in her ear, "My God, Carrie, you are a flame. A beautiful searing flame." He laughed softly. "I knew it. I knew how you would be."

He rolled from her body, but she could not let him go. Her arms clasped him close. "I didn't know, Justin. I didn't know!" There was an incredulous wonder and joy in her voice, and although she did not realize it, hunger in the kisses she pressed upon his face.

He took her once more, though much later. Then she lay flushed and panting beside him, her tears spilling over.

He raised himself and looked down into her face. "Crying, Carrie? Why?"

She pressed her head against his shoulder. "Tears of joy, my darling. It was so wonderful, so beautiful! I love you, Justin, love you!"

"And I love you, Carrie."

She knew he did not. A man in love could not speak so lightly, so casually. But at this moment it did not seem to matter. She was content to lie beside him, to touch him in wonder. There was time, she told herself. Somehow, in some way, she would make him love her alone. How this was to be accomplished, she did not ask herself then. She would think of it later.

Lost in her dream, she was startled into attention by Justin's quiet voice. "You know, Carrie," he said, "I really do not think I can take much more of this unending monotony."

"Three weeks, Justin. That is only a short time."

"It seems more like three years. Things never change here. Years from now, it will probably be just as uneventful. No, I can't take it. I have been studying you of late, and I don't think you can, either."

This was so true that for a moment she could not answer him. Then she said in a faint voice, "What is to be done about it?"

"Wait. I have something to show you." He got up. Picking up a silk robe that lay at the foot of the bed, he put it on and belted it around him.

Caroline covered herself with the sheet, watching him as he crossed the room. He stopped before a small ornamental desk. Opening a drawer, he took something from it. She was quite unprepared for what he had to show her. Seating himself on the bed again, he held up a necklace of diamonds and rubies. The diamonds winked blue-white in the candlelight and the rubies glowed a fiery red. "Justin!" Caroline exclaimed. "It is exquisite. Did it belong to your mother?"

"No," he said calmly. "I stole it."

"You what!"

"I stole it," he repeated. "Why so surprised? You know who and what I am."

"Yes, but . . ."

"Come, Carrie, don't look so shocked." Before she could ask more questions, he began to talk at length. His dark eyes vivid with excitement, he told her of his plans for the future. Stunned, she listened to him. He had no idea of giving up the dangerous thrill of his old life for the quiet and peace and security that Bewley Grange and his estates represented. Rogue Lawrence was back! And this time his plans had a wider scope. Among other things, they included kidnap for ransom. "Only, it will not be a real kidnapping," he explained. "For after a few days I shall let the victim go and return the money anonymously to its owner. I don't need the money. I just want to see if I can get away with it."

"Why, Justin?" she exclaimed. "Why must you live this way?"

"I told you," he said impatiently.

"For the excitement and the thrill. Yes, Justin, I know. But surely there are other and safer things you can do?" She sat up and clutched at his arm. "What of the news Chobham brought? What if you should be discovered?"

"I will not be."

"Justin, you must listen to me! You escaped the rope once. But if you are caught again, and you could be, you will not escape it a second time."

His face darkened with memory, and he put a groping hand to his throat. But the next moment his laughter had thrust the uneasy memory aside. "Do not hope to make sense of me, Carrie. Even I have never been quite certain of what drives me." He smiled his brilliant smile. "What is to be will be—that is my philosophy. But as I told you, I do not intend to be caught again."

A thought came to her. "The law is hunting for Paul. Surely you do not intend to involve him again in your mad schemes?"

He had no intention of involving Paul, but he did not tell her that immediately. It amused him to see the angry flash of her brown eyes. "Paul is my concern," he said smoothly. "As he has always done, he will follow my lead."

"Oh, you are despicable! Do you really intend to drag Paul into this thing?"

"I am not sure." He smiled at her. "Perhaps."

"No! You will not, if I can help it. Rather than that, I would ride with you myself."

"The law is looking for you, too," he reminded her.

"Do you think I had forgotten? But I owe Paul a great deal. He is happy with this quiet life. Let him stay happy. Let the risk be to me rather than to him."

"Do you think Paul would agree to that?"

"No. But he need not know, need he?"

Laughing, he seized her hands. "Would you really ride with me, Carrie, love?"

Drawing her hands from his, she stared at him aghast. He was actually excited by the idea. "Yes," she said faintly. "If you will leave Paul out of it."

"You and I together. Think of it!" Justin laughed exultantly. "A pretty pair of rogues we will make, Carrie Fane." He held out his hand. "Is it a pact?"

"A devil's pact," she said, putting her hand into his.

"Aye. So it would have been."

"Would have been?"

He grinned. "Did you expect me to take you seriously?" he said, releasing her hand. "You actually believed I would allow you to put yourself in danger for my sake?"

"Yes."

"What the devil do you take me for?"

He sounded angry, but she knew that for those few moments he had meant it. He had been carried away by the idea. "And Paul?" she said quietly.

"Not Paul, either. I will do this thing on my own. The less either of you is involved, the greater my peace of mind."

Illogically, now that she knew he would not hold her to it, she wanted to ride with him. She had become infected with his restlessness and his craving for excitement. If he was mad, then so was she. She would do it. She would defeat all his arguments. For quite suddenly she found that she cared nothing for the peril in which she might find herself.

She thought of the blameless life she had led before Thomas was murdered. But her blameless life and her innocence had not prevented the law from finding her guilty of Thomas' murder. She had been humiliated and cruelly punished. If Paul had not rescued her, she would have been taken to Tyburn and hanged for a crime she had not committed. Justin had been right about her—she was like him. She would ride with him, and be damned to the consequences!

"What are you thinking about so deeply, Carrie?"

She smiled at him. "You spoke of your peace of mind, Justin. But you gave no thought to mine."

"To yours? What do you mean?"

"I mean that I will not sit back with my hands folded while you expose yourself to danger. You are a fool, but then, so am I. I ride with you, Rogue Lawrence."

"No, Carrie!"

"Yes, Rogue. I want to."

"I can't let you do it." But even as he said it, she saw that the bright gleam of excitement was back in his eyes.

"You have no choice. Don't forget that I could expose you at any time I wished."

He began to laugh. "I told you that you were like me! All right, we ride together."

"I was sure you would see it my way," she said, straight-faced.

"Carrie!" He pulled her into his arms and kissed her lips. Her lips clung, and the fire between them began to build rapidly.

Justin released her and divested himself of his robe. "You know, Carrie, love," he drawled, "that sheet is not going to protect you from me."

Laughing, she threw the sheet aside and opened her arms wide to receive him.

Chapter 7

The Bewley Grange servants were all agog over the rash of crime that had broken out in Edgerton, the small town that lay to the east, just a few miles from the village of Bewley. On the heels of several daring robberies, Judge Benson had inexplicably disappeared. When, suddenly, he reappeared, it was learned that he had been kidnapped by two masked men. Though one of the men, the judge gave it as his opinion, was too small and slight to be a grown man, and was undoubtedly a youth who had fallen into bad ways. The ransom money had been promptly paid by Mistress Benson, the judge's anxious wife, and after three days the judge was released. The mystery of the affair was that the ransom money had been returned with the judge. Inside the bag of money was a note. It read: "Thank you. I am much indebted to you for the practice afforded."

The excitement over the judge's experience and the cool nerve of the rogues who had kidnapped him died down as a new wave of robberies began. Lady Catherine Brookfield, of Malvey Hall, in Edgerton, had had her diamonds stolen. The thieves had taken everything—the necklace, the twin bracelets, and the tiara. The diamonds had been in Lady Brookfield's family for generations. They were flawless stones, and said to be priceless. The Ramsey emeralds had also been stolen. It seemed there was scarcely a palatial home in the district that had escaped the attention of the thieves.

Lady Brookfield's maid, Mary, who was sister to Amy Bellows, Mistress Caroline Fane's maid, had come over to Bewley Grange in a state of great excitement. She told Amy all about the robberies. Impatient with her sister's tepid reception of her story, she related it to cook, the other maids, and Chobham. Encountering Paul Lawrence in the hall, she again told her story.

Amy told the cook that her sister Mary was upset over the way Master Paul had treated her. "Just stared and frowned at Mary. Didn't even thank her for telling him about the robberies. Just turned away and left her standing there. It was different when she told Master Justin. He smiled at her and gave her a kiss on the cheek." Amy laughed. "He told Mary that she was a pretty thing. Mary was all excited, especially when he kissed her again. Had a fancy, she has, for Master Justin, from the first time she seen him."

Sighing, cook put a hand to her large breast. "He's a lad, is Master Justin. There ain't a lass what claps eyes on him that don't fancy him. He ain't shy at obliging 'em, neither."

"I know one lass that can't abide him."

"And what lass would that be?" cook snapped, looking almost personally affronted.

"Mistress Fane, that's who. I seen her come down the stairs when he was kissing Cassie Dale. Oh, my, if looks could kill!"

"Jealous, I shouldn't wonder. Anyway," cook added indignantly, "what right's she got to hate him? And her a guest in his house!"

Amy giggled. "I was in that little dressing room what leads off Mistress Fane's bedchamber. Getting her bath ready, I was. I was still in there when I hears Master Justin's voice. He says to Mistress Fane . . ." Amy broke off, dissolving into giggles again. Then, meeting cook's choleric blue eyes, she hastily resumed her story. "Master Justin says to her, 'Keep the bed warm for me, Carrie, love. I'll be visiting you tonight.' Mistress Fane must have forgot I was there, for she answered him quite loud and sharp. 'What! After I caught you with that pop-eyed creature who is always mooning after you? You sadly overestimate your charms, you devil! Come near me again and I'll do you a mischief. I swear it!'"

"There!" cook said triumphantly. "If that don't prove she's jealous, I don't know what does. What did Master Justin say?"

"He just laughed in that way what he has. Anyway, there was silence for a bit; then I heard a loud slap. 'Swine!' Mistress Fane called him. 'I may follow where you lead, you bloody bastard!' she shouts at him, 'but I am in great hopes they will catch you and hang you!' Master Justin answered her quite good-natured. 'You know you don't mean that, Carrie, love. And jealousy ill-becomes you. A mere kiss to a troubled little girl. Be reasonable!' Mistress Fane goes on shouting at him. 'Liar! Her only trouble is that she is always hanging on your coat sleeve, waiting for you to notice her. She stares at you so with those great eyes of hers that it makes me want to vomit! And you are only too willing to oblige her with a kiss and a caress, and only God knows what else, you bastard!' "

Cook frowned. "Swearing! Taking the Lord's name in vain! Fine goings-on for a lady, I must say. But then, it's always them quiet ones what's the worst." She eyed Amy eagerly. "What do you suppose she meant about him being caught and hanged?"

"Just something to say, I suppose. After that, I heard sounds like they was fighting, so I peeped into the room. Master Justin had her down on the bed. It looked like he was trying to kiss her. She ups with her doubled-up fist and hits out at him like a man would. Caught him a great clout on the nose. Oh, my, you ought to have heard him swear!"

"Fine goings-on," cook said again in a scandalized voice. "Well, what happened then?"

Amy went on eagerly. "The look on his face scared me. Like the devil might look, it was. He grabbed her up from the bed and he shook her so hard that her hair came tumbling down. Then he lands her a smack around the face that you could have heard from here to Edgerton."

"Served her right," cook said shortly. "What do you mean by telling me she can't abide him? Seems plain enough to me that her and Master Justin are sleeping together. Her and her fancy manners! I know her kind, I do."

"You don't know nothing," Amy snapped. "Mistress Fane's a nice lady. I like her. Anyway, what if they were sleeping together? It's nothing to do with you and me."

"That's as may be. After Master Justin give her the slap," cook went on, her manner changing, "what did she do?"

Amy gave a delicate shiver. "As soon as he let her go, she flung herself at him. Strong though he is, she gave him a fair old tussle for a bit. 'Wildcat!' he called her. 'Bitch!' And a whole lot of other things what made me go red in the face. I thought they were going to murder each other, the way they were going at it."

Cook tutted and frowned. "Well, I never!"

"I made a noise then, just so's Master Justin would know I was there. He turns around and grins at me, just like he'd never lost his temper at all. 'Hello, sweet Amy,' he says to me. But then, when he turned back to Mistress Fane, he looked like the devil again. 'As for you,' he tells her, 'I'll be back. Make no mistake about that.' "

Since she had no more to tell, Amy set about her duties. Mistress Fane had breakfasted in her room. She would have finished her meal by now and be wanting to dress. Bidding cook a hasty farewell, she went on her way.

Brushing out Caroline's hair, Amy chattered on happily about the robberies in Edgerton. "My sister Mary told me that Lady Brookfield saw them thieves with her own eyes. Two of 'em, there were."

Caroline, who had not appeared to be listening, started violently and gave her full attention to the maid. "How did ... how did Lady Brookfield happen to see the thieves? I understand, from the tales going around, that they come and go so quietly that no one except Judge Benson has laid eyes on them."

Amy looked curiously at Caroline's face. "You mustn't worry, Mistress Fane," she said soothingly. "If them thieving devils come here, we've got Master Justin and Master Paul, to say nothing of Chobham, to defend us. Chobham's old, but he's still got some fight left in him."

"Yes, yes. Answer my question, Amy."

"This time the thieves didn't move so quietly, and that's how Lady Brookfield came to see 'em. One of the rascals knocked over a vase, and it woke her up. Back for the second time, them thieves were, and this time they got away with her sapphires. Cheek of the devil, they've got!"

Caroline's hands clenched. Why had she listened to Justin? Why had she allowed herself to be talked into burgling Malvey Hall for the second time? It could not go on! Already her nerves were stretched to the breaking point.

"They was gone in a flash, Mistress Fane." Amy's voice sounded in her ears again. "Done up in caped greatcoats, they was. And they was masked, with tricorne hats pulled down low. Pity she never got a look at their faces."

That vase! Caroline thought. That cursed vase! How could she have been so clumsy?

"I will dress now," she said, rising.

"But your hair!"

"I will wear it loose today."

Amy, thinking she had finished her mistress, went on to another topic. "Lady Brookfield's had trouble with her butler, too. Gave him a little holiday, she did. So off Carter went to London. He was going to pay his little sister, as he always calls her, a visit. He came back to Malvey Hall yesterday, and he was that upset. "The 'spirits' had made away with his sister."

Caroline stared at the girl, wondering if she might have been tippling at cook's strong blackberry wine. "I don't understand you, Amy. Are you referring to ghosts?"

Amy laughed. "No, mistress. Ain't you ever heard of 'spiriting'? I thought everybody knew about being 'spirited.' It's sort of like kidnapping, see. These people, 'spirits' they're called, they get hold of folks and they talk to 'em all nice and sweet. They tell 'em if they'll just sign a little paper, they can sail across the seas to the colonies, and they can have themselves a fine old time out there. Grow rich and everything, the 'spirits' tell 'em. All they got to do is to give their services for a few years to them folks out there in them American colonies. Mostly, I heard, they go to someplace called Virginia, where the tobacco plantations are. The folks what are 'spirited' over the seas are called indentured servants. Once they've finished working for them planters, or whoever, they get given fifty acres of land so's they can start up on their own." She frowned. "I wonder if that's true, mistress? The part about the land, I mean."

"I have no idea, Amy. But if the people sign a paper and agree to go of their own free will, it can scarcely be called kidnapping."

"But folks don't always want to go of their own free will, mistress. That's why it's called 'spiriting.' If them folks don't want to sign a paper, I hear tell that they get knocked on the head and taken aboard ship just the same. When they come to again, it's too late. They're well on their way to this Virginia or one o' the other colonies. Don't seem right, do it?"

"No," Caroline agreed. "I would have thought such trickery was against the law."

"Well, so it is, mistress. But them 'spirits' is usually too slippery for the law to get their hands on. It's going on all the time, and more and more folks get 'spirited' over the seas. I even heard tell as there's 'spirits' what works secretly in King William's court."

"Oh, Amy, that's nonsense."

"I'd not be surprised to find it true. There's some who'd do anything for money."

"I wonder how Carter's sister will like living in the colonies?" Caroline said absentmindedly, her mind really on the Malvey Hall robbery and the vase.

Amy shivered. "I wonder too. A man I know once went out there. He wasn't 'spirited,' he went out on his own. He told me that this America is a great big land. So big that it could swallow up England a thousand times or more. Beautiful, my friend said it is, and full of wonders. There's lots of savages living out there. Indians, he said they was called. Painted-up savages what'd kill you as soon as look at you. I wouldn't like to go and live among them savages. Would you, mistress?"

Caroline thought of the hate-twisted, jeering people who had surrounded her at the cart-tail procession. Once again their voices rang in her ears. "Murderess! Whore! Filthy trollop!" The lash seared her back savagely again and again. And still the people were not satisfied. They cried out for her blood. More and more blood.

"What's the matter, mistress? You look sort of pale."

"I'm all right, Amy. I was thinking that we all live among savages. They are not all in this America, I assure you. They are here, too." She paused, the memories still vivid. "You may go, Amy."

"I'll get out a gown for you first, mistress. Which one shall it be?"

Caroline gave her a vague smile. The girl meant well, but she wanted to be rid of her for the moment. She had to think. "No, Amy," she said, "you need not bother. I will attend to myself."

Chapter 8

Reclining on the long couch beneath the window, Justin seemed to be half-asleep. But watching his restlessly pacing brother, he had never been more alert. Paul's feelings always showed in his face, and at this moment, Justin knew, he was full of suspicion and fear. He had said nothing as yet, but Justin did not doubt that he would shortly be asking some very pointed questions. Ever since the Edgerton robberies began, Paul had been uneasy. It was unfortunate that he had encountered Lady Brookfield's maid. Her story had seemed to turn the balance. Suspicion had all but become certainty.

Justin linked his hands behind his head and frowned thoughtfully up at the ceiling. He had never lied to Paul before, but this time he must. On no account would he allow the youngster to become involved in this particular part of his life again.

Thinking of Carrie, a wry smile touched Justin's lips. She had told him in no uncertain terms that he was selfish, no good, a fool. If he were really concerned for Paul's peace of mind, she had said, then he would turn from crime and settle down like any normal man. She was right. He agreed with her on all counts. And that being so, why could he not think and behave as a normal man? Was he a little mad, as Carrie sometimes said? The truth was that he felt only half-alive unless there was a spice of danger in his living. The things he did had no real point in them. It was for the thrill, and only for that. Because he secretly agreed with Carrie's summation of his character, he had been stung into only a mild defense. "It is my neck I am risking," he told her.

Because she had angered him, he refused to tell her what had been in his mind lately. It was time to think of someone other than himself, and Paul was very dear to him. And, if he were honest with himself, so was Caroline. And so he had all but decided, because of that affection he bore them both, to give up his dangerous pastime.

He smiled. Warm and tender, or angrily storming, like always called to like, and Carrie, deny it though she may, was very like him. She was as drawn to danger as he was himself. Though he thought she had not fully realized this herself until six months ago, when she had begun to ride with him. This did not, however, prevent her pleading with him to give up his way of life.

"What is amusing you, Justin?" Paul's serious voice roused him from his thoughts.

"Nothing of importance, lad." Justin swung his legs to the floor. Sitting up straight, he prepared to give his full attention to his brother. "Something is disturbing you, Paul. Out with it."

Paul sat down slowly on a chair. Looking into Justin's eyes, unsmiling now and intent, he felt the hot blood flushing his face. Now that he had been invited to speak, he felt unsure and miserably inadequate to deal with the situation. He hesitated. Always before it had been Justin who led, and he who had unquestioningly followed. But he must have some reassuring answers to the doubts and suspicions that had been plaguing him for some time now. Justin could not be implicated in the robberies, could he? He must be wrong. He had to be wrong! Besides, he had heard there were two thieves. Where, in this quiet place, would Justin manage to get himself a partner? It must not be Justin. Let it not be him!

"Well, youngster?" Justin's voice was very gentle.

Paul swallowed. "I . . . I want to talk to you about the robberies in Edgerton." He paused, not realizing how pleading was the expression in his eyes. "Justin"—his words came out in a rush—"are you . . . are you mixed up in those robberies?"

Justin's eyes softened. He could say: "Yes, Paul. I am. But you no longer have cause to worry. Tonight, the job at Maidenfair Manor will be the last job. After that I abandon my criminal life." But how could he say that to him? He could well imagine his alarm. Paul would no longer be at peace with his world and himself. He would be constantly listening for the knock upon the door that would herald disaster. No, there was no other course open to him but to deny it.

"How can you ask me that?" he said lightly. "You know that I am a reformed character."

Paul's hands gripped the arms of his chair, his knuckles showing white. "Are you, Justin? I want very much to believe that! Tell me the truth, please. Whatever you have done, we will face it together. You know that."

"Aye, lad, I do know it. But it is not like you to doubt me."

"I don't want to doubt you, Justin," Paul said miserably. "It is the last thing I wish to do. Give me your word that you know nothing about these robberies. I will believe you."

Justin picked up a silver snuffbox from the table beside the couch. He flicked open the lid, snapped it closed, flicked it open again. "Will you really believe me, lad?" he said at last.

Paul stared at the thin restless hands toying with the snuffbox, and for some inexplicable reason he suddenly felt the older of the two. A wave of emotion washed over him. Nothing must happen to Justin! He had almost lost him once, and he had never been able to forget his agony of mind. It must not happen again. He could not endure it. "Yes, Justin," he said earnestly, fighting to keep his voice steady. "I know that you have never lied to me."

Justin carefully replaced the snuffbox. He was giving up his old bad ways, he thought with a touch of wry humor. And after the job tonight, though he perished of boredom, he would abide by his decision. Ten minutes ago he had not been sure. It was the misery in Paul's face that had decided him. So, in a way, he would not be lying to him now. "No, Paul," he said quietly. "I am not involved."

Paul's taut hands relaxed. Feeling almost limp with relief, he pulled his kerchief from his pocket and wiped his sweating forehead. "Thank God for that, Justin!"

Justin looked at him curiously. Paul was well entrenched in, and obviously more than content with, his quiet life. Did he ever miss the old days? "And if I had been, Paul?" he questioned. "What then?"

"How can you even ask me that? We have always been together. We have always shared everything."

No, Paul hadn't changed. Now, as always before, he was perfectly willing to put aside all that he loved and valued for the sake of a scapegrace brother who was entirely unworthy of such devotion. Looking at the sincerity in the young face,

Justin felt a sting at the back of his eyes. Frowning, he cleared his throat loudly. "One brother puts his head into the lion's mouth, and the other must do the same, eh? You know, Paul, I never thought to find a bigger fool than myself. But I do believe I am looking at one now." His frown lifted. "It must run in the family, this urge to run headlong into trouble." Smiling, he rose from the couch and strolled over to the door. "I think I'll take a turn about the grounds. It might help to blow the cobwebs from my brain."

The door closed behind him. About to rise from his chair, Paul suddenly sank back again, giving in to the vague worry he felt. Something was wrong. What had it been that had so managed to elude him in the conversation, and was only just now striking him? Had it been an expression on Justin's face, a look in his eyes, an inflection in his voice? He sat very still, trying to place it. His breath caught in his throat. He knew! Those restless hands, the faint and unusual flush in Justin's swarthy face. No, Justin had never lied to him before. But he had lied to him now.

Chapter 9

The stallion was impatient with the long inaction imposed upon it. Tossing its head, it snorted gustily through flaring nostrils and pawed nervously at the ground.

Paul put out a quick, reassuring hand to the animal. Stroking the heavy black mane, he whispered. "Be still, Hereward. We must not be seen."

He stared at the two mounted figures poised on the top of Shooley Hill. They were obviously resting after a hard gallop. To the eyes of a casual observer, Paul thought, they would have looked innocent enough, but there was nothing innocent about either of them. Only yesterday Justin had said to him, "I am not involved." Not involved! How calmly he had lied to him. He was involved in every crime that had taken place these past months. Only, Paul had not known then that Caroline, his Caroline, was Justin's partner in crime.

Paul's eyes stung with tears. Caroline! How he had dreamed of her! In his mind she had become to him "his Caroline." He loved her. He had hoped one day that she would return his love. Shock hit him again, mingling with his pain, as he thought of the events of last night. Knowing that Justin had lied to him, he had followed him. He had seen Caroline join Justin, and he had heard their laughter. She had been clad in masculine garments, her bright hair tucked up beneath a tricorne hat. She was as one with Justin on his dangerous road. And more than that, she had become his mistress. He had heard enough of their conversation to understand that.

There was an uncomfortable lump in Paul's throat. Angry with his tears, he brushed his hand across his eyes. Looking at Justin's erect back, Paul knew that nothing had changed. Justin's deception, his own love for Caroline, could not change his devotion to his brother. It was too deep-rooted.

He restrained a sudden impulse to step out of his hiding place and confront them with his knowledge. Perhaps even now they were discussing the emeralds they had stolen last night from Maidenfair Manor. Tonight, at the dinner table, he determined, would be the best time to face them. He would tell them that their activities must and would stop.

Justin turned his head and looked at Caroline. "It would have been only a question of time before Paul found out," he said. "I was gambling with Paul's happiness as well as fate, but I refused to see that. I will risk many things, but not that lad's happiness. So it's over, Carrie. Maidenfair Manor was our last job. It is time for me to grow up, don't you think?"

Caroline's smile was warm. "High time. There is hope for you yet, Rogue Lawrence," she said lightly. "I had not ever thought to hear you put someone before yourself. Do you really mean it?"

"I mean it," he said curtly. "But I would not have you start believing me to be some kind of saint."

"I would scarcely do that," she said dryly. "That very remote possibility need cause no concern at all."

He laughed. "I should have known better than to say a thing like that to you. It is comforting to know that I can always count on you for the telling answer, Carrie."

"Justin. What will you do with your life?"

He shrugged. "I shall travel a great deal. There must be plenty of adventure waiting for one who is determined to find it. Perhaps I will put up my sword for hire. One thing is certain. I must do something, for I'm damned if I'll stay here and just molder away."

For a moment she could not speak; the pain consuming her was too intense. How could she bear to lose him now? And yet his words had seemed to slam a door in her face. She moistened her dry lips. "Is ... is there no longer a place in your life for me, Justin?"

He gave her a quick sidelong glance. "I will return to England from time to time, Carrie. We will see each other then." He laughed. "Unless, of course, I find you married and busily rearing a brood of children."

How could he speak so? As if she could ever marry any other man! Oh, God! Had he no love for her at all? She took a deep breath before speaking. She was gambling everything, her whole life. "Why not marry me yourself, Justin? You can be sure then that I'll always be waiting. Or better still, I could travel with you."

He laid his hand over hers. "Carrie, love," he said gently, "if I could make any woman my wife, it would be you. But I have told you many times that I have no intention of marrying now or ever."

Yes, he had told her, she thought drearily. She could not say that he had deceived her. She had not meant to reproach him, for she hated a whining woman, but she could not seem to stay the words. "You have never loved me at all, have you?"

"I have a warmer and stronger feeling for you than I have ever had for any other woman, Carrie. But I do not believe I have it in me to sincerely love any one woman."

"Justin, I have an odd feeling about you." She turned her face to his, and he saw her brightly glittering dry eyes. "I sometimes wonder if you would recognize love if it came to you."

"Perhaps not." He frowned thoughtfully, his eyes on the carriage coming along the road below. "Are you saying that I am in love with you and don't know it?"

"You might be." She tried to laugh, to make her words sound lighthearted. "And why not, I should like to know?"

"Why not indeed," he answered her in the same tone. "I will give some thought to it."

"You are too kind, sir."

He did not answer her. She saw that he was looking at the carriage again, and she followed his gaze. The lumbering vehicle lurched awkwardly over the potholed road. It was near enough now for her to see the scarlet-and-gold colors emblazoned on the side panel. The driver, seated on his high perch, tooled the vehicle with some difficulty. The sun shone on his scarlet coat and the scarlet cockade at the side of his tall black hat. Behind the carriage came two outriders. Unlike the coachman in his gay scarlet coat, one man was dressed in drab brown, and the other in gray.

"London carriage," Justin commented. "Must be carrying an important personage."

She cursed the carriage for coming along and taking his attention from her. She had so much she wanted to say to him. "What makes you think so?" she answered, forcing the words.

Justin pointed downward at the two men bringing up the rear. "Hired protection. You can always tell. If they belonged to the household, they would be wearing livery. The very way they carry their muskets gives away their profession. See? They carry them before them, in a pocket in the saddle."

"Yes. I can see them sticking out."

Justin's eyes glowed with a light she knew well. "Doubtless something of great value is being carried, hence the hired protection. I wonder what it might be?"

"That is no longer any concern of yours," Caroline said sharply. "Remember your promise."

He laughed ruefully. "You have no need to remind me, Carrie. I have vowed to turn my face away from crime. You may trust me to do a thorough job on the reformation of Rogue Lawrence. Come on, wench. I'll race you down the hill."

"Race? But the carriage is too near, Justin," she protested. "We will collide with it."

"Not we. We will cut sharply to the right and come out ahead of it. Just follow the master horseman, and you cannot go wrong."

Suddenly she felt gay and lighthearted, full of hope and confidence. Somehow she would make him see that she was the woman for him. "You are a reckless fool," she said, laughing. "All right. I'll race you."

With a loud yell, he was off. He tore down the hill at breakneck speed, with Caroline following. The wind whipped at her long, unbound hair as she tried to close the distance between them.

The carriage was level with the base of the hill. The driver took one startled look at the two riders thundering toward him, and he knew he could not hope to outrace them. "Bloody fools!" he bellowed. Completely losing his head, full of panic and confusion, he sawed frantically at the reins and brought the carriage to a stop.

Caroline's heart lurched. Justin had misjudged; she knew that he had. Even were he to pull up in time, she could not. Her horse was all but bolting, and she no longer had any control over the animal. She felt the sickening lurch as her mount stumbled. A scream tore from her throat as she was thrown. She rolled over and over down the hill, to fetch up bruised and breathless almost under the wheels of the vehicle.

"Christ almighty!" the driver shouted. "That's Rogue Lawrence. It's him or his bloody ghost!"

Caroline's hands were shaking badly, but she managed to pull herself to a safer position. Her eyes dilated as she saw the two outriders stiffen in their saddles. Their muskets seemed to jump into their hands, so swiftly did they move. She knew then what would happen. She could see it beginning to happen.

Unlike Caroline, Justin, with his superb confidence, believed himself to be in complete control. He had pulled up just in time to avert a collision. He was laughing, his dark eyes very bright and his face glowing with the excitement of the race. He pulled on the reins, and his horse, infected by the excitement, reared up. A shock of surprise and anger went through Justin's body as the first musket ball struck the animal in the side.

The wounded horse was dancing on its hind legs. Flecks of foam began forming at its mouth. Its eyes rolled wildly, and its front hooves lashed frantically at the air.

Caroline screamed wildly and despairingly as Justin was thrown heavily to the ground. The desperate sound she made mingled with the high, agonized scream of the dying animal. Finally, after one last frenzy of action, the last it would ever make, it toppled over on its side with a sighing grunt. Save for the spasmodic twitching of muscles, it was very still, its glossy coat already dulled and darkening with its death sweat.

Caroline's eyes went from the dead horse to Justin's crumpled form. He was lying so still. "Oh, no!" Her voice was raw and quivering with pain. "Not dead! Let Justin not be dead!"

There were voices all about her now, rough, excited, one voice sharply commanding. Caroline's whole being was concentrated on Justin, and she heard the voices only dimly as she crawled toward him. Was he dead? If she found it to be so, there was no reason for her to go on living! She bent over him, and she gave a great wrenching gasp of relief as she saw his eyes open. Seeing his faint smile, she burst into a storm of tears. "Oh, Justin, you fool!" she sobbed. "You damned hairbrained fool!"

A shout from behind them caused them to start to attention. "Watch out! Here comes another of 'em!"

Justin's eyes turned to the hill. "Paul!" He tried to raise

himself. "No, Paul, no!" His voice was hoarse and shaken with fear. "Stop, lad, stop!"

Paralyzed, Caroline crouched there beside Justin. Whether or not Paul heard Justin's frantic cry, he could neither stop nor turn the horse about. Where had he come from? Caroline had just time for the irrelevant thought to enter her mind before it was wiped out completely by the whine of the musket ball.

Paul took it full in the face. Caroline's frozen brain struggled to reject the sight, but she could not. Dear God! Paul's face was a mask of blood. Where his features had been, there was nothing, nothing! His figure, as though borne upward by wings, was lifted in the air, and then he was rolling toward them. A helpless rag doll of a figure without a face.

Caroline neither felt nor saw Justin move. He was suddenly there beside his brother. He gathered him into his arms and pressed the shattered face tightly against his breast. She saw his tears fall on the boy's bright hair, and the naked agony in his voice would live with her forever. "Paul, Paul! This is my fault, all mine. Oh, God, forgive me!" He rocked his brother in his arms. "Paul! Oh, my God, Paul!"

Obeying the command of a thin, impatient-sounding man in blue breeches and a brighter blue-satin jacket, the outriders approached Justin. One of them grasped him by his black hair and forced back his head so that he might peer into his face. Justin did not seem to notice. He was aware of nothing but the boy cradled in his arms. The man released his grip on his hair. "It is Rogue Lawrence," he shouted.

"Then what are you waiting for?" the man in blue called sharply. "Bind him and put him in the carriage." He moved toward Caroline's crouching form.

She stared first at the blue-satin shoes with their high red heels and their carved steel buckles. Then her gaze traveled slowly upward, and she looked into his cold gray eyes. The man smiled, showing uneven teeth, the front two broken and stained. "So," he said in a soft, satisfied voice, "we have caught two pieces of scum together. A very good day's work, I would say." Caroline's hand moved, and he placed his shoe over it, grinding the red heel into her fingers. She did not cry out, merely looked at him. Annoyed by her lack of reaction, he raised his voice to an angry bellow. "I recognize this woman. It is Caroline Fane, no less! Bind her, too."

His words meant nothing to Caroline. She was watching Justin. The two men had managed to pry his arms loose from Paul's body, and they had dragged him struggling and fighting to his feet. He was straining to get back to Paul. Paul, who would never hear him again! She could not watch Justin's agony anymore. It was too much! Paul, so young, so shy, so endearing, his life ended in a shattered waste. Quickly she averted her tear-blinded eyes.

"Stop that scuffling!" the man in blue barked. "Knock him on the head!" He surveyed Justin's slowly collapsing force. "That's right, Payton, that was a good hard blow. Now, bind the damned madman before he comes to. Be quick about it."

"Don't hurt him, don't!" Caroline screamed out in agonized protest.

The man in blue lifted his hand and cracked her hard across the mouth. "Quieten down, whore. You, Chudleigh, get yourself over here and bind up this wench good and tight."

Caroline was lifted to her feet. Her split lip dripped blood, but she did not feel it. Her arms were dragged behind her back and her wrists lashed tightly together, the thin cords biting into her flesh, but still she felt nothing. It was as though all feeling, all pain, all terror had died. Paul was dead, and Justin would hang. And she? They would hang her, too. What did it matter? Nothing would ever matter to her again. In these few minutes her life, everything that was important to her, had crumbled into dust.

The man in the drab-brown coat picked her up roughly. Stalking over to the carriage, he threw her through the open door. She landed on the leather-upholstered seat with a small jar. Justin, she saw, was already there, half on the seat, half on the floor. The dammed-up feeling came flooding back in a hot, hurting wave at sight of his pale, unconscious face, the blood on his head that still trickled and splashed on his shirt. Her tightly bound hands writhed against the bonds in an effort to break them. "Open your eyes, Justin! Oh, my darling, open your eyes and look at me!"

The man in blue entered the carriage. He hesitated; then, seizing Justin's legs, he heaved them on the seat. Without looking at either of them he slammed the carriage door and seated himself. "Name's Judge Forsythe," he said. "Maybe you'll remember me?"

The judge at her trial! Caroline stared at him without answering. How could she have forgotten those thin lips, those cold, gray, merciless eyes?

Judge Forsythe did not seem to expect an answer. He turned those unnerving eyes on a small boy who sat hunched in the opposite corner of the carriage. "You are quiet, Eastley. I had begun to think you were asleep." He put a hand to his head. "Owing to this encounter, my nerves are in shreds. Take up your fiddle, Son, and play me a nice soothing tune. But before doing so, you will tell that woman on the seat facing you the name I am known by."

The boy hunched his shoulders and said sullenly, "I would rather not, Father."

"I said tell her!" the judge barked.

Seeing no way of avoiding it, the boy said in a low voice, "He is known as 'the hanging judge.' "

No reaction came from Caroline, and the judge was angered. "The fiddle, Eastley," he said sharply. "Play something."

The boy looked incuriously at the prisoners, then back at his father. "Very well," he said reluctantly.

He picked up the fiddle, hesitated, then cradled the instrument beneath his chin. The stubby little fingers, remarkably skilled, plied the bow deftly. The tune he played was "Greensleeves." The words of the song ran through Caroline's mind, but sadly jumbled and out of sequence.

> Alas, my love, you do me wrong
> To cast me off discourteously.
> Green Sleeves was my only joy
> My lovely Lady Greensleeves . . .

The tune ended, and the boy thankfully laid the instrument on the seat again.

To Caroline the wheels seemed to continue to pound out the words. "Greensleeves," she thought bitterly. It would be their funeral dirge!

Caroline closed her eyes. Justin knew she loved him, but he did not know the strength of her love. There was more to it than just making love. There was the wish to love and to share all things with him, to become a dear and intimate and familiar part of his life. Even were Justin to become as impotent as Thomas Fane, it would make no difference to her. He would still be her one and only love. Her thoughts turned to God. For a long time now she had not really believed in Him, but now she found herself praying fervently. She prayed that it might be true that there was another world. A world where she and Justin might meet again to love and quarrel and love again, just as they had done on this earth they were soon to leave.

Part III
The Transportation

Chapter 10

At first light, the prisoner was led out into the gray gloom of the courtyard to receive the prescribed punishment of flogging. He had been flogged several times before, and it was an effort for him to put one foot before the other. He stumbled and fell, causing the little procession to come to a halt.

"Pick him up," came the command.

The two prison officials who had been walking on either side of the prisoner bent over him. Grabbing an arm each, they hauled the emaciated figure to his feet and led him over to the flogging post.

Jeremiah Crowley, the head turnkey of Newgate Prison, frowned as he stared at the drooping figure. "All right," he said curtly, "tie the prisoner to the post. You, Hale, remove his shirt. Look sharp about it!"

Shivering in the early-morning chill, Crowley waited with ill-concealed impatience as the prisoner was made fast. Hale, with a sidelong glance at Crowley, ripped the shirt away.

Crowley stepped forward to examine the prisoner's lacerated back. The examination was routine, but it made no sense to him at all. Whatever the man's condition, the flogging would still be carried out. Aware of the concentrated gaze of the other two men, Crowley poked a tentative finger here and there at the inflamed back. His eyes widened slightly as he saw the pus dribbling from several open wounds. Poor swine! he thought, feeling an unexpected twinge of compassion. Much more of this sort of treatment, and he'll die. The frown between his eyes deepened. He was powerless to stop the flogging of this particular prisoner, for the order had come from someone in higher authority than he, Judge Forsythe himself.

Crowley looked at the tall burly man standing to the left of the post, and his eyes lingered for a moment on the heavy whip clutched in Newman's hand. "Lawrence is due for transportation, Newman. Remember that." He hesitated, afraid of appearing weak before his men. "Because they can use every man they can get out in the colonies, it is against the king's law to beat a transportee to death. If Lawrence should die, we would be in a lot of trouble." He hesitated again, then added in a flat voice, "We only carry out orders. But for all that, we would get all the blame."

"Are you telling me to go easy on the prisoner, sir?" asked Newman.

Crowley nodded. "Exactly, Newman. It is for our own preservation."

"If you say so, sir."

"I do say so." Crowley turned to Hale. "Another thing. The prisoner looks half-starved to me. When did he last eat?"

"He gets the same as the others," Hale answered in a sullen voice. "It ain't nobody's fault if he can't keep nothing down."

Crowley shuddered inwardly. Prisoners such as this wretched man Justin Lawrence, and one moreover who was guilty of the added crime of cheating the hangman, were placed in the condemned hold to await either their death, or, in some cases, transportation as white slaves to unknown masters in the New World. Unless the condemned had money, and Lawrence, because he had been seized so abruptly, did not have any, the rations consisted of a slice of maggoty bread and a half-cup of water. This was given to them in the morning, and the same again in the evening. Small wonder, then, that Lawrence, in his condition, could not retain it. Throughout, the man had remained stubborn. He would see no one, and if any came to see him, he still issued an adamant refusal.

Forgetting Newman, who awaited his command for the punishment to begin, Crowley stood there deep in thought, his hand rasping across the coarse stubble on his chin. He was wishing that he had the courage to disobey the needlessly sadistic instructions of Judge Forsythe. But he had never been a courageous man, and to order that Lawrence be untied and returned to his cell would be to bring censure down on his own head.

Besides, he thought, hurriedly stirring up his anger, Lawrence had brought some of these punishments upon himself. From the moment he had entered Newgate Prison he had proved himself to be not only a troublemaker, but violent in the extreme. He did not seem to care if he lived or died. Three times he had attacked the turnkey. If he had not been forcibly dragged off, he would have killed him. If Lawrence had not been already condemned, he would have gone to the hangman for this crime alone. The turnkey's story was that he had offered the prisoner no provocation at all. His story did not agree with that of the other condemned prisoners, who stated that Rogers, the turnkey, had been unnecessarily rude and insulting. Lawrence, however, had apparently borne all this in silence. It was not until the name of his brother, Paul, the youngster who had been killed by Judge Forsythe's men, had been included in Rogers' insults that he had begun to behave like a wild man. Even after the first attack, Rogers, the prisoners said, would not let up on Lawrence or his brother. The result of this had been two more savage attacks upon his person.

Crowley sighed, despising himself. The truth was that he had been inclined to believe the story told him by the prisoners. But a man in his position, he had decided, must side with his colleagues. As a consequence, he had been forced to add further punishments to those already ordered by Judge Forsythe. And then yesterday Judge Forsythe had made one of his periodic tours of Newgate Prison. In the men's condemned hold, the judge had stood looking about him with those wintry gray eyes of his. It was then that Justin Lawrence had opened his eyes and caught sight of him. Scarcely able to walk, Lawrence had somehow found the strength to hurl himself at the judge. "Murderer!" Crowley could still hear Lawrence's raised voice.

Order had finally been restored and the judge rescued. Outraged, breathing fire and vengeance, he had ordered today's punishment.

Crowley looked up. "Hale, step up to the prisoner and raise his head. It has been ordered that he must know the reason for his punishment and the number of strokes he is to receive."

"Yes, sir." Hale saw Crowley's frown as he grasped the prisoner's dark hair and pulled his head upward. So old man Crowley thought he was being too rough with Lawrence, did he? He gave the hair a vicious twist.

"I told you to raise his head, Hale," Crowley said coldly, "not pull it from his shoulders."

"Sorry, sir."

Crowley ignored him. Again he felt that twinge of compassion as he looked into Justin Lawrence's gaunt face. There was little trace now of the exceptionally handsome looks that had distinguished Rogue Lawrence, as he had for so long been known. Suffering had set faint traces of gray here and there in his hair. His face was badly bruised and his cheeks sunken. The dark eyes that looked out at him from between puffs of swollen and discolored flesh had an unfocused look. His lips were swollen to twice their size and the skin cracked. Crowley saw that Lawrence's lips were moving, as though he had something he wanted to say.

"If you wish to speak, Lawrence," Crowley said abruptly, "I am ready to listen."

There was no answer. Hale had momentarily relaxed his grip on the prisoner's hair, and his head drooped again. With an exclamation beneath his breath, Hale forced it up again.

"Justin Lawrence," Crowley began in a deep solemn voice, "you are guilty of attacking the person of Judge Forsythe with violent intent." He looked down at the paper in his hand. The notation stated that the prisoner, Justin Lawrence, was to receive twenty strokes. "For that crime," he continued calmly, "you are to receive ten lashes." Had Hale and Newman seen the paper? Crowley wondered. Did they know that he had deliberately lied? He looked at Lawrence again. "Have you heard and understood?" he demanded.

Justin was dimly aware of voices. Someone was saying his name. He tried to listen, but the effort was too much for him. His mind slid back to Paul. Paul! God, in Your mercy, let me turn back time. But, no, he could not turn back time. Paul was dead, and he could think of nothing but the terrible shattered bloody mess of his face. That boyish freckled face with its shy smile. If only he had been open and honest with Paul, it would never have happened. Paul would have been alive today. It was as much his own fault as of those bastards who had killed Paul. He could not go on living with Paul's death on his conscience, and he would not. But before putting an end to his life, he would get those other men who had killed his brother. In the meantime, with that purpose in mind, he would do whatever was asked of him. He was to be transported to the New World. And so he would slave in the colonists' fields. He would plant their tobacco and whatever else was required of him. And then one day, if he could trust the promise made to him, he would be free. Free to pursue his plan of vengeance, to ruthlessly hunt down and destroy those men who had murdered Paul. Another face rose up in his mind. He saw smiling brown eyes set in a fresh, lovely face. He saw the sheen of blond hair as the face came nearer. Carrie! What have they done to you, Carrie? What have I done to you? I have destroyed your life as well as Paul's. I am twice a murderer. He felt the cold loneliness of despair and grief and need all through him. He needed her. He needed to feel her soft lips touching his, the warmth and comfort of her arms holding him close. Carrie! Her name rose up like a sob, like a cry for help. I need you, Carrie. Forgive me! Help me!

Crowley stepped back. "Release the prisoner's head, Hale," he instructed. "Newman, let punishment begin."

Newman nodded. Gripping the butt of the whip tightly for better purchase, he raised his arm and brought the lash down across the prisoner's back. The thin body jumped convulsively, but the groan that came from the swollen lips was faint, as though there was not sufficient life left for a louder outcry.

Crowley flinched as the weighted leather strap whistled through the air again. He did not know why this particular prisoner should so profoundly affect him; he only knew that he did. Gay, laughing Rogue Lawrence, who had become this pitiful wreck before him. He saw the blood dripping from the cuts Newman was making on Lawrence's suffering flesh, and the fresh blood that came welling up from the unhealed cuts already there, and he was sickened. Why in the name of sweet Christ must Newman hesitate so long between each stroke? It seemed to him that the man was enjoying prolonging the agony. "Newman!" he snapped. "Hurry it up, will you?"

Justin gritted his teeth against the searing agony. They were tearing him apart! They were killing him! But he must not die yet, he would not! His breath came pantingly from his lips. Help me, Paul! Carrie! Somebody help me. I can't stand this pain! Pain, day after day. Every hour, every minute I live is a torment. How easy it would be to give in, to die. How tempting that thought was. No, I will not. I will hang on, and someday I will look into the faces of your murderers, Paul. Someday, somehow! He could feel the blood, sticky and hot against his tortured back. Oh, God, no more, no more! He could not see through the swirling blackness before his eyes. He felt the rough wood of the post against his cheek, and he turned his head and tried in vain to sink his teeth into it. Anything to suppress his cries. Anything to show his persecutors that he could and would endure.

Crowley saw Lawrence's tensed body sag and the contorted look leave his face. He had fainted on the tenth stroke. "All right," he roared, as he saw Newman draw back his arm again. "Can't you count, man? I said ten strokes."

Newman dropped his arm. "Sorry, sir, I lost count."

Crowley did not believe him. "Cut the prisoner down and return him to his cell."

His expression glum, Crowley watched as Justin Lawrence was cut down. The two men carrying the body disappeared. Crowley walked slowly after them. It would be a wonder to him if Lawrence lived. It was doubtful, very doubtful indeed, if he would ever set foot in Virginia, the place to which he was to be transported. And somehow, even if he survived this last beating, Crowley could not see slavery sitting too well with Rogue Lawrence. He had heard, too, that, given a choice between hanging and transportation, Caroline Fane, who had admitted to being Rogue Lawrence's mistress, had chosen transportation. Had she or had she not killed Thomas Fane, her husband? Shrugging, Crowley put the thought aside. It was nothing to do with him. He did not sit in judgment upon the prisoners. The law said she was guilty, and that was good enough for him.

Caroline Fane stared up at the ceiling. Her mind was divorced from the filth and squalor all about her, the nauseating reek of unwashed bodies and the overflowing pail of urine and excrement; there was room in her mind only for Justin. Oh, Justin, my love, my love! Tears overflowed her eyes and washed pale tracks in the grime of her face. Five months now she had been imprisoned, and in that long and agonizing time she had heard through various channels that Rogue Lawrence was seriously ill, dying. That he was dead. Someone had told her that he had been buried in an unmarked grave. Ever since then, she had lain unmoving on the hard plank that served her as a bed, and she had prayed passionately that she might die too. Justin! She saw him again in her mind's eye, his dark eyes glowing, his quick-striding walk. He had had almost boyish enthusiasms, her complex Justin. Sometimes she could say and do anything, and he would only smile and lift his dark brows in that quizzical way of his. But at other times he would blast her with his hot temper. Oh, God! She had heard that he had been beaten to death! That he had died like some poor wounded animal, alone, friendless, with not a soul present to mourn his passing.

She put her arm across her eyes and felt her tears cold against her flesh. She would mourn him forever, her dear love! Her mind tortured, she seemed to hear that husky, whispering voice sounding in her ears. "Carrie, love. Carrie, love."

That night, when he had taken her for the first time, he had awakened in her body a flaming desire. She had felt him deeply within her, and she had become a woman. Yes, she had been the passionate, ardent, loving woman that Justin had always known she could be. But she had not known how deep and enduring was her love for him until they had once more been captured and brought back to grim Newgate Prison, this place of misery and death and despair.

Justin dead? Even now it was impossible to think of that vital life as being no more. Her hands clenched, and her long, ragged fingernails dug into her palms. How long had it taken them to beat him to death? How long had he lingered in his excruciating agony? Justin was a strong man. Death would not have come to him quickly.

She closed her eyes tightly, shutting out one thought, letting in a memory instead. The day they were tried in that dreary courtroom. The crowds that had packed the benches and stared with fascinated eyes at the prisoners, some of whom might be proved innocent and set free, and others who would be condemned. The smell of perfume, musty clothes, and perspiration that came from the closely packed audience. The frightened murmuring, the restless movements, and the low, nervous laughter of the prisoners who sat beside her and behind her. The rustling of paper as, here and there, packages of food were unwrapped. The woman on the front bench, who had devoured meat and bread with noisy gusto, and without once taking her round brown eyes from the prisoners.

The stuffy, dusty atmosphere. The tension, the fear. And then, finally, Justin.

When they brought him in, he had been loaded down with chains. They called him violent and dangerous, and they were taking no chances on his escaping. Violent? Dangerous? He could barely manage to shuffle to his position. Her heart had throbbed with love and pity as he made his painful way forward. How gaunt and ill he had looked! Four months in Newgate Prison, four months of brutal treatment, semistarvation, and the burden of his grief had aged him. She had sworn to herself to be calm, but she could not hold back her tears when she saw the deep lines of suffering in his face and the gray that sprinkled his hair. "Justin!" His name had been torn from her.

The murmuring in the courtroom rose in volume as Justin looked up sharply at the sound of his name. "Justin!" she said again in a strained whisper.

He had stared at her, but his eyes seemed not to register her image. His blank eyes appeared to be looking through her. She had the painful feeling that they were deliberately blank because the sight of her reminded him too poignantly of Paul. Perhaps, if he had determined to be done with everybody and everything that had led up to the terrible moment of his brother's death, it was a form of self-protection against added pain.

She could not look away from him. She could not stop herself from willing him to recognize her. She wanted him to give her some sign, however small, that she had once existed for him. Her concentration was so great that she had not heard when her name was first called.

"Caroline Fane!" A hand grasped her arm and jerked her out of her seat. "You have been called."

She looked at Justin again, but he was still staring blankly before him. She turned her eyes to the hard-faced man gripping her arm. "What did you say? I did not hear you."

The man did not answer. Heedless of the iron anklets she wore, he propelled her roughly forward. Twice she almost fell. It was only the man's painful jerk on her arm that saved her.

"That's Caroline Fane, the murderess," a woman's voice said loudly. "Her what escaped."

"Silence that woman!" a cold voice rapped out. "She will keep her mouth closed, or she will leave this court."

That voice! The voice that sounded through all her nightmares. Frozen, Caroline felt the full weight of fear as she looked up at the man who was to decide her fate and Justin's.

Judge Forsythe sat high above her. His face was expressionless. The eyes meeting hers were as cold and as gray as she had remembered them. Her head reeled as her mind rushed her back to that fatal day when Paul had been murdered. The carriage that was bearing Justin and herself to prison and to death. The judge, the sullen-faced little boy, and the tune he had played.

Caroline tried to concentrate on the proceedings, but it was difficult. Judge Forsythe was leaning forward; he was saying something to her. She knew that he was, because his eyes were fixed upon her, and his thin lips were moving. She stared at him, her heart pounding so heavily in her ears that she could not make out the words. Calm! She must be calm. To achieve this calm, she had used an old trick that she had employed many times before. She began to think of irrelevant things. The crossed scarlet-and-gold banners on the wall behind the judge. The dingy green of those walls. The coughs, the sighs, the rustlings, the varied noises made by a group of people who were crowded tightly together.

"Bastard!"

The loud voice caused Caroline to jump. She saw the judge stiffen, and she swung around in alarm. The word had come from Justin. He was on his feet, and his eyes were no longer blank. They blazed with a murderous fury. "You swine! You murdering bastard!" Justin shouted at the judge. He lunged forward, but, impeded by the heavy irons, he fell.

Judge Forsythe hammered his fist on the desk before him. "You, Wentworth, pick up that man and return him to his seat. You are to gag him. Later, he will be given permission to speak. But for now, I will hear no more from him." Despite his hammering on the desk, even then the judge's face was expressionless and his voice cold and precise.

Justin seemed to go mad then, and it was as if the hatred brought about by his sudden recognition of the judge had given him back the strength that had once been his. It had taken three prison officials to overpower him.

Caroline had watched, her heart aching for him. "No!" she cried as Wentworth bent over Justin and stuffed a rag into his mouth. "No, no! Leave him alone!" She was never able afterward to remember how she got there, but suddenly she was standing before Justin and looking deeply into his tortured eyes. "Stop it!" she screamed at Wentworth. She tore desperately at his arm. "Take that gag from his mouth!"

"Bring that woman back here to me!"

She heard the babbling excited voices of the people as her arms were pinioned at her sides and she was half-carried, half-dragged to where the judge awaited her. Trembling violently, her head hanging, she stood there. This time, when he began to speak, she heard him.

"Caroline Fane, you have already been given a fair trial. The verdict brought in against you was guilty. You will therefore be returned to your seat to await my disposal of your case."

With her eyes on Justin, she had sat there as the long afternoon had worn itself away. Sometime later, the gag had been taken from Justin's mouth. He stood next to her, before the judge. She had wanted so much to stretch out her hand and touch his. That frightening blaze was back in his eyes as he concentrated his whole attention upon Judge Forsythe. Behind Justin stood two prison officials. They were tensed up and alert for any sudden move Rogue Lawrence might make.

There was a faint smile on the judge's lips as he began to speak. His voice was almost contemptuous as he offered them a choice between life and death. Yes, astoundingly, she, Justin, and three other prisoners were being given that choice. Death by hanging. Or life in one of the colonies of the New World. If they chose life, the five of them were to be transported to Virginia.

She had stood very still, not daring to look at Justin. She thought of Amy Bellows' description of the painted-up savages to be found in the New World. "Indians, they call them," Amy had said. She knew then that she did not fear the perils of the New World. It was being parted from Justin that she feared. And so she waited to hear his choice. Death or life? Whatever he chose, she would choose too.

Her heart had begun to beat very fast as Justin spoke out. He declared for life. Thinking of it afterward, she had realized why. He wanted them dead, the three men who had killed Paul. While they walked about freely, unconcerned over their murder of a young boy, death was not for Justin.

Caroline put her hand to her shaking mouth. Those men still lived, but Justin was dead. Why couldn't she die too?

A woman wandered over and seated herself on a plank beside Caroline's. "Woken up at last, 'ave you, dearie?" She smiled and put a hand to her snarled dark hair. "I been picking out lice from me 'air," she announced. "Got a lot of 'em, too." Stretching out a skinny hand, she picked up a strand of Caroline's hair. "You got nice 'air, dearie, but you got lice too. I know, 'cause I seen 'em crawling. If you like, I'll 'ave a go at it for you." She chuckled. "We don't want no lice when we gets aboard that ship, do we?"

Caroline pulled her hair free. "Leave me alone, please," she said in a toneless voice.

Disappointed that her offer had been rejected, the woman frowned at her. "Ain't you a bleeding little friendly soul, then? What's the matter with you? If you was to ask me, you don't care about nothing." She paused and eyed Caroline with open curiosity. "You been saved from 'anging, ain't you? What more do you want? Ain't you even excited about sailing out to this 'ere New World?".

"No."

Annoyed, the woman rose to her feet. Wandering to the other side of the dark cell, she transferred her attentions to another of the inmates, an enormously fat woman whose abundant flesh overflowed the plank upon which she was seated. The fat woman was naked to the waist, and her fingers were dreamily stroking her breasts.

" 'Allo," the woman announced her presence. "What the 'ell you doing?"

The fat woman looked up and smiled. "Ain't doing nothin'. I just been sitting 'ere and dreaming about all them men there's bound to be out in that Virginny. I ain't 'ad a man for a long time."

"Won't do you no good if there's men all over the bleedin' place. Them men'll want a proper woman, not a fat old bucket o' guts like you."

The fat woman was not in the least affronted by this plain speaking. "I'll find me a man, so don't you be worrying about that."

"I ain't worrying, and I never come over 'ere to talk about men." She pointed at Caroline. "That one there, she's mad. Lies about all day long, don't talk, ain't got no interest in nothing. What you think's wrong with 'er?"

The fat woman looked across at Caroline. "She ain't mad. She's just pining for 'er man. That Rogue Lawrence, what died."

"Loved the Rogue, did she?"

"Aye, seems like. But she'll get over it." Chuckling, she began to stroke herself again. "She'll get 'erself another man, you just see if she don't. Me too. I'm getting me a man, you'll see."

Chapter 11

The ship that was to carry them to the New World was inappropriately named the *Merryventure*. The vessel, with its scaling paint and patched sails, looked old and shabby, as though it had limped through this trip a hundred times or more, and with each successive crossing, through lack of care, had deteriorated just a little more, taking on the weariness and hopelessness of its passengers. A ship, like a woman, needed love and care, and the *Merryventure* was dying of neglect. In size, it looked scarcely capable of accommodating the six hundred convicts to be transported. To make the crowded conditions worse, many of the women convicts who had small children depending upon them had been allowed to take them along on the voyage.

With a gruesome effort at chivalry, or perhaps a heavy irony, it had been decreed that the women prisoners and the children were to board the ship first. The men were lined up to the left, awaiting their turn.

Caroline stared straight ahead as she stumbled up the rough gangplank, impeded by the iron fetters about her ankles. Her face, beneath its coating of dirt, was gaunt and very pale. Her eyes, like her face, were drained of all expression. The creaking of the timbers was loud in her ears, and above her head the screeching seabirds swooped and circled over the Portsmouth waters. Behind her, the other women giggled together, pushing at each other good-naturedly in their efforts to be first aboard. To hear them, Caroline thought bitterly, one would think they were off on some long-anticipated holiday. Seven months of hell had passed since the sentencing. Seven months! And now, finally, they were brought to this moment.

Some sailors who were halfheartedly attempting to swab down the scuffed and grimy deck stopped their work as the women prisoners came aboard. Leaning on their mops, they eyed the dirty, bedraggled collection of humanity appraisingly.

"This lot's just as scummy as the last," one of the men remarked, his nose wrinkling with disgust.

"Aye," the short blue-eyed sailor standing next to him agreed. "Pity the wind's in this direction. You can smell 'em a mile away. The least they could do is give them flossies a bath before letting 'em aboard. The ship smells bad enough as it is."

The third sailor, his eyes inspecting Caroline boldly, said in a harsh voice, "That one there wi' the blond 'air don't look too bad. But like you say, she needs a barf." Picking up his pail, he approached Caroline. "You'd like a barf, wouldn't you, dearie?"

Caroline's expressionless eyes inspected him from head to foot. She said nothing. Behind her, the women shuffled and tittered uneasily.

Caroline's calm inspection, her very lack of emotion, angered the sailor. His face flushing a brick-red, his brown eyes gleaming, he suddenly raised his voice to a bellow. "I said, you'd like a barf, wouldn't you? You answer when I speaks to you, whore!"

"What would you like me to say?"

The man gaped at her. "Listen to 'er, mates. Jus' listen to 'er fancy voice! We got a lady come a-visitin' us, we 'ave. Only right that a lady should take a barf, ain't it?"

The other two men began to laugh. "Go on, Joe," the short sailor cried, "give it to her, then. Hurry up. The men are coming aboard."

"Right!" The man lifted the pail and flung the dirty water full in Caroline's face. "Now you're all nice and clean, dearie."

She recoiled from the impact, gasping as the water went down her throat and clogged her nose. A spark of anger glowed in her eyes, and she took a half-step forward. Then, the anger dying as quickly as it had been born, she shrugged and stared listlessly ahead of her.

The sailor felt curiously deflated as he stared at the thin girl with the muddied water dripping from her face and hair and spangling her lashes. With would-be jocularity he remarked to his companions, "Here, Bill, Pete, they've forgot to bury this one, I reckon. The bloody cow ain't got no life nor feelin' in 'er."

The other two men laughed uneasily. The men prisoners were filing aboard now, their heavy fetters clanking. Joe, ceasing his baiting, stepped back. "All right, you men," he shouted to the prisoners. "Get your arses over here to the left. Line up. You women stay where you are, but you form a line too, see. Cap'n Dennison'll be 'ere in a minute to inspect 'is cargo. An 'e ain't goin' to like it if you ain't in place."

The short sailor waited until the two lines of prisoners were in place; then he hurried forward and nudged the man's arm. "I thought you said as the blond wench hadn't got no life in her, Joe," he whispered. "Take a look at her face."

"What you talkin' about, Pete?" Annoyed at the interruption, Joe irritably shoved the short sailor aside. Glancing casually in Caroline's direction, his gaze became fixed.

She was looking at one of the men in the line-up, and her face was glowing, radiant with life.

Joe's eyes turned to the man who had wrought such a transformation. He saw a tall, painfully thin man with a swarthy face deeply indented by gaunt lines of suffering. He had intense dark eyes beneath a mop of gray-flecked curling black hair, and a mouth that was folded into a straight bitter line. Like all the other men, he was filthy, his body reeking. His shirt, once white, had taken on a dingy gray look, and it hung on him in tatters. His breeches, obviously intended to fit a much larger man, were held in place at his waist by a piece of frayed rope passed through the cloth loops and tied in front in a heavy, clumsy knot. He was barefoot, and there were open, festering sores on his ankles caused by the continual rubbing of the iron manacles. Joe's eyes narrowed as he noticed that the manacles on his wrists and ankles were heavier than those worn by the other prisoners. Dangerous character, he deducted, and determined to speak to Captain Dennison about it at the earliest opportunity. Captain Dennison particularly hated dangerous characters aboard his ship. They were liable to start a mutiny.

"Justin!" Caroline said his name with wonder and joy. Her incredulous eyes fixed on his face, she took a step forward, then another. "They told me you were dead!" She held out her manacled hands pleadingly.

"Here!" Joe sprang forward and seized Caroline by her hair. "You get back in line. No talking, bitch!" Still gripping her tightly by the hair, he glared at the dark man. "You're going on report! What's your name?"

"Justin Lawrence."

Joe twisted Caroline's hair. "And you, bitch? What's your name, eh?"

"Let her go!" Justin Lawrence spoke in a quiet, deadly voice. "Release her at once!"

For answer, Joe twisted Caroline's hair so cruelly tight that tears of pain started to her eyes. "An' what if I don't feel like lettin' 'er go, Lawrence?" he jeered. "What you reckon you c'n do about it?"

"I shall do my best to kill you!" The quietly spoken words held far more menace than a raised voice. "Release her, I said!"

"Oh, no, Lawrence, I ain't goin' to do nothin' of the sort. Come on, what you waitin' for? Whyn't you 'ave a go at me?"

"Justin, no!" Caroline cried out in despair. "You will be punished! That is what he wants. Stay where you are. Do nothing!"

Justin ignored her. He lunged forward. The sailor, who had not believed that the prisoner would have the courage to attack him, was taken by surprise. He automatically released Caroline in order to meet the challenge. He gasped as the heavy iron manacles were wrapped tightly about his neck. Dark eyes, frightening eyes, full of murderous light, blazed into his.

The sailor's hands clawed frantically at the manacles, loosening them a little. Straining back, he managed to shout, "Christ Almighty! The bastard's tryin' to choke me. Get the mad swine orf me!"

Caroline screamed as the other two sailors sprang to their companion's aid. She hobbled forward clumsily, trying with her body to block their advance. She was swept to one side. She fell heavily to the deck and lay there half-stunned.

Released from the choking manacles, Joe charged in to the attack, and all three men flung themselves upon Justin.

The prisoners, both men and women, were whistling and stamping and shouting encouragement. Her head clearing, Caroline did her best to aid Justin. Like the wildcat Justin had once named her, she clawed at the sailors' legs, trying to pull them off. She doubled up her fists and hit out at them. "Leave him alone! Cowards!"

The short sailor gave a yell of anguish as he felt sharp teeth sink into his leg. He tried to shake free, but Caroline, like a fierce terrier worrying at a bone, hung on. His blue eyes hot with rage, the sailor bent over and dealt her a blow on the side of the head. "That'll teach you, you crazy bitch!" he shouted as she fell backward. For a moment he continued to glare at her; then he went back to the attack.

Her face drained of all color, her eyes wide open and staring, Caroline heard the sickening contact of knuckles on flesh. Have I found him again, she thought, only to lose him? They will kill him! Oh, God, help him. Please help him!

As though in answer to her frantic prayer, a pistol shot was heard. Complete silence descended. The sailors, releasing Justin, straightened to attention. Their eyes, riveted on the tall portly man coming toward them, the pistol in his hand pointed upward, looked frightened.

"Jackson, Taylor, and Lovering, at it again, I see," the tall man said in a soft, almost gentle voice. The soft voice rose to a roar. "You dirty swabs! How many times must I tell you to leave the punishing of prisoners to me? You, Jackson, come forward. What have you to say for yourself?"

Joe Jackson stepped forward and saluted smartly. He was obviously frightened, but he spoke up clearly enough. "Prisoner attacked me, sir. I was just defending myself, Cap'n, sir."

"And Taylor and Lovering were lending you a hand, eh?"

"Aye, Cap'n, sir. Bastard tried to choke me with 'is manacles."

"Did he, now? Now, that is interesting." He looked down at the battered and bloody man. His eyes were closed, and his head rested on the lap of a girl with tangled, dirty blond hair and wild brown eyes that stared at him challengingly. Captain Dennison smiled at the girl. "These swabbies telling the truth, wench?"

Caroline looked into wide blue eyes incongruously set in a heavy red face. The blue eyes were framed by thick black lashes, and they blinked at her mildly and inquiringly. "He, that man there"—Caroline pointed a trembling finger at Jackson—"he provoked Justin into attacking him."

Captain Dennison took off his cap. Shifting from one foot to the other like an awkward and bashful boy, he rumpled his short carroty red hair: then, sighing, he replaced his cap. "Justin?" he said in his gentle voice.

Caroline nodded. She looked down at Justin and placed a hand on his hair. "Yes, Captain. His name is Justin Lawrence."

"Ah!" Captain Dennison rocked backward and forward on his heels. "Would he by any chance be the famous Rogue Lawrence?"

Caroline's heart plunged. But of what use was it to lie? "Yes," she said in a low voice. "But he . . . he is paying for his crimes."

"So he is, and so he will." Captain Dennison knelt down beside Justin. "He's a hard case!" he snapped. "A very hard case!" Caroline caught her breath in horror as he suddenly pressed the muzzle of the pistol to Justin's temple. "Do you know what we do with hard cases, wench?"

"No, don't!" Caroline grabbed for the captain's fleshy wrist. "He was provoked. Don't shoot him, don't!"

"Take your hand off me, wench." The gentle note was back in the captain's voice. "Convicts are not allowed to touch me. Not ever, do you understand?" He stood up abruptly. "Lovering," he barked, "run to my cabin and fetch me my preparation of healing herbs. You will then cleanse my hand of this whore's dirty and diseased touch."

"Aye, sir." Lovering started away.

"Wait, lad," the captain called after him. "Before you go, I would wish you to hear my judgment on this case."

"Aye, Captain, sir." Trembling, Lovering came back and stood to attention again.

The captain's smile, like his eyes, was wide and candid. The smile dwelt first on the three sailors. "After you have cleansed my hand, Lovering, you will be lashed to the mast. You, Taylor, will give him thirty lashes. Then, Taylor, I greatly fear that it will be your turn. Thirty nice hearty lashes delivered by Jackson." The guileless eyes rested on Jackson. "For you, lad, I have reserved the privilege and the honor of punishment at your captain's hands."

Caroline glanced at Jackson's blanched face. Instinctively she bent protectively over the unconscious Justin. God help you, my darling! she thought. God help us all!

"Wench," the captain's voice said, "I am about to address you. Look at me, if you please."

Slowly Caroline raised her eyes. "Yes?"

"Yes what, wench?"

"Yes, Captain."

"That is much better." The captain pointed at Justin. "That man, that godless and scandalous man, will be placed in the solitary hold for ten days. A hard case must be taught that it does not pay to cause riot and rumpus on my ship. You agree, my dear?"

"Please!" Caroline begged in a choked voice. "Please don't do that to him. He has been very ill. I beg you, Captain!"

"And you beg very prettily indeed. However, punishment must be carried out."

"Could you not overlook it this time? Could you not punish me instead of Justin?"

"Carrie, don't!" Justin's weak voice came to her. She saw that his eyes were open. His hand made a groping movement, and she took it in hers, feeling the weak clasp of his fingers.

"Yes. Don't, wench. You'll only worsen things for yourself." The captain's voice was as smooth as cream. "And that won't do, since you already have punishment enough coming to you."

"She has done nothing!" Justin tried to raise himself, but the effort was too much for him. "Double my punishment, but leave her alone."

Tears crowded Caroline's eyes. Justin might not love her as she desired to be loved, but he did care about her.

"Very gallant of you, Lawrence," the captain said, smiling. "But I hope that I am a just man. I would not think of doubling your punishment. Like yourself, the wench will endure."

Justin's fingers tightened on Caroline's hand. "My fault. I'm sorry, Carrie."

"No, darling, no!" She bent over him in an agony of love. "We will come through this together." She lifted her eyes and looked steadily at the captain. "You may do whatever you will with me. I care naught!"

"You will care, sweetheart. I promise you. Every night, accompanied by one of my crew, you will be taken to the solitary hold. You will feed this man his meal. After that you will be returned to the women's quarters."

The swine! The fat, cruel swine! So that was it. He wanted to make sure she witnessed Justin's suffering. But the joke was on him. The fact that she would see Justin took away the sting. Her slight smile was scornful. "I quite understand, Captain."

"I thought you would, Pretty Poison. Under that coating of filth, I think you might have an ounce of intelligence, and perhaps some beauty to go with it." The captain turned abruptly on his heel. "Two of you men take Lawrence to the solitary hold. The rest of the punishments will be carried out when we are well out to sea. Prisoners are to be lined up to watch punishments. That is all."

Caroline watched the tall, portly figure walk away. The silence he had inspired still lingered on after he was out of sight. Justin's hand fell away from hers as Taylor and Jackson lifted him. They did not look at her as they bore him away.

Dully, she watched as other sailors came forward, instructed the men prisoners to form an orderly line, and herded them away to their quarters. Then the sailors returned for the women. As Caroline went down the steep, rickety ladder to the dark, cramped cabin they were to occupy on the long voyage, her stomach turned over at the nauseating stench that assailed her nostrils. It seemed to be composed of sweat, vomit, urine, old stale breath, excrement, diseased flesh, and the sharp, sweet, rotting odor of death. Wide wooden shelves jutted one above the other from three walls. The sailors told them that the shelves were for sleeping upon.

Betsy Buford, a lame woman who had killed her husband and her three children, and, after being caught, had tried to kill herself, hobbled toward a young sailor. "Don't we get nothing to put beneath our heads, nor nothing to cover ourselves with?" she demanded in a shrill voice.

The young sailor looked wistfully after his three companions, who were already ascending the stairs. This was his first voyage, and he was feeling ill at ease and at a loss. His eyes returned to Betsy Buford, and he quailed before the mad glitter in her narrowed brown eyes. "I . . . I got no orders about that," he stammered. As Betsy put out a thin, clawlike hand, he turned about and bolted up the stairs, almost falling down again in his panic.

Betsy stood there, her cackling laughter following him.

Above them, the hatchway slammed closed. Except for the feeble glimmer of a candle in a bracket upon the wall, they were enclosed in airless darkness.

"Ma!" A scream came from a little girl who was crouched on the filthy floor. "Ma, make 'em let me out. I can't see, I can't breathe!"

"Hush, Jennie," a soft voice with a country burr said. "It's not so bad. You'll get used to it."

"Something crawled over my foot. Something furry! I felt it!" The child began screaming again. "I'm frightened, Ma. Make 'em let me out!"

Dimly, Caroline made out the small form as the child jumped to her feet and hurled herself up the stairs. "I want to get out! Let me out!" She clawed at the hatchway.

"Come down, Jennie. Come down!"

Sobbing hysterically, Jennie remained where she was for a long time, her thin, broken voice still pleading to be let out. At last, realizing the hopelessness of it, she crept down the stairs and sought her mother.

A high-pitched scream came from a young woman who had hitherto been silent. "Rats!" she shrieked. She began beating her manacled hands against her ragged skirt. "Oh, God help me, the thing's ran up my skirt!"

Caroline hobbled toward the screaming woman. "I'll help her," she cried. "The rest of you get on the bunks." She waited until the women rushed eagerly to obey her. Then she took a fold of the woman's skimpy skirt in her trembling hand and began to shake it violently. There was a tearing sound, and a large brownish-gray rodent fell heavily to the floor. The creature crouched there for a moment, a piece of the cloth of the woman's skirt gripped between its bared yellow teeth. Its dingy fur bristled, its beady eyes darted from side to side, before, to the vast relief of the hysterical women, it scampered away from the circle of candlelight and disappeared into the darkness.

Caroline caught her breath sharply. She felt a cold, quivering sensation inside her and an upsurge of panic. As if her plight had just become real to her. She and Justin and all the other miserable souls on the sea, crossing oceans to reach a vast, savage, and strange land. And when they arrived, it would be to slavery. A scream rose in her throat, and she lifted her manacled hands and bit down hard on her wrist to stop herself.

Later, Caroline found that she had lost all count of time. It was all one to her now. But how much time had passed? It had been broken at intervals by the opening of the hatch. Sailors had thrust small wooden bowls of soup at them, soup so thin and flavorless that it might have been water, and rough hunks of bread. The sailors would retreat immediately, leaving them shut into the darkness again, the smells, the groans, and the despair.

Trying to choke down the soup and the coarse bread, Caroline wondered why she had not been called upon to take Justin his meal. Was it not supposed to be part of her punishment to see him suffer? Justin! The miracle of seeing him alive! How was he now? What was he thinking and feeling?

Time. The slow and relentless passing of time, the dragging minutes and the plodding hours that kept her separated from Justin. When would she see him again? Or was he once more lost to her? No! She would not think that way. She was being foolish. She would see him! She must see him! She must keep on telling herself that.

She heard the creaking of the old ship's timbers. Her body slid forward and then sideways, and she had to catch at the splintered edge of the shelf to steady herself against the lurching and the heaving of the vessel. The ship seemed to steady itself; then it shuddered, dipped down, and reared up again. Rough weather, she thought, desperately trying to concentrate on something other than herself. It was no use. With each movement of the ship, she had the sensation that her stomach was dropping away. It was stiflingly hot in the women's hold, and yet she was shivering beneath the cold perspiration that dewed her face and her body. She could hear the sounds of suffering all about her. She clenched her teeth together, willing herself not to be sick.

Above her, the hatchway was thrown open, startling her. A stentorian voice bawled a command. "All prisoners out on deck to watch punishment. Come on, move! Get your scabby arses up here!"

With the other women, Caroline climbed upward and stumbled out on the deck into bright daylight. After the prolonged darkness, her eyes narrowed in a painful effort to adjust to the light. They were all half-blind, and many of them were sick from the motion of the ship, but it made no difference to the sailors. The women and children were herded together and marched off to the scene of punishment. As they marched, Caroline took a hasty shuddering look at the sea. The waves were certainly high, but there was no sign of the rough weather she had imagined. If she felt like this now, how would it be with them all if they should run into rough weather? A storm at sea! How would they be able to endure it?

Lovering, the first man to be flogged, was already lashed to the mast. His back showed the pale ridgings of healed scars, mute testimony to previous punishments.

Captain Dennison looked around as the women prisoners came to a clanking halt. For a brief moment his eyes encountered Caroline's. Frowning, as though the sight of her annoyed him in some way, he turned his attention to the flogger. "Taylor," he shouted, "begin punishment!"

As Taylor stepped forward, Caroline closed her eyes. She had no mind to see a man tortured, even such a man as Lovering.

Caroline started as a hand touched her chin and fingers squeezed painfully. Reluctantly she opened her eyes and looked into the grinning face of a sailor. "You just keep them eyes open, wench," he bade her in a voice that was half-jocular, half-bullying. "The cap'n's give orders that all prisoners are to watch punishment. He means what he says."

She did not answer him. The sailor, still grinning, released her chin. Throwing her a warning look, he moved back into position.

Then there were to be no exceptions, Caroline thought bitterly. All must watch, even the children. They, surely, might have been spared the gruesome sight? She watched in mounting horror as Lovering's body jumped beneath the smashing impact of the blows that were reducing his back to a pulped and bleeding mess. "Christ Almighty!" Lovering screamed out in anguish. "Oh, Christ, help me!" He cried out again, but this time his words were incoherent. He began to sob, and after a while the sobs turned into screams.

Lovering received the thirtieth stroke. Strangely, for a man who had endured so much, he was still conscious, but his eyes rolled wildly as he was cut down and thrown to the deck.

With the sound of the children's frightened sobbing in her ears, Caroline looked quickly about her, hoping to catch a glimpse of Justin. There was no sign of him. Captain Dennison had said that all prisoners must watch. Why wasn't he present? Was he all right? He must be! He had to be! She felt a surge of hatred as she stared at the captain. That fat pig! He enjoyed cruelty! Almost as though he had eyes in his back, Captain Dennison swung around. He stood there, his hands planted on his hips, staring straight at her.

Her face flushing, Caroline returned the stare. It was another scream from Lovering that broke the spell. Lovering was lying on his stomach, and two sailors were dousing his torn back with buckets of seawater. Caroline watched as the sailors lowered their empty buckets on ropes. They drew up a fresh supply of water and placed the brimming buckets to one side.

"Eyes front!"

Caroline watched dully as Taylor's punishment began. Seeing, and yet trying not to see. Automatically, she began silently counting the strokes—twenty-eight, twenty-nine, thirty.

Taylor was cut down, and, as Lovering had been, he was delivered over to the rough attentions of the sailors. The shrinking Jackson was seized. Despite his obvious terror, he made no outcry as he was fastened securely to the mast. But the look on his face was more eloquent than a scream.

Smiling, Captain Dennison moved forward with the whip. Before he drew back his arm, he turned once more to look at Caroline. Her heart gave a great leap of terror. Why did he keep looking at her? Was it something about Justin? Was he looking forward to the pleasure of telling her that he was dead?

Caroline felt that the whip, wielded by Captain Dennison's hand, had taken on the evil she had sensed in the man, a malevolence, a viciousness, and a terrible power. It was like a nightmare, she thought, her limbs trembling. The high whine of the whip, the violent contact with flesh, and Jackson's high, tortured screams. It was far worse, far more horrifying than the punishments that had gone before. This was a show put on for them by a monstrous man who delighted in cruelty for its own sake. Jackson's back had been laid open on the fourth stroke. On the tenth, he shrieked out, begging for mercy. The captain's smile broadened. He paused long enough to wipe the great pearls of sweat from his forehead; then he applied himself with renewed vigor to his task of breaking Jackson. And he did break him! There was no more sound from Jackson. On the thirtieth stroke, Caroline knew that he was dead. His terribly torn flesh hung down in ribbons. Blood spouted from the gaping wounds, dyeing his rough brown breeches and spattering the deck. There was even blood on the clothing of those sailors who stood nearest to the scene of carnage.

"Cole!" Captain Dennison flung the whip from him. "Get over here and examine this man."

Cole, a short sailor with a halo of blond hair and brilliant blue eyes, sprang to Jackson's side. He seemed hesitant about putting his hands on the shattered body, but, shrinkingly, he did so. After a few moments he turned a haunted face to the captain. "He . . . he's dead, Cap'n, sir."

"Well, then, cut the body down and heave it over the side."

Cole's eyes flickered nervously. "Yes, Cap'n, sir."

Jackson's broken body was dragged over to the rail by Cole and another sailor. A woman screamed out as the body was raised up and sent splashing into the water. "Oh, my God!" she babbled. She stood there swaying for a moment; then her eyes rolled up in her head and she fell heavily to the deck.

Another woman stood there as if frozen. "Not even a prayer! He wouldn't even allow him a prayer!" Her wild eyes went to the sea, then came back to the prone figure on the deck. "The devil's on this ship!" The color drained from her cheeks, and a strangled sound came from her throat. Retching, she bent over and vomited.

Captain Dennison turned slowly from the rail. His lip curled in disgust as he eyed the vomiting woman. "You, swabbie"—he beckoned to a sailor standing nearby—"throw a bucket of water over that filthy bitch. After that, have her clean up her spew." His thumb jerked toward the unconscious woman. "A bucket of water for that one, too." He turned about. "Two of you lads come forward. Pick up the punished men and get them below. Hurry, now! Don't dally. There's good lads."

The thrown water toppled the still-retching woman. She lay there on the deck, her limbs twitching.

"Women prisoners line up to the left. Men to the right."

Caroline lined up with the others. Useless though she knew it to be, her eyes searched the row of men. Justin was not there. Why? Tears rose in her eyes, and she bit her lip to keep herself from breaking down.

Captain Dennison strolled forward, coming to a halt beside Caroline. With his wide blue eyes fixed on her face, he spoke in his soft voice to the sailor who was to escort them back to their quarters. "Hobbs, lad, we are well out to sea. Have Jamieson go with you. The pair of you may strike off the women's irons." He paused. "I think we will not have too much trouble with them."

Dennison was standing so close to her that Caroline could feel the warmth of his body. Without willing it, she raised her eyes and stared at him unflinchingly.

Dennison did not seem to be offended. "You have lovely eyes," he said, smiling at her. "I am right, I think—there may well be beauty beneath your filth." His hand came out as though to touch her; then he drew it back hastily, as if he feared contamination. "Tell me, wench, are you diseased?"

"Diseased?" A flush mounted in Caroline's face, and he saw the angry flash that came into her eyes. "I have no notion of your meaning, Captain."

"Indeed?" Dennison laughed. "Then for a whore you are extraordinarily innocent."

"A whore?" Caroline repeated coldly. "You are mistaken, Captain. I am no whore."

"But of course you are. Do you forget your reputation?"

"The reputation forced upon me by injustice and by lying, malicious tales. No, Captain, how could I?"

Dennison's eyes narrowed as he contemplated her. Let her continue to deny it, if it pleased her. She was both whore and killer, but the thought only added a spice of anticipation. He would have her, come what may, he decided.

With the thought of Justin in her mind, Caroline swallowed her anger. It would not do to antagonize this man too much. She must see Justin. "Captain," she began, "might I ask you—?"

Instantly he was arrogant. He cut her off with a wave of his fleshy hand. "You may ask me nothing!" he snapped. "You will not speak to me unless I invite you to do so. Is that clear?"

Before she could answer, Dennison turned on his heel and

moved away. "Hobbs, come with me," he said. "Parker, lad, step over here and watch the women until Hobbs returns."

"Aye, aye, sir." Parker, a tall, rangy man, was instantly beside them. He stood stiffly to attention until Dennison was out of sight; then, with a grunt of relief, he relaxed.

Waiting for Hobbs to come back, Caroline noticed the glances the women were stealing at her. Her face flushed hotly as she saw the hostility in their eyes. Did they think she had wanted the captain to notice her? She loathed the gross beast! Thinking of the hand he had put out as if to touch her, she shuddered. Had he put his hand on her, she would have felt unclean. More so than she did now, with her body stinking and her matted hair filthy and infested with lice.

Some moments later Hobbs came hurrying back with another man beside him. "You can go, Parker," he said, dismissing the man. "Me and Jamieson'll take over now."

Jamieson's face was gloomy as he took his place at the rear of the column, but Hobbs, striding by the side, his arms swinging, wore an expression of undiminished cheerfulness. He had one of those faces, Caroline thought, that looked cheerful under all circumstances. And yet she knew him to be a brutal man. She had seen him double up his fist and knock down a woman who had refused to look at the flogging. And even worse, for this act he had received a beaming nod of approval from Captain Dennison. What kind of men were they? she thought with a little shudder. They all seemed rough and brutal. She thought of one man she had seen in the front of the crowd. He had a gentle expression, and he had looked pale and rigid with shock while the floggings were in progress. He was a member of the crew, though obviously in a higher position than an ordinary sailor. She had heard the captain address him as Cameron. She stole a glance at Hobbs's smiling face. Outwardly, he too looked like a decent man, so one could not go by appearances. Probably Cameron was as bad as the others.

"Get along, get along," Hobbs shouted. "If you want them irons off today, you'd better swing them arses!"

The women at once increased their shuffling pace, almost colliding with each other in their anxiety. "That's right, me beauties," Hobbs boomed his loud approval. "Now you got the idea."

They were halted by the entrance that led to their quarters.

Flinging back the hatchway, Hobbs gave an exaggerated stagger and doubled over, coughing, as the foul air from below rushed upward. "Phew!" He held his nose, winking at the women. "No place like 'ome, is there?" He met Caroline's eyes. "Don't like my little joke, eh?" He shrugged. "Can't please everybody, I guess." He saw the angry look some of them cast at Caroline, and he laughed. "She's a fine lady, is that one, and she don't like being with us common folk. Never mind, we won't take any notice of fine airs and a nose stuck up in the air, will we?"

There was a murmur of agreement. But little Jennie, who was standing next to Caroline, moved closer to her and gave Hobbs an angry look. "She's a nice lady," she said defiantly. "You're a bad man to say things about her. I don't like you!"

"Hush, Jennie!" Caroline said quickly.

"So you don't like me, eh?" Hobbs's face was not pleasant now. His hands reached for the child. "You know what we do with brats like you?"

"N-no." Jennie shrank back, on the verge of tears.

"Why, we feed 'em to the sharks, that's what we do. How'd you like 'aving a shark crunch up all them bones o' yours? How'd you like to 'ave that big fish tearing at your flesh? Water'd be red with your blood, it would."

"No! No!" Jennie screamed. "I want my mum. Please, I want her!"

"Your mum's back there." Hobbs chuckled and rubbed his hands together. " 'Ad a bucket o' water flung in 'er face for messing up the nice clean deck. Likely the captain's 'ad 'er flung to the sharks. Maybe you'd like to join 'er?"

Caroline took a step forward and placed herself in front of the sobbing child. "Leave her alone, you rotten swine!"

"The fine lady speaks!" Dull color suffused Hobbs's face. "But we ain't got no time for fine ladies on this ship. So 'ere's what we do with 'em." Balancing himself, he drew back his arm, waited for a moment while his eyes roved the faces turned to him, then slapped his hand hard across her breasts.

For a moment Caroline felt paralyzed. Then, as agony struck, her legs collapsed beneath her. She rocked herself backward and forward, moaning, trying to subdue the pain.

Hobbs glared down at her. "Think yourself lucky that I never touched your bleedin' face!" he roared. "You deserved to 'ave your tits mangled up a bit, you bleedin' cow!"

Jamieson stepped forward. "Hobbs!" His voice was low, but it had a powerful effect on the other man.

Hobbs blinked, swallowed, and the high color faded from his face. He looked almost frightened as he hauled first Jennie and then Caroline to their feet. "You fell an' 'urt yourself. Do you 'ear me?" he muttered in Caroline's ear. "If anyone should ask you, you fell. You say anything else, an' I'll make you sorry!"

Caroline stared at him, unable to speak. She tightened her lips to hold back her moans.

"You'd better listen to me, cow!" Hobbs hissed. "You tell on me, an' it won't only be you who'll be sorry, it'll be Lawrence too." He drew his finger across his throat. "Aye, it'll be Lawrence too!"

He gave a soft chuckle as he saw the look of terror in her eyes. Satisfied that Caroline wouldn't talk, he became businesslike. "Line up, you bitches. We'll 'ave them manacles off you."

The task was accomplished almost in silence. At a nod from the gloomy Jamieson, one by one the women and the children climbed over the hatchway and disappeared into the darkness below.

Hobbs had purposely left Caroline to the last. His touch was unnecessarily brutal as he released her from the heavy irons. "You remember!" he warned.

"Leave it be, Hobbs," Jamieson said.

Growling something beneath his breath, Hobbs pushed Caroline forward. "Get on down to your 'ole, you cow!"

The last thing Caroline heard before the hatch slammed closed was Jamieson's voice. "Between your threats an' the cap'n's, the wench ain't in for a jolly time o' it."

Locked once more in the stinking darkness, Caroline was a prey not only to pain but also to a formless terror. Lying on her hard wooden shelf, she pondered Jamieson's words. What had he meant? Why had Hobbs looked frightened? And what had she to do with Captain Dennison? She thought of the way his eyes had kept turning to her, and she began to tremble. Why did he look at her that way? His words came back to her: "Tell me, wench, are you diseased?"

The terror was beginning to take on form, the reason for the captain's interest was knocking at the door of her mind, but she refused to open that door and admit it.

The candles guttered lower, and a heavy, brooding silence fell. It was broken now and again by the wrenching groans of the seasick. An occasional burst of weeping came from little Jennie, who was missing her mother and terrified that she would not return. On the shelf below Caroline, a baby boy who was attempting to suckle at his young mother's empty breasts set up a frustrated wailing cry.

Poor baby! Caroline thought. The boy, who had been born in Newgate Prison, was alarmingly frail, and his delicate skin was marred by red spots. How long could he, how long could any of them, survive these conditions? There were interminable days and nights of this misery to endure before they reached the New World. And at the end of the long voyage, slavery awaited them.

The baby, exhausted, fell silent. Caroline turned over on her back and closed her eyes. She would slave, her thoughts roved on, she would do anything, be anything, as long as she could be certain that Justin still lived. Her heart plunged as she thought of them being parted, perhaps going to different masters. But even that she could somehow endure, because if he lived she would find him again. No matter how long it took her, she would find him.

She had fallen into a light, restless sleep, which was disturbed by the opening of the hatch. She heard Betsy Buford begin to cackle as Hobbs and Jamieson came clattering down the steep ladder.

"What you want, dearies?" Jumping down from her shelf, Betsy rushed toward the two men. "You come to give Betsy a nice kiss, 'ave you?"

Without answering, Hobbs lifted his fist and punched her shoulder. The blow spun her about and sent her crashing to the floor. Screaming with pain and rage, she lay there, glaring at them with malignant eyes.

"Fane," Hobbs said in a loud voice. "Where are you? Come with us."

Unresisting, Caroline let them pull her along. Her feet moved one after the other, but it was as if someone else walked between the two men, not she. She felt numbed, tired, and drained of strength. In the dark hold, she had been starved for air, but she could take no pleasure now in the cool breeze that touched her hot face. Passing sailors stared at her curiously, and she looked back at them with blank eyes. She felt the tight grip that Hobbs and Jamieson had on her arms, and she did not care where they were leading her. Her eyes went to the restless sea. If she should find that Justin was dead, there would be nothing left for her in this life. The sea, the restless sea, it was the answer to all her problems. Drowning, she had heard, took little time.

They halted her before a door, and Hobbs tapped on it.

Captain Dennison rose to his feet as the sailors ushered her in. At a sign from him, they released her arms and stood to attention.

Jamieson noticed that the whites of the captain's eyes were tinged with yellow, his usually firm mouth looked loose, and his hands had a faint tremble. His altered appearance might be due to the anticipated rape of the girl, or it might be that he was ill. Jamieson hoped that it was the latter. If the captain fell ill, too ill, it was to be hoped, to run the ship, then Blair Cameron would take over. Once before, when the captain had been stricken with a fever, Cameron had been in command. Cameron was firm, and he saw to it that his orders were obeyed. He liked to run a taut ship, but he was a decent and reasonable man and did not ask the impossible of his men. He was not like Dennison, who was, in Jamieson's opinion, more than a little mad. Cameron would punish if no other alternative presented itself, though he rarely ordered a flogging. Dennison, on the other hand, punished frequently, and from the sheer delight that the sufferings of others afforded him.

Dennison was saying something to the men. Caroline heard the murmur of their voices, but she did not listen to the words. She looked about her, her mind registering impressions. The lamplit cabin was small and cozy, a little island of comfort compared to what she had thus far seen on this ship. The furniture was sparse, and what little there was of it was bolted down. There was a bed covered with a crisp white coverlet, a desk, and a desk chair with a padded seat. A rich red carpet, an incongruous note, covered the tiny floor. On the desk was a pile of neatly rolled parchments, a folded map, and a small statuette of a dancing woman. On the floor, a little way from the desk, stood a large hip bath filled with water. The bath must have been brought into the cabin quite recently, for steam was still rising from the water. Next to it were several towels. After the stifling women's hold, the air in the cabin smelled fresh, and the atmosphere was pleasantly warm. Captain Dennison, it seemed, was a man who liked his comforts. Her eyes returned to the bath and lingered there.

"The bath is for you, my dear." The captain's voice, breaking in on her thoughts, caused Caroline to start.

"For me?" She turned her head and looked at him. "Why?"

"Why? A strange question, girl. I am a fastidious man." He gestured toward the bath. "I like my women to be clean as well as willing."

"I am not one of your women!"

The revulsion in her expression stung Dennison to anger. That cheap slut, that murderess, how dare she look at him so! His anger faded as self-pity took its place. All his adult life women had worn that same expression whenever he approached them. Even when he visited the whorehouses, he had seen it in the faces of the whores. It was as though his gold was not good enough for them, as though they feared to be near him. The fear he could understand, for he knew himself to be a man to inspire it, but the revulsion he could not understand. He was not a handsome man—he admitted that freely; but neither was he ugly. So why the repulsion? Anger stirred again. "Hobbs!" he barked. "Place yourself in front of the door."

"Yes, sir." Hobbs sprang to obey.

Dennison turned to Jamieson. "Strip her. Put her in the bath!"

Caroline retreated again, almost colliding with Hobbs, who thrust her roughly forward. Her face burning with humiliation, she put out her hands to ward Jamieson off. "Keep away from me. Don't you dare to touch me!"

Uncertainly, Jamieson stopped short. He was unused to defiance of the captain's commands. He looked at Dennison with inquiring eyes.

"One moment, Jamieson." Dennison was conscious of a heady sense of power. The wench could fight him now all she pleased, but in the end, because she would find no other course open to her, she would come to him willingly. He smiled faintly, feeling a tinge of admiration for her fiery fighting spirit. "Come, Mistress Fane," he said smoothly, "you are wasting time. I am looking forward to taking a clean and beautiful and willing woman to my bed."

Willing! The man was mad! "I hope you will find this woman," she cried, giving him a hard, defiant look. "It will not be me!"

Dennison sighed. "You are being foolishly stubborn, but I will correct those faults in you. Jamieson, proceed."

"Wait, please!" Desperately Caroline fumbled at the buttons on her bodice. "I see that it must be. But at least let me undress and bathe myself."

Dennison hesitated. Then, because he admired her courage, he found that he was not unwilling to make this concession. It would all come to the same in the end. "Very well. I will allow that."

Despite her humiliation and the fixed stares of the three men, Caroline enjoyed the luxury of the warm, soapy water. Trying to shut her audience from her mind, she washed herself thoroughly. Without being prompted, she soaked her hair in the vinegar provided, and then washed it.

As she was rising from the bath Dennison leaned forward. Grasping her hands, he drew her from the bath. He swathed her shivering body in a large towel. "There. Now you are sweet and clean." He smiled at her. "I pronounce you to be fit for my bed."

"Go to hell!" The words were out before she could stop them. And at the look on his face, she knew real fear.

"I like spirit, wench, but perhaps not quite so much of it," Dennison's soft voice said. Lifting his hand, he lashed her hard across the face. "Let us have an understanding between us," he continued. "Should you be rash enough to speak to me in that way again, I will have you tied to the mast and flogged."

Her hand held to her burning, throbbing face, Caroline said nothing. But the hatred in her eyes spoke for her.

Recovering himself, Dennison went over to a cupboard that was set in the left wall. Opening it, he drew out a gown. "My sister once took a short voyage with me," he explained, handing the garment to Caroline. "She left this behind. You may wear it."

The print gown was shabby, but it was clean. Thankful to escape from the staring eyes, Caroline pulled it hastily over her head. Smoothing the material down over her hips, she felt a despair so great that she had difficulty in holding back her tears. The thought of Dennison's gross body coupled with her own was more than she could bear.

Dennison's eyes traveled slowly over Caroline. Her figure, although a shade on the thin side, was good. And her face, except for the bruises that marred it, was quite lovely. Her hair, clean and freed from lice, shone golden against the faded blues and greens of the gown. He congratulated himself on sensing the beauty that had lurked beneath the grime. He had released that beauty, and for the length of this voyage Caroline Fane would belong to him.

Caroline flushed beneath his appraising eyes. She opened her lips to speak, then closed them again.

"You want to say something?" Dennison asked.

"Yes. Justin Lawrence. Is he . . . is he . . . ?" She broke off, unable to go on.

"Ah, the famous Rogue Lawrence. His condition is not of the best, I fear." He laughed as he saw the look in her eyes. "You thought he was dead?"

"I . . . I didn't know what to think."

"Not dead, no, but suffering. And you must not think I have forgotten the punishment I promised you. Beginning tomorrow, you shall see him suffer. But for tonight, you and I will have some wine, and then we will retire to our bed. I will send the lads away, so you need not fear an audience."

"No!"

Dennison strolled across to her and put his hand on her shoulder. "I have heard you were Lawrence's mistress, so such resistance does not suit you. In any case, your emotion is wasted. I have told you that you will come to me willingly."

Caroline's eyes met his. "I won't. Your strength is greater than mine, of course, and you can force me. But don't delude yourself that I will ever come willingly."

"You will, my dear, and in all haste, I promise you." Without looking away from her, Dennison lifted a beckoning finger. "Hobbs, open the drawer in my desk, take out my pistol. When I tell you to do so, you will go to the solitary hold, and you will shoot Lawrence."

"Aye, Cap'n."

Caroline looked from Dennison to Hobbs. She saw the malice in his eyes, his grin as he hefted the pistol. "Captain

Dennison, please!" Her voice was a strained whisper. "You . . . you would not murder him?"

Dennison shrugged. "My dear, it is my duty to keep the law aboard this ship. Lawrence is a hardened criminal, a hard case if ever I saw one. He is also a rabble-rouser, and an inciter to mutiny. I would be justified in either hanging or shooting him."

"And that . . ." Caroline took a deep breath. "And that would be your story?"

"It would. And let me assure you that my version of the story would be believed."

"But these men?" She gestured wildly at Hobbs and Jamieson. "They have heard. They know!"

"Of course. But they know better than to say anything. And even if they did, the word of common sailors against the captain of the ship would have little weight."

It was true. Of course it was true. Caroline tightened her trembling lips. "You look desperate, wench," Dennison's amused voice said. "But there is really no need for desperation. Lawrence's life is in your hands. You can save him or not, just as you please."

She did not waste time in futile argument. Dennison meant exactly what he said. Forcing herself to be calm, she said in an expressionless voice. "So it is."

"And your decision?"

Caroline turned away from him and walked over to the bed. Without looking at him, she sat down on the edge. "I am willing, Captain."

"I rather thought you would be." Dennison went to her and took her cold, trembling hands in his, and she did not attempt to withdraw them. "Look at me," he bade her. "Smile. You would not want me to think you unwilling, would you?"

She let her lips stretch into a mirthless smile. "But why would you think that, Captain?"

"I wonder." He saw the hatred in her eyes, he sensed the fear she was keeping under such rigid control, and it excited him. Now it was his hands that trembled. Her tongue had spoken the words "I am willing." It was a lie, but she had said it. It was enough for the moment. Experience had taught him that it was the best he could expect from any woman. And who knew, given time, but that the lie might not turn into truth? Releasing her hands, he laid his own upon her breasts. His excitement growing, he pressed her back and lifted her legs onto the bed. "We will have the wine later. Much later. What do you say to that, my dear?"

Caroline did not answer. She lay where he had placed her, unmoving. "Hobbs," Dennison called, "put the pistol back in the drawer. You are both dismissed. Go about your duties."

"Aye, Cap'n, sir."

Caroline heard the tramp of their feet, the closing of the door behind them.

"And now," Dennison said, "I will sample my willing woman." He undressed quickly, flinging his clothes carelessly to one side. "Take off that gown," he said in an uneven voice.

Without a word, she obeyed. Lying down again, trying to keep her mind a blank, she waited.

Dennison stood there a moment, his eyes going over her body; then he threw himself upon her. Parting her legs, he entered her at once.

Caroline did not look at him; she lay like a statue, her head turned to one side. His climax was building rapidly, his strokes quickening. He rode her like a demented man. Strangled cries came from him, broken words couched in the language of the gutter. Her mind closed against him. She would not hear. She would not feel. She was not a woman to him. She was a convenient thing to be used.

With a sobbing breath, Dennison collapsed against her. Lying rigidly beneath his weight, Caroline thought she heard Thomas Fane laughing.

Chapter 12

For eight days, just as dusk was falling, the same sailor had conducted Caroline to the solitary hold. His name was Jimmy King. He was a tall burly man with bright-blue eyes and a slow, seldom-seen smile. Caroline, perhaps because she needed so desperately to believe it, thought she sensed in King a certain sympathy to the prisoner in the solitary hold. But if sympathy there was, King kept it well hidden. Other than telling her his name, he had volunteered no remarks at all.

It was on the ninth day that King, surprising her, broke his taciturn silence. With the key clutched in his hand, he stopped before the entrance to the solitary hold and eyed the bowl of thin gruel held in Caroline's right hand and the hard biscuits she held in her other. "Lawrence ain't so good today," he commented gruffly. "That grub you got there ain't going to help him much. As for them biscuits, they got the weevil in 'em."

"I know." Caroline turned her pale face to him. "But what can I do? There is nothing else to give him. We are all fed the same thing."

"Even you?"

"What do you mean?"

"Captain's whore, ain't you?"

Caroline felt as though he had punched her. So he knew! And Justin—did he know?

Reading her thoughts, King said, "I ain't said nothing to Lawrence, if that's what's worrying you."

Caroline inclined her head, silently thanking him. "I . . . I am not what you called me, King. He . . . the captain, he forced me. I had to do it or he would have had Justin shot." She looked at him. "But even so, I do not eat with the captain. I share the same food as the other prisoners."

181

It was true. The captain had used her. He had made her feel soiled and cheap. But he did not believe in pampering her body to the extent of feeding her his good food. Consequently, she was as gaunt as the other prisoners. Surely King should have seen that for himself? Even now she could not be sure that he believed her; he was looking down at the deck, and he seemed to be thinking deeply. She felt a wave of indignation. If she had food, did he think she would keep it for herself and not share it with Justin?

"I got something to put to you, wench," King said at last. "Can I trust you?"

Caroline forgot her indignation and her resentment of the term he had applied to her. So far as she knew, King had not been as brutal and unfeeling as some of Justin's other jailers. In his own way, he had been kind to him. He had even gone so far as to remove his fetters now and again, and to rub salve into the festering sores on his ankles and wrists. Thinking of this, she answered him simply. "Yes," she said.

King nodded, taking her word for it. "The captain's ill," he said.

Caroline's eyes widened. So that was why Dennison had not sent for her in the past three days. He was ill. She had felt gloriously free, and despite the conditions under which they were forced to live, and her constant nagging worry over Justin's welfare, she had been almost happy. She could endure anything as long as Dennison did not touch her. She smiled at King. "I'm glad he's ill. I hope he is suffering."

"The cap'n's off his victuals. Don't seem to fancy 'em nohow. So I thought to myself, if he can't eat 'em, why not Lawrence?"

"King!" Hope rose in her. "Do you mean—?"

"Aye," he interrupted hastily. "And keep your bloody voice down. I pinched the stuff what was meant for the cap'n, seeing as he didn't want it, and I got it hid in the hold. Even Lawrence don't know about it yet. I ain't said nothing to him. Just in case, see?"

"In case?"

He ignored the question. "I got real nourishing grub for Lawrence, and a nice bottle of red wine. How'd you like the sound o' that?"

"I like the sound of it very much!"

"I can get more, too. We'll soon have Lawrence fighting it."

"It is kind of you to do this for him, King."

King's eyes shifted. "I ain't exactly doing it for him. I'm doing it for myself, see."

"I don't understand."

"Well, if I do this for Lawrence, I got to get a little something out of it for myself. And what I want is some of that what you give to the cap'n."

Oh, God! she thought. Not again! She stared at him, and there was something in her eyes that made King uncomfortable. "I see," she said in a bitter voice. "And if I don't give you what you want, what then?"

"Then I'll eat the grub myself, or I'll chuck it in the sea. It's up to you, ain't it?" He took her arm in a hard grip. "I'm risking punishment to do you and Lawrence a favor. Anyway, seeing as you give it to the cap'n, why not to me?" His eyes narrowed. "I already told you, Lawrence ain't so good," he said, giving her a sly look. "You don't want him to die, do you?"

If Justin were to have a chance to survive, she knew that she could not refuse King. She felt a profound despair. Was she to sell herself from man to man in order to keep her love alive? Was she to become the whore that King had called her? Even as she asked herself the question, she knew the answer. Yes, she would give herself to every man on the ship if it would keep Justin alive. There was nothing she would not do to ensure this, nothing! But Justin must never know. If he learned that she was bartering her favors to keep him safe, it would be death to his pride, and that would surely kill him.

Her eyes were full of tears as she looked up at King. "No," she whispered. "No, I don't want him to die. But Justin mustn't know, King. Promise me that you'll say nothing to him!"

King felt sorry for her in that moment, but he was nonetheless determined to have his way. A favor for a favor—that was his motto. "I won't say nothing to him," he promised in a rough voice. "And what's more, if it'll make you feel any better, I won't say nothing to the lads, either."

"You mean that, King?"

"I mean it. And when I gives my word, I keep it." He smiled. "Besides, it wouldn't do to say nothing to the boys.

Word of it might get to the captain." His smile faded. "Well, what's it to be? Yes or no?"

She nodded. "Then I suppose it must be yes."

"Then there's no time like now." He seized her hand. "Come on."

"No, wait!" She tried to hang back. "We'll be seen."

"No, we won't. Lads is all busy, and them that ain't is having their grub. Don't no one come near this spot I'm going to take you to, not after dusk."

She did not believe him—there were always sailors about; but she went with him. Strangely enough, she found that King was right. All through the quick, furtive, and fumbling operation, no one did come by. As she had done with the captain, she tried to keep her mind a blank while King plunged inside her.

Her lack of response meant nothing to King. He had got what he wanted. He was satisfied. Rising to his feet, he pulled up his breeches. "Come on. I'll get that grub for Lawrence."

They made their way back to the solitary hold in silence. King was about to unlock the hatchway when a sudden thought struck him. "You made me promise to say nothing to Lawrence, but how do I know you'll keep your mouth shut?"

She gave him a bleak smile. "You may be certain I'll say nothing. I'm not very proud of it."

"If the cap'n gets well," he persisted, giving her a doubtful look, "will you be saying anything to him?"

"Nothing." Without interest, she added, "What is wrong with the captain?"

King seemed uncomfortable. "Don't know," he said, shrugging. "One o' my mates told me he's too weak to hold a cup to his lips. He's come out in a rash, and now and again he's delirious."

Caroline stared at him. The same symptoms as the baby who had died the sixth day out to sea. The same symptoms as the three women who had followed the baby to his watery grave. The same symptoms as Betsy Buford, who was even now tossing and moaning and rambling on her hard wooden board in the women's hold. A chill went through her. Just as the dead baby's and the three women's, Betsy's lips had the same scaly crust about them, and her tongue was thick and swollen and furred with brown. Epidemic! The word leaped frighteningly into her mind and would not be dismissed.

"King," she said huskily, "the baby who died, the three women—they had the same symptoms as the captain. Do we have an epidemic aboard this ship? Tell me the truth."

King's eyes avoided hers, and he cursed himself for his loose tongue. She was sharp, this wench. "I shouldn't have said nothing," he mumbled. "Doctor don't want no panic."

"King, what is it? What is the captain suffering from? Don't pretend that you don't know!"

King was silent for a moment. "I reckon it's typhus," he said in a low voice.

"Typhus!" Caroline exclaimed in horror. "Oh, my God!"

"Shut up!" King brushed her to one side and hastily unlocked the hatchway. Motioning to her, he pushed her through the small opening.

"Carrie!" Justin's manacles clanked as he started forward. Unlike the other prisoners, who had been released from their manacles, he was still forced to wear his. He had sprouted a dark heavy growth of beard, his hair was unkempt, and he seemed to Caroline's anxious eyes to be thinner than ever. The solitary hold was dark and narrow, so narrow that one could touch the walls with outstretched hands. It was stiflingly hot, and it reeked with the stench from the bilges. Locked away, his only air coming from the narrow grating in the hatchway, Justin's face continually ran with perspiration, and his tattered shirt and the ill-fitting breeches were plastered to his body.

"Justin." Caroline smiled tremulously. "How do you feel?"

He smiled so rarely these days that his faint return smile startled her. "I feel as weak as a rat. Weaker, for the rats I have seen look remarkably healthy. And I am sick to death of my prison." He lifted a hand to check her as she took a step forward. "Not too near to me, Carrie. I stink."

Usually, out of respect for his ingrained fastidiousness, she pushed the food toward him and kept her distance. But today she ignored the ban. She ran to him. Flinging her arms about him, she hugged him close. "And so do I, my darling. So neither can be offended by the other." Her heart ached as she felt his sharply jutting bones. Despite his little speech, longer than he usually attempted, she knew that he was much weaker. She kissed his bearded face. "King and I have a little surprise for you. Some real food at last."

He did not answer her at once. "Then you eat it, Carrie,"

he said at last. "You look worn to a shadow." His eyes on her gaunt face were suddenly very tender. "Don't be so good to me, Carrie, love. I don't deserve it. You have sacrificed enough for me."

"I have sacrificed nothing. King got this food especially for you, and you will eat it. Besides, I . . . I have had some of it."

"Liar!" She was alarmed by the unsteady note in his voice. His spurt of strength deserting him, he sank down on his hard bedboard. She heard his panting breath as he struggled to get the next words out. "I am not a fool, Carrie. I can see that you are half-starved. Eat it yourself, please."

She sat down beside him and put her arms about him. "I will do nothing of the sort. It is for you."

She felt his trembling, and she knew that he was very near to utter collapse. Her arms tightened fiercely and protectively about him.

"Carrie!" Suddenly his head was resting against her shoulder, and his tears were soaking through the thin fabric of her tattered gown.

She stroked his hair, encouraging him to spend his grief, hoping that in some way it might melt the hard core of bitterness inside him. "It will get better, my love, my darling," she whispered. "It will, you will see!"

She felt the shake of his head. She looked quickly for King, not wanting him to see Justin broken and weeping. He had retired discreetly to the head of the stairs; she could see his waiting shadow.

"Weakness." Justin's shaken voice was trying to excuse himself. "S-sorry."

"Don't be sorry, love. You will feel better afterward."

His small, difficult laugh was as painful to her as his tears. "N-never cried in a lady's arms before. New ex-experience."

She laughed too, rallying him now. "Whatever you choose to do in a lady's arms from now on, it had best be this lady's arms."

Justin sat up straight. He did not look at her as he wiped his face on his ragged shirt. "But you are not a lady, Carrie. I . . . I have told you that before."

"Never you mind. You heed my warning, Rogue Lawrence." She glanced at him. He had himself reasonably under control now. King, who had evidently been listening, felt it safe to come down the stairs. "Here." He tossed a crumpled kerchief to Justin. "It's hot in here, lad. Wipe the sweat off your face."

"Thanks." Justin wiped his face again and blew his nose. "Where is this feast you promised me?" he said with forced lightness.

"I'll get it." King went up the stairs again. They could hear him fumbling. A moment later he returned with a tray. "Stew's cold, o' course," he said, placing the tray carefully on Caroline's lap. "But cold or hot, it's good and nourishing." He looked at Justin. "I'll take them manacles off your wrists for a bit, lad. Then you do as the lady says. You eat up all that stew, and drink all the wine too. It'll put fresh heart into you."

Justin looked longingly at the food, he even picked up the horn spoon obligingly supplied by King. Then, shaking his head, he laid the spoon down again. He could not be persuaded to eat unless Caroline ate also.

She stared at the round dish of brown stew, and she ached to fall upon it and cram it into her mouth, but, obstinate as he, she would take only tiny mouthfuls, chewing them longer than was necessary.

Justin saw that she was not to be moved. With the taste of the stew in his mouth and the red wine glowing inside him, he surrendered to temptation. He began to eat like a starving man.

King spoke only once. "Not so fast, lad," he warned. "Or you'll suffer for it later. Besides, with the captain ill, I can manage to sneak more to you. Though, in a manner of speaking, it's not really sneaking. Cookie's a pal o' mine. He'll get the captain's food ready just the same, because he ain't been told not to. But he'll look the other way when I make off with it." After this—for him—unusually long speech, he folded his arms and lapsed into silence.

Justin finished the last of the stew. Picking up the half-empty wine bottle, he offered it to Caroline and King. When both refused to drink, he hesitated; then, tilting the bottle, he drained the contents. He felt light-headed, with the fumes of the wine mounting to his brain, but at the same time he felt curiously relaxed, and for the first time since Paul had died, almost at peace with himself. "The captain is ill, you say?" He smiled, amused at the slurring of his tongue. "What is wrong with him?"

"It don't matter," King said uncomfortably.

"Tell him, King." Caroline's eyes on the man's face were compelling.

"Why? Ain't he got enough to worry about?"

"He is shut away from everything here. He has a right to know."

Justin looked from one to the other. "Tell me what?"

King shuffled his feet and muttered unwillingly, "There's typhus aboard ship."

As though a bucket of icy water had been flung over him, the pleasant lassitude occasioned by the food and the wine left him. "You are sure it is typhus?" Justin said sharply.

In that moment he sounded so much like his old self that Caroline gaped at him in surprise.

"Oh, aye." King nodded gloomily. "I knows typhus when I sees it."

"Any dead?"

"Four. Three women and a baby. And there's two men sickening."

"And another in the women's quarters," Caroline put in.

Justin turned on her so quickly that she started back in fright. "Have you been tending this woman, Carrie?"

"I have helped."

"Let me see your tongue."

"What?"

Justin frowned impatiently. "Do as I say. Let me see your tongue."

Slowly Caroline put out her tongue. Justin stared at it for a minute. "All right. No sign there, as yet."

"But Justin, what . . . ?"

Justin touched her forehead, her cheeks, and the back of her neck. "No fever. But these things can begin quickly. You can be well now, but raging with fever by nightfall." His hands grasped the front of her gown and pulled it open. "No spots."

King's eyes were bright and interested. "You sound as though you know something about typhus, lad."

"I should. We had a bad epidemic of typhus in London a few years back. I was staying with a friend of mine, a doctor, at the time. I stayed on and helped him with his patients."

"You know a cure?"

"No, and neither did he. But there are ways of bringing

the fever down and making the patient more comfortable. Usually, if the fever breaks, the patient will recover."

"Dr. Langley'll be interested to hear that," King said eagerly. "It looks like he's in for a bad time of it. He'll welcome any help he can get."

"No!" Caroline cried out in sharp protest. "Justin must not be exposed."

"Be silent, Carrie. I am not a child that must be coddled and protected."

"But you have been ill. Justin, you are very weak. You just cannot—"

"I said be silent." Justin looked at King and smiled ruefully. "But Carrie is right in one thing. In my weakened condition, I would be little use to anyone."

"Listen, lad. With the captain ill, Blair Cameron is in command. And Cameron's been through some epidemics himself. He ain't like Captain Dennison, he's a decent and reasonable man. I'll speak to him and Dr. Langley about you. With decent food, you'll soon be fit."

Justin's voice took on a faint touch of excitement. "A bath," he stipulated, "and clean clothes?"

"If you know something about typhus, an' can help 'em, I reckon you can have anything you want."

Justin looked at Caroline. "Wherever you are on this ship, Carrie, love, you are going to be in danger of infection. So you might as well be at my side." He nodded to King. "I will have Carrie as my assistant. She gets decent food too."

King was already moving toward the stairs. He looked back at Caroline, hesitating. "I ought to take you back to your quarters." Making up his mind suddenly, he shrugged. "No, stay. I told you Cameron's a good man. He won't say nothing. He's human, see."

He clattered up the stairs. The hatchway slammed behind him.

"Justin!" Caroline was near to tears. In her mind she saw Justin stricken by the disease. His body sewn into a sack and committed to the sea. She saw the upright fins of the sharks circling, waiting, patiently waiting. As they had waited for the pathetic body of the baby. She saw once again the sickening flurry, the bright streaking of blood upon the water. "Justin, don't!" She clung to him tightly. "You're not strong enough. You will die!"

"I'll die when it's my time, not before. Besides, typhus is no respecter of persons. It can strike anywhere. I could just as easily die here."

"You don't have the strength. You can't do it!"

"Perhaps not. But I intend to try."

It was some time before King returned. When he did, it was with news. "Captain Dennison's dead," he said without preamble, and there was no regret in his voice. "Captain Cameron's in charge now. If you meant what you said, and you do know something about typhus, then he's agreeable. He says you're to get good food. You'll be moved into quarters near to Dr. Langley."

Justin's hand gripped Caroline's hard. "And Carrie?" he said in a breathless voice.

King's grin did not diminish. "Captain Dennison's sister used to sail with him now and again. She had a little cabin all to herself. The wench is to have that. Captain Cameron's taking your word that she'll help out."

Despite her fear for Justin, Caroline could not help being dazzled by their sudden good fortune. She looked at him speechlessly. To be out of that dark and stinking hold, to be away from the screaming and cursing and the constant violent quarrels. It seemed almost too good to be true.

Justin's hand gripped tighter. "We progress, Carrie," he said with an attempt at humor. "We progress."

Progress? Caroline's joy faded, and she lowered her head to hide the tears in her eyes. She tried not to think of the poor baby's contorted limbs and the openmouthed death mask of agony his little face had become. It was no use; she could see him still. The harsh, rattling breathing of the dying women sounded in her ears again. She saw the circling fins of the sharks. Blood. Blood upon the water. We progress, Justin had said. But to where, to what? To an agonizing death? To a grave in the sea?

She raised Justin's hand and pressed it to her lips.

Justin started as he felt her tears against his hand. "Carrie, what is it?"

She kissed his hand again, and then held it cradled to her cheek. "It is only that I love you so much!" she said huskily. "So very much!"

Chapter 13

The *Merryventure* was a floating death ship. And now, with the failing of the wind, the vessel had lain becalmed for five days, its sails useless. Water was low. Food must be doled out sparingly if there was to be any hope at all of survival. Sometimes it was no more than a few hard biscuits that were practically inedible, laden with weevils and other dead insects. And this fare must be forced down the throats of sick and well alike. From a sky of bright hard blue a merciless sun beat down upon the dead and the dying, who lay in every available space. It almost seemed as if nature mocked at the puny efforts of man to alleviate the suffering, for still the death toll continued to mount.

Mocked by nature and forgotten by God, Caroline thought bitterly. Leaning wearily against the rail, her eyes on the glassy sea, she thought of Dr. Langley and of Justin. In their fight with death, the two men were aided only by herself and a few frightened and unwilling sailors, but both were unsparing in their efforts to stem the typhus that ravaged the ship. Alarmingly thin, their hands trembling with fatigue, their eyes haunted above vinegar-soaked masks, they continued to work over the stricken. Despairing of a cure, but hoping for a cessation in the alarming number of deaths. Now Justin Lawrence, that haggard man who worked furiously as if he had a personal vendetta with death, bore little resemblance to the gay and charming and audacious thief Rogue Lawrence. It was as though two entirely different men lived in the same body.

Caroline's hands clenched tightly over the rail. Where would it all end? They were on a ghost ship, a floating island peopled with the dead and the dying. Fear! It was everywhere. It stalked by the side of death, twin grim specters. Eyes avoided a direct glance at another, for fear that person might be the next to go. Whose turn will it be today? Tomorrow? The unuttered words seemed to hang in the air like letters of fire. Hands furtively touched cheeks and foreheads, feeling for the dry blazing heat that would herald the onslaught of the disease. Tongues were continually examined for that fatal brown furring, and the faintest spot on the skin was the signal for immediate panic.

Caroline rubbed at her tired eyes with the heels of her hands. Out of the six hundred convicts and the twenty-four children who had sailed, two hundred adults were dead, and all twenty-four of the children. And still, shockingly, unbelievably, the monstrous disease continued on its savage path. Soon, now, Captain Cameron would be calling all hands together. In his soft, attractive voice that somehow made the words even more horrifying, he would once more read the burial service for the dead. Captain Cameron, a gentle man, who was, in Caroline's opinion, out of place on this convict ship. He cared too much. He took every death as a personal blow. He was very different from the brutal Dennison, whose diseased body had long ago been consigned to the sea and the attention of the sharks.

The sharks! Caroline bit down hard on her trembling lower lip. She had tried, but she could not put the terrible scene from her mind. It was with her when she worked over the sick. It haunted her snatched moments of sleep. The nightmare that came to her then would repeat the scene again in every detail. The sailors told off for burial detail, standing stiffly beside the pile of dead bodies, their eyes frightened, trying not to cringe as they picked up the bodies and placed them on the board for their last journey. She saw the dead sliding downward, she heard the splash as they hit the sea. And then the sharks. Moving in swiftly, avidly, tearing at dead flesh. The thrashing sounds of their furious activity. The water about them would be red with blood. She had seen a severed foot, and a head torn from a body, floating on the widening red circles. Mangled flesh and limbs, borne up by the water, lapped against the sides of the ship, and in her ears would be the hysterical screaming of the women and the half-sobbed cursing of the men. And then, after an interminable time, the terrible activity would cease. The water would resume its natural hue. Only a piece of flesh here and there gave proof that the horror had ever been.

Caroline's thoughts scattered at the sound of Captain Cameron's voice. Turning from the rail, she was immediately taut. What further blows were about to descend? Her eyes sought Justin first, and she felt weak with relief at seeing him still on his feet. The captain, with Justin, Dr. Langley, and several sailors, was proceeding toward the already sacked dead.

Caroline drove her nails into her palms in an effort to still her trembling. Forcing her tired limbs to move, she hurried to join them. The burial service was about to be pronounced, and all who could be, must be present. Dear God! By now, she knew every word by heart. Under the prevailing conditions, another man might have ordered the bodies to be simply thrown into the sea, denying them those last words. But no matter how many deaths might occur, no matter how he might flinch from it, Captain Cameron was punctilious in his observance of the courtesy due to the dead. The soft voice continued to ask the mercy of God on thief, murderer, prostitute, and simple sailor alike.

Drawing nearer to the men, Caroline found herself struck by the air of suppressed excitement that seemed to emanate from them. She stopped before them and looked at them inquiringly. Above the vinegar-soaked masks they wore, their eyes were glowing.

"Caroline!" It was Captain Cameron who spoke first. "We have wonderful news. The fever has broken in several of the patients, and one or two of them are talking rationally. We are winning!"

"Carrie!" Justin was beside her. "How many times must I tell you that you must always wear your mask?" He jerked it up roughly to cover her nose and her mouth. "Damn you, you fool! Must you deliberately court danger?"

She stared at him, seeing the top half of his swarthy, sharpened face through a mist. His dark eyes burned like coals, but she saw in them the same hope as in Captain Cameron's. How strange, she thought, that despite his tireless work, he was much stronger now than he had been. In that much, at least, God had decided to stay His hand. Justin, like herself, seemed to be immune from the disease. Immune? Yes, but for how long? At any moment Justin could be stricken. The mist before her eyes thickened, and Thomas Fane's face, like a spider poised in his web waiting to strike, appeared before her. Thomas! An evil omen. Swaying, she put out a hand and grasped at Justin's sleeve. "Justin, no!" Her voice seemed far away, unreal. "Don't die! Please don't die!"

"Catch her, Lawrence!" Dr. Langley's voice was an explosion of sound in her ears. "She's fainting." The sound dwindled and died, and she was falling into a black pit.

She came back to her senses to the feel of Justin's arms tightly about her and his voice saying, "It's all right, Carrie. It's not typhus. You are just tired and overworked."

She nodded, content to lie there. She felt safe and happy in the security of his arms, and for this one moment she could tell herself that they were far away from the *Merryventure*. There was no hungry sea about them, only the peace and the soft green of the Yorkshire countryside. There was no stalking death. No pleading upturned faces disfigured by rash, mouths crusted, and tongues brown and swollen. No more gusts of foul breath, or limbs that thrashed in the death agony. There was only this cherished moment plucked from terror and devastation.

Captain Cameron's voice solemnly intoning the burial service shattered the dream. Whimpering, she cowered as she heard the splash of the bodies hitting the water.

"Pull yourself together, Carrie." Justin's voice braced her.

"I will. You must not worry about me." She forced her head to turn. Captain Cameron, looking much older than his thirty years, was bent over his prayerbook, and the wind was ruffling his short-cropped prematurely white curls.

The wind? Caroline jerked herself upright. "Wind, Justin!" Her voice was shaken and shrill with excitement. "The wind is blowing, it's blowing! Do you hear me?"

Justin laughed. "I wondered when you would notice. Yes, Carrie, love, the wind is rising. Look above you."

She glanced up. Sailors, like so many agile monkeys, were swarming in the rigging. She could hear their laughter and their excited shouting as they pulled on ropes and manipulated this part and that. Beneath their combined efforts the sails filled with the gradually strengthening wind, ballooning out full-bellied. Caroline thought it must be the most glorious sight she had ever seen. She collapsed back into Justin's arms. "Are we really going to come through this?" she asked in a breathless voice.

He looked down at her. Her eyes seemed to take up most

of her thinned face. Her blond hair was dull and her lips
brown and cracked. Near-starvation had obscured her shining
beauty, and she looked plain, almost old, and yet, perversely,
he had never cared for her more. How could he answer her
question with the brutal truth, kill that flicker of hope in her
eyes? If the wind kept up, if they were not blown off their
course by storm or some other act of God, it might be that
they would arrive in the New World alive, but just barely.
They had, it seemed, temporarily triumphed over the disease;
now, unless good fortune attended them, they were facing
slow death from starvation and lack of water.

His expression frightened her. "Justin," she repeated, "will
we come through?"

He pulled her tightly into his arms and buried his face
against her hair. "Yes, darling, we will come through."

"Justin!" She pulled away from him and looked into his
face. "You called me 'darling'! You have never said that before. Do you perhaps care for me just a little?"

His eyes were full of pain for her, so changed was she, but
he managed to force a laugh. "What has happened to my
fiery fighting Carrie that she can ask me a question like that
in such a humble voice?"

"She lived a long time ago, that girl. A lifetime ago."
There was a great weariness in her voice. "All that remains
of her is the shell. I am so tired, Justin. Much too tired to
fight with you."

"But she is still there, my stubborn fighting Carrie, I know
it. Once she is well-fed and rested, she will return. Damned if
she won't!"

"And the old Rogue Lawrence? Will he return?"

"Perhaps." A shadow darkened his face. "But I fear he will
never be quite the same again."

"Whatever he is now, or might become, I will always love
him." She touched her hand to his face. "Justin," she insisted,
"do you care for me just a little?"

He felt the burn of tears, and he swallowed hard. "Ah,
Carrie, Carrie, much more than a little."

"Do you . . . do you love me?"

He heard her caught breath as she waited for his answer,
it really mean so much to her? His brow wrinkled. But he did
and he felt the rapid pounding of her heart against him. Did
not know what love was. Perhaps it was the strong feeling he

had for this thin and overburdened girl in his arms. Or perhaps it was something quite different, something that was far removed from anything he had ever felt before. It might be that one day he would find out. In the meantime, a lie, if lie it be, would be the kindest. "Yes, my darling, my Carrie," he said softly. "I do love you."

Life and joy animated her gaunt face, and for a fleeting moment he caught an aching glimpse of her buried beauty. "Justin!" She leaned her head against his chest, and he heard her quick, shallow breathing. "Now, for the first time, I am truly happy."

Happy? If only she could be. With him, or with some other man, as long as her life be happy and fulfilled. Justin's arm tightened about her as he looked up at the blue sky. He saw the tracing of clouds here and there, the darker ones forming to the west, presaging rain. He began to pray silently and fervently. Lord, if You exist, let Carrie live. Don't let her die here on this stinking tub! The blame is not hers, it is mine alone. It was my thoughtlessness and selfishness that killed Paul and brought Carrie here to this disaster. If Your desire is for more deaths, then take my life. But if You have justice and pity and love, spare her!

"Come, Carrie." Justin rose to his feet and drew her upward. "We still have patients. We are still needed."

She went with him like a docile child, her hand tightly clasped in his.

Captain Cameron greeted them with a friendly smile. Justin made conversation for a moment, trying to hide his exhaustion; then he said abruptly, "The sick need attention, Captain. Do I have your permission to go?"

"You have it," Cameron said quickly. He smiled ruefully. "One day I hope to cure myself of meddling. But may I say one thing more, Justin?"

At the captain's utterance of his first name, Justin turned about and looked at him in surprise. "What is it?"

"If we make it to the New World, you will take care of Caroline? You will be good to her?"

Justin's eyes softened and his hostility fell away. His genuine liking for Cameron showed through as he answered, "In the New World, I doubt we will be in control of our own actions and destinies. But yes, Blair, if I am given the opportunity to do so, I will take care of her, I promise."

Blair Cameron smiled. "That's good enough for me."

Down below, in the stifling hold, Justin found Caroline bending over Jimmy King.

King's eyes were wide open. Their bright blue hue had faded and they appeared to be more gray than blue. Caroline wiped his slack face with a damp cloth. This man had used her, just as Dennison had done, but she could feel nothing but pity for him now. She was startled to hear his voice emerge clearly. "Don't go away. Don't leave me!" His fingers plucked at the rough blanket that covered his body. "I'm— I'm frightened."

"It's all right, King," Caroline whispered. "I won't go away."

"S-s-sorry," King panted. "Sorry about a—a lot of things."

"I know. Hush! Don't think about it now. Just rest."

King's mouth twisted into a parody of a smile. "You're a . . . a good wench. I'm glad you're here with me."

On an impulse, Caroline bent closer and laid her face against his cheek. "Everything will be all right, King."

Justin's hands jerked her roughly upright. "What do you think you're doing, Carrie! You must be out of your mind to put your face so close to his!"

She looked at him with tear-blinded eyes. "I'm sorry. It's just that there is so little we can do for him, for any of them!"

"Glad you came," King said loudly and clearly. His eyes closed, and his body jumped convulsively, then was still.

Justin bent over him. "He's gone, Carrie." He gently closed the staring eyes, then took her hand in a firm clasp and drew her along. "Come," he said in a voice roughened with suppressed emotion. "There are others needing us."

And others, Caroline thought as she stumbled along beside his tall, spare figure, and still others. They will keep calling out to us, pleading for the help we don't know how to give. It must stop, it must! I can't stand any more! She felt as though she were choking, as though she were fighting against a great flood. Justin had said the disease was abating, but people were still dying. How could she believe that it was abating? How could she believe in anything?

Leaving Caroline and walking to the deck, Justin saw that the sky had darkened. An arrow of lightning streaked across the sky. It was followed immediately by an ear-shattering crash of thunder. The wind caught at his hair and ruffled it, and the first heavy drops of rain fell on his upturned face.

Unmindful of the curious stares of the hurrying sailors, who, instructed by Dr. Langley, were pulling tarpaulins over the patients sprawled on the deck, Justin continued to stand there. He was used to the milder rains of England, and he was dazed by the fierce torrential fury of the rain that now deluged them. Soaked, half-blinded, battered by the downpour, he still could not bring himself to move. He stood there like a man turned into stone. Then, as the deck heaved up and then fell away again, he stumbled forward, almost falling. Recovering himself, he began to laugh, high, crazy laughter that caused the sailors to freeze in position. A storm at sea! Justin thought. Disease! Near-famine! And now a storm!

The sailors watched him, their eyes blinking in the rain, this normally calm and collected aide of Dr. Langley, on whom they had come to rely. At this shattering of his monumental calm, they felt a thrill of superstitious fear.

It was Captain Cameron's hand on his arm that stilled Justin's laughter and brought him back to reality. "Get a hold on yourself," Cameron urged. "Storms, like fire, can cleanse, so you must not fear. I have ridden out far worse storms than this one promises to be."

"I fear for Carrie," Justin answered him in a dazed voice, "not for myself. For Carrie!" he repeated.

"I know." Cameron pressed his arm urgently. "You are tired, Justin, much too tired. Get below. Try to get some sleep."

Part IV
The New World

Chapter 14

With Captain Cameron standing to her left and Justin to her right, Caroline clung to the ship's rail, her knuckles showing white with the strain. A little farther along stood Dr. Langley. It was pride and the stubborn will to endure that kept Caroline and the three men on their feet. Without being told, they knew too that now, having at last arrived at their destination, after those five grueling, death-haunted months at sea, the convicts who lay sprawled on the deck behind them silently looked to them to show an example. While the four who had battled to keep death from them still stood, their fears were somehow lessened.

Caroline's hands loosened and slipped, but she tightened them immediately. They had actually arrived! They were alive! Out of the six hundred convicts and the twenty-four children, only three hundred and fifty adults remained. The survivors were weak, dirty, starving, verminous, and wild-eyed. They were waiting now to be claimed by the masters who would carry them off to slavery in this strange land. And Caroline knew that they feared their eventual fate even as she did. White slaves to white masters. Englishmen and Englishwomen who had never before been enslaved! Hatred and resentment temporarily drowned out her fear. It was not a life sentence, for eventually they would be freed, even given land so that they would have the same opportunity as their masters, if they cared to work for it, but it was still slavery until they obtained that release. What were the convicts thinking? Caroline wondered. Was their fear, like hers, turning to fury?

Caroline glanced quickly about her. The three men, herself, the convicts behind them—how would their hollow-eyed appearance, their yellowed skins, and their starved, almost fleshless look impress the sleek and prosperous men who were even now being rowed toward the ship?

The spark that had momentarily lit Caroline's eyes died as

she watched the boats. The sleek men sat at their ease while the oars were handled by men in strange leatherlike fringed clothing and round fur hats with tails hanging down behind. Strange apparel, she thought, turning inquiring eyes to Cameron.

Anticipating her question, Cameron smiled at her. "The men at the oars are wearing buckskins, Caroline," he said. "Their hats are coonskin. Backwoodsmen. They are very proud and independent, but they sometimes hire out their services."

"Buckskins," Caroline repeated in a wondering voice. "Coonskin."

The lounging men in the boats were in high good humor. Voices and laughter echoed over the waters of the Chesapeake Bay. Instinctively, Caroline edged nearer to Justin. He turned his head, smiling reassuringly, and then returned his fascinated attention to the panorama before them. Behind the men in the boats, like some vast backdrop, could be seen in the distance great rearing mountains whose peaks were hazed in purple. Below the mountains, falling steeply away, were slopes covered in dense mats of greenery. On the far bank, lofty trees lifted leafy arms to a sky of cloudless blue.

Captain Cameron's voice broke into Caroline's concentration. "You will find this a land of abrupt changes, Caroline."

"Then it is not always so hot?"

"No. March, April, and September are usually rainy periods. In the winter, it can be piercingly cold. But you will find that conditions are ruled by the direction of the wind." He smiled at her. "And the winds, believe me, can be extremely variable."

Narrowing her eyes against the sun dazzle on the water, Caroline drew in a deep breath of the clean, strong air. She leaned forward, staring at the darting silvery flashes of the fish breaking the water. A bird rose up, startling her with its size and its pure white plumage. Looking at it more intently, she saw that it was faintly tinged with pink on the breast, and its long, thin legs were of a rosy hue. Her attention was caught by another bird that had just darted into view. She watched it as it skimmed low over the water. It was a great deal smaller than the white bird. Its plumage was of a vivid blue, and its wings were marbled in an odd pattern. The bird gave a harsh, discordant cry that was scarcely in keeping with its exotic appearance, and flew off, to lose itself in the distance. Quite suddenly she was frightened by the strangeness about her. They had not even left the ship, and yet her first impression was of a vastness that was intimidating. This land to which they had come, this Virginia, was too alien, too big, too bright and burning and colorful. How would they, coming from the grays and the greens and the autumn bronzes of England, ever get used to it? She thought of the painted-up savages, as described by Amy Bellows, and she shuddered. It was too much! How big were the lands of the New World? Did they spread out endlessly beyond Virginia, sprawling north, south, east, and west? Going on and on, too vast for the mind to encompass?

The first of the boats bumped against the ship, and instantly Justin's hand came out to squeeze her shoulder, trying to impart something to her. Reassurance. Courage, perhaps. Courage? Aye, they all had need of that to face whatever fate might now be about to befall them.

The talk and the laughter rose in volume as men began clambering up the rope ladder. The first to set foot on the deck was a short man clad in a black broadcloth jacket and breeches and a frilled white shirt. Beneath a tall beaver hat his face was round and rosy. His medium-length light-brown hair was tied at the nape of his neck with a red ribbon. Several rings glittered on his plump, well-cared-for sun-browned hands. Compared to the convicts, he looked like a being from another world. He bowed to the captain; then, as his gaze fell on the group of men and women lying on the deck, his eyes opened wide in shock. Recovering himself with some difficulty, he announced himself to be Hugh Walker, of Suntrail Plantation. He stepped back as more and more men came to crowd the deck.

Captain Cameron, himself hardly able to stand from exhaustion, had instructed the convicts earlier. Holding tightly to the rail, he gave the prearranged signal for them to get to their feet and form two lines facing each other. The sailors ranged behind them watched their efforts. Then, at a nod from the captain, they came forward and assisted the convicts to rise. Glances were exchanged between the prospective owners as they noticed that the sailors were in the same starved and exhausted condition as those they sought to help. Shocked faces were turned to the captain.

Caroline took her place beside Justin, her heart thumping so rapidly that she could hardly breathe. They faced now the thing that she had resolutely thrust into the back of her mind, and panic overwhelmed her. She and Justin had come through so much together. How could she bear it if they were parted now? She stole a quick glance at his sober face, and wondered if the same thought was in his mind. Did he really care if it came to a parting of the ways? He had said he loved her, but perhaps his words at that time had been meant only to comfort her. Shaken with doubt, trembling, she put out a blindly seeking hand. Justin did not look at her, but he was aware of her movement. She was faintly reassured as his hand closed about hers.

Captain Cameron's dragging, weary voice began explaining the conditions that had existed during their long and tragic voyage. Explaining, soothing, reassuring. "No," he said, "there is no typhus now. The prisoners are very weak, but they are free of disease."

A man with dark, hawklike features said in quick concern, "But you are ill yourself, Captain."

Cameron's smile thanked him for his concern. "No more so than the rest. It is nothing that food and rest will not cure."

Caroline's thoughts scattered as the men began to pace up and down the two wavering lines. Their faces were frowning and doubtful as they made their examination. Bitter complaints were heard, and various derogatory remarks were made about the poor lot they had been sent this time. It was as though the captain had never spoken at all, so uncaring did many of them seem to be of the conditions that had existed.

A small man dressed in bright green with a black silver-laced tricorne hat set rakishly upon dark-auburn hair stopped at the end of the line and exclaimed in a shrill, indignant voice, "Damned riffraff! In agreeing to take in England's refuse, we are risking our lives and the lives of our women and children, and how are we repaid? We were promised strong hands for our tobacco fields, and they send us this stinking riffraff! By God! It is more than we should be expected to bear!"

Captain Cameron drew in a deep, gasping breath. "Have you no thought for their sufferings, sir? Is it impossible for you, with your well-fed body, your plantation, and your rich lands, to visualize all that they have had to endure?"

The little man drew himself up. "You are insulting, sir! There is not one of us here that has not known suffering. We came to this land, and we had the guts, sir, the courage, if you will, to claw out a livelihood from the wilderness. Erstwhile friendly savages suddenly turned into enemies, and so we fought them. Are still fighting them. Perhaps you have heard of the massacre of the white people back in 1622? What we have now, we have earned."

"It was not my intention to be insulting," Captain Cameron said quietly. "I am well aware that it takes brave and courageous men to settle new lands. I only meant that, having known suffering and privation yourself, can you not have pity on theirs?"

As he stared at the captain, the little man's anger faded. "My apologies, Captain Cameron. You do right to remind me."

Caroline shrank back as a man in a buff coat and white breeches stopped before her and eyed her keenly. "What's your name, wench?" he asked in an abrupt voice.

Caroline stared at him. Her throat worked as she tried to answer, but no words came.

"Your name?" the man repeated. The straw hat he was wearing threw dappled light over the harsh planes of his face. His bushy black brows met in a frown over cold eyes as he waited for her to answer. "You are not a mute or an idiot, are you? That, I think, would be a little too much." He placed the tip of a short silver-handled whip beneath her chin, tilting up her head so that she was forced to look at him. "Well, wench?"

Justin stiffened. "She is neither a mute nor an idiot," he said, his husky, whispering voice tight with anger. "You are frightening her. Have the goodness to take your whip away from her chin."

The man stared at him in outrage. "Curse your insolence!" he growled. "Your captain should have informed you that you do not speak unless spoken to."

Justin said nothing, but his slight, scornful smile drove the man into a paroxysm of temper. "Insulting scum!" Lifting the whip, he lashed out, opening a cut on Justin's cheek. Eyeing the blood oozing from the shallow cut, he said in a tone of satisfaction, "That should teach you your place. If you do not profit from this lesson, you can expect much more."

Captain Cameron saw the blaze in Justin's eyes, and the jumping of the muscle beside his mouth. Foreseeing what was about to happen, he went forward as quickly as he was able. Grasping Justin by the arm, he whispered urgently, "Be sensible, Lawrence. You are in no condition to tangle with him. He would cut you to pieces. If he cared to, he could order you to be publicly whipped."

"Does the scum wish to fight?" the man with the whip said in a taunting voice. "Let him come forward. It might be amusing."

Justin tried to push the captain aside. "Move, please. I will fight him."

"No, Justin!" Caroline's voice was agonized. "Please don't!"

Justin turned on her furiously. "Be silent, Carrie! I am not an animal, and I'll be damned if I'll submit to being treated like one!"

"Quite right, lad," a deep, pleasant voice said. It was the man with the dark, hawklike features. His ice-blue eyes flickered briefly and contemptuously over the man who had caused the scene; then he turned back to Justin. "However, it would be wrong of you to judge us all by Tom Keene here."

"Now, you look here, Markham!" Tom Keene took a menacing step forward. He halted again, stopped by something in the eyes that were again turned his way. "I suppose you think, because you are the head of the Planters' Association, that you have all the say here," he blustered. "Let me tell you that you are much mistaken." He looked about him, as though expecting backing from the other men. When nobody moved or spoke, his face fell ludicrously.

Tobias Markham smiled. Taking off his broad-brimmed black hat, he mopped at his sweating forehead with a red-and-white-silk handkerchief. Replacing the handkerchief in the pocket of his long-skirted silver-buttoned fawn coat, he said in an amused voice, "I am indeed the head of the Planters' Association, Keene. May I advise you, before you make an even bigger fool of yourself, to think about that very carefully. The position, as you know, carries with it some power. And, if forced to, though I would greatly regret it, I am not above using that power."

"Blackmail!" Keene growled.

"But of course. How clever of you to understand that." The amused note left Markham's voice. "Behave yourself and mind your manners. It is men like you that give the rest of us a bad name."

"And if I go against you, I would find it hard to get a market for my tobacco. Is that what you are trying to say, Markham?"

"You have put your finger on the nub of the matter, Keene. We do not need men of your kidney in Virginia. I must confess that if action of mine would cause you to seek other pastures, I would not pine."

"Don't count on it. Here I am, and here I stay." Keene smiled unpleasantly. "As your nearest neighbor, Markham, I am in the position to know something of your domestic affairs. It is a pity that the power you wield does not extend to Miss Biddy. I understand you find it hard to keep her under control, and that she is drinking more than ever."

There was a white line about Tobias Markham's mouth, but he had himself well under control. "I note that my sister-in-law, Miss Selina, keeps you well supplied with the latest gossip. However, Keene, I think we will not discuss my wife."

Caroline stared at him as he presented his elegantly clothed back to the fuming Keene. She saw a man who was perhaps in his middle fifties. He was of medium height, broad-shouldered, and somewhat stocky of build. His curling dark hair was frosted with white, and, unsmiling, he was sternly handsome. The sternness left his face as he smiled at Justin, giving him a warm and pleasant look. Caroline sensed that he could be ruthless to his enemies but that there was a deep essential kindliness to his nature that offset the streak of ruthlessness.

"My name is Tobias Markham," he said to Justin. His blue eyes warmed. "You look to me like a walking skeleton, lad, but for all that, I believe you would have tried to thrash Keene."

"You are right. I would have tried."

Tobias Markham laughed. "I admire your spirit. I do indeed! I have told you my name. May I know yours?"

"Justin Lawrence."

Markham considered him for a moment. "Would you like to work for me, Justin Lawrence? My plantation is a ways from here, fronting the Rappahannock. It is the Montrose Plantation."

"The Rappahannock?"

Markham cocked an amused eyebrow. "Aye, the Rappahannock River. You find the word strange on your tongue?"

"I do."

"You are not alone in that. When I first came here, some years ago now, I found many of the Indian names not only strange, but almost unpronounceable. But one grows accustomed in time. Well, do you think you would like to work for me?"

Justin smiled. "Since work I must, yes, Mr. Markham, I would like to work for you."

Markham was startled by the difference the smile made in the haggard and yellowed face. Again he was amused. Justin Lawrence, he guessed, was a man accustomed to command, for his tone had been that of one conferring a favor. He said dryly, "Thank you, lad. You are too good to me."

Somewhat taken aback by this, Justin said quickly, "I regret if my manner offends."

"Not at all. Think nothing of it." The blue eyes turned to Caroline. "I take it, from your violent protest a while ago, that you would not like to be parted from this young lordling? You are fond of him, girl?"

"I . . . I . . . Yes, I am fond of him."

"And you would not think kindly of me if I parted you, eh?"

Confused by his manner, Caroline reddened. "I would rather not be parted from him."

Her eyes turned briefly to Justin, and Markham found himself moved by the look on her face. What must it be like to be loved like that? he wondered. When he had made Biddy his wife, he had believed himself to be loved. He had quickly been shown that he deceived himself. Dismissing thoughts of Biddy and his disturbing stab of emotion, he smiled at Caroline, his teeth showing white and even against the deep brown of his face. "You would rather not," he repeated in a faintly amused voice. "That, I believe, must be the famous English understatement at its very best. What is your name, girl?"

"My name is Caroline Fane."

"Mindy, my cook, tells me that she has need of a kitchen girl. You may have that position."

Now that glowing look was turned upon Markham, and

again he found himself unwillingly moved. "Thank you," Caroline said. "You are very kind."

"Nonsense! I am not kind at all. But I do have the ability to recognize good workers when I see them." Markham turned to Cameron. "My bid on these two, sir."

Cameron smiled. "An excellent choice, Mr. Markham. You could not do better."

Markham noted the warmth in Cameron's voice, and again he congratulated himself on his ability to pick out the best. "These two are special to you, I know," he answered understandingly. "You need have no fear for their welfare. If I know anything of Mindy, my cook, she will immediately take them under her wing. She is not happy unless she has one stuffed like a turkey." He grinned. "Mindy is very fat, very black, and excessively kind."

After that, things went by in a blur for Caroline, so quickly was everything settled. Before she knew it, she was saying good-bye to Captain Cameron. There was sadness in the parting, for she had grown fond of him, and she believed, too, that she and Justin held a special place in his regard. They had been through so much together.

Seated beside Justin in the boat that was rapidly rowing them away from the *Merryventure,* Caroline found that she was trembling. Slaves! She could not blink at the fact. She and Justin were to be slaves to a man who might, conceivably, hold the power of life or death over them.

She started as Markham leaned toward her. Her eyes widened as he began to speak, for he seemed to know exactly how she was thinking. "On Montrose, Caroline, no one is a slave. They are simply workers." Markham's glance at the silent, grim-faced Justin included him in the conversation. "Simply workers," he repeated. "And I have never seen the need to treat my workers, be they black or white, as other than the human beings they are."

Caroline gave him a faint, grateful smile, but she said nothing. She moved nearer to Justin, her fingers nervously pleating and unpleating the skimpy skirt of the evil-smelling rag she wore.

Markham subsided. Frowning, he wondered why he had found it so imperative to reassure Caroline Fane. She was a convict, he told himself. A prostitute, perhaps. He remembered the look on her face when she had glanced at Justin

Lawrence, and he was suddenly quite sure that whatever else she might be, she was not a prostitute. Caroline Fane's crime was listed on the paper in his pocket, but he had not yet glanced at it. He would try to guess at her crime. Thief? Murderess? Numerous possibilities began to present themselves. His thoughts moved from Caroline to Biddy, his wife. Biddy would have laughed to hear him trying to reassure a convict. She was always telling him that he was a soft and gullible fool. He was neither of these things, but she firmly believed it. He thought of her pinched and narrow face, of her thin lips that were constantly opening to accuse him. His frown deepened. As he had told Caroline Fane, he did not treat his workers as slaves, but apparently, in his frequent and necessary absences from Montrose, Biddy more than made up for his tolerance and leniency. He had heard disquieting rumors of her treatment of the salves and the indentured workers, but thus far he had been able to prove nothing against her.

Justin watched Tobias Markham closely, without appearing to do so. The man's startling ice-blue eyes that were set so incongruously in his dark-skinned face rested constantly on Carrie, and Justin wondered if he might have something planned for her that was not domestic. The thought brought with it a hot rage. Gradually, as his rage died, he began to think clearly about the position in which he found himself, and with the dying of that rage, he found that on the whole he was inclined to trust Tobias Markham. There was a certain hardness about Markham, but he seemed to be a reasonably decent man. But decent or not, Justin would not remain in bondage to any man, not for too long.

Tobias Markham exuded strength and confidence, Caroline thought, and because he had taken the trouble to ease her mind, she believed that he was kind. For the moment she was content to lean upon that strength. She was tired, so tired that she felt almost mindless. Let Tobias Markham direct and order her. As long as she did not have to think for herself, she would be happy to obey. Sighing, she closed her eyes. She never wanted to think for herself again.

Justin looked at Caroline's closed eyes. He felt the faint trembling of her body against his own, and he understood all that she was feeling now. She was subdued, without fire, but that state of things would not last for too long. The old Carrie would return.

Chapter 15

Eliza Harris pushed back her fine pale-blond hair from her heated forehead. Her thin, plain face was faintly flushed with impatience and suppressed excitement as she waited for cook to finish her task. But the enormously fat black woman was apparently in no hurry. Her thick lips in her prune-black face were pursed thoughtfully as she continued to stir the contents of the brown earthenware bowl.

What could Mindy be thinking about? Eliza wondered. Usually she was brisk and bustling, always kind, but driving everybody to finish their allotted tasks. But today, the very day that Master Toby was returning to Montrose, Mindy seemed to be in some kind of dream.

In a fever of impatience that was rapidly mounting to an almost physical agony, Eliza dug her small white teeth into her lower lip and prayed that Mindy would soon dismiss her. She dared not leave without that dismissal. Suppose Mindy sent somebody to look for her? Suppose she was discovered with Moon? Her darling Moon? When would she be able to slip out to the fields and be with him for a few precious moments? He must be wondering what had happened to her, and he would be worried. He always worried so much about her.

Eliza fixed her eyes on Mindy's broad back and tried to will her to turn. Why was she such a coward? Why could she not simply say, "I have finished my tasks, Mindy. May I go?"

Eliza blinked tears of frustration from her pale-blue eyes. The only one she was not frightened of was Moon. She loved him so much! He was so big and protective, so gentle. It was impossible to fear him. She did not really fear Mindy, if the truth be told. It was simply that she was in awe of her. Except for those times when Mindy was impatient and her heavy hand would deal one a smart box on the ear, she was never unkind. After one of these infrequent bursts of temper, Eliza was always wrapped in the warmth of the black

woman's arms, and Mindy would cry genuine tears of remorse. To show the depths of her penitence, she would set
about making Eliza's favorite dish. Eliza's appetite was poor
at best, and under Mindy's fond regard and her beaming
white smile, she was forced to choke down every morsel. She
knew well that if she did not, Mindy would bridle and become offended, suspecting that a slur was being cast upon her
cooking.

Eliza looked about her, checking to make sure she had
really finished all her tasks. She had prepared the vegetables.
In the big black pot she had helped Mindy wrestle onto the
iron rack, the pudding, wrapped in a clean linen cloth, had
been cooking for the last hour in the briskly boiling water.
The dishes were washed and stacked, the kitchen was swept,
and the copper kettle stood on the hob, steam issuing from its
long spout. Before the great hearth, Andy, the small black
boy who helped out in the kitchen, was engrossed in his task
of basting the whole lamb on the spit.

As Eliza watched him, Andy, his tongue protruding between his teeth, dipped his big iron ladle in the pan below the
spit. Carefully, he poured the hot fat over the roasting meat.
Then, with a sidelong look at Mindy, he returned with a sigh
to his task of turning the spit.

Eliza looked sympathetically at the great beads of sweat
standing out on Andy's forehead. The boy was scowling, and
his lower lip was thrust out petulantly. It was only natural
that a nine-year-old boy should resent the tasks imposed upon
him. No doubt he was anxious to be at play with the other
and luckier boys.

Eliza sat up straighter on the stool as she caught the half-
turn of Mindy's white-turbaned head and the flash of the gold
hoop earrings that Tobias Markham had presented her with
on her last birthday. The steady scrape of the spoon against
the bowl began again, and Eliza, disappointed, slumped back
to her former position.

Mindy's brown eyes were heavy with worry as she automatically continued her stirring. Homecomings were never
joyful occasions for Master Toby—his drunken slut of a wife
saw to that—but this time it would be worse than ever. Miss
Biddy was cruel to the servants. Master Toby suspected it,
but he could prove nothing. None of the servants would talk
against Miss Biddy for fear of reprisals.

Mindy's hand clenched about the wooden spoon as she thought of the disgraceful scene that had happened yesterday. She had been passing through the hall when she had seen Miss Biddy standing at the top of the stairs.

Miss Biddy was very drunk. She was clutching at the banister with one hand, and about her light-brown eyes were so distended that they seemed about to pop from her head. Seeing Mindy standing there looking at her steadily, she had shouted belligerently, "Well, you black ape, what are you staring at?"

"Are you all right, ma'am?" Mindy had answered.

Miss Biddy had taken no notice of the question. Mindy had felt a wave of disgust. Her mistress's frilled white wrapper was stained and creased. It was unbuttoned at the top, and her blue-veined breasts, big breasts for so small a woman, swung heavily forward. Her hair looked as though it had not been brushed in many days, and she looked old. Far older than her forty-nine years. Mindy, at her own age of fifty-five, felt that she looked younger than Miss Biddy.

Patiently, Mindy repeated her question. But Miss Biddy's mind seemed to have wandered. Hiccuping, she looked at Mindy vaguely. Then, as the words registered, she blurted out, "Mind your own business, you fat black fool!"

"Very well, ma'am. If you don't want mah help, then ah ain't got no time to waste."

"You dare to talk to me like that! I'll . . . I'll have you whipped!"

Mindy shook her head. "No, ma'am, you cain't do it. Ah ain't no slave, and you knows it. Cain't have me whipped."

Biddy's eyes blazed. "How many times do you intend to remind me that you're a free woman, you damned smirking fool? Slave or no slave, it makes no difference to me. I'll have your back flayed raw!"

Mindy shook her head. "You just cain't, Miss Biddy. Master Toby would never allow it." She turned away. "I'll be getting back to mah kitchen."

"Mindy!"

Mindy turned back. "Yes, ma'am?" she said politely.

For whatever reason Biddy had recalled her, it went out of her head as she looked down at the impassive-faced black woman. Her eyes lost their blaze of anger and dulled over. Swaying dangerously, she gave an explosive belch. "I'm sick, Mindy," she whimpered. A thin line of brown moisture dribbled from the side of her mouth. "I'm so sick! Send somebody to attend me."

For a moment Mindy did not move. With her eyes on the swaying woman, she thought: Just a little more forward thrust and she will come tumbling down these stairs. Maybe she will break her neck and free Master Toby from his hateful marriage.

In the recesses of her muddled and reeling mind, Biddy became dimly aware of her danger. Her face twisted as another painfully violent belch tore from her. Retching, she sank to her knees and vomited on the turkey-red carpet.

Master Toby would not be pleased, Mindy thought. The carpet, at great expense, had been imported from England.

Gulping, Biddy turned watering eyes to Mindy. "I'm dying, you ape!" she shrieked. "Send somebody to me!" Her body convulsed as the retching began again.

Dying? Mindy thought. No such luck! She shrugged resigned shoulders. "Ah'll 'tend you mahself," she said trudging heavily up the stairs. She made no attempt to touch the miserably vomiting woman until she deemed the spasm was over. Then, looking with disgust at the mess on the carpet, she hauled her to her feet. With the sound of Biddy's noisy sobbing in her ears, she conducted her staggering steps to her bedroom.

As was usual in Biddy's room, the windows were closed and the heavy green-velvet draperies partially drawn. Depositing Biddy none too gently on the bed, Mindy marched across the room and pushed back the draperies; then she opened the windows wide.

"I'm dying!" Biddy moaned.

Shuddering, Mindy leaned out of the window and took a deep breath of the clean, sweet air. Poor Master Toby!

Thinking of him, Mindy's eyes softened. Master Toby was only a day older than herself. They had both been born in the great house. She, the child of a slave woman, and Master Toby, the son of the master. They had played together as children, and they had been unaware of any difference in their skins, such was the strength of the bond of affection between them. They had done other things together, too. When he was fifteen years old, Master Toby had made his first fumbling attempt to explore her body. He was a shy, rather diffident boy in those days, and she could easily have rebuffed him had she cared to. But she adored him, and so she had lain down willingly and allowed him to have his way. Her hands, by some age-old inherited instinct, had guided him. When he was inside her, she had felt a pang of disappointment. She had expected to feel so much more. After that, he tried several times, becoming increasingly confident. And then, one day, she had known rapture. He came to her many times. Their hands linked, laughing together, they would run to the grove that they had made their special place. And there, with the moon filtering through the leaves of the surrounding trees and sending little dancing spearpoints of light over their naked bodies, he would take her hungrily.

Mindy sighed. She had been slim and pretty then. Master Toby used to love to kiss the deep dimples in her cheeks. She was fat now, but Master Toby still thought her pretty. He had said so many times. Occasionally, when he was worried or unhappy or restless, he would still come to her room. It was as though his eyes did not see fat, fifty-five-year-old Mindy, but only the young girl she had once been. After he had entered her body and satisfied himself, he would lie spent but content with his head pillowed against her ample breasts. With a happiness known to her only when he was with her, she would tighten her arms about him. Holding him close, she would encourage him to talk. His reticence fled when he was with his old and trusted friend. Her anger with Miss Biddy would grow as she heard of the misery and horror his life had become with this crude woman who had no delicacy or fastidiousness at all.

If only she would die! Mindy thought. Her death would set Master Toby free again. It might be, if he were happy with another woman, that he would never come to her room again. But she could bear that pain if only she knew he was happy. She wanted happiness for him so much!

Meeting Mindy's eyes, Biddy gave a weak belch and said, "Something I ate has disagreed with me."

"Yes, ma'am."

"I know what you're thinking! You think I'm drunk, don't you? Admit it! Don't you!"

"Ah don't think nothing, ma'am. It ain't mah place to think." Leaning over, Mindy twitched the wrapper over the exposed breasts. Before she could straighten up, Biddy drew in a deep gulp of air and deliberately belched in her face.

Mindy recoiled beneath the gust of foul breath, and Biddy broke into weak laughter. Her sly eyes on the black woman's face, she tore the wrapper open again. "You leave me alone. I like to feel the air on my body." Her smile was more of a leer as she squinted up at Mindy. "Your precious Master Toby will be home soon. That will please you, won't it?"

"Yes, ma'am," Mindy answered her tonelessly. "It will please me. Ah'm always happy to see Master Toby."

"And happier still when he's in your room, you fat black bitch!"

Mindy's eyes went blank. And why shouldn't he come to me? she thought. All he has from you is misery and despair. It is all he has ever had. She tightened her lips against the words struggling to be uttered.

Biddy looked down at her breasts. Cupping them in her hands, she said, "Look at them, Mindy. They are big and nicely shaped, aren't they? Toby used to love my breasts. If ever I allowed him to touch me, he would love them again. But I won't let that animal near me!" She began to laugh again. "I don't want him to touch me ever! That is why I don't mind when he comes to you. Two animals together. I should like to bore a hole in the wall and see him trying to climb up your great mountain of flesh."

Mindy's hands clenched. "Ah don't have to listen to that kind of talk, ma'am."

Something flickered in Biddy's eyes, and Mindy knew that she had belatedly remembered caution. With her sly eyes on Mindy's face, she put a hand to her sweating forehead. "I declare, Mindy, I feel so ill that I just don't know what I'm saying."

"Yes, ma'am." Mindy walked over to the door. "If you should get to feeling ill again, ma'am, ah've placed the chamber pot right handy."

"Mindy, wait!"

Without turning her head, Mindy went out into the corridor and closed the door firmly behind her. She heard Biddy moaning loudly and retching again, but she did not pause. I hope you strangle! she thought.

Downstairs, she found three of the servants grouped together. The noise Biddy was making came to them plainly. They looked frightened but resigned. "Joe," Mindy said, turning to a slender young black man, "get a bucket of water and clean up that mess at the top of the stairs."

Joe looked sullen. "More of Miss Biddy's mess?"

"More," Mindy said.

"I cleaned up after her the last time. Why cain't somebody else do it?"

" 'Cause ah'm telling you to do it, Joe Williams."

Muttering, Joe went away to find a bucket. He would have liked to defy Mindy, but he did not dare. She was more than a cook, she was in charge of the whole household, and, in Master Toby's absence, the true seat of power. They all of them obeyed Miss Biddy out of fear. But they obeyed Mindy out of awe and respect.

That same day, Mindy had felt suddenly desolate with the weight of the responsibility that was hers each time Tobias Markham went away. But for all the power Master Toby reposed in her, what could she really do about Miss Biddy? Unless perhaps Miss Selina could be awakened to the fact that there were certain matters of which she must take charge. With a faint stirring of hope, she had sought out the woman.

Selina, Biddy's sister, was in her room. Grudgingly, she had allowed Mindy to enter. Selina, two years older than Biddy, did not resemble her in any way. Her dark-brown eyes were set in an angular, sallow face. She was tall, scrawny, and invariably acid of expression.

Watching the quick, furtive peeps Selina kept darting at the mirror, Mindy felt that she had made a mistake in coming to her. She appeared to be listening to the account of Biddy's increasingly disgraceful conduct, and yet, Mindy knew, she was not really listening. There was an unusual flush in Selina's sallow cheeks, and she continually ran smoothing hands over her untidy bird's nest of mouse-brown hair. It was obvious that her thoughts were far away. No doubt with Tom Keene, of Ballymore Plantation, who would be returning home at the same time as Tobias Markham. Miss Selina, Mindy knew, hoped to marry Tom Keene. In her opinion Miss Selina, at the age of fifty-one, was desperate to be married, but only to avoid the title of "old maid." Left to herself, she felt that Miss Selina would gladly have continued on in her untouched virginity. She was afraid of sex. Not like her sister, Miss Biddy!

Miss Biddy refused her husband his rights. And yet, during Master Toby's absences, when she locked herself away in her room with a bottle, she was not always alone. Mindy, when unable to sleep, had taken to wandering through the house and checking to see that all was secure. And once she had seen Nigel, the black man in charge of the lower tobacco field, come creeping from Miss Biddy's room. He had been buttoning his breeches as he went. Stunned, not wanting him to see her, Mindy had drawn back. Another time it had been Ben Cranwell, the trashy white indentured servant whom Mindy had learned to despise. Creeping noiselessly up the stairs and along the corridor, she had found Miss Biddy's door standing open. Cautiously, she had peeped into the room. Miss Biddy was lying on the bed, snoring. She was naked, and her legs were spread wide. As though, Mindy thought bitterly, she still believed Ben Cranwell to be between her thighs. Going farther into the room, she had seen that the black-silk bedspread was spotted with semen. She had not attempted to touch her mistress. She had left the room and closed the door quietly behind her. She had never told Master Toby of her discovery. He had been hurt enough.

Miss Selina was patting her hair again. Watching her, Mindy thought that if Miss Selina looked for marriage with Tom Keene, who was ten years her junior, she was due for disappointment. Tom Keene, Mindy had heard, laughed at Selina and called her names that were scarcely loving.

Selina was suddenly caught by the expression on Mindy's face. "Why are you still here?" she demanded in a shrill voice. "What is it you want?"

She had not meant to tell Miss Selina about the black men that Miss Biddy invited to her bed, but suddenly the burden of her own painful knowledge was more than she could bear. The words came tumbling out, and she saw Miss Selina pale and begin to shake.

"Liar!" Selina shouted in a furious voice. "How dare you make up such lies about my sister?"

"Ah don't tell lies, Miss Selina," Mindy said, unmoved by this show of rage. "Ah seen them men with mah own eyes."

"You are a liar!" Selina said again.

"Ah sorry you think that, Miss Selina. If you ain't willing to do nothing 'bout it, then maybe ah better speak to Master Toby when he come home."

Selina caught her breath. Mindy must be silenced. If it came to Tom Keene's ears, her hopes of marrying him, though admittedly slim, would be gone altogether. Despite her angry words, she had not the slightest doubt that Mindy was telling the simple truth. Oh, Biddy, she thought, you drunken, promiscuous fool! You filthy slut! Swallowing her dismay and anger, she said in a placating voice, "We must talk, Mindy. Will you sit down?" She indicated a Turkey-worked chair.

Mindy shook her head. "If it all the same to you, Miss Selina, ah rather stand."

Selina nodded. She was wondering how best to get Mindy to keep her silence. She decided to appeal to Mindy's weak spot, her devotion to Toby. "I think, Mindy," she said in a gentle voice, "that it would be better to say nothing of this to Master Toby. He has quite enough to bear, and you would not wish to give him a new hurt, would you?"

Struck by this, Mindy wavered. She said uncertainly, "But something got to be done 'bout Miss Biddy. Ain't fair to Master Toby if she go on this way. This time, Miss Selina, ah think ah should speak out."

"No, no!" Selina said desperately. "I will talk to Miss Biddy. I . . . I will try to get her to mend her ways. If I try my best, will you promise to keep your silence?"

"You think you can get her to change, Miss Selina?"

"I can try, Mindy. I promise you that I will try."

"Then ah won't say nothing to Master Toby this time. But if it keep on happening, ah got to tell him. Ain't right if he find out his ownself. It shock him bad."

"Yes, Mindy, I know." Smiling, Selina rose. "Come with me, Mindy. We will go together to Miss Biddy's room. You shall hear for yourself what I will have to say to her."

"It ain't necessary, Miss Selina."

"Please. I insist."

So once again Mindy had gone unwillingly to the room she hated. Miss Selina, walking in front of her with her back straight and her meager shoulders squared, had looked almost militant. "We will get this matter cleared up, Mindy," she had said. "You will see."

They had walked in on a shocking and unbelievable sight. Even now, recalling it could still make the sweat break out on Mindy's forehead.

Miss Biddy was lying on her back on the floor. She was naked, her legs wide open. From her sagging, dribbing

mouth, raucous snores issued. In between her legs sat a
naked, sobbing black boy. Mindy recognized him as ten-
year-old Bobby, a lad who was often seen at play with her
kitchen helper, Andy. Even in sleep, Miss Biddy had not
relaxed her grip upon him. Her right hand held the boy's
hand firmly clamped to her breast. Her left hand was grasping his tiny penis.

Mindy thought Miss Selina was going to faint, and she
moved forward to catch her. "Oh, my God!" Selina moaned.
"Oh, God! Oh, God!" She sank down in a chair and hid her
face in her hands.

For the first time since she had known her, Mindy actually
felt sorry for the spiteful and troublemaking Miss Selina. But
her first concern was Bobby. With an exclamation of pity,
Mindy started forward. "Don't cry, Bobby, honey. Don't
cry."

Stooping, Mindy forced open the fingers of Miss Biddy's
right hand, then her left. "Hush, boy, hush!"

But Bobby was not to be hushed. His eyes terrified, he
flung himself against Mindy and clung tightly to her legs.
"M-miss Biddy look out of her window and she c-call to me
to come up to—to her r-room," he sobbed. "She say we p-
play a game together."

"You don't have to say any more, boy," Mindy soothed.

Bobby was deaf to her voice. Spurred on by terror, afraid
that he would be whipped, he babbled on desperately, "When
I come into the r-room, she hadn't got any c-clothes on.
And she—she made me take off mine." Overcome, his arms
clung tighter.

Miss Selina lifted a ghastly face, but she made no attempt
to stop the boy's revelations.

"Then Miss Biddy, she got down on the f-floor," Bobby
resumed. "She was on her h-hands and knees, and she started
laughing, and—and then she lay down on her back and said I
w-was to sit between her legs. She said for me to put my
mouth on her—her breast and k-kiss it." He raised his head
and looked up at Mindy. "But I c-c-couldn't do that!"

"No, boy, of course not."

"Then she grab for my hand and m-made me hold her
there. And then she took my—my—"

"All right, boy," Mindy interrupted hastily. "Ah knows the
rest."

"Will I get whipped, Mindy? Will I, Miss Selina?"

"No," Selina said in a dull voice. "Put on your clothes and leave this room. You are to say nothing of this to anybody. If you do, I promise that you will be whipped."

"I won't, Miss Selina. I won't say nothing."

Bobby scrambled hastily into his clothes, and hurriedly left the room. They could hear his running feet along the corridor.

Mindy waited for a word or a movement from Selina, but she continued to sit there in the chair, her shocked eyes staring straight ahead. She made no move to help when Mindy, with much effort, heaved Biddy back on the bed.

Biddy awoke partially as Mindy was struggling to force her flaccid arms into a fresh wrapper. Grunting, she struck out with ineffectual fists, but almost immediately fell asleep again.

Lifting, pushing, rolling the inert figure, Mindy finally managed to get her into the wrapper. She smoothed the wrapper down over Biddy's legs, did up the buttons, and tied the sash. After wiping the stained mouth with a damp cloth, she stood there looking down at her mistress. Heavy with hopelessness, Mindy turned away from the bed and went over to the door. Selina's voice stopped her.

"Remember your promise, Mindy. You are to say nothing to Master Toby."

"Ah don't know," Mindy said, shaking her head. "After what ah seen here today, ah just don't know."

"You've got to give me a chance. You promised!"

"Ah'll see, Miss Selina. Ah'll think 'bout it."

Her face set like a stone, Mindy went on her way, the sound of Miss Selina's desperate sobbing following her.

Only yesterday, it had been, Mindy thought. She must give Miss Selina a chance, but she doubted if she could accomplish anything. Miss Biddy, in her opinion, was too far gone.

Mindy sighed heavily, thinking of another worrying thing. It seemed that Miss Biddy was not satisfied with Betsy, the black girl who was being trained as her maid. Miss Biddy, Betsy had told her, wanted a white girl to maid her. Mindy's thoughts went anxiously to Eliza Harris, the only white servant in the household. Poor frail little Eliza—how would she be able to endure the woman? No, she must not keep on worrying so. Today Master Toby would be coming home, and all would be well.

Today? Mindy started and dropped the wooden spoon into the bowl. Here she stood, deep in thought, and he might come at any time. She turned quickly. "Eliza!"

Relieved that Mindy had at last come out of her dream, Eliza Harris jumped lightly down from the stool. "Yes, Mindy?" With her habitual nervous gesture, she pushed back her pale hair from her forehead.

"Don't keep up that fiddle-faddling with your hair!" Mindy said sharply. She saw Eliza's flinch, and she was sorry for her sharpness. She put out a plump hand and patted the girl's thin shoulder. "There, girl, ah'm sorry. Have you done all your jobs?"

Eliza nodded and smiled. "All done."

"Good. Stir up the fire and put on some more wood. After you've done that, you can go rest."

Eliza ran to the wood bin. Filling her arms with logs, she felt the familiar glow of happiness. She could go! Very soon she would be with Moon.

Mindy watched with frowning brows as Eliza returned to the fire and began carefully placing the small logs upon the sunken glowing red heart. The licking flames, leaping up instantly, lighted the delicate face with a ruddy glow. Trouble! Mindy thought, her heart heavy. And far worse trouble than Eliza's possible promotion to Miss Biddy's bedroom. If the persistent rumors that Eliza and Moon were meeting secretly had any truth in them, it could result in tragedy. Terrible tragedy! Moon, the big black so named because of the half-moon-shaped scar on his left cheek, a powerful man who stood well over six feet three inches in height, and fragile little Eliza? It must not be true! Moon, consorting with a white girl! Mindy felt clammy with fear. If it became known, Master Toby would be powerless to help them. The law was the law, and it had been clearly stated that whites might not mingle familiarly with blacks. The fornication of a white girl with a black man was a death warrant for one and banishment for the other. Moon would be taken away and hanged. But in a way, the punishment for timid little Eliza, who had come to Montrose only last year as an indentured servant, would turn out to be even more cruel than death by the rope. Mindy doubted if the frail girl would be able to endure.

Mindy caught her breath as she remembered the case of the white girl on Hawkeye Plantation, some miles from Montrose. The white girl—Margaret Ross, her name had been— had been caught in the act of fornication with Tambo, a black field worker. Tambo had been hanged. Margaret Ross had been taken to the market square. First her hair had been shaved from her head, and then she had been stripped naked. Her ears had been nailed to a wooden board, and a sign had been placed before her. The sign had stated in bold letters: "This white trash has been used by a nigger!"

Mud, rotting vegetables, and all manner of filth had been hurled by the screaming crowd at the tortured girl. And finally, when the sun had gone down, Margaret Ross, half out of her mind with pain and fear, had been publicly banished. Injured, without food or clothes, with not one person to turn to, Margaret Ross, a stranger in a strange and savage land, had died from hunger, exposure, and terror.

Mindy did not know if the case of Margaret Ross was true, or an exaggerated distortion of the truth, but she had certainly been banished. Her dead body, naked and deeply gouged by the claws of some animal, had been found in the forest by a party of trappers.

"Eliza," Mindy said impulsively, "is it true that you and . . . ?" She stopped, unable to go on.

"Yes?" Eliza turned her flushed face her way. "What were you saying?"

"Nothing," Mindy answered shortly. It was best if she kept her own counsel. And if it should be true about Eliza and Moon, she could only pray that others would follow her example of silence. She would ask no questions. The less she knew about the affair, the better off she would be.

Mindy's eyes met Andy's wide and curious stare. He was crouched before the now-blazing fire, his small hands idle. She frowned at him formidably. "Ain't you got nothing better to do than to sit there staring at me, Andy? Ah ought to take a broom to your skinny behind. Baste that meat some more. Cain't you see it's gitting dry?"

Andy was not deceived by the frown. He knew that later on Mindy would regret her burst of temper, and she would console him with some of her special syrup cakes. It had happened many times before. He grinned at her. Then, seeing her threatening forward movement, he hastily picked up the big ladle and began to baste the meat.

Chapter 16

Moon stood in the narrow path between the two fields of tobacco. The field on his left had been planted with Orinoco,
and the field to his right flourished with the tobacco plants
known as the "sweet-scented." His mind roamed, remembering how he and his crew had labored to break up the earth in
the fields, finally laying them out in long, shallow furrows.
He had taken pride in his work, and he had looked with
some satisfaction at the fields that stood ready and waiting.
After the May rain, he and his crew had taken the prepared
tobacco seedlings from their beds of special mold and had
transplanted them in the fields.

Moon looked carefully at the plants. Once, before the coming of Eliza, he had lived, thought, and even dreamed of tobacco. Its cultivation fascinated him. The sowing of the seed
in winter, the careful nursing of that seed. The hoeing, the
plowing, the weeding, the frequent loosening of the soil, and
the job he had been doing today. The topping of the plants to
prevent too wild a growth, and the removal of the sucklers
from the base of the stem.

Moon yawned and stretched. The plants would be yellowing soon. Then would come the cutting and the curing.

He grinned to himself, aware that he was only allowing his
mind to dwell on the cultivation of tobacco in order not to
think and worry too much about the possible reason for
Eliza's failure to meet him at the arranged time. Was she in
trouble of some kind? he wondered now. Was she ill? Moon's
huge black hands clenched at this last thought, and he felt a
stab of fear. She was so thin and frail, his Liza! He could not
help worrying about her.

Moon shaded his eyes and looked toward the distant plantation house. From here, Montrose looked like a toy house.
So did the wagon that was coming along the road that di-

vided the house from the lower fields. Someone coming calling? Or perhaps Master Tobias home at last? Thinking of the
distance, another possibility suggested itself. Perhaps Liza had
failed to get a lift in one of the field wagons.

Moon looked about him. If Liza came, he was certain they
would not be disturbed. The hands were either eating or
resting after their long, hard day. They saw enough of the
fields, and they were unlikely to come wandering this way.
He and Liza, as they usually did, would talk for a while. And
then they would go to his little cabin behind the trees. He
would be able to hold her in his arms and kiss her lips. And
later, their passion rising, they would lie together, his ebony-
black body in startling contrast to hers. Liza always laughed
at his never-ending wonder at the color and the fine texture
of her hair, the blue of her eyes. "Your eyes are like the sky
when the rains have washed it clean and pure and blue," he
had told her once.

He had been surprised and shocked when Liza had burst
into tears. "Nobody has ever said anything like that to me before," she had sobbed. "All my life I have been plain and un-
loved."

"All your life?" he had answered her tenderly. "You are
only fifteen years old, my Liza. I am ten years older than
you."

"Fifteen years can seem like a lifetime when you have
been brought up in a home for unwanted children. And when
you are without beauty or talent, it is doubly hard." She had
clung to him suddenly. "Oh, Moon! Had it not been for the
charitable organization that sent me out here to the New
World, I would never have met you."

He had folded her in his arms, stilling her trembling. "But
you are here, and we did meet. You are not unwanted now. I
want you, Liza. I love you. With all my heart, I love you.
And never say to me again that you are not beautiful. In my
eyes, you are as beautiful as a rose. So beautiful that it makes
a pain in my heart."

"My darling! If only we could be together always! I want
so much to be your wife."

He had hated to be the one to put the fear into her eyes.
But he had had to make her understand their position. "We
can never be married, Liza. We cannot even be friends. Only

by sneaking can we ever be together. Do you know what the white men would do to us if we were found together?"

She stared at him. "No," she whispered.

"They would kill us."

"Moon!" Her eyes looked into his, wide and very blue. She was so pale that even the delicate tint of color in her lips had faded. "Don't say that. Don't!"

It was like slapping a trusting child, and he had to force himself to go on. "They would kill us, Liza," he repeated in a hard voice. "Our love would be an outrage against white society."

"Master Tobias is not like that!" she had cried out in protest.

"There are many good and decent white men, Liza, and Master Tobias is one of them. But for all the good men, there are twice as many who are without understanding or compassion. To that kind of man, a black man is not human. He is an animal."

Liza, shivering violently against him, had cried out passionately, "Then from now on I shall hate all white men!"

"That would be wrong and very foolish. Have I not told you that there are many good white men?"

"Yes, but—"

"It is simply that evil is always so much stronger than good." He looked at her sadly. "That is why we must always be careful, my Liza. Do you understand?"

He could see in her a longing to repudiate all he had said. She was a child, and despite her hard life, untouched as yet by the evil in man. Then he saw by the droop of her shoulders and the clouding of her expressive eyes that he had won her understanding. "Yes, Moon, I understand," she had said, and there had been an undertone of horror in her voice.

Moon sat down on the dusty path. Drawing up his knees, he folded his arms about them. His eyes dreaming, he thought back, remembering the first time he had seen Liza. One of her jobs was to bring food to the field hands. Until Liza came, it had been carried to them by Rosie, the black woman who sometimes helped out in the Montrose kitchen. Engrossed in his work, he had not noticed her. Then he heard a light, rather breathless voice say, "Excuse me, sir. I have brought food. Are you hungry?"

Sir! He had never been called sir before. He had looked up

sharply. To his sun-dazzled eyes she had wavered in an out-line of gold. He had seen white women before, but never this close, and never had they looked at him with such candid eyes and such a friendly smile. The tool in his hand slipped, and he felt a sharp stab of pain on his instep.

"You have cut yourself!" Eliza's voice had cried out in distress. Then she was down on her knees beside him, her little hands gently touching his injured foot. She looked up, and he was taken aback by the tears in her blue eyes. "Does it hurt very much?"

He could not believe that this girl was touching him so ten-derly, actually crying for him. Shaken, he shook his head and stammered out, "N-no, ma'am, it doesn't hurt h-hardly at all."

"But it must be attended to at once. It is bleeding."

He felt a wave of relief as he remembered that John Put-nam, the white overseer, was in one of the lower fields. "It is nothing," he answered her.

But Eliza, forgetting her natural shyness before what she thought of as his pain, insisted. "Come, sit in the shade. I will bind your foot."

He was alarmed and dazzled and fascinated all at the same time. "Bind it, ma'am?" he said. "What with?"

"I will tear a strip from my petticoat."

Now the alarm was predominant. "No, ma'am, don't! It will be all right."

For answer, Eliza took his hand and began leading him to the tree, a little distance away. And he had thought then that it was as if a flower had come to life and taken his hand. A fragile golden flower leading a black giant. Oblivious of the staring eyes of the other hands, he had gone with her meekly. Submitting to having his foot bound, he could not seem to take his eyes from her face.

Suddenly she had looked up and met his eyes. A faint pink had tinged her cheeks. "I hope your foot feels better."

"Yes, ma'am," he had answered her in a hoarse voice.

"Please don't call me that. My name is Eliza."

"Liza," he mumbled the name.

"No, Eliza," she corrected. She smiled at him. "But you may call me Liza, if you wish."

Without answering, he continued to stare at her.

"What is it?" her voice said. "Why do you look at me like that?"

"Like what?"

"As though . . ." She hung her head, unable to go on.

He could not help himself. "As though I have never seen anyone quite like you before. Is that what you were going to say? I never have, ma'am. That is the God's truth!" It was as though someone else had spoken, not he.

Her head came up very slowly, and the blue eyes looking into his were shining. She said with shy pleasure. "I know from the way you said it that you mean it in a nice way. But I am really very ordinary."

Ordinary! She was to him like a flower. A pink and golden and perfect flower. And her eyes, those blue and shining eyes! Surely the sky had lodged itself in them? He shook his head in protest at her words. "No!" he said. "No, ma'am!"

She smiled at his vehemence. "I am new to Montrose," she said, placing her hand lightly over his. "Do you think we could be friends?"

The innocence of her! Her almost incredible naïveté! But it would not last. Plantation life and the particular circumstances under which white and black lived rather uneasily together would combine to take away that shining innocence. He felt a poignant sadness at this last thought, and he was unaware of the tears in his eyes.

"What is it?" she exclaimed in distress. "Are you feeling ill?"

He looked at her in surprise. "No, ma'am." He looked down at her hand.

Eliza flushed scarlet and removed her hand. She had the embarrassed feeling that perhaps she had been too forward. But there was something about this big man that drew her. She had no idea what it might be. His color was strange to her, his race alien, and yet she had the feeling that she had always known him.

"What is your name?" she asked shyly.

"I am called Moon." He touched the scar upon his left cheek. "I was so named because of this mark."

"Moon." She said the name as though she were savoring it. "It suits you." She began to smile again. "I am usually very shy with people, Moon, but I think that I could never be shy with you."

It was as if love had grown between them from that very moment. Black eyes looked deeply into blue, and their awareness of each other was mirrored there. Words were started and then quickly stilled as they continued to hold each other's gaze.

There was so much he could have told her. He could have spoken of prejudice, deep-rooted prejudice. Of the white distrust and fear of the black man. But he said nothing. She would find out soon enough for herself. It was not his job to enlighten her; that was for the whites to do. No, he would not be the first to instill into her distrust, prejudice, and unreasoning hatred. As he turned away, he found himself mourning for the innocent open-heartedness of her that would shortly be stripped away. "I must get back to my work, Miss Liza, ma'am." He walked away and left her standing there.

She had come the next day, and he knew from the expression in her eyes that she had received her warning on how to conduct herself in a black man's presence. But that darkening of her eyes was not reflected in her smile and her friendly approach. As clearly as if she had told him, he knew that she had set herself to leap the gulf between them.

He tried to hold back, for he was afraid of the happiness that filled him. Although she had been warned, it was obvious to him that she had no real conception of the dangers of the relationship she was trying to establish between them. He felt her love, even though it was as yet unuttered. His own love, mute too, rushed out to meet it. A white woman—not even a woman, a girl—and a black man! This feeling that was growing and strengthening between them must stop. He must find a way to stop it! Such a situation, tragic in all its implications, could have only one end for both of them. Death.

He found that he could not sleep for thinking of her. He ate little. His work suffered, bringing down on his head a stern rebuke from John Putnam, the white overseer. But still he could not keep his eyes from straying and seeking that spot where she would first appear. And yet, when she came, so demure-looking in her quiet gray gown, her pale hair peeping from beneath a little winged white cap, her eyes as always seeking him out first, he could not bring himself to look at her. He did not want to meet that look in her eyes, for fear that his own might respond. He did not want foolish and ill-considered words to be torn from him. But above everything else, he was afraid for her.

One day she had come to his side and handed him a package of food, and he heard her low voice speaking words that filled him with a sense of fatality. "After work is over for the day," she said, "I will come to the fields. Please meet me."

He took the food from her, aware of the eyes of the white overseer, who was standing a little distance away. He stole a quick look at her, and he knew what it had cost her to speak first. She was not a forceful person, she was by nature timid and self-effacing, but her love for him was stronger. She was determined to grasp at happiness. But didn't she know that there could never be anything for them?

"Will you, Moon?" Her voice again, quiet, insistent.

His fingers clenced about the package of food. "No! You do not know what you are doing."

"I do know. I will be there."

He would not meet her, he had told himself. It was for her sake. Little foolish Liza, who was rushing headlong into calamity. And yet he did meet her, as, in his subconscious mind, he had known he would.

After that first time, they met frequently. Hidden from prying eyes by a thick screening of trees, they would talk of many things, but never of love. He knew that words of love trembled on Liza's lips, but he would not, dared not let her say them. He would rush into conversation, saying anything that came into his head. He could not help wondering if the other field hands knew of these meetings. If they knew, they had said nothing. The brotherhood between them was strong, and they would protect him if they could. Yet, if a white man had reason to suspect and questioned the hands, they must either speak out or deny all knowledge. Tobias Markham was a kind man, and he did not encourage floggings, but he must stand straight in the eyes of the law and the community. If punishment were indicated, it would be carried out. A flogging for those who had concealed the truth, death for himself, and cruel banishment for Liza.

On that night when, without a word being exchanged between them, he had taken Liza's hand and led her to his cabin, he had thought afterward that he must have been suffering from a form of insanity. But at that time, he knew only that he was happy to have her there. They belonged together. Surely God would pity and protect them?

At first he did not touch her. He was content just to see her seated in this rough place he called home. Seating himself beside her, he talked to her of Virginia, the place that from now on would be her home. "If she lived!" The words trembled inside him, but he ignored them. He spoke of the great trees, the cedars, the oaks, the cypresses, and the maples, which, he believed, must surely be greater in girth and height than anywhere else in the world. He told her of the variety of nuts to be found. The chinquapins, the chestnuts, hazels, and many others too numerous to mention. There were wild fruits. Strawberries, cherries, grapes, plums, persimmons, raspberries, and blackberries. Flowers grew everywhere in the Virginia forests, mingling their colors and their perfumes, so that they all but blinded the eyes with their beauty and set the head to reeling with their fragrance. There were crystal streams to be found in almost every valley, and these streams were crowded with fish of every description. His eyes glowing, Moon talked on, describing for her the wonders and the ever-changing seasons and beauties of Virginia.

Watching him, Eliza knew that despite his slavery, he had come to love this land. He spoke of it as though it were a kind of Eden. A savage Eden, for there were hidden dangers and cruelties, as well as beauty. And listening to him, she was herself convinced. Here, in this vast and beautiful land, love had created for her yet another kind of paradise. Now she longed for Moon to stop talking. She wanted to feel his arms about her, his lips on hers.

Moon did stop talking. He looked at her in silence for a while. Then he opened his arms and said simply, "I love you, Liza. Come to me."

"Moon!" Her face seemed to be lit from within with a glowing beauty. She gave an inarticulate cry, and then she was in his arms. It was meant, he told himself again. She belonged to him. And yet he still could not forget caution. That was when he warned her. That was when he told her of what the white man would do to them if they should ever be found together. Her face paled and her eyes were darkened and solemn. Her fear was apparent, but her arms did not stop holding him. He won her understanding, that night, of the

danger in which they had placed themselves. She became as
cautious as he. But there was one thing she could not do,
even when he implored her for her own sake to try. She
could not put him out of her mind. She could not stop loving
and wanting and needing him.

"Can you forget me?" she asked him.

"No, never!"

"Can you stop loving me?"

He looked at her with hopeless eyes. "You know that I
cannot."

"Then why do you ask the impossible of me?"

"It is for your own sake. Do you think that I—?"

She had stopped his mouth with her kisses, and she had
laughed when he tried to free his mouth. Flushed, happy, in
love, she became bold, and the hidden facets of her personality emerged.

That had been the true beginning of their love. For that
night he had possessed her completely. The beginning! Sitting
now on the path, waiting, hoping she would come, and yet, as
he always was, consumed with fear for her, he prayed passionately that there would be no end.

Eliza peered from between the trees, her eyes searching for
Moon. Her heart leaped as she saw the tall figure in the loose
osnaburg pantaloons and the thin cotton shirt. It was getting
late, and she had been half-afraid he would be gone to his
bed. She had not dared, without an excuse, to beg a ride on
one of the field wagons. Besides, there would have been only
a slim chance of catching a ride, for most of the wagons had
been put up for the night. Also, she was running out of excuses. From now on she would walk. Her eyes rested on him
with love, enjoying this moment when he was unaware of
her. Her Moon towered above the other field hands. His
shoulders were broad, his waist narrow, and his hips lean.
Standing there so still, he was like an ebony statue. He did
not have the broad features of some of the other black men.
His nose was thin, the nostrils flaring, and his mouth, although full, was not excessively so. But, in common with the
others, he had the same tightly curling cap of black hair. He
was love and beauty and poetry to her. He was everything
she would ever want or need. At the thought of being without
him, her eyes misted over and her heart began a terrified
beating. Stop it! she cautioned herself. You are not without

him. He is there, waiting for you. This is a time for happiness, not for fear.

Smiling again, she picked up a small stone and tossed it in Moon's direction.

Moon's sharp ears caught the tiny rattle. It was Liza's signal. She was here! He swung around, his eyes searching for her.

Liza laughed softly as he came through the trees. "Moon, I am so sorry to be late."

"You are here. It is all that matters." He took her in his arms and held her close against him.

"Master Tobias has come home," she said against his chest. "He came just as I was about to leave, and I had to stay for a while. He brought with him a white man and a white woman."

"Guests?"

"No. I heard him telling Mindy that they came on the convict ship. When they are well again, the girl is to work in the kitchen with Mindy. The man will become one of the field hands."

Moon, as always, was instantly alert for anything that might endanger Eliza. "What do you mean, when they are well again?" he questioned her sharply. "What is wrong with them?"

Guessing what was in his mind, Eliza raised her head and smiled at him tenderly. "You are always so fearful for me, Moon, and you must not be. They are not suffering from anything infectious. It is just that they are so terribly exhausted. Mindy was quite shocked when she saw their thin, worn appearance. She has vowed to Master Tobias that she will fatten them up." Eliza was silent for a moment. "Then, just as I was getting ready to come away," she continued, "Master Tobias said that I must meet my fellow workers, and of course I had to stay. The man's name is Justin Lawrence. The girl is Caroline Fane."

"Oh." Moon was uninterested in Justin Lawrence and Caroline Fane. He lifted Eliza into his arms, smiling at her. "Shall we go to the cabin?"

She nodded. "But I can't stay too long tonight. It is already so late."

"I won't let you walk alone through the darkness. I will see you almost all the way home."

The fear that he himself had instilled into her leaped up. "No!" Her hand clutched his shirt. "If you are going to insist upon walking with me, I will go now. There is still some daylight left, and I will be perfectly safe." Her hand released its clutch upon his shirt, and she began to stroke his chest coaxingly. "But you don't want me to go now, my darling. Tell me you don't."

He hesitated, frowning at her. "It is wrong to let you walk alone through the darkness."

"But what can happen to me? Please, Moon, let us go to the cabin."

Ben Cranwell smiled unpleasantly as he watched them walk away. Earlier, intrigued by something in Eliza's almost furtive manner, he had followed her on a whim. He had wondered what the little runt might be up to, but he had not expected to find anything like this! His lips pursed in a soundless whistle, and his small blue eyes narrowed. Bedding herself with a nigger, by Christ! He had always thought of Eliza Harris as a plain, skinny, cold piece. When she had first arrived at Montrose, he had considered her, and then rejected the notion of bedding her. He had never liked these thin and ugly females. They had no juice, and he had proved more than once that that type were hardly worth the trouble of a man unbuttoning his breeches. But perhaps he had been wrong about this Eliza wench. Seemingly there was more to her than he had thought. But to do it with a nigger!

Following slowly and cautiously after them, Cranwell felt moral indignation as well as anger. A white girl and a nigger. By Christ, the two of them should be strung up! If she could let a stinking nigger prod her, then she was nothing but a filthy whore! And she must be hard up! Cranwell ran a complacent hand over his smooth brown hair. She was in for a treat. He'd show her what it was like with a white man. He grinned to himself. The dirty little cow didn't know what a treat was in store for her. He'd prod her so good that she'd be begging him for more.

Moon laid Eliza gently down on the pallet. "Shall we talk, my Liza? Or would you like me to love you?"

Her eyes were soft with love for him. He was always so considerate. He had never touched her without first inquiring her feelings in the matter. Sometimes he had wanted her so much that he had trembled with the force of his wanting. But always he would make that gentle query. And he meant it, she knew. His need would be subdued to meet hers. She smiled at him. "Love me, Moon, please."

His startling white smile flashed out. "I will, my honey." He bent down and kissed her mouth. "I adore you, my white bud!"

White bud. He often called her that. She watched him with dreaming eyes as he removed his shirt.

Ben Cranwell watched them through a rent in the old piece of sacking that covered the window. The window was a square without glass, and he could hear as well as see. He looked at the naked, towering black man, and his lip curled in disgust. Filthy, stinking nigger! he thought venomously. Tobias Markham coddled his workers too much. If he hadn't given this one a cabin to himself, he wouldn't be prodding a white girl. He looked more intently at Moon. That heap of dung had got a body on him, all right. But it wouldn't look so good after he'd been broke up. He'd like to flog him himself, and then put a rope about his neck! Seething, Cranwell considered bursting open the door and confronting them. He could just imagine the look on their faces. The impulse died. That nigger was a giant. And if he'd gone so far as to dig it into that little bitch, he might not stop at laying hands on a white man. It was better to wait and watch. He would think about the best time to use his knowledge, and the best and most profitable person to reveal it to.

Cranwell's eyes turned to Eliza. Smiling, she stood naked before the black man, her arms held out. Skinny she might be, Cranwell thought, but damned if she didn't have a lovely pair of tits on her! He eyed them greedily. They were small but well-shaped, and the nipples were so prominent that they stood out like tiny red spears. She was ready, all right!

"Liza!" Moon breathed her name huskily. He came to her and held her close. "My Liza! My little sweet Liza!"

Eliza felt the thrusting urgency of him against her. "Come. darling," she said.

Cranwell sucked in his breath as Eliza lay down on the pallet. The black man began to kiss her body. A moan came from Eliza as his lips touched her breasts and lingered there.

Cranwell felt his own penis throbbing and swelling as the black man entered her. In a frenzy of excitement, he put a clutching hand over it. His eyes glittering, he watched the black man driving faster and faster. He saw the girl's legs twine and cling, and he heard her broken cries of ecstasy. And then suddenly it was over. With a shuddering sigh, the black giant collapsed against her.

Christ Almighty! Sweat rolled down Cranwell's forehead and dripped into his eyes. His need to relieve himself was a grinding pain. He would have her tonight!

Chapter 17

Caroline Fane awakened with a start. She lay very still in the hard bed, her confused mind unable for the moment to recall where she was. Then it came back to her. She was at Montrose, in the room she was to share with the other white servant, Eliza Harris.

Caroline smiled. She felt warm and sleepy and content. For the first time in a long while she was comfortable, her belly replete with Mindy's good cooking. It would not take her long to recover her strength, she thought with a surge of optimism. Tobias Markham had said that she must rest for as long as she desired. But she could not take his words seriously. He was very kind. But after all, she was to be a servant in his house. She could not very well lie around like a fine lady, and certainly she had no desire to do so.

Caroline turned over on her back and stared at the dark square of window. A pale sliver of moon rode high in the sky. The stars were like diamonds scattered across black velvet. Everything seemed bigger here in the New World. The stars, the birds, the trees. She felt dwarfed by the massive grandeur all about her. She found it frightening, and yet at the same time it exulted her. The very air, the strong, wine-sweet air, seemed to throb and tingle with challenge. There was something wild and reckless in her that longed to meet that challenge. Brave New World! When they were free, she and Justin would surely be a part of all this exciting magnificence. They were both fighters. What could they not achieve together! She had the sudden sure feeling that their destiny lay here, in the New World. But what that destiny was to be, only the years could show them.

Caroline turned over on her side again, her thoughts going to Justin. He had been very quiet when the wagon had driven along the curving dusty road that had brought them finally to

Montrose. He had not exclaimed, as she had, or shown any
interest in the big plantation house with its rearing white-plas-
tered walls and its cypress-shingled roof. Its many windows
had glistened in the fading sunlight. Trees heavily burdened
with white blossoms grew on either side of the house. Flowers
bloomed in long, narrow beds, and, starting from the entrance, bordered the house in beauty. Behind the house was a
grouping of smaller buildings. The stables, and some well-
built wooden huts. The huts, Tobias Markham had explained,
housed many of the household servants. The dairy was there
too, and an outdoor kitchen, where Mindy, the cook, did her
baking in the worst heat of the summer months.

 Frowning, Caroline pondered on Justin's strange mood. His
quietness had continued. And in spite of the good meal a
beaming and solicitous Mindy had placed before them, he ate
little. His eyes seemed always to be upon Tobias Markham.

 Markham, instead of taking his leave, had lingered in the
kitchen, to Mindy's obvious delight. When he had turned to
Caroline, his smile had been warm and friendly. "There is no
hurry to begin your duties, Caroline," he said. "Remember
that. You must rest all you can, and build up your strength
with Mindy's nourishing food. You are already looking much
better. And I know that I can rely upon Mindy to complete
the cure."

 "You sure can, Master Toby," Mindy put in, "Ah happy to
do it."

 Markham glanced at Justin. "That means both of you,
mind." His eyes returned to Caroline. "When you are well
enough, you might enjoy seeing some of the scenery. I have
horses in my stables that do little more than eat their heads
off. They are at your disposal."

 Taken aback by this amazing and surely most unusual generosity of master to servant, she had stammered out her
thanks.

 "No, don't thank me, Caroline." Markham had placed his
hand on her shoulder and squeezed gently. "You will enjoy it,
I know."

 Justin had been almost rude. He said curtly, "It is very
generous of you, Mr. Markham. But you must not be too
good to us, or you will spoil us as servants. You have remembered that we are servants, sir?"

 Justin had laid emphasis on his last remark, and Tobias

Markham had flushed dully. He said coldly, "I would not wish you to misunderstand, Lawrence. My only object was to make up to you a little for all you had been through."

Justin smiled at him, a smile that did not reach his eyes. He looked at Markham's hand, still resting on Caroline's shoulder. "I understand you entirely, Mr. Markham. I assure you that I do."

As though something had stung him, Markham had snatched his hand away. "I see. Well, my offer is open, if you care to avail yourselves of it." He walked stiffly over to the door. "Good night to you both. I hope you sleep well." The door closed behind him.

She had been angered by Justin's hostile attitude. "What is the matter with you, Justin? What possessed you to speak to him like that?"

He had looked at her, a smoldering anger in his eyes. "I ask you that same question, Carrie. What is the matter with you?"

"I don't know what you mean. Mr. Markham was only trying to be considerate. There was no need for you to be so rude."

"Rude? Damn you for a fool, Carrie! Do you tell me you are really so blind as to his intentions?"

"His intentions? I don't understand you."

"Don't want to understand, is more like it! Are you to be bought and sold so easily, Carrie? Do your creature comforts mean so much to you?"

"Don't talk to me like that!"

"If it will knock some sense into that wooden head of yours, I'll talk to you any damn way I please! Think for a moment. Would you offer to supply your servants with horses and various other comforts?"

"No. But this is a different matter. You heard what Mr. Markham said. He wants to make up to us a little."

"Bah! We are servants, Carrie, not guests." He met her eyes. "No, not servants," he burst out bitterly. "Slaves! That bastard could sell us tomorrow, if he had a mind!"

"Don't call him that. He has shown us only kindness."

Justin's lip curled. "But scarcely disinterested kindness." He shrugged. "Suit yourself, Carrie. If you have no objection to being Markham's bedmate, then it is scarcely my place to interfere."

"You are mad! How dare you say that to me?"

All Justin's smoldering anger and bitter resentment had been in his voice when he answered her. "If you are reconciled to slavery, Carrie, I am not. I do not seek kindness. I seek freedom! I am a man, not a bloody puppy dog to be whistled to heel and told to do this and do that!" He banged his clenched fist on the table. "For a time I might be confined by circumstances, but not for long. As for you, think over what I have said. Markham's intentions toward you are clear enough to me. And unless you have entirely lost your wits, they should be to you. Don't forget for a moment that it is in his power to order you to his bed. If you refuse, you can be punished. Never forget for a moment that you are a slave!"

They had continued to shout at each other, and Caroline wondered now where they had found the energy. Both of them had entirely forgotten Mindy's presence. They were startled when she came waddling toward them, her eyes flashing angrily.

"Now, you look here, boy." Mindy glared at Justin. "Ah ain't standing for that kind of talk 'bout Master Toby. He a good man, you hear me? If he say he want to be kind, then that all he want. You got a nasty mind, that what you got!"

"This is ridiculous!" Justin said stiffly.

"Ain't nothing ridiculous 'bout it. Ah say you got a nasty mind, and that what ah mean. What's more, you ain't got no charity in you heart. What you know 'bout Master Toby? What you know 'bout the way he think and feel?"

"Now listen to me—"

"Ah ain't listening to you! If there one thing ah cain't stand, it a smart-talking mouth." Mindy lifted her hand and cuffed Justin's head.

Justin stared at her with dropped jaw. Mindy's action had reduced him to the level of a rude little boy. Caroline, who knew him so well, saw the glint of laughter appear in his eyes. The humor of the situation had struck him, dissipating for the moment his anger and bitterness. It was the old Rogue Lawrence, whom she had so yearned to hear again, who replied now to the irate Mindy, "Think shame of yourself, madam, you have brutally struck a sick man, and one, moreover, who is incapable of defending himself."

The underlying laughter in his voice seemed to elude Mindy. The change in her was startling. Her glare faded at once. "If you feeling poorly, boy," she said in a distressed voice, "then ah right sorry to be losing mah temper like ah done."

With the audacity that had characterized him in the past, Justin had immediately taken advantage of the situation. Leaning his head against Mindy's big comfortable breast, he had replied in a weary voice, "You must not be concerned, madam. As soon as my head stops reeling from the force of your blow, I daresay I shall be quite all right. I would not want you to feel guilty. I forgive you."

He should have been an actor, Caroline thought. She had no doubt that his anger would return, but for the moment he was enjoying himself. Watching Mindy's concerned face, she was forced to smother a laugh. The appeal that Justin had always had for women was working. Mindy's fat, dimpled hand pressed his head protectively against her breast. "Ah sorry ah hit you, boy," she said gently. "But that ain't the only reason why you is feeling poorly. It 'cause you ain't ate no more'n a smidgen. But don't you worry none, ol' Mindy's going to take right smart care of you." She looked up and met Caroline's smiling eyes. "What for you smirking, wench?" she demanded. "Here, you just hold this boy's head and soothe it. Ah'll fetch him some of mah special tonic."

She walked quickly away. Caroline rose from her chair and bent over him. "Fraud!" she said softly. "You should be ashamed to take advantage of that nice woman."

Justin smiled and touched her hand. Caroline knew that this was a mute apology on his part, at least for the moment. The matter had not been forgotten. "I only take advantage of those I like," he replied. "And I like her."

"I'll remember that." She touched his smiling face with caressing fingertips. Her love for him showed in her eyes. His thin face had harsh lines of suffering in it that had not been there before, and his dark hair was threaded with gray, but the brilliant smile was the same. Rogue Lawrence's smile. She pressed her cheek to his for a brief moment.

Carrying a stone jar and a big spoon, Mindy hastened back to Justin's side. Opening the jar, she thrust the spoon into it and ladled out a thick sticky black mixture. "Ah soon have you right," she crooned. "This mah special tonic for ailing folk, and it do you all the good in the world. Open up your mouth, boy."

"No!" Justin started back and looked at the mixture with horror. "I don't need it. I am feeling much better."

"No, you ain't," Mindy said firmly.

"I am."

"You hush your mouth. It 'pears to me, boy, that you got better right quick."

"Yes," Justin said hastily, his wary eyes on the spoon. "It comes and goes, you see."

"Ah don't see nothing like that. It don't make sense." The spoon advanced toward his mouth. "You open up, boy."

Resignedly, Justin opened his mouth, and Mindy promptly jammed the spoon inside. "You swallow down all of mah tonic. That right. Don't it taste good?"

Justin's throat moved as the mixture went down. His eyes widened, and an appalled expression crossed his face. Caroline smiled. "Does it taste good, Justin?" she inquired sweetly.

"Of course it good, wench," Mindy said indignantly. "It make rich blood." She stroked Justin's hair with a heavy hand. "You tell her, boy. It good, ain't it?"

Shuddering, Justin removed the empty spoon from his mouth and placed it on the table. For a moment he seemed to be unable to find his voice. Then, his eyes watering profusely, he gasped out, "If you love me, Mindy, never do that to me again!"

Caroline saw the glint in Mindy's eyes, and she knew that the woman had not been deceived. Mindy's huge bulk shook with her chuckling. "That teach you a lesson, boy. That teach you to mind you manners. Mindy ain't no fool. But still, for all ah seen through you, ah done it for the sake of you health. Mah tonic good for folks."

Still shuddering, Justin wiped his watering eyes. "It occurs to me, Mindy, that you have a heart of stone."

Mindy beamed at him. "You a rogue, that what you are. But ah like you, boy."

Caroline's eyes met Justin's. "Welcome home, Rogue Lawrence," she said softly.

Mindy looked from one to the other, puzzled by the sudden clouding of Justin Lawrence's face. The laughter was gone from his eyes, and it was as if the mention of that name had brought bad memories back to him. She asked no questions, however. Shortly after that, she had bustled them off to their rooms. Caroline, Mindy said, was to sleep in Eliza Harris' room. And the Lawrence boy, as she dubbed Justin, was to share a room with Jimmy, a young black man who waited on table.

Caroline stretched luxuriously in the bed. She felt wide-awake now. Her mind began to stray over the events of the day, and as she thought, uneasiness tightened her muscles. She was suddenly quite sure that Justin was right about Mr. Markham. Markham had proved that he could be kindhearted, but he was nonetheless a hardheaded businessman. Some of his remarks and certain of his attitudes on the long and wearying journey to Montrose had clearly shown this. He was not a man who gave something away without expecting something in return. Why, then, did he tend to treat Justin and herself more like guests than servants? His horses were at their disposal! Why, it was ridiculous! Then what was behind his easiness and affability? Did he have plans for her other than her domestic duties? Since he knew how she felt about Justin, for she had made no attempt to hide her feelings, was his easy attitude to him merely the bait to catch her off guard?

Caroline's eyes opened wide at this last thought. But if that were so, why? Markham's eyes must see beyond her haggard appearance, for there was certainly little about her now to inspire passion in a man. She was looking better than she had, that much was true. On the long journey to Montrose they had been treated with consideration and kindness. Whatever Markham's reasons, they had been well fed, and they had been allowed to rest most of the time. Her figure was not quite so gaunt, the yellowing of her skin had faded, and with the fading a little of its former tone had returned. Her appearance had been further improved by frequent bathings in the bathhouses encountered on the way. Her hair, freed from lice, was soft and bright again, but there was no denying that she still looked haggard and plain.

Caroline's thoughts, as they always did sooner or later, turned to Justin. He was still painfully thin, but, unlike herself, he had picked up amazingly. Even in this short span of time, he was already beginning to look like his handsome self. When he had bantered with Mindy, he had even sounded like his old self. But she did not delude herself. She knew that Rogue Lawrence belonged to the past. Justin, with his haunted eyes, was a driven man. Paul's tragic and unnecessary death was a wound that would never heal. Tonight, for a few poignant moments, she had been given an aching glimpse of the charming, smiling Rogue Lawrence. And that was all it would be, just fleeting glimpses. But she loved him! Not for what he had been, but for what he was now. For what he might be in the future.

What of herself and Justin? On the journey to Montrose, he had been tender, and he had taken as much care of her as he was able. But for all that, no further words of love had been spoken. Did he love her? Would she ever be certain? On board the *Merryventure* they had both been so worn and exhausted, so nearly at the end of their endurance, and it might be that Justin's confession of love had been prompted by pity. Caroline drew in a sharp breath. There was such pain in that thought.

She moved restlessly in the bed. Could it be that he had determined not to speak to her again of love until they were both free, until he could be certain that they had a future to look forward to? She smiled, vaguely comforted. But how would Justin get on at Montrose? He, who was so fiercely proud and independent? Servitude and Justin Lawrence. It was unthinkable! The two simply did not go together. Sooner or later the old restlessness would overtake him, and one day she would awaken to find him gone. This New World, this America, with all its exciting possibilities, with the lands that were still to be conquered, with the savage elements to be fought, would beckon to him. Rebellion against being bound would prevail. He would inevitably attempt to escape. If his attempts were thwarted, he would make a fight for his freedom. She knew him, she knew how he thought. And his fight would go on until he was either free or dead.

Caroline's hands clenched at this last thought. Hastily she forced her thoughts away from that grim possibility. She thought instead of Tobias Markham. Markham, who had said, "On Montrose, no one is a slave. They are simply workers." But for all his words, one could not disguise the fact that they were slaves. Were they to run away from Montrose, the law governing slaves would punish them. Their white skin would not protect them. Contracts of their servitude to Tobias Markham had been signed, and those contracts were in his possession. He could enforce the terms laid out in them.

As runaways, they could be brought back in chains. They could be flogged. The term of their servitude lengthened. She liked Markham, and she believed that Justin, despite the hostility he had displayed, liked him too. But Markham, she had the certain feeling, could and would be harsh. She believed that he was a man who would hold on firmly to what he thought of as rightfully his. And the law would be on his side, it would uphold his claim, for in the eyes of the law, she and Justin belonged to Tobias Markham.

Caroline turned over again, and her eyes were caught by the empty bed next to her own. She had no idea of the time, but it must be quite late. Where was Eliza Harris? Eliza, of course, was an indentured servant. She was not a convict like herself. But were the rules so relaxed for indentured servants that they could stay out until any hour they pleased? She did not think it could be so. There must be a specified time when they should be in their beds. Why was Eliza not in hers? Where could she be?

For a while Caroline debated on what she should do. Should she awaken Mindy and mention the girl's absence? But then, if she did, Eliza might get into trouble. She did not want to be the cause of that. Uncertain, troubled, Caroline finally fell into a light, restless sleep.

Shivering in the cool night air, Eliza Harris glanced nervously about her. If it had not been that her desire to see Moon was greater than her fear, she would not be here now, walking alone through the darkness. The night had always terrified her. When she was smaller, she had believed that the darkness was full of ghosts and goblins, and that if she were not very careful, they would spring upon her and destroy her.

Frowning, impatient with herself, Eliza hastened on. She was not much different now. She was still afraid. It was time she grew up. Moon loved her, and she loved him. And Moon's love had turned her from child to woman. Afraid of the dark? She was a fool!

Eliza slowed as she rounded the last bend. Her legs felt heavy and tired, and hurrying had given her a pain in her side. It was not much farther now. She had only to go through that small grove of trees, then down the small incline, and she would be on level ground, in sight of the house. Lengthening her stride, she walked on.

Ben Cranwell's alert ears caught the rustle of leaves and the small, sharp report of a snapped twig. Grinning, he pushed himself away from the tree against which he had been leaning. The Harris bitch was coming. Was she in for a surprise! His face flushed hotly with a mingling of anger and indignation. Nigger's whore! The taunting words ran through his head. He'd call her that, because that's what she was. She had something coming to her, did that one!

Eliza stopped short, her heart palpitating with terror, as a dark form suddenly detached itself from a tree. Then, as it lunged toward her, she screamed.

"Shut up!" a voice snarled. A hard hand clapped itself across her mouth. "Ain't no need for that bellowing. It's me. Ben Cranwell."

Cranwell! Eliza's eyes dilated. She hated him! She hated his leering smile and his little cunning eyes. He pressed closer against her. She could feel the heat from him, an animal heat, she thought. Her sensitive nostrils caught the strong odor from his unwashed body. Sickened, she began to struggle. Instantly his hand moved upward, covering her nose as well as her mouth, cutting off her air.

"If I take me hand away, wench," Cranwell hissed, "you going ter scream?"

Eliza's thoughts whirled rapidly. Maybe she could run for it. Once in sight of the house, then she could start screaming. She would be punished for being out so late, but she didn't care. She knew what he was going to do to her, and she could not bear it! This was not the first time he had lain in wait for a girl. She had heard all the stories about him. Yet no one so far had told on him, because they were afraid. If he touched her, she would tell. She would scream the truth aloud. This time he would be caught and punished. But first she had to get away from him.

"You deaf?" Cranwell jostled her with his body. "I asked if you're going ter scream?"

She shook her head.

"You sure 'bout that?"

Her head shook again.

"You try screaming, and you'll get a clump on the head what'll set your ears ringing for months."

Eliza was about to nod to show that she had understood, when Cranwell's next words froze her. "I seen you up there n that cabin, you bleedin' nigger's whore! Aye, I seen everything what you and that stinking nigger done." He felt the slump of her body against his, and he cautiously removed his hand. That had taken the fight out of her. "Don't like hearing that, eh? What if I tell about you and him?"

Eliza did not move. She could not. "Please!" she said in a strangled voice. "Please!"

Cranwell laughed. "That's scared you, ain't it, you dirty little bitch."

She turned her head and looked at him. Her mouth moved, but no words came. Cranwell pushed his body forward in an obscene attitude, his finger pointing downward. "If you don't want me to say nothing 'bout you and the nigger, you'd just better do as I say." His hand struck her shoulder. "Get them clothes off."

"Not that!" she whispered. "I'll . . . I'll do anything you say, but not that!"

He was outraged. "A decent white man ain't good enough for you, eh?" His lifted hand slapped her face, rocking her head and bringing from her a whimper of pain. "Rather have a nigger, would you?" Cranwell slapped her again. "Get them clothes off, or by Jesus I'll tear 'em off you!"

She did not hear him. Sobbing, she sank to her knees and buried her face in her hands. What was she to do? She rocked backward and forward in her anguish. Cranwell would tell about her and Moon. She couldn't let him do that. Her hands dropped, and she lifted an imploring face to him. "Don't tell, please! They will take Moon away. They will hurt him!" Her voice rising hysterically, she grasped at his legs. "Don't tell, don't tell!"

Cranwell kicked her away, sending her sprawling backward. Crouching down beside her, he hit her again. "That's for bellowing so loud. Sounds carry at night. Aye, they'll hurt the nigger. But they'll do more'n hurt him, Liza. They'll kill him."

Liza? He had called her Liza! Moon's name for her. It sounded profane on Cranwell's tongue.

"I told you to take them clothes off. I meant what I said." Cranwell's voice held a snarling note. "Reckon I got ter do it for you." His hands plucked at her clothing. She heard a tearing sound, and still she could not move. She could only lie there, feeling dead and hopeless inside. He pushed at her,

handling her roughly, pulling and ripping until at last she
lay naked before him.

The wind was cold against her skin. If she could only die
now, this moment, before ever he could touch her! But she
would not die, and she would be forced to accept this animal
inside her.

Cranwell flung himself upon her. His tongue licked at her
face, flicked into her ear. "Ain't that nice?" he panted.
"Ain't it, wench? Tell old Ben it's nice."

"Oh, don't! Please let me go!" She pushed at him with
feeble hands.

"You want me ter tell?"

The fight went out of her. She shook her head despairingly.
"I'll do anything you say, if only you will not t-tell!"

"Maybe I won't," he grunted. "Just maybe." He began to
maul her again. His teeth bit at her breasts, bringing a moan
of pain from her. The sound seemed to excite him. He moved
quickly, his hands forcing her legs apart, and then he was inside her.

She bit back her screams as fiery pain shot through her.
She could feel something warm and wet against her legs.
Blood! He had torn something inside her. He continued to
thrust and force himself upward. He began to move faster,
faster, his body pounding against her own, and she could feel
the warm wet trickle increasing. He was tearing her apart. He
was killing her!

Suddenly it was over. He withdrew. His panting body
rested heavily against her. She could feel the racing of his
heart. He began to chuckle. "Had quite a surprise, eh,
wench? I ain't too big a man, but I'm big down there, ain't
I?" When she did not answer, he bit her ear. "Ain't I?"

"Yes," she managed to whisper.

Still chuckling, Cranwell raised himself. "You said you'd
do anything what I want. That right?"

She nodded. Cranwell was silent for a moment; then he
said in a roughened voice, "You'll come whenever I'm in the
mood for a bit of fun and prodding?"

To be forced to come to him whenever he beckoned! She
would go mad! But she had to do it. It was for Moon, her
darling! She must keep telling herself that. It was for Moon!
"Yes," she whispered.

His hands touched her breasts and squeezed hard. "You ain't going ter try backing out?"

"No, no!"

He rose to his feet and pulled on his shirt and breeches. "That's good. 'Cause it'll be too bad for you and that nigger if you do." He squatted down beside her again. "How'd you like doing it with a white man?"

She did not answer him. His hand lashed across her cheek. "When I speaks, you answer, hear? Now, then, you bleedin' filthy whore, I asked you how you liked doing it with a white man?"

"It . . . it w-was all right."

"All right!" His fingers pinched hard at her nipples. "Say it was better than with the nigger! Say it, bitch!"

"Yes." Her voice was barely audible.

"Yes, what?" His fingers tightened, twisting viciously at her nipples, making her body arch with the pain. "Yes!" she gasped. "Yes, it . . . it was b-better."

"I should just think so," Cranwell said triumphantly. "Doing it with a nigger is the same as doing it with a horse or a bull. Niggers is animals, ain't they?" He saw the hatred in her eyes. "You don't like me saying that, eh?" He crushed her breasts, laughing as she gave a stifled scream of pain. "That's right. You know better'n to make a noise. You like me, don't you, wench? Say you like me!"

She nodded. Cranwell let his hands hover over her breasts, his fingers making pinching motions. "I don't want no nod. I want to hear you say it. You like me, don't you?"

Tears blinded her eyes. "Yes. I l-like you."

Cranwell got to his feet. "You just remember that you got to come to me whenever I say, and you'll be all right. Don't tell no one 'bout this, hear?"

She nodded. Cranwell squinted down at her. In the shaft of moonlight that came through the trees, he saw the dark stain on her legs. "Bleeding, eh?" He grinned at her. "It your time?"

"N-no."

"Like I told you, I seen you with the nigger, so don't you go trying ter fool me that you're a virgin. If it ain't your time, how come you're bleeding?"

Her mouth trembled. "It . . . it is because you h-hurt me."

"Did, did I?" Cranwell got down on his knees and dabbed

a finger in the blood. "Reckon that shows I'm more powerful than the nigger, don't it?" He stared hard at the blood, and again he touched it with his finger. "Hurt you that much, eh?"

Eliza saw a tremor go through his body. She felt sick as the moonlight showed her the bright glitter of his eyes. Her pain was exciting him! What manner of man was he who could be excited by another's pain? His shuddering increased. She cringed as he began to unbutton his breeches with violently shaking fingers. "Open up your legs, wench," he said in a thick voice. His frenzy overcoming him, he did not wait for her to obey him. He seized her legs and wrenched them apart. Moaning like a man in torment, he plunged into her.

Pain! Pain! It was almost more than she could endure. Her outflung hands tensed, her fingers dug themselves deeply into the soft earth. She must not scream, must not! He would tell, and then Moon would die. She began to pray silently. Help me! Oh, God, help me. Let it be over soon, please!

Cranwell was breathing in gasps when he withdrew. "I'll need you tomorrow night," he said in the same thick voice. "'Bout this same time." He arranged his clothing and then turned away.

"I can't!" Eliza cried out desperately. "I can't be out late every night. I'll be missed."

"I can always find a good excuse for being out of my bed. You do the same." He looked at her threateningly. "You be here!"

For a long time after he had left her, Eliza could not move. When she finally managed to get to her feet, it seemed to her inflamed imagination to take her hours to dress. Her feet dragging, she stumbled in the direction of the house. Once or twice she fell. Struggling to her feet again, she went doggedly on. She wondered what she would do if Mindy, contrary to her usual custom, had fastened the kitchen window. Mindy usually left the window open. "Ah likes to air out mah kitchen," she was always saying.

The kitchen window was open. With a little sob of relief, Eliza hoisted herself up. The pain between her legs flared up so violently that for a moment she thought she was going to faint. She sat very still on the wide sill, waiting for her head to stop whirling. If only she did not have to move again! It was desperation, fear for Moon, that forced her onward. Gasping, crying, she crawled over the sill and jumped down into the room.

Creeping silently up the back stairs, she knew that she could never tell Moon about Cranwell's assault. Moon's head would not rule him. Disregarding danger, he would go after Cranwell. He would kill him! So she would never tell him, never! She would lie. She would make up excuses for this pain Cranwell had put into her, anything but the truth. Moon's safety was the only thing that mattered to her. But it might be that the pain would pass, she thought hopefully. If it did, she would not have to make excuses to Moon for rejecting his lovemaking.

The opening of the door awakened Caroline. The door closed again, shutting off the faint gleam of light from the corridor. Something overturned with a loud crash. Caroline heard the sound of quiet but desperate sobbing as the person who had entered went blundering clumsily across the room.

Caroline sat up in the bed. "Eliza? Is that you?"

With a stifled scream, Eliza swung around. "Oh! I . . . I had forgotten that you were to share the room."

Caroline flung back the covers and got out of bed. "What is it, Eliza?" She reached the shadowy figure. "Tell me what has happened," she said, gently touching the girl's shoulder.

Eliza drew back with a sharp intake of breath. "Nothing," she muttered. She flung herself down on the bed. "Go back to bed. I'm all right."

"But why are you crying? Has someone hurt you?"

"No! I have told you that nothing is wrong."

Caroline heard the note of hysteria in Eliza's voice. Hesitantly, she moved over to her own bed. Getting in, she drew the bedclothes over her. "If there is anything you want to talk about, Eliza," she ventured, "I am ready to listen."

"There is nothing."

"You are sure that I can't be of some help?"

"No! No one can help me."

Uneasily, Caroline lay down again. She could not very well continue to insist when the girl obviously wished to be left alone. But there was a note in Eliza's voice that worried her. She would stay awake for a while, just in case she should be needed.

Her swollen eyes staring unseeingly at a patch of moonlight on the floor, Eliza lay there stiffly. Cranwell—that man with his smelly, sweaty body! Cranwell, after the wonder and magic of Moon! She pressed her hand between her legs, trying to still the pain of his assault. The pain was bad, and she could still feel the warm trickle of her blood. She could not tell Moon, she told herself again. He would kill Cranwell. She shuddered as she pictured Moon's fate if he should kill a white man. A sense of such overwhelming despair swept over her that for a moment her eyes were blinded and she had difficulty in breathing. There would be no end to Cranwell's demands. If she did not go to him each time he beckoned, he would expose her love affair with Moon. It was no idle threat on his part. He would do it.

For a long time Eliza lay there with her bitter, sorrowing thoughts. She must get up; she could not just continue to lie here. She must wash, cleanse herself of Cranwell's touch. Slowly, carefully, she turned her head and listened to Caroline Fane's soft breathing. Had she fallen asleep? Was it safe to move? With some difficulty, Eliza raised herself. "Caroline," she said softly, "are you awake?"

Caroline made no reply. Instinct told her that Eliza was hoping that she slept.

Caroline was asleep, thank God! Eliza crawled from the bed and began to remove her garments. Naked, she went over to the washstand. She held her breath in alarm at the faint clink the china made as she removed the full jug from the basin.

Through half-closed eyes Caroline watched as Eliza set about the task of washing herself. Somehow the girl's actions, so slow, so difficult, as if each movement pained her, reminded her of the time when she had crept from Thomas Fane's bed and had done just as Eliza was doing now. The memory brought with it a stab of pain. She had been trying to wash herself clean of Thomas' touch and his stale old odor. Was that what Eliza was doing? Was she trying to erase the memory of some brutal violation?

Long after Eliza had crept shivering to her bed, Caroline remained awake. So much had happened to her since Thomas' murder and the horror that murder had set in motion. But out of horror, there had come one bright and shining thing. She had found Justin. She forgot Eliza. "Please love me, Justin!" she whispered.

Low though the whisper was, Eliza heard. Justin. Eliza repeated the name silently. Justin Lawrence, of course. The man with the intensely dark eyes and the smile of startling brilliance, to whom Master Tobias had introduced her. She had liked him.

Eliza felt a touch of sympathy for Caroline, but it quickly died as she thought over her own predicament. They were in love, she and Moon, but they could not be together because his skin was black. Her hands clenched on the coverlet. It wasn't fair! No one had the right to make rules or laws that forbade you to love where you willed.

Bitterness and pain brought hot tears to Eliza's eyes. Moon had told her that all white men were not the same. He had said that there were many who were good and kind and compassionate. But to Eliza, in her despair, all white men had one collective head, bigotry and intolerance. She did not want to be white. She wanted to be black, like Moon. She wanted to love and to be loved. The tears were still sliding down her cheeks when sleep finally overcame her.

Chapter 18

Shivering in the chill wind that, blowing up unexpectedly, had scattered the balmy days, Caroline Fane stood at the open kitchen door and watched the bustle of activity going on in the yard. A ginger-haired stable hand was backing two sturdy chestnut horses into the shafts and deftly hitching them to Tobias Markham's light farm wagon.

Watching, Caroline frowned. For some reason that she could not define, it made her uneasy to know that Tobias Markham was going away. A matter of business had come up, Mindy had told her, which would require him to sign several papers. He would be gone for a few days. It annoyed him to be forced to leave at this particular time, for today saw the start of the annual sowing of the tobacco seeds. First the seeds were to be placed in their prepared beds of special mold. After that came the backbreaking task of spading up the fields and laying them out in even furrows. The earth must be continually inspected and kept free of weeds and encroaching wild plants. After a specific time had passed to allow the seedlings to grow, the earth would then be ready to receive the growing and carefully nutured seedlings.

Tobacco! Caroline thought. Nobody seemed to think of anything else. Nobody, that was, except Justin. Justin's thoughts were occupied continually with plans of escape. It was as she had known it would be with him. He had never before had to serve in a humble position, and his pride was in continual revolt. He was bitter and unhappy, and continually watching for a chance to escape. She had the feeling that one day, ignoring the dangers, he would turn his back on Montrose and walk away. It would be like Justin to do that. He would have only one objective in view, to be free. The search parties that would inevitably be sent after him would not worry him at all. Once he walked beyond the boundaries of Montrose, he would trust in his luck, and he would travel fast and far.

Caroline clenched her teeth. To be with Justin, she was prepared to face any danger. But would he take her with him? That was the big question that exercised her mind. Did he love her enough?

She sighed. In the four months they had been at Montrose, she had seen little of Justin. Had it not been that she had taken over Eliza Harris' job of delivering the food to the field hands, she would have seen even less of him. Justin, working side by side with Moon, the big black man with the friendly smile and the soft, unhappy eyes, had little to say to her. He seemed to have drawn into himself, and she sensed that thoughts of escape were the only reality to him. But he must not go without her. They belonged together. If he left, she would somehow contrive to follow him.

Behind Caroline, Mindy's voice rose in an outraged shriek. "What you doing here, boy?"

Caroline swung around quickly as Justin's cool, amused voice answered her. "Aren't you going to say you're glad to see me, Mindy?"

"No, ah ain't. You get yourself in bad trouble one o' these days."

Caroline stared at him. He was in his sweat-stained clothes, his black hair uncombed and falling untidily over his forehead. He had obviously just come straight from the fields. It wasn't like him to come to the main house in work clothes. "Justin!" she ran toward him. "Is something wrong?"

Justin shrugged. Ignoring Mindy's fierce frown, he seated himself at the kitchen table. "Is nobody going to say they are glad to see me?" he said in a plaintive voice.

Mindy saw the laughter in his eyes. "You a rogue, that what you are," she said grimly. " 'Nother thing. You come into mah kitchen by the other door, and that mean that you come into the house by the front way. Why you do that?"

"Why not? There was no one about. And I am not accustomed to using the back entrance."

"Well, ah never did!"

Caroline felt excitement stir. Justin looked more alive than she had seen him for some time. Had he made a plan to escape? Had he come to tell her about it? Her hands trembled as she pulled up a chair and sat down beside him. "Justin."

She placed her hand on his. "You are here for some reason. What is it? Did Putnam send you with a message?"

"Putnam did not send me." Ignoring Mindy's snort, Justin lifted Caroline's hand. Turning it over, he pressed a kiss on her palm. "Putnam couldn't very well send me. He is absent from the fields, you see."

"And so you just walked off?"

His dark brows quirking with amusement, Justin released her hand. "Correct, Carrie. I just walked off."

"Justin! You must go back at once. Mr. Markham has not yet left. What if he should see you?"

"Calm yourself, Carrie. I will take my chances on his seeing me."

"Oh, you will, will you?" Mindy came nearer to the table. "It ain't for the likes o' you to just up and leave that field. Master Toby, he won't like it nohow. How you going to 'splain to him if he catches you?"

Unperturbed, Justin leaned back against the chair. "I have no idea."

Mindy sternly suppressed a smile. "Now, then, ah been hearing 'bout you. You a troublemaker. Mr. Putnam, he tell Master Toby so. Master Toby, he real put out when he hears what that Putnam say, and ah don't blame him none."

"You don't, eh?" Before Mindy could move away, Justin's arms went around her waist. "Tell me you love me," he said, hugging her close.

"You stop that, boy. Ah ain't going to tell you no such thing. Leave me go. What you want here anyhow?"

Smiling, Justin released her. "A few moments alone with Carrie."

Mindy hesitated. "If ah let you talk to Caroline, then you go?"

"Then I will go."

"Ah don't like it. Master Toby might come in." Mindy's eyes went to the larder door. "Get yourself in that larder and take Caroline with you. Don't you be making no noise, now, or ah get into trouble."

"Not a sound, Mindy, love." Rising quickly to his feet, Justin planted a kiss on Mindy's cheek. Laughing, ignoring her protest, he dragged Caroline to the larder door.

Mindy's hand tightened on the handle of the carving knife she was holding as the larder door closed behind them. It would not do for Master Toby to see Justin Lawrence, especially not when he was shut away with Caroline. Master Toby had said nothing to her, but she knew that he was taken with Caroline. Mindy's eyes went to the larder door. Who would have thought that the gaunt Caroline Fane would turn into such a little beauty? Poor Master Toby! If only there was something she could do to help him!

In the cool dimness of the larder, Justin took Caroline in his arms and held her very tightly. "Are you pleased to see me, love?"

"What a question!" She touched his tumbled hair and smoothed it back from his forehead. "I don't live until I see you."

"Or I you."

She strained back against his arms. "Is that true? Do you really love me?"

It seemed to her that he hesitated. "I have said so, have I not?"

"Yes, you have said so." She could not help the tinge of bitterness that crept into her voice. "But how can I believe it? You are never tender to me. You speak no word of love, and when I do see you, you almost ignore me."

He frowned impatiently. "Come, Carrie, you must know that I have much on my mind. A fine position we are in to speak of love, are we not? Once we are free, I will very quickly let you know how I feel." He hesitated. "I ask you to trust me, Carrie. To be sure of me."

"Sure of Rogue Lawrence? What woman could truthfully say that?"

"This woman can say it." He bent his head, and his lips fastened hungrily on hers.

Even when he released her, she still clung to him. It was as though she could not get enough of the feel of him. Her hand touched his hair, his face. "Justin," she said at last, "have you thought of a plan yet? I want to get away from here. I want to be with you, to start really living!"

He seemed to withdraw from her. "I am turning over several plans in my mind."

"And am I included in those plans?"

"Always, Carrie. But there is just one thing. It may not be wise for both of us to run at the same time. I think—"

"No!" She would not let him finish. She was afraid to hear

what he had to say. With Justin alone in that wilderness, with adventure beckoning, he would be lost to her. "I won't let you go without me. I won't!"

"Damn, Carrie! Haven't I asked you to trust me? I will do nothing without letting you know about it."

His words did not comfort her. They implied that if he thought it best, he would go off without her. She said no more. She would make her own plans. He would not get far before he found her beside him.

Justin kissed her again. "I came here for two reasons, Carrie. To see you, and also to seek Eliza."

"Eliza? Why?"

"I have a message for her."

"You have?" She looked at him suspiciously. "A message from whom?"

He touched her nose with a teasing finger. "None of your business."

Caroline thought of the way Eliza cried in the night, of her cough and her perpetual look of pain, and she found herself telling Justin of her anxiety on the girl's behalf.

Justin listened without comment, but she wondered at the intent look in his eyes. All he said at the end, however, was, "If you see Eliza, Carrie, tell her that he will be waiting for her in the usual place. Same time."

"He? Who, Justin? Who will be waiting?"

"Never mind. Just tell her."

She knew from the set of his lips that he would say no more. He was shielding somebody. Who? Obliged to swallow her curiosity, she said quietly, "I will tell her."

"Good. Come here." Justin took her into his arms again and kissed her long and fiercely. Then, just as abruptly, he released her. "Must go."

Justin pushed open the larder door and stepped into the kitchen. Caroline followed him reluctantly.

"Is it safe?" he said, smiling at Mindy.

Mindy's gay scarlet turban wobbled and the gold hoop earrings swung as she tossed her head. "Safe!" she snorted. "What you care 'bout safe? You all the time taking so many chances that ah wonder you ain't been flogged or killed!" Her suspicious eyes went to Caroline's face. "What you been doing to that girl? She looking flushed."

Laughing, Justin took a step toward her. "Would you like me to show you what I've been doing?"

Mindy retreated before him. "If ah a few years younger, ah be glad to let you show me, boy. But ain't getting any younger, and ain't got no time for foolishness. Out o' mah kitchen before Master Toby see you. Git!"

"Mindy, you will never grow old." With a smiling salute, Justin left them.

Watching him out of sight, Caroline noticed that he made no effort at concealment. He walked as he had always done. As if he owned the earth.

Seated on a bench beneath the rose arbor, Tobias Markham thought that it was time to be on his way. Even so, he made no movement to rise. Staring down at the ground, he wondered if it was his fate to be drawn to women who had something to hide. He loved Caroline Fane. Whether she be innocent or guilty of the murder of her husband, he loved her. She had ridden with Justin Lawrence—Rogue Lawrence, as he had been known. She had probably been his mistress. Whatever the way of it, it was obvious that she had a good deal to hide. His lips twisted into a mirthless smile. He was fifty-five years old, and in love with a young girl.

Once he had been in love with Biddy. When he had first met Biddy, she had been so lovely, so full of bubbling life that he had been dazzled by her. Before he knew it, he was married to her. It was not long before he realized the terrible mistake he had made. Biddy, he found, was only a beautiful shell. Beneath that outer covering of beauty, she was sly, intemperate, and immoral. Selina had tried to warn him against the marriage, but of course he had not heeded her. He was too much in love. Biddy, Selina had told him, had been slyly drinking without her parents' knowledge since the age of eleven.

On their four-week honeymoon, he found that everything Selina had told him was all too true. Little by little Biddy's true personality began to emerge. She was unashamedly drunk every night. She was coarse of language and lewd of manner. Now she made no pretense of loving him. He had been a means of escape from her family, she told him. To get away from them and the restrictions of her narrow life, she would have married an ape!

Her words, so cutting, so baldly put, had hit him like blows. He had thought he would never recover. But to a certain extent, he had recovered, and in sheer self-defense, arming himself against her lashing tongue, he kept assuring himself that he loved her still. She was his wife. He would influence and change her.

In a certain trembling of the spirit, for he had married without his parents' knowledge, he had taken her to their home in Virginia. The Virginia countryside, so wild and unsettled, so savagely beautiful, had for a time appealed to Biddy. To his delight, she seemed to change. She drank less, her coarse manners gentled, she tried to win his parents to her side. One night, in an excess of remorse, she even told him that she had lied to him, that she really loved him. That the lie had been prompted by a feeling of unworthiness. He had believed her because he so badly needed to believe, and that night he had taken her in tenderness and genuine desire. It was the one and only night there was real tenderness between them, as it turned out, for he was to find that it was not in Biddy to really change.

The climax came one night when his father, as he always did, was making the rounds of his property. Opening the door of one of the stables, he had found Biddy naked beneath Jethro, a black field hand. There was no question of Biddy having been forced into the action, for her voice, husky with passion, had been inciting Jethro on.

His father had been unwell for a long time before that night, and the shock of the experience had resulted in a heart attack. He had died that same night. In a way, his mother's death could be put to Biddy's account too. For his mother had quickly followed after his father. Without him, she had had no desire to go on living.

Markham frowned, feeling again the pain of that long-ago hurt. Perhaps it had never been real love he had had for Biddy, because it was from that moment he had stopped loving her and hatred had been born in its place. Since then there had been many Jethros in Biddy's life, he was sure, though no one at the plantation let on, and he had no doubt that before she died, there would be many more.

Before she died! Markham was shaken with a flare of hope. She was drinking heavily, more heavily than ever before. Surely the drink must kill her soon. If only she would die. If only!

Markham rose slowly to his feet. He did not wish to see Biddy, but with that ingrained courtesy that had always dictated his actions, he felt that he must take his farewell of her. Going toward the house, he told himself that for the time he was to be away on business he must put Biddy completely from his mind. He would not even allow himself to think of Caroline Fane. Caroline! He would have her if he could. But when he returned to Montrose would be the time to think and plan. To be rid of Biddy. To have in her stead the loveliness, the strength and sanity, the love of Caroline Fane! Somehow he would make it become a reality.

Chapter 19

Eliza Harris stood very still, afraid that a sudden movement might awaken Miss Biddy. Sprawled out naked on the bed, the woman was sleeping the sleep of utter exhaustion.

Miss Biddy had sent for her well before dawn. When she had entered the room, trying to hide her yawns, she had found Miss Biddy stumbling drunkenly about, clutching at chairs or at anything that would aid her uncertain steps. She had been in a state of considerable agitation, and Eliza, knowing what this portended, had felt her heart sink. Listening to the moaning sounds Miss Biddy was making, she was not surprised when the woman tore off the one flimsy garment she was wearing and threw herself on the bed. She began caressing herself, bringing her already hungry body to a fresh peak of desire. The scene had been repeated so many times before Eliza that she knew she should be used to it by now. But somehow she never could get used to it.

Although Miss Biddy had sent for her, she had not yet addressed one word to her, nor would she until she was ready. The summons came, as Eliza had known it would. The moans had turned now to small shrieks, and Eliza was able to discern one word—"Jem."

Knowing that Miss Biddy would begin to scream if she lingered, Eliza ran from the room. Jem, the black stable hand, had been sleeping in his quarters above the stable. Cursing, he made ready to accompany her to the house. Eliza was not deceived by his expressionless face, for she had glimpsed the fear in his eyes. It was obvious that he would have liked to ignore the command, but he did not dare. The black people were all afraid of Miss Biddy's vindictiveness. The more so today, for they knew Master Toby was going away for a while.

Entering the room, Jem took one look at Miss Biddy's

writhing body; then, without a word or a glance in Eliza's direction, he moved over to the bed. He was slow to accommodate Biddy, and she cursed him. Even when he was inside her she was still not at peace. He could not seem to satisfy her. Eliza wondered if any one man could do that.

Finally Biddy was satiated. Jem was glad to escape from the room. Just before she had fallen into a deep sleep, Miss Biddy had instructed Eliza to put out her lavender gown. To-day, she had informed her, she intended to take a drive about the plantation.

Eliza stared down at the gown. A dark spot appeared on the material, and she realized that she was crying. She rubbed her hand over her eyes. She must not think of Cranwell, or she would go mad. But despite her determination, she could not seem to shut out the memory of his sharp, cunning face, the feel of his rough hands upon her body, the rank smell of him. She had tried everything to gain her release from him. She had even offered him the small hoard of money she had managed to save. It was no use; he would not let her go. So she was still bound to him by her fear for Moon. She knew, if she should once fail to meet him, that he would tell everything. Because of Cranwell, because of the pain he had caused her, she had had to refuse Moon. They had not been intimate for more than a month now. Moon was bound to get suspicious, or worse, begin to feel Eliza didn't love him. And now Cranwell had put more than pain into her body; he had also put his seed there. Eliza stifled a sob. She was pregnant with that filthy animal's child! What was she to do?

Eliza started as a knock sounded on the door. Hastily she wiped her tears away. Before she could move, the door opened and Tobias Markham entered. Shrinking back into her corner, she hoped that he would not notice her.

Markham did not glance Eliza's way. Picking his way through a litter of empty jars that had contained peach brandy, he approached the bed.

The opening of the door had awakened Biddy. She stared up into the face of her husband with sleep-confused eyes. Automatically, as though she could not keep her fingers from straying, she began to caress her breasts. Under the caressing, the nipples stood out prominently. "Toby!" Whimpering, she moved her body restlessly.

Markham looked down at her with disgust. "I have come

to say good-bye," he said in a harsh voice. "I shall be away for several days."

"Away?" Biddy frowned, not understanding. She moved to make room for him on the bed. "Been a long time, Toby," she said in a slurred voice. "W-want you." Her arms reached for him. "Come here to me."

He struck her arms away. "Keep your hands to yourself, you filthy slut!"

"Want you, Toby, want you!"

He did not answer her for a moment; then he said in a dead voice, "Are you going to live on forever in your filth and your lewdness? Anyone else, abusing their body as you abuse yours, would be dead by now. Why don't you die, Biddy, why don't you?"

The very lifelessness of his voice broke through the alchoholic haze more effectively than a shout. Raising herself, she began to scream at him, "I'm your wife, you bastard! I'm not dead, and I want you now!" Opening her legs, she arched her body upward, her heels digging into the sheets. "Take me now, and I'll never send you from my bed again."

"You must be mad to think I would touch you. When I look at you I can feel nothing but revulsion!"

Staring at him, seeing the hatred with which he regarded her, she slumped back on the bed. "Toby," she whispered. "There's a fire inside me. Can't help it, never could! Born with the fire inside me. Don't hate me. Can't help it. Put the fire out, Toby. Put it out!" She blinked moisture from her eyes, and then tried to reach his hand. "Help me!"

"I'll help you, Biddy! I'll help you into your grave, you bitch!"

Biddy began to scream at him. "Whoremonger! Bastard! I know all about you and that prison scum you're so fond of. Maybe it will be your stinking convict mistress who goes to her grave first. But it won't be me!"

Markham's head moved stiffly, and a muscle at the side of his mouth began to twitch. He was surprised that Biddy was not so dulled by alcohol that she could perceive feelings he had never expressed to anyone—his feelings for Caroline. "So you know. But I warn you, Biddy, no harm had better come to Caroline."

"Does it thrill you when you open up her legs and start in

prodding her, you pathetic old fool? Does your baby murderess like it, old man?"

"Shut up!" His fist knotted, and he lifted it as though he would strike her. "Shut your filthy mouth!"

"Caroline Fane killed her husband. I know, I've seen her papers. She'll kill you too, old man. Have you seen the way she looks at Justin Lawrence? He's been inside her. Take my word for it!" She began to laugh as she saw his expression of pain. "Fool! Did you think you were the only one?"

"I have never touched her."

"Liar!"

Eliza's heart thudded in fear and distress. Caroline Fane, a murderess? It did not seem possible. Not Caroline. It could not be! There must be some mistake.

The color had drained from Markham's face. Only his eyes seemed to be alive. "Remember, Biddy. If you harm Caroline, you will pay for it!"

After he had left, Biddy broke into a storm of hysterical weeping. After she had calmed, she lay very still on the bed, staring up at the ceiling. Eliza stayed where she was, hardly daring to breathe for fear Biddy's wrath might turn on her.

But there was no wrath left in Biddy. She was consumed with fear. What she had told Tobias was true—she could not help her sexual craving. She could not remember when she had first become aware that she was a slave to her body, but she had been very young. It had started long before she had met Tobias Markham. She had made many efforts to control herself in those early days, but the more she tried, the more the fire inside her built. The fire, which was the only way she could think of to describe the terrible thing that drove her, was her master. Even when she had a man making love to her, even as his body worked to put out the fire, she knew it could never be entirely quenched. Soon it would begin to build again, driving her to a frenzy, making her go to any length so that she might know a little peace.

Sighing, Biddy turned over on her side, hiding her eyes with her hand. Peace! She had never known it. She had another master too. Alcohol. Even when she gagged on it, even when she vomited, she still continued to drink, for this too was a craving that she could not still.

Oddly enough, despite the hatred that existed between them now, she had fallen deeply in love with Tobias Mark-

ham from the first moment she had set eyes on him. She had
had many doubts about the marriage, but she had told herself
that marriage with Toby would cure her.

Toby was an ardent lover, but he was also a healthy and
normal man. He could not keep up with her demands. Afraid
of disgusting him, she drank herself senseless. And so it began. A vicious circle, and she was powerless to stop, even
though she yearned to. When had Toby's disgust turned to a
deadly hatred? When had her own hatred leaped out to meet
his?

Biddy pressed her fingers into her temples. Another terror
had been added lately. She had a conviction that she was going mad. She seemed to see and to hear things that were not
really there. Sometimes she would see Jethro's dangling body,
the black man who had been hanged because he had copu-
lated with a white woman. But it had not been poor Jethro's
fault. He had not wanted to take her. He had been afraid.
But she had forced him by means of threats. She had told
him that whether or not he took her, she would swear he had
forced her against her will. So big Jethro, shaking with fear,
had given in. And he had been hanged. But she, who had
caused it all, was looked upon as a tragic and innocent victim
of a black man's lust. But not by Toby. He knew her now for
what she was.

She had not thought her craving for sex and alchohol
could grow worse, but it had. Until now, as she suspected,
the sexual promiscuity had affected her spirit and the alcohol
had begun to affect her brain. She had thought of killing herself, but she was afraid to take that final step. The fear that
drove her came out in cruelty, in vile language, and in a
coarseness that, like her body, she could no longer control.
She thought of what might have been, had she been born
with normal urges, and a wave of self-pity swept over her.
She began to cry again.

Eliza heard the muffled sound of Biddy's weeping, but she
did not go to her. She stayed where she was, her fingers
pressing into the slight swell of her stomach beneath the
white apron. There would be bad trouble when Miss Biddy
found out that she was pregnant. The truth she had tried so
hard to keep from Moon would come out. Would he believe
that she had gone willingly to Cranwell? No, he could not
think that. He had more faith in their love for each other.

But Moon would go after Cranwell, and he would kill him. And then Moon in his turn would be killed.

Tears filled Eliza's eyes. There was nothing she could do to save Moon from that final tragedy. Sooner or later, Cranwell would speak out and tell all he knew. But before Moon died, he must know that she had been forced into a betrayal of their love. He must know that the love between them was a shining wonder, a sweetness, and a perpetual joy in her heart.

Eliza became aware that Miss Biddy's sobbing had ceased and that she was calling her. "Harris. Go downstairs. Bring me back a dozen jars of the peach brandy. When you return, you may dress me for my drive. Hurry!"

When Eliza returned to the bedchamber some fifteen minutes later, the bottles of brandy clinking together in the rush basket she carried, she found Miss Biddy sitting up in bed.

"Harris," Miss Biddy ordered, "pour me a drink."

Biddy was on her third drink when the knock sounded on the door. Annoyed at the interruption, she shouted, "Come in!"

The door opened. "May I speak with you, Miss Biddy?" Caroline Fane said, entering the room.

Biddy's eyes narrowed. So here she was, Caroline Fane, the slut that Toby was mooning over. Her face flushing with angry color, she said imperiously, "Well, Fane?"

Caroline indicated the basket over her arm. "I have to take the lunches to the hands, Miss Biddy," she answered. "The other carts are in use, and I wondered if I might obtain a lift from you. Mindy told me that you would be visiting the upper fields. She suggested that I ask for permission to ride up with you."

Biddy stared at the girl's lovely, slightly flushed face. "Mindy suggested that, did she? That bloody black ape should keep her big mouth shut! My plans have nothing to do with her. And you, Fane, what is wrong with walking? Are you too lazy?"

Eliza was startled by the momentary flash that came into Caroline's eyes. Then she told herself that she must have imagined it, for she saw that she was smiling. "I am not too lazy, Miss Biddy," Caroline replied calmly. "Usually I enjoy walking. But if I walk now, the food will not arrive on time, and the men will go hungry."

Caroline's tone was respectful, but there was something in her eyes, something that Biddy perceived as contempt, that set an angry pulse hammering in her forehead. She was about to reply heatedly, when a sudden idea came to her. She smiled inwardly. She would fix that slut! "Very well, Fane," she replied graciously. "Now that you have explained, I understand. You may ride with me."

"Thank you, Miss Biddy."

Biddy felt the boiling of anger again. Yes, Caroline Fane would shortly be very sorry indeed. She was nothing but prison scum, a murderess, for all that she bore herself with the airs and graces of a duchess. "Well, Fane," she said sharply, "don't dawdle. Go downstairs and wait."

Smiling, Caroline inclined her head. She left the room and closed the door gently behind her.

Chapter 20

Jasmine smiled broadly as he settled Caroline Fane in the back seat of the cart. He patted her knee gently with his gnarled black hand. He had an almost fatherly feeling for this young white girl with the eyes of brown velvet and the sunshine in her hair. He was getting old, and she always treated him with consideration. She never passed him without giving him a word and a smile. He liked that. It made him feel good, like he was somebody. But Miss Biddy, now, she made him feel like dirt. Thinking of her, his smile vanished. He said in his rumbling voice, "That ol' devil be down soon, will she?"

Caroline did not reprove him. It was not her place to do so, and her sympathy was with him. "She will be here shortly. Tell me, how is the pain in your joints?"

Sighing, Jasmine rubbed a hand over his seamed black face. Shaking his bald head, he said dolefully, "Them pains is cruel bad, Miss Ca'line, ma'am. Master Toby, he done promised me a bottle of good rubbing oil. He going to buy it and bring it back with him."

Caroline nodded. In an effort to distract him from his woes, she said, "Why are you called Jasmine? How did you get your name?"

Jasmine chuckled. "Ah called Jasmine 'cause mah mammy, she done birthed me 'neath some jasmine bushes." He chuckled again. "When ah a young buck, ah had me lots of fights with the other bucks on account of mah name. But ah always win them fights."

"I'm sure you did." Caroline hesitated. "You are not a slave, are you, Jasmine?"

"No, Miss Ca'line, ma'am, ah ain't no slave, and ah ain't never been one. Ah free." He looked at Caroline with that mixture of pride and expectancy that she had come to recog-

269

nize. "You know when the first black slaves was brought here
to Virginny?"

Jasmine was a mine of information, and he liked to air his
knowledge. She did not disappoint him. "No, Jasmine,
when?"

"The first black men, they come here as slaves in 1619.
Brought here on a Dutch ship."

"I think that is sad. No man should be a slave to another."

"It sad, all right, Miss Ca'line, ma'am, and it get sadder.
Soon more and more black men come, 'cause they be captured and made to come. All us black men be slaves pretty
soon."

Changing the subject, Caroline said quickly, "Did you ever
work in the tobacco fields?"

Jasmine shook his head. "No, ah ain't never worked the
fields. But ah knows all about growing tobacco. You know
who first started in growing tobacco?"

"Who?"

"He a white buck, name of John Rolfe. He husband to Pocahontas."

She repeated the strange name slowly and experimentally.
"Pocahontas."

"You ain't never hear tell of Pocahontas, Miss Ca'line,
ma'am?"

"No."

"Well, Pocahontas, she an Indian maiden. She the daughter
of a big and 'portant chief by the name of Powhatan."

Indians! Caroline felt a shiver chase down her back. The
savage red men who wore little more than a breechclout, who
striped their faces with paint, hung themselves with barbaric
ornaments, and decorated their long black hair with feathers.
They resented the white man's intrusion into their land, the
injustices that many of them suffered, and their resentment
and hatred would often erupt in its full fury upon the white
settlements.

Caroline's eyes turned to the purple-hazed mountains in the
distance. She had the feeling that before this vast new land
could be settled, it would be soaked with the blood of the
white settlers and the Indian warriors. There seemed to be no
peaceable way out. She thought of the way the avenging Indians were reputed to come. Silently. Like drifting shadows.

And when they came, they killed men, women, and children. They pillaged and burned and scalped.

Scalped! Caroline had heard of the massacre of the white people back in 1622. And she had heard of more Indian uprisings just lately. The last one had been not very far from Montrose. Often in her troubled sleep she would dream that the Indians were raiding them. She would hear their wild, spiraling cries. She would see a lifted tomahawk glittering in the sun. The tomahawk would descend, and then, rising again, its glitter would be dulled with blood. A feathered arrow would wing silently through the air, and Justin would fall at her feet, the arrow buried deeply in his breast.

The dream would end there, and she would awaken with his name on her lips. "Justin! Justin!"

Caroline shuddered. She, who had thought she could never be frightened of anything again, was frightened of these alien people, a people she had not yet laid eyes on. There was something horrifying about the thought of those silent, stealthy figures advancing upon their unprepared prey. How nerve-shattering it must be to hear that sudden savage war cry. What must it be like to see your own death written in the fierce painted faces of the warriors? She had heard that the Indians did not always kill. Sometimes they took prisoners. But if the stories of the savage torture they inflicted upon those prisoners were not exaggerated, it would be far better to be dead.

"Something wrong, little missy?" Jasmine's worried voice cut across her thoughts. "You sick?"

"No, Jasmine, I'm all right. I was thinking about the Indians. Are they really so cruel?"

Jasmine pulled a stained clay pipe from his pocket. His brow furrowed in thought, he placed the empty pipe between his lips. "They cruel, all right," he said, the pipe quivering as he spoke. "But Master Toby, he say they got their reasons for raiding the white folk. He say that promises have been made to the Indians, and often them promises have been broke. He say they got a bellyful of them broken promises."

"But to kill innocent women and children!"

Jasmine took the pipe from his lips and restored it to his pocket. "Indian women and children have been killed too. The Indians, they were right friendly when the white man first came here. Now they ain't so friendly." Jasmine shook his head. "Faults on both sides, Master Toby tell me. He say if them promises was kept, instead of broke, we could have peace. He say the Indians have got honor, and they always keep their word. White man ain't so honorable, seems like. Ah don' know Miss Ca'line, ma'am. It a puzzle, and ah wouldn't be knowing the right of it."

"Jasmine!" The old man started as Miss Biddy's imperious voice sounded behind them. "I am ready to go."

"Yes, ma'am," Jasmine said, turning to face her. "Sho am ready for you."

Caroline watched Biddy advance. Walking beside her, her eyes downcast and her hands folded before her, was Eliza Harris. In her gray gown and her plain white bonnet, Eliza looked small and frail and very insignificant. Biddy was weaving unsteadily on her feet, and her face was flushed. She was resplendent in a lavender-silk gown and a bonnet of the same color with a curling white feather decorating the brim. A necklace of garnets circled her throat, matching earrings dangled from her ears, and clasped over her long white gloves were wide bracelets studded with the same stones. She looked, Caroline thought, as though she might be going to some fashionable London party rather than for a tour about the Montrose estate.

As Biddy, breathing raspily, stopped beside the cart, Jasmine stared at her as though he could not believe his eyes. It was the first time in ages he could remember seeing her so neatly dressed and even halfway sober. He wondered what the occasion was.

After some struggle, during which Miss Biddy fell back several times and managed to knock the fashionable bonnet askew, Jasmine finally settled her in her seat. Miss Biddy patted his wrinkled cheek and pursed her lips as though she would kiss him; then, letting her hand linger caressingly on his shoulder, she fell back against the seat. His face taut with disapproval, Jasmine moved away from her hand and went to help Eliza. Picking her up, he desposited her gently on the seat beside Caroline. "Ain't got no more meat on your bones than a picked chicken," he grumbled, giving Eliza a severe look. "Ah declare that mah arms didn't hardly feel you."

Several times during the drive, Caroline glanced at Eliza. The girl was too quiet. What was Eliza Harris really like? she wondered. What went on behind the pale mask of her face?

Then Caroline remembered the message she had promised to deliver for Justin and made a note to herself to deliver it as soon as she and Eliza had a moment alone.

Arriving at the lower fields, Caroline momentarily forgot Eliza Harris and the mysterious problems that caused her to weep so desperately during the night hours. Frowning, she stared at the bent backs of black men and white men. The sun shone on their sweat-glazed bodies as they labored to break up the earth and form it into near furrows. Behind the diggers, other men crawled on their hands and knees as they diligently searched for weeds.

Approaching the last field, just before they took the narrow path that led to the upper slopes, Biddy ordered the cart to stop.

Biddy was particularly interested in this field. It was controlled by Kedlow, who had once had the freedom of her bed. Kedlow, a short black man with a powerful physique, broad, flat features, and a mop of kinky hair, had liked being her lover. His reign had been short, but he still retained a certain tenderness for her because of this, and because she had been instrumental in helping him get the coveted position of overseer.

Kedlow was by nature brutal, and the position of power over other men was one that suited him well, but he had gratitude, at least to her, Biddy thought, and he would do almost anything she asked of him. She stole a sly look at Caroline, and then returned her eyes to Kedlow.

Kedlow was strutting importantly up and down the rows of stooping men, his heavy whip grasped in his right hand. She would speak to him now, Biddy decided. With a commanding look at Jasmine, she indicated that he was to help her down from the cart.

Flapping her hand now and again to attract attention, Biddy wove her unsteady way to the overseer's side.

Relieved of the woman's restricting presence, Caroline turned to Eliza, but the girl was gazing off into the distance. Caroline changed her mind, and occupied herself with watching Biddy. Whatever Biddy had to say to the overseer, it was obviously very interesting, for their heads were close together. What could they be talking about so intently? she wondered. It must be amusing, too, for they kept glancing toward the cart and laughing immoderately. Caroline saw

Kedlow nod and flourish his whip, and for no reason that she could think of, she had a sudden feeling of foreboding. Something was going to happen. Why else would she feel this way? To rid herself of her sudden and unreasonable dread, she tried taking herself sternly to task. She was being ridiculous. After all, what could happen? Did she feel this way because Tobias Markham had left Montrose? But in a few days' time he would be returning, and all would be normal. Nevertheless, for all her reasoning, she could not quite shake off the feeling.

When Biddy finally returned to the cart, she was accompanied by a grinning Kedlow. Biddy was still laughing, and her laughter had a high, hysterical sound.

Caroline flushed as Kedlow looked at her. She had never liked the man, ever since she had witnessed the brutal way he treated the men who worked beneath him. Coolly, she returned his stare, then haughtily turned her head away. Her flush deepened as she heard his soft laugh.

"Jasmine"—Biddy's voice turned querulous as she addressed the old man—"I have seen enough for today. I will return to the house. Kedlow will come with me. I have something of the cart, Fane. It will not hurt you to walk the rest of the for him to do." She looked at Caroline and Eliza. "Get out way. When you have delivered the food to the workers, return to me at the house at once. Harris, you may accompany Fane, if you wish."

If she wished! Eliza was astounded at this unusual concession on Miss Biddy's part, but she did not pause to examine her motives. I will see Moon! she thought with a burst of joy as she climbed down from the cart to stand beside Caroline. I will see Moon!

Jasmine glanced over his shoulder at Kedlow, who was seated on the front seat beside Miss Biddy. His face grim with disapproval, he backed the cart and drove away.

With a sense of freedom, the two girls began to make their way to the steeply winding path that led to the upper slopes. Listening to the sound of Eliza's difficult breathing as the path became steeper, Caroline thought she knew what was troubling Eliza.

They were almost at the top when Caroline stopped short and caught at Eliza's arm. "You are ill, aren't you?" she said, looking into the girl's drawn face. "Won't you tell me if there is any way in which I can help?"

Eliza stared at her, fighting to recover her breath. When her agitated breathing calmed, she did not say the evasive words she had meant to say. Instead, it was almost as though she were driven to speak. As though she could no longer contain them, words came bursting forth, and she told Caroline the whole story.

Caroline said nothing at first. Then, after a few moments, she said quietly, "Justin knows, doesn't he? About you and Moon, I mean?"

Eliza nodded. "Yes, he knows, Caroline."

"And so Moon is the 'he' that Justin's message was from?"

"Message?" Eliza asked.

"Oh, I'd nearly forgotten." Caroline relayed the message Justin had given her that morning.

Something in what Caroline said, or perhaps in the way she said it, caused Eliza to break into desperate tears. Her situation loomed hopelessly before her.

Caroline took the girl into her arms and stroked her tenderly until the sobbing stopped. Then she bit her lip thoughtfully. "Justin will help you if he can. And so will I. I will speak to him. Perhaps we can find a solution."

The white, scared look was back on Eliza's face. "It is hopeless. Moon is a slave. There is nothing he can do to help himself, or me."

"And so you will just fold your hands and wait to die?" Caroline said scathingly.

"What else can we do? I could run off, I suppose. But I will not leave Moon. Cranwell will tell, if I run off. I know he will!"

"Run off?" Caroline said eagerly. "That's it! Justin must arrange for you and Moon to escape."

"Escape? Caroline, you are dreaming! Do you really think it would be that easy?"

"Nothing is ever easy. But if you want it enough, it can be arranged. Besides, you do not know the ingenious Rogue Lawrence."

"But even if Moon did escape, what then? For the rest of his life he would have to hide."

"This is a very big country, Eliza. Pursuit can only go so far. Don't worry, Justin will think of something. Listen to me, you must find a chance to speak to Moon. You must tell him—"

"No! I will not tell him about Cranwell, or . . . or the child I am carrying."

"Of course not," Caroline said impatiently. "That must come later, when you are well away from here. I was going to say that you must tell him about our conversation. It would be best to give him time to digest and get used to the idea of escape."

"Caroline . . ." Despite her misgivings, Eliza's voice held a tremulous note of hope. Caroline and Justin were her only chance. "Do you really think it can be done?"

Caroline did think so. Her faith in Justin was high. If anyone could plan and carry through this escape, it was he. Smiling inwardly, she thought: To make the impossible job possible, apply to Rogue Lawrence. "We will do it, Eliza," she said firmly. "The plan should go something like this. Moon and Justin will escape first, and then, before the alarm can be raised, you will slip away to join them. A safe meeting place can be arranged beforehand. Later, when I think it is safe, I will come to you."

Eliza's doubts were swept away by the glow in Caroline's eyes, the excited flush in her cheeks, and her overwhelming enthusiasm. She so wanted to believe they could escape. She said, "I would like to be like you, Caroline. You are so strong and self-reliant."

"I had to learn to be." Laughing, she went on. "Imagine it! Rogue Lawrence and Carrie Fane together again in planning another coup. It makes me feel alive again! Don't have a worry in the world, Eliza. Somehow or other Rogue and I will pull it off."

"But Justin? Perhaps he will not—"

"He will. He is like me—he too needs to feel alive again."

Eliza smiled for the first time. "And you call Justin a rogue. I think you are a pair of rogues together."

"But of course we are. That is why we are so well-suited. I will tell you something else, Eliza. I do not intend to allow Rogue Lawrence to get away from me. I will manage to hobble him to me, never doubt it. We belong together. And I believe in his heart he knows that too."

"If he does not," Eliza said with a flash of mild humor, "I am quite sure you will convince him."

"I will indeed!"

Eliza's smile faded. "You will despise me, I know, Caroline, but I can't help being afraid."

"Of course I don't despise you. Do you think I have never been afraid? I was very afraid once. Afraid of life, afraid to be myself. But then I met Rogue Lawrence. He taught me to be bold and fearless. But more important, he taught me how to be myself." Caroline took Eliza's hand and squeezed it tightly. "You must not be afraid. Trust Justin. Trust me."

"I do trust you, Caroline. Whatever happens, I am glad I told you."

"And you will not be afraid?"

"I will try very hard not to be."

"It is just as well. When the Rogue sets his mind to a thing, no one has time to be afraid. You are young, Eliza, but you must grow up very quickly. Moon will need his woman to be strong."

Caroline walked on, and Eliza followed, her mind full of hopes and dreams. In the excitement, she had completely forgotten the conversation she had overheard between Miss Biddy and Master Toby. If she had remembered, she would have put her fear for Caroline down to her imagination. Caroline was strong and bold and fearless. How could that woman hope to hurt her or overcome her?

Chapter 21

Moon sat quietly in his chair, his eyes on the restlessly pacing Justin Lawrence. Not once in the ten minutes allotted t them for rest had Justin ceased his pacing of the cabin floo Moon likened this man whom he called friend to a cage panther. He was lithe and strong now, and as brown as a Indian. And with his thick untrimmed hair hanging almost t his shoulders, his handsome, somewhat hawkish features, an his intensely dark eyes, he might well pass for an India Justin was not meant to be confined. He did not take order easily. Good-natured though he appeared to be, there was dangerous quality about Justin. He could be a staunch an true friend—he had proved that; but he would also make bad enemy.

Justin was unaware of Moon's eyes upon him. His hand were clenched together so hard that his nails dug into hi palms. He wanted freedom. He wanted to explore Virgini and the lands beyond. This urge had been steadily growin over the weeks, until it was now an obsession. Freedom! Th word seemed to hang in his mind like a glittering golden bau ble. To be his own man again. To strike out with power an purpose. To roam these wilds with Carrie by his side. Tha would be living again.

Justin frowned. Despite his declaration of love on boar the *Merryventure*, he was still not certain if he truly love Carrie, but he did know that he wanted her. At first he ha thought of going off alone, for he had not wanted to start th great adventure hampered by a woman. Then, second thoug had shown him that Carrie was no ordinary woman. Sh could shoot straight and true, and she could ride like th devil. And he not only wanted her, he needed her. It wa the first time in his life he had ever needed a woman fo

278

more than her body, and he was momentarily disconcerted. If need might be construed as love, then he loved Carrie.

"You are thinking of escaping, aren't you, Justin?" Moon's quiet voice broke in on his thoughts.

"What?" Justin swung around to face him. "Now, how the devil did you know that?"

Moon smiled. "Be easy. You are not that easy to read. But to me, who have come to know you so well, your thoughts are transparent."

"The devil they are!"

"Will you take Caroline with you?"

Making no attempt to evade the issue, Justin grinned at him. "Since you know so much, friend, yes. If it can be managed, you can be sure that I will take her."

"I'm glad. You two belong together. And if anyone can plan an escape and carry it through, it is you, Justin."

"Perhaps. We shall see." A flare of excitement lit Justin's eyes as he studied his friend. "I have not yet thought of a way," he said quickly, "but when I plan, I plan on a grand scale. If inspiration should come to me, will you and Eliza come with us?"

Escape! Moon turned his head away so that Justin might not see his hopelessness reflected in his eyes. Had things been different, he would gladly have taken a chance. But a black man of his stature with an unusual and betraying scar on his cheek had little chance of going unrecognized. "When you have thought of something," he answered in a low voice, "we will talk again." He rose from the chair. "It is time to go back to the fields."

"Bah!" Justin said impatiently. "You are too conscientious. Since Putnam is absent from the field, we could have taken a few more moments."

Moon shook his head. "True. But I like to get my work done with." He paused by the door. "Well? Are you coming?"

"I suppose so." Frowning, Justin followed after him.

Back at his task once more, Moon's movements were automatic. The thought of Eliza was always in his mind, but today more so than ever. He became conscious of a niggling, uneasy feeling, but he could not put a name to it. She had not let him make love to her in a month. He dug his spade deeply into the earth he was turning, trying to rid himself of the uneasiness. It persisted. He was thinking so deeply that when he looked up and saw Eliza and Caroline approaching, he was not sure for a moment if they were really there. Staring at Eliza, he heard Caroline's voice explaining why they were late.

Impatiently Justin flung down the tool he had been using. "The devil with you, Carrie! If you had walked in the first place, you would have been here long before this."

Annoyed by his unreasonable attitude, Caroline answered him sharply. "No doubt the pangs of hunger are clawing at your belly. Which would account for your exquisite manners. Another thing. Look to yourself before you criticize me, Rogue Lawrence."

Justin grinned at her. "Have you come here to quarrel with me, Carrie, or to distribute the food?"

Frowning, Caroline studied him. There was something different about him today, a softer look in his eyes. Never before had he looked at her quite like that. On any other man than Justin, she would have said it was the look of a lover. Nonsense! She brought her chaotic thoughts sternly to order. How could she ever be sure of Justin, curse him! The hot color mounting to her face, she said hurriedly, "I do not see Putnam. Where is he?"

"Other side of the field," Justin said indifferently. "Be off with you. The men are waiting to eat."

"All right. When I come back, I want to talk with you. It is important."

"Hurry, then. There is something I have to say to you, too."

Some of the men gave Caroline a surly look as she approached them, but most of them greeted her with a smile when she handed them the packets of food. Her mind was not on her task; Justin had something to say to her. What was it? That look in his eyes. Had she been imagining it? The seesaw of her emotions swung upward again. Surely he must love her! Why else would he look at her in that way? With a new confidence, she returned to Justin's side.

"Moon!" Justin's loud, wrathful voice cut into Caroline's pleasant thoughts. "What the devil are you doing with that spade? Are you trying to cut your foot off, you great lummox?"

Caroline swung around. Blood was oozing from Moon's

ankle. "He has hurt himself, Justin. You might be a little more sympathetic." She took Eliza's arm and pressed it gently. "Don't look like that," she soothed. "It's only a surface cut."

"Caroline is right." Moon smiled at Eliza. "I wasn't looking at what I was doing."

"But . . . but will you be all right?" The tears were bright in Eliza's eyes. "I can't bear you to be hurt."

"Of course he'll be all right," Justin answered for him. He took Moon's arm. "I'll take you back to the cabin and bind it for you."

"But Putnam—" Moon began.

"Never mind about Putnam. He's not looking this way."

Eliza's eyes went to Moon, seeking reassurance. Smiling, he nodded at her. "I can hardly feel it, Liza. Go back to the house now. Come tomorrow, if you can."

Caroline looked quickly about her. No one was looking their way. "Can we come with you, Justin?" she said quickly. "I told you I have to talk with you."

"No," Justin said. "Putnam is sure to miss us if we're gone too long." He helped Moon walk toward the cabin.

Caroline linked her arm in Eliza's. "Come, I will take you back to the path. Putnam won't see me if I double back through those trees. I am going to make sure that Moon is all right."

"No, Caroline, you must not!" Eliza looked at her with horror. "Justin said—"

"Never mind what he said," Caroline snapped. "I am going."

Eliza was still putting up a feeble argument when Caroline left her at the path. Heedless of the dust, Eliza sat down, her hands clenched over the basket that Caroline had thrust at her. She bowed her head and wept bitterly for Moon, for herself, and for something that could never be. She had allowed herself to be upheld by Caroline's confidence and courage, but in her heart she knew that she and Moon were reaching an end. If Caroline could see her now, she would believe that she wept for Moon's small accident, but her tears were for all that she had hoped and dreamed, for the waste of two lives. Things could not change. She had been foolish to believe that they could, even for one moment.

Caroline was breathless when she arrived at the cabin. She

looked cautiously about her, and then gave a gentle tap on the door. It opened at once. "Carrie!" Justin glowered at her. "Damn your stubborn hide. I told you to go back to the house."

"It's Eliza. She's frightened. Is it a bad cut?"

"No." Justin pulled her inside and banged the door shut.

Moon looked up with a smile. Without any words having been exchanged, it was obvious to Moon that Caroline knew about his affair with Eliza, and he could sense that she was a solid, loyal friend. "It's nothing," he said. "Try to convince Liza of that."

Caroline nodded. "I'll tell her. Justin, now that I am here, can we talk?"

"No!" Justin answered her sharply. "I want nothing to interfere with a certain plan I am making. It would be disastrous if you were found here." He took her arm and turned her toward the door. "Out with you!"

"Justin, please listen to me. I think—"

"Think?" Justin cut her off. "When the devil did you ever stop to think?" With a swift movement he pulled her into his arms and kissed her fiercely. "God knows why, Carrie," he said in a shaken voice, "but I love you."

"Do you?" She looked at him with shining eyes. "Do you really, Justin?"

"I have said it, have I not? Now, get out!" Justin opened the door and peered outside. "All clear." He slapped her sharply on the behind. "Off you go, pest."

"Tomorrow?" Caroline said in a soft voice.

"Tomorrow." He closed the door in her face.

As she walked on, it seemed to Caroline that she could still feel the hard, tingling pressure of his lips on hers. He had said he loved her, and for the first time, she found herself believing him without question. She was still smiling when she rejoined Eliza. Her smile died as she looked down at the crouching girl. "Eliza!" she exclaimed. "Everything is all right. Moon told me to tell you so."

"Thank you, Caroline." Without looking at her, Eliza rose to her feet and began to walk down the path.

"Wait!" Caroline caught up with her. "Tonight, when you come to bed, we will discuss plans. And tomorrow I will talk to Justin. It is unfortunate that I could not do it today. But tomorrow will do just as well."

Eliza shook her head. "Something will always intervene, Caroline. I know it. There will never be anything for Moon and me."

Caroline could understand Eliza's despondency. But she felt that Eliza was not as weak as she appeared to be. The fact that she had kept her suffering to herself made Caroline feel that there was, in fact, a strength about Eliza that would blossom when she was away from Montrose, free, and with her lover. She decided to speak no more about it until the girl had had some time to think. She took Eliza's hand in hers and led her down the path toward the house. She still had to keep her appointment with Biddy.

Chapter 22

Tom Keene's cold eyes dwelled on Biddy Markham's flushed and excited face. "You sent for me, Miss Biddy, ma'am," he said. "How may I serve you?"

"Ah, Tom, always so formal!" Biddy's smile widened. "I will get directly to the point. I wish to sell a wench. She is one of the two white slaves my husband acquired aboard the ship the *Merryventure*. Her name is Caroline Fane." She flourished the papers she was holding in her hand. "I have here her contract of servitude. Are you interested in buying it?"

Remembering Markham's intervention when he had approached Caroline Fane, he felt his interest quicken. He did not really want the girl, but it would be pleasant to score over Markham for once. He said casually, "I might be interested. Why does Tobias wish to sell her contract?"

Even before she replied, he knew from her deepened color that Markham knew nothing about it. He smiled inwardly. So much the better. "It is my own idea," Biddy answered harshly.

Keene's amusement deepened. Obviously Markham was too interested in the girl to suit Biddy, and the selling of Caroline Fane's contract was undoubtedly an action of spite on her part. "Hmm!" Keeping her on tenterhooks, he pretended to ponder. "I am not sure, ma'am. I will give you a definite answer by morning."

Biddy was dismayed. She thought uneasily of her husband. It would be like Tobias to cut short his business and return unexpectedly. He had done so many times before. As for Caroline Fane, Biddy was not yet finished with her, but she had hoped to have her away from Montrose before nightfall. "Very well," she said reluctantly. "But be sure to let me have your answer by morning."

"Be assured that you will have it, ma'am." Keene moved over to the door. "I bid you good day, ma'am."

Mindy sat at the kitchen table gazing listlessly before her. For once she felt at a loss. She had always tried to protect Master Toby's interests in his absence, but with this thing Miss Biddy was planning to do with Caroline Fane, she did not quite know what she could do about it.

Mindy's hands clenched in helpless anger. She had known Miss Biddy was up to something when she had seen Tom Keene enter the house. She had crept quietly to the parlor door. Her ear pressed against the door, she had listened to the conversation between them. Miss Biddy was going to sell Caroline Fane to Tom Keene. Tom Keene would accept, she knew. He hated Master Toby, and he had always coveted everything he had. Mindy's brow furrowed. There was one thing she could do; she could warn Caroline. It would make no difference, of course. If the contract was sold to Tom Keene, Caroline would be obligated to go to Ballymore. But at least she would know.

Mindy started as she heard the door open. She turned her head sharply as Caroline and Eliza entered the kitchen. To hide her emotion, she said in a grumbling voice, "What for you creep up on me like that? It like to scare me out o' mah growth!"

Because of her enormous bulk, this was one of Mindy's favorite little jokes.

Caroline gave the required smile. "I'm sorry, Mindy. We did not mean to creep."

Mindy chuckled, then sobered suddenly. "Ah got something to tell you, girl," she said abruptly. "Don't know no other way o' telling you, 'cepting straight out."

Caroline looked at her apprehensively. "What is it, Mindy?"

"Ain't no use you looking at me like that." Mindy snorted, attempting to cover the fact that Caroline's fear had moved her. "Cain't do nothing 'bout it. Would if ah could, but cain't."

"Yes, Mindy, I know. But what is it?"

"It Miss Biddy. She going to sell you contract to Tom Keene, him what owns Ballymore Plantation."

Caroline stared at her, her thoughts flying wildly in confusion and fear. Tom Keene! That cold-eyed, cruel man whom she had first seen aboard the *Merryventure*. Tobias Markham's intervention had saved her from him then. Who would save her now. "But can Miss Biddy do that?" she stammered.

"Can," Mindy said mournfully. "When Master Toby, he first married up with Miss Biddy, he have to be away a lot. So he make it that Miss Biddy's signature be legal like his. Never remembered to change it, ah reckon. It lawful, what Miss Biddy do. Lawful as Master Toby's signature."

What was she to do? Caroline looked at Mindy with stricken eyes. She would be parted from Justin, and she could not bear it! Only a few miles would lie between them, but it might just as well be hundreds. The escape! She grasped at the thought with desperate eagerness. It must somehow be planned now. There was no time to lose. The four of them—she and Justin, Eliza and Moon—they must get away from here. But how? How was it to be managed? Caroline put her hand to her head. If only her brain did not feel so heavy and confused. She must have time to think!

Mindy looked at her pityingly. "It bad, girl, ah know. But don't you go worrying yourself too much. Master Toby, he get you back from that Tom Keene. Ain't going to 'low you to be sold off. When he know, he—" Mindy broke off as the kitchen door opened again. She stared indignantly at the short black man framed in the doorway. "What you wanting, Kedlow?" she said in a belligerent voice. "Ah don't want no dirty field hands in mah clean kitchen. Git along with you! Scat!"

Kedlow ignored her. His eyes fixed on Caroline, he came farther into the kitchen. "You," he said, stabbing a thick finger in her direction. "You got to come 'long o' me."

Caroline's heart was beating wildly. "Why? What do you want with me?"

Kedlow came close to her and glared into her face. "Don't want no back talk from you, you white bitch!" He grasped her arm, attempting to pull her forward. "Get on outside!"

"Take your hands off me!" Caroline felt Kedlow's grip relax, and she tore her arm free. "I'm not going anywhere with you."

"Ain't you now, bitch? We just see 'bout that." He turned his head and looked at the trembling Eliza. "You got to come too."

"No!" Eliza shrank back.

Grabbing up her cleaver from the kitchen table, Mindy advanced on Kedlow. "What you think you a-doing, nigger, a-scaring them girls? Get out o' mah kitchen!"

Kedlow whirled on her. His eyes gleamed as he saw the cleaver in her hand. "You thinking o' using that thing, Mindy, gal?"

"Ah use it," Mindy threatened. "Ah use it to split your thick skull in two 'less you get out of mah kitchen and leave us alone. You wait! Master Toby, he going to hear of this. You be in big trouble!"

"Master Toby!" Kedlow sneered. "He away. He ain't got nothing to say this time. I take my orders from Miss Biddy."

"Miss Biddy?" Mindy fell back a step. "What she got to do with this?"

"Drop that cleaver, woman!" With a sudden spring, Kedlow was upon her. His hand fastened on her wrist and twisted. "You hear me? You drop that thing!"

"Ah won't!" Mindy breathed in gasps as she struggled against him. "You gone mad, nigger," she panted. "That what you done!"

"I said drop it!" Kedlow snarled.

Big though she was, Mindy had little strength. She was no match for Kedlow. Her fingers opened, and the cleaver clattered to the floor.

"That better." Kedlow's smile was unpleasant. He grabbed Eliza and hurled her toward Caroline. "Miss Biddy, she want you two outside. Now, git!" He took a menacing step forward. "If you ain't out that door 'fore I count to three, you going to get it."

Caroline stared scornfully at Kedlow. What did Miss Biddy want of them? she wondered. Why had she sent this brutal man to fetch them? The feeling of foreboding she had experienced earlier rushed over her again. Something terrible was going to happen! Was it possible that Miss Biddy had already sold her to Tom Keene? That she would be forced to leave at once for Ballymore Plantation? Her thoughts flew to Justin. If only he were here! She took a deep breath. But Justin was not here. Whatever awaited them, she must see it through herself.

"Get on over to that door." Kedlow's voice was menacing.

Caroline's mouth was dry with fear, but she would not let

Kedlow know that she was afraid. "Come," she said, putting a comforting arm about the trembling Eliza. "We will go and see what Miss Biddy wants. You must not worry, Eliza. Everything is going to be all right."

"It won't be!" Eliza began to sob. "Oh, Caroline, what is happening? I'm so afraid!"

"Hush! We are probably frightening ourselves for nothing. I daresay it is something quite trivial." Struggling to control her own fear, Caroline urged Eliza over to the door. She paused there and looked back at the prostrate cook. "Eliza and I will be back later to attend to you, Mindy."

"Lawd Jesus!" Mindy's voice was despairing. "What happening? Why Miss Biddy send this ape after you? Ah frightened for you. Ah got this bad feeling in mah heart!" Mindy's eyes rolled in Kedlow's direction. "Kedlow, you stop that grinning. You tell me what Miss Biddy want with these wenches."

Kedlow strode over to the door. He pushed Caroline and Eliza outside, and then turned to grin at Mindy. "If you so interested, gal, you can watch through the glass o' the door. But you ain't coming out and interfering, 'cause I locking it, see."

"Wait!" Mindy raised herself and grasped at the edge of the table. Then, gasping with the effort, she struggled to her feet. "Listen to me. Whatever Miss Biddy want you to do, don't you do it." Her hands stretched out in pleading as she staggered toward him. "She a-wanting you to hurt them wenches, ah knows it. But she mad, Kedlow, she mad! Ah tell you now that she get you into big trouble with Master Toby."

"You shut your mouth, woman!" Kedlow put his hand on her forehead and pushed hard. Unable to keep her footing, Mindy fell heavily, striking her head against the edge of a chair.

Kedlow stared at the motionless woman. Her eyes were closed, and for a moment he wondered if he had gone too far. If she died, he would be hunted down and hanged. Tobias Markham would be very vengeful. Kedlow felt the dryness of fear in his mouth. Then, as he saw her hand move, his confidence came back. She wasn't dead. All that fat on her body would have cushioned her fall. She had struck her head, and there was a thin trickle of blood seeping from the cut, but that was nothing. His grin returning, he stepped outside and locked the door. That should hold the old fool for a while. All that fuss over a couple of skinny white bitches!

"Where are you taking us?" Caroline said as Kedlow came toward them.

"Nowhere," Kedlow answered. "Don't need to. Right here is where it's going to happen."

"What do you mean? What is going to happen?"

Ignoring her, Kedlow put two fingers into his mouth and whistled shrilly.

As though she had been awaiting her cue, Biddy appeared around the corner of the building and approached them. She was carrying a length of rope and a whip.

Caroline did not hear the conversation between Kedlow and Biddy. Her eyes were on the whip clutched in the woman's hand. She felt the long-healed scars on her back begin to tingle and burn, and the tightly leashed-in terror almost overcame her. Staring at that whip, she knew what was going to happen. Once again the foul stench of Newgate Prison seemed to be in her nostrils. Once again she saw the vengeful people lining the London street. Their faces were avid, hating, condemning, as they waited to see that punishment was carried out on Caroline Fane. She could hear their curses and their insults as she went stumbling past on her bleeding feet. "Murderess! Whore!" On that day, the June sunshine had been hot. It had burned down on her half-naked body. She remembered her agonized screams as the searing lash cut into her flesh. Was it to happen all over again?

"Why, Fane," Biddy's sharp voice said, "how pale you are." She held up the whip. "You seem to be most interested in this. Perhaps you have guessed the use it will be put to."

"Don't, Miss Biddy," Eliza's trembling voice broke in. "Oh, please don't!"

"Be silent, Harris!" Biddy snapped. "You are only here to watch punishment carried out on this trollop. If you do not behave yourself, the same will happen to you."

"Why do you call me a trollop?" Caroline said in a steady voice. "What have I done?" Even as she spoke, she was amazed at her calm. But it was the calm before the storm, she knew, for nothing would make her submit tamely to this kind of punishment. "Why am I to be punished?"

Biddy did not like the girl's calm. She considered it to be

unnatural. "I'll tell you, Fane," she snarled. "You came into my home, you harlot! And then, like the convict scum you are, you fornicated with my husband."

Caroline's head lifted in her old proud gesture. "That is a lie, and you know it."

"Lie, is it, you dirty trollop! We'll see about that!"

Eliza wrung her hands together in an agony of fear. "Please, Miss Biddy, please!"

"Shut up!" Kedlow turned a threatening glare on Eliza. With a swift movement he turned and pressed his hand over her mouth. "One more word out o' you and I'll break your skinny neck!" His hand pressed tighter, and he gave a grunt of satisfaction as he saw the terror in her eyes. "Well? You going to be quiet?"

Tears rose in Eliza's eyes. She could not help Caroline. There was nothing she could do. She nodded. Looking at her suspiciously, Kedlow released her and pushed her away.

"Keep away!" Caroline cried as Biddy tried to crowd her against the wall. Her clenched fist flashed out and caught the woman on the cheek.

Gasping, Biddy fell back. "You dare to touch me, you filthy scum!" she cried.

"You keep away!" Caroline's voice had lost its calm; it was ragged with fear and defiance. "You stupid, drunken old fool! I'll kill you!"

"Now!" Biddy screamed at Kedlow. "Grab her!"

Kedlow's rough hands seized Caroline's arms. Pulling them up behind her back, he twisted them cruelly tight. "If you don't want both your arms broke," Kedlow snarled, "you'll keep nice and still!"

"Convict!" Biddy's openhanded blow rocked Caroline's head. "Dirty, murdering bitch!"

There was a thundering sound in Caroline's head as Biddy continued to strike her, but something inside her refused to give in. As soon as the blows ceased, she spat in Biddy's distorted face.

Trembling with fury, Biddy wiped the spittle away. "Bind her to the laundry post," she snapped at Kedlow. "Hurry!"

Kedlow shrugged. He was beginning to be bored with the whole business. The girl had done nothing to him. Miss Biddy was mad, all right, he thought, looking at her glittering eyes and her working face. But still, he had been ordered to punish Caroline Fane. Best to get it over and done with. Thankful that the yard was always deserted at this time of the day, he pushed the struggling girl toward the post.

Mindy heard the voices outside. Feeling nauseated, she put a hand to her throbbing head. Then, with an effort that turned her faint, she got to her feet and stumbled over to the door. Pressing her face against the glass, she saw Caroline's sagging form bound to the post. There was blood streaking her back, and her head was lolling as though she had lost consciousness. "Oh, Jesus God!" she breathed in an agonized voice. "They been flogging that girl! Master Toby, he going to kill Miss Biddy for this. He kill her! If he don't, ah will!"

Mindy saw Kedlow raise his arm again, and she battered at the glass in a frenzy. "No more!" she shouted. "You going to kill that wench! Ah tell Master Toby, ah tell him!"

Kedlow paused. "I think Mindy right." He nodded at Caroline's sagging form. "We done cut her up good, I'd say. Time we stop."

Angry color flushed Biddy's face. She would have liked to order Kedlow to go on with the flogging, but she had the uneasy feeling that he would not obey her. "All right," she said sullenly. "Cut her down." She turned malevolent eyes to the kitchen door. "Take Fane down to the root cellar and lock her in," she instructed. "After that, I want you to teach that fat black fool a lesson."

"Do it if you say so," Kedlow grunted. "It an order?"

"It is, Kedlow."

"Right. Ain't killing her, though. Man who kill Mindy'd hang. Your husband see to that. Sets a lot o' store by Mindy, he do."

"No one asked you to kill her. Cut Fane down. Get on with it!"

"You'll take the 'sponsibility, Miss Biddy?"

"Yes, yes!"

Kedlow said no more. Taking his knife from his pocket, he sliced through the rope that bound Caroline. Picking her up, he strode away. "I see to Mindy," he called over his shoulder. "Don't you worry none, Miss Biddy."

The tears streaking her face, Eliza stared after him, Caroline was badly hurt, and now Miss Biddy had ordered that Mindy was to be beaten. What could she do to aid them?

Biddy stared at Eliza. "Get on back to the house, you sniveling bitch!" she shouted.

Not daring to look at Mindy's face framed in the kitchen window, Eliza crept away.

Chapter 23

Eliza stood by the window, her eyes fixed on the slowly lightening sky. The long, terrible night would soon be over, giving way to the day. But daylight, Eliza thought, could not banish the nightmares for her. As long as she lived, she would always see Caroline's limp, bloodied form. She would always hear poor Mindy's frantic cries for help.

Eliza shivered and put a hand to the bruise on her jaw. Another memento from Kedlow. At Kedlow's request, Biddy had sent all the house servants away. They were to eat and sleep elsewhere for this one night, she had told them. Arrogant as always, she had offered no explanation. And the servants, startled but obedient, had gone meekly, almost thankfully. They were always uneasy when Tobias Markham was away. No doubt, Eliza thought, they had sought food and shelter in the cabins of the field hands. And so, with the house emptied of the servants, there had been no one to hear the sound of overturning furniture and the crashing of pots and plates. There had been no one to respond to Mindy's screams as she scrambled to get out of the way of Kedlow's fists.

Gradually Mindy's screams had dwindled, finally dying away altoghter. An uneasy silence had descended over the house. Anguished, her imagination racing, Eliza wondered if Mindy was dead. Or if Caroline, lying untended in the cold cellar, had died of her injuries. She herself could not get out of the room to investigate, for the door was locked. She had begged Miss Biddy to give her the key, so that she might tend Caroline, but her mistress, sprawled naked and drunk on the bed, had only laughed and had kept the key clenched in her hand. Short of fighting a woman who was much stronger than herself, there was nothing she could do about the situation in which she found herself.

Later, when she heard footsteps approaching the door, she had been alert. She watched closely as Miss Biddy staggered across the room to admit Kedlow. But Miss Biddy, after embracing Kedlow, had relocked the door. Collapsing back on the bed, she had flung the key on a side table.

Eliza had felt a return of hope when Kedlow quickly disrobed and flung himself upon Miss Biddy. But Kedlow's mind seemed to be quite divorced from the passion he brought to his performance. He seemed to know what was in her mind, and whenever she came near to the side table, he watched her every movement. She knew, had she reached for the key, that he would have stopped her.

And so the night hours had worn away. Kedlow was apparently indefatigable. He needed only a short rest before he was ready to enter Miss Biddy's frantic and willing body again. Eliza's nerves were stretched so taut that she had to bite her knuckles to keep herself from screaming. Would they never sleep? Would they never grow tired of the act they had made so coarse and raw and ugly?

Dawn was streaking the sky with the first vivid colors before they slept. Hearing the snoring coming from the bed, Eliza turned slowly and stiffly. She was almost afraid to look in case Kedlow had made the sound only to taunt her.

Kedlow lay on his back, his eyes closed and his mouth sagging, one arm flung across the sleeping Miss Biddy. His snoring began to grow in volume, and Eliza's eyes flew to the key on the side table. Kedlow had placed two other keys there. Now there were three keys—to the kitchen, to the root cellar, and to Miss Biddy's bedchamber.

Eliza snatched them up and ran noiselessly across the room. With a shaking hand she unlocked the door and slipped outside. Relocking the door, she walked firmly to the stairs.

Her steps faltered as she approached the kitchen door, for she was suddenly terribly afraid of what she would find. The key grated loudly in the lock as she turned it. "Mindy!" She flung the door wide and stepped into the disordered kitchen.

Mindy was conscious. She was sitting up, her back against the wall. Her face was so puffed and discolored that it was scarcely recognizable.

Tears of relief running down her face, Eliza ran across the kitchen and fell to her knees beside her. "Oh, Mindy, I was so afraid!" She put her arms about Mindy and held her closely. "I thought Kedlow had killed you!"

Mindy released herself gently from the clinging arms. "It take more'n Kedlow to dead me, so don't you take on." Mindy's voice was slow but clear, and Eliza had never been so glad to hear that softly slurred accent. "He hurt me some, an' Master Toby see that he pay for that, but far's ah can tell, ain't nothing busted."

"Oh, Mindy, I wish Master Toby would come home!"

"He be home soon, don't you fret." She patted Eliza's shoulder and gave the ghost of her old chuckle. "You a good chile, but you ain't none too strong. It be a hard job for you, but see if you can he'p me to mah feet."

Eliza was panting audibly before this was finally accomplished. Seated on her stool, Mindy managed to hold herself erect, but Eliza knew that this was a gallant effort that hid pain. "Now, then," Mindy said, "what them two done to Caroline? Where she at?"

"Caroline!" Eliza's hand flew to her mouth in dismay. "I must go to her."

"Where she at?" Mindy repeated.

"Kedlow locked her in the . . . the root cellar."

Mindy nodded. "And where them two at? What they doing?"

"They are sleeping in . . . in Miss Biddy's bed."

"That what ah thought," Mindy said grimly. "They sleep long time when Master Toby get he hands on 'em. Now, you get 'long and get Caroline out o' that cellar. Take her to mah room. Ah tend to her. After you done that, ah wants you to get the servants back to the house. Find that lazy Rose. Tell her she got to do the cooking in mah place. Now, scat!"

"Justin Lawrence should know about Caroline. Should I go to him?"

"Ain't we got 'nough trouble?" Mindy said in a horrified voice. "That Lawrence boy, he a savage when he roused. He ac' before he think. He get his hands on that Kedlow, he kill him. Don't want that, 'cause ah saving that pleasure for Master Toby."

"What about Miss Biddy?" Eliza asked hesitantly. She displayed the key in her hand. "I've . . . locked her door."

Mindy nodded approvingly. "That good."

"What if . . . what if Miss Selina comes along and wants to get into the room?"

"Miss Selina, she won't be doing no interfering. She ain't here. After Miss Biddy left for her drive, that friend of Miss Selina's, Mary Messinger, she stop by with her brother. Miss Selina, she go off with them for a visit. Said she'd stay with them for a few days. Tol' me to tell Miss Biddy, only ah never got the chance to tell her."

Eliza nodded. "Mindy, should I go back and unlock Miss Biddy's door?"

"After you done what ah tol' you, you get on back and lock yourself in again, like you ain't never left. Wish ab could keep Miss Biddy locked up till Master Toby get back, but cain't. Still, she going to be sick and sorry when she wake. She going to think twice before she do any more harm."

Eliza looked at her doubtfully. "What about Kedlow?"

Mindy's eyes flashed. "He get what coming to him. That Kedlow, he ain't as clever as he thinks."

Forcing herself to move, Mindy got off the stool and went over to the drawer where she kept her best candles. Deliberately, knowing the joy that Eliza found in the exquisite odor, she took out a long candle of myrtle wax. "Ah have me a boil-up of them myrtle berries two days ago," she explained her generosity as she fitted the candle in a pewter holder. Lighting it, she smiled at the girl. "There! Don't that smell good?" She turned away. "You going to need a light. That cellar mighty dark."

The tiny candle flame cast a trembling light over Eliza's face as she moved over to the door. Smiling at Mindy, she left the kitchen.

Eliza's fingers felt cold and clumsy as she fitted the key into the lock on the cellar door. "Caroline!" she called in a faint voice.

Her relief was almost overwhelming when Caroline answered at once. "Eliza! Is that you?"

"Yes, it's me, Eliza." Brushing tears of relief from her eyes, she started down the steep steps.

Caroline was crouched in a corner of the cellar, nearest to the narrow vent that let in weak puffs of air. Her face and her lips were blue with cold, and her knees were drawn up and her arms wrapped tightly about them. The position she had assumed, Eliza guessed, was meant not only to favor her back but to shield her naked breasts from Kedlow's gaze should he return to mete out further punishment.

There was relief in Caroline's eyes as Eliza came into view. "I thought . . . I thought it was Kedlow." Her arms dropped away, and her lips moved into a faint smile. "I . . . I thought I was going to be left to die here."

Eliza held the candleholder higher. Caroline was a pitiful sight. There were deep lines of pain in her face. Her hair was limp and dulled with sweat, and despite the faint smile, the eyes that regarded Eliza were hard and lightless. "Did Kedlow send you?" she said in a wary voice.

"Kedlow? Oh, no, Caroline! How could you think I would do his bidding?"

"I have lain here for hours," Caroline said bitterly. "When you did not come, I did not know what to think."

Eliza set the candle on the floor and knelt down beside her. "I was locked in Miss Biddy's room. Kedlow is still there, but they are sleeping now, and so I . . . I stole the key."

Caroline winced. "The pain is rather bad . . . it makes me say things I do not mean. I should have known you would come if you could."

"I know," Eliza said in a compassionate voice. "I understand." She touched Caroline's shoulder gently. "Your back needs Mindy's attention. Do you think you can manage to climb the steps?"

Caroline's eyes met hers. "I have had worse beatings. I will get over this. What did Kedlow do to Mindy? I know he hurt her. Even down here I heard her screams."

"He beat her with his . . . his fists."

Caroline turned her face away. "I am leaving this place, Eliza. I am going now. Will you help me?"

"Caroline!" Eliza's voice was shocked. "I understand how you feel. But in the state you are in, you can't just leave. Mindy is a little recovered now, and she is going to tend your back. I am to take you to her room."

"No," Caroline said in a hard voice. "My back will heal itself. I will not stay another moment in this place."

"But . . . but Justin?"

Caroline's face changed. "You must tell Justin what has happened to me," she said urgently. "He will understand why

I had to go. Tell him he is to do nothing about it. He is to wait for a message from me. Somehow I will get one to him."

"And if he refuses to do nothing? If he goes after Kedlow?"

Caroline seized Eliza's hand and held it tightly. "It would ruin everything. You must make him promise to wait for my message!"

Eliza stared at her. She was to make Justin Lawrence promise that instead of doing anything to avenge Caroline, he would wait for a message! It would be like pitting the will of a rabbit against that of a panther. "Perhaps it would be better to tell him nothing of the flogging, Caroline," she ventured. "If he knew of that, I could not possibly stop him going after Kedlow. You must know that for yourself?"

Caroline looked thoughtful. "Yes," she said after a moment, "you are right, of course. I wasn't thinking. Then just tell him of Miss Biddy's plan to sell me to Tom Keene. But he must wait for a message. If he jumps one way and I the other, we might never find each other again."

"Don't go like this, Caroline." Eliza drew her hand away. "Wait until your back is healed."

"No!" Caroline's voice was stubborn. "Will you help me?"

Sighing, Eliza nodded. "I will do whatever I can."

"Good. Go to our room and bring me a gown. And if you can avoid Mindy, some food from the kitchen. If, after I am gone, anyone should ask, you know nothing about it. Can you get the key of the cellar back before Miss Biddy wakes?"

"I think so. I hope so."

"Then it will be easy to say that you know nothing about it." Caroline's eyes were fierce and challenging. "Will you help?"

Eliza rose to her feet and moved reluctantly over to the steps. "You make it sound so easy," she said, turning to look at Caroline. "You will simply get on your feet and walk away from Montrose. But it will not be that way at all, Caroline. Master Toby can be kind, but you are wrong to take him for a fool. As a businessman, he has an investment in you, and he will protect that investment. He will send out search parties. Never doubt that."

Caroline did not doubt it. Lying on the cold stone floor in the stifling darkness, her back an agony, she had made her plan to escape. But even as she had made it, she had known how Tobias Markham would react. He was, as Eliza had just said, a businessman, and he was not one to let go easily.

"Nothing in life is ever easy, Eliza," Caroline said roughly. "But one must be prepared to take a chance. I shall watch for search parties. I will keep out of their way."

"I see it's no use talking to you, Caroline. Whatever I say, you will go your own way." The door at the head of the steps closed firmly behind Eliza.

Caroline rested her head against her knees. Her decision to escape had been formed in hatred and resentment and anger, but even then she had not been blind enough to think that it would be easy. She had known she was being foolhardy even to think of leaving the safe and familiar confines of the Montrose Plantation. But that safety was only an illusion if Miss Biddy made good her threat to dispose of her to Tom Keene. She must leave! With her mind made up, she had managed to thrust her doubts and fears into the background. Justin, she knew, would not have hesitated to strike out for parts unknown. He was a male, and strong. And what she had to prove to herself and to him was that a female could likewise survive in the wilds. She would show him that she could be as hardy and enduring and fearless as a male. If she and Justin were to make their home in this wild and untamed country, it was essential that she display courage and fortitude. She would be no weak and whining and lagging female, no, not she! She would be his partner, his full partner, in the great adventure. Others, she had heard, both male and female, had traveled that great forest that edged the plantation. Some had lived and some had died. She would travel it, and she would live! There would be ways of keeping in touch with Justin, and she would find those ways. She had no intention of losing him. For to do so would be to lose everything.

Caroline jumped violently as a rustling sound came from the opposite corner of the cellar. Her sudden involuntary movement sent darts of agony through her raw back. The rustling sound, she knew, was made by rats. Rats. How she hated them. They had infested the *Merryventure* and had added to the nightmare of the sick and the dying.

Caroline laughed shakily. Afraid of rats! She must remember that when she left here she would be entering the dark and mysterious forest. If she were not to be discovered and brought back to Montrose, it was the only way she could go.

There were things in that forest that were far more frightening than rats. There were wolves, for instance. Sometimes the wolves would come quite close to the boundaries of Montrose. Lying safely in her bed, she would shiver at the howling sounds they made.

She had spoken of the wolves to Mindy. Mindy had told her that the wolves had been known to devour unwary travelers. She had told her of one man who, finding himself too tired to travel farther, had made his bed in the forest. Before sleeping, he had built a bright fire to keep the wolves and other beasts away. The fire had saved him. But his horse, which had been tethered just outside the circle of firelight, had not been so lucky. The man had been jerked rudely from his sleep by the demented screaming of the madly plunging and rearing creature. The horse was struggling to fight off a pack of wolves. The snarling wolves, their fangs gleaming, foam dripping from panting mouths, were attacking the horse from all angles. They were at its throat, they scrabbled over its sweating back, they clung to its soft underbelly, ripping and tearing. They were everywhere. Paralyzed with horror, the man could only watch. When, at length, his palsied hand managed to snatch up his pistol and fire off a shot, it was already too late. The horse was dead. The snarling wolves were tearing at the carcass and dragging their spoils into the underbrush. Before his very eyes, the creatures had torn the animal to pieces. Later, telling his story, the man had said that the eyes of the wolves had glowed fiery gold in the firelight.

Mindy had told Caroline much of the forest, and she had always found the tales fascinating. Bears made their home there too. But they were more to be found near the looming shadows of the great mountains. Wildcats, minks, and polecats inhabited the forest, mingling with the gentle deer, the foxes, the squirrels, and the raccoons. Beavers made their homes in the streams, as did the moccasin snakes. The bite of the moccasin, Mindy had told her, was deadly. There were other snakes, too. The blacksnake, the horn snake, and the puff adder. There was danger everywhere in the forest, according to Mindy. If you did not become the prey of some hungry animal, you were likely to be stung to death by the teeming insect life. But the greatest danger, in Mindy's opinion, came from the Indians. She had stories to tell about the cruelty and the savagery of the Indians that could literally make your flesh crawl.

Shivering in the dank air of the cellar, Caroline slowly and painfully moved her position on the stone floor. The pain in her back seemed to recede as she thought of what Justin had said to her just yesterday. Yesterday? So much had happened to her that it seemed to be a long time ago. But for all that, his words came back to her as fresh and as bright as they had been on the moment of their utterance. "God knows why," he had said, "but I love you, Carrie."

Caroline smiled. It had been a grudging statement, as though he loved against his will, and one would scarcely call the words loverlike, but it was Justin's own unique way of expressing himself. He had made a similar statement before, of course, and she had never really believed him. But this time there had been something in his eyes, and, despite the grudging words, an undercurrent of sincerity in his voice that had convinced her. Justin! They would be together very soon, for she had a sure conviction that she would not, after all, be alone in the forest. Once he knew she was gone, he would not be far behind her. With Justin by her side, she would not fear the wild beasts that prowled, or the quick death-dealing strike of the snake, for he would keep harm from her.

The door at the top of the steps creaked open once more. Eliza came swiftly, bringing with her a delicious wafting perfume from her myrtle-berry candle. "I did not see Mindy," she said, setting the candleholder on the floor. "She is resting in her room. The servants will return later."

"The servants? Where are they?"

"Miss Biddy sent them away. She did not want them in the house last night. I have brought you a gown, shoes, your gray cloak, and a little food." Eliza paused. "I have also brought with me a bowl of warm water and some of Mindy's salve. No matter what you say, Caroline, your back must have some attention."

"It is early yet. I will get the things." Ignoring Caroline's "There is no time!"

further protests, Eliza turned away and mounted the stairs again.

In a frenzy of impatience to be gone, Caroline nonetheless was forced to submit to Eliza's careful ministrations. Light

though her touch was, Caroline bit hard on her lip to keep
back her cries of pain. But at last it was done.

The dew was still wet on the grass when Caroline left
Montrose. But despite the early hour, the plantation was already beginning to stir to its accustomed busy life. The sun,
slowly climbing higher in the blue, cloud-flecked sky, shed a
faintly warm pale-yellow shimmer over sleepy workers who
were reluctantly issuing forth to begin their long day of labor.
Their voices, some weary, some grumbling, some good-
natured, echoed hollowly in the thin morning air. From
somewhere near at hand a mockingbird set up a shrill, scold-
ing clamor.

Eliza, who had managed to creep back into Miss Biddy's
bedchamber without awakening its occupants, who slept so
soundly, watched Caroline from the window.

Caroline walked boldly, without any attempt at concealment. Her head was held high. It was as if she knew exactly
where she was going and why. She walked steadily, calmly, as
if she had a perfect right to be traversing that narrow dusty
road that was leading her away from Montrose. One or two
glances were thrown her way, but they were incurious. If
those that saw her go gave any thought to her and her destination, the basket she carried over her arm would indicate
to them that she was going to the edge of the forest clearing
to gather the late berries.

Eliza watched until she was out of sight. She was full of
admiration for Caroline's performance. She knew what it
must have cost her in pain to walk so boldly and erectly. She
thought of Caroline's words of hope. But she knew—how
could she help knowing?—that it was already too late for
Moon and herself. "Too late!" she whispered. "Much, much
too late! Good-bye, Caroline. God bless you." The mockingbird began to scold again as Eliza drew back from the window.

Chapter 24

Lounging by the open kitchen door, Ben Cranwell narrowed his eyes and looked from the idle Mindy to the bustling Rose. He was consumed with curiosity. What had been happening here? he wondered. Last night, when the servants had been turned out of the house, he had questioned one or two of them, but they had given him only a stupid look. Either they did not know why they had been turned out or they refused to say. To add to the mystery, here was Mindy, who usually refused to let anyone else touch her precious cooking pots, sitting idle at her table while Rose hurried to prepare the lunches for the field hands. Mindy's face was swollen and bruised. Her left eye was almost closed. Her hands, resting on the table, were trembling.

Mindy became aware of Cranwell's eyes on her hands. Throwing him an angry glance, she hastily hid them in her lap. "What for you still here, Cranwell?" she said sharply. "Ain't ah done told you that the lunches for the hands won't be ready for a while? You git on back to your work, or that Jaxon, he ain't going to be too pleased with you."

Cranwell scowled at this mention of his overseer. "Let the bastard wait," he answered Mindy in a surly voice. "Ain't my fault them lunches ain't ready. Why'd I have to come for 'em anyway? Where's the girl, that Caroline Fane? It's her job to bring 'em."

At this mention of Caroline Fane, Mindy's heart leaped in alarm. What would Miss Biddy say when she found that Caroline had run off? What was she to say to Master Toby, who set such store by the girl? There was only one way out. She would tell him the truth about everything that had occurred. And this time she was determined not to hide Miss Biddy's part in it. Turning her head away from Cranwell's too penetrating eyes, she said gruffly, "Caroline ain't feeling so good."

Cranwell's grin exposed his yellowed teeth. "Ain't that a bleedin' shame? I has to work when I ain't feeling good, so why the 'ell can't she?"

"Ain't none o' your business, far's ah can see."

Alarmed by her expression, Cranwell retreated. "What 'bout them lunches? I ain't no nigger to be wearing out my legs. They ought to be ready."

"Well, they ain't. Scat! Wait outside till ah call you."

Rose gave the scowling Cranwell a frightened look. "They be ready soon," she called in her high, thin voice.

"They'd bloody better be!" Cranwell snarled. He turned his scowl on Mindy. "I'm going to take me a walk. If them lunches ain't ready when I get back, you'll have to tote 'em yourself. Aye, you can haul that fat black arse o' yourn. Or maybe you can send the Harris wench." Grinning, Cranwell stepped outside. "I been wanting me a word with that little bitch. You tell her that."

Mindy's answer was to slam the door in his face. Studiously avoding Rose's eyes, she went back to her seat. If only Master Toby would get back soon, she thought wearily. Everything was going wrong. Caroline had run off. Eliza, released at last from Miss Biddy's room, had hidden herself somewhere. If Miss Biddy should ask for Eliza, she wouldn't know what to tell her.

A pot dropped, and Mindy looked up with a frown. "Be more careful, Rose," she rebuked.

"Yes, ma'am."

Mindy's thoughts returned to her worries. Frowning, she thought of the story Eliza had told her. Caroline had run off, Eliza had said. She was going to make her way through the forest. The forest! The good Lord alone knew what would happen to her! As for Miss Biddy, she was still drinking steadily. The hour was early, but no doubt she was already drunk. Kedlow, she was sure, had left hours ago.

Another pot dropped from Rose's hands and clanged to the floor. Looking miserable and guilty, Rose began babbling nervously, "It all right. Wasn't nothing in that pot."

"You pick it up, girl," Mindy said sternly. "And you 'member this. Ah don't want no dents in mah good pots." Mindy's eyes softened as Rose began to sniffle. "It all right this time, girl. Ain't your fault nohow. You nervous, ah ex-

pect. Tell you what, you see if you c'n find Eliza. Tell her ah
wants to see her."

Still shaken with sobs, Rose departed. Mindy continued to
sit for a moment more, then got to her feet. Hobbling painfully, she gathered ingredients together. "Better ah do the
work mahself," she muttered. "That Rosie wench, she like to
drive me out o' mah mind."

His hands thrust into his pockets, Cranwell whistled
through his teeth as he slouched down the narrow road.
Whenever he could, he liked to walk on this road. It gave
him a sense of freedom.

Cranwell frowned fiercely. Freedom? He had yet to work
out the term of his indenture. Two years, two long years before he could call himself free, before he would be given fifty
acres of land.

Cranwell's eyes were suddenly caught by a flash of scarlet.
What was it that made that brilliant flash? He hesitated, then
moved toward it.

The flash of scarlet proved to be the lining of a gray cloak.
The same cloak he had often seen wrapped about Caroline
Fane. The cloak was dry, he could see that, so Fane must
have passed this way not so very long ago. But what was
Fane doing in the forest? Mindy had told him she was feeling
poorly, and he had thought that she must be in her bed.
Where was she now? How far had she gone into the forest?

Cranwell stared at the basket lying beside the cloak. Flop-
ping down on his knees, he pushed the cloak to one side and
reached for the basket. It contained two packets of food.

Cranwell's eyes narrowed in thought. To his mind, this discovery could mean only one thing: Fane had decided to run
off. Perhaps the cloak had been too heavy, and that was why
she had left it behind. But he couldn't imagine her leaving
the food too. A person had to look out for himself in the
forest, by all accounts that he had heard. No, unless something was wrong, she would not have left the food. Had she
been taken up by Indians? Cranwell shook his head, instantly
rejecting this idea. It was too close to civilization. Indians
would not come this far. Then what? Perhaps, as Mindy had
said, she was sick. Cranwell grinned. More than sick, he
would think. She'd have to be delirious to leave the food behind. Whatever had happened to the wench, he had no inten-

tion of going after her. He'd not run the risk of being scalped by Indians, or likely making a meal for a prowling wildcat or some other animal. If the bitch wanted to run, let her look out for herself.

Crouching there, Cranwell remembered the look on Mindy's face when he'd asked her about Fane. He'd thought nothing about it at the time, but now he knew that the fear he had surprised in her expression meant that she knew Fane was gone. Did Miss Biddy know? He shook his head. No, it was not likely that she knew, or there would be no reason for Mindy to fear. The problem would no longer be hers. What if he went to Miss Biddy and told her that Fane was gone? For that matter, he could tell her about Eliza and the nigger. Perhaps, as a reward for telling, he would gain an immediate release from his indenture. He had heard that it was the practice of a grateful master to release an indentured servant before his time. And surely Markham would be grateful to know of the filthy morals of Eliza Harris? Freedom! His fifty acres of land! If it had happened for others, why not for him? A white girl doing it with a nigger! Yes, Markham was bound to be grateful to learn of this. But he wouldn't wait for Markham's return. He would tell Miss Biddy first.

Cranwell rose to his feet. Looking quickly about him, he made his way back to the road. Almost as though his thoughts had conjured her up, he saw Eliza Harris standing there. Startled, he blurted out, "What you doing here? You spying on me?"

Eliza shrank back. "No. I . . . I was just taking a walk."

"Come here, you!" Cranwell seized her roughly by the arm and pulled her toward him. You an' me's going back to the house."

"Why?"

The terror in her eyes amused him. "You know why, you filthy little cow. I'm going to tell Miss Biddy 'bout you and the nigger."

"No, don't! You promised!" She touched him with trembling fingers. "I'll do anything. Anything at all!" Desperately she swayed her hips, trying to make her childish figure inviting. "Take me behind those trees. You can have me as many times as you want."

He pushed her away from him. "I don't want you no more. I said I'm going to tell, and I am."

"No! I won't let you!" She launched herself at him and tried to hit him with her clenched fists. "You must not! No, no, you must not!"

Cranwell held her off easily. Laughing, holding both of her thin wrists with one hand, he cuffed her head sharply with the other. "There! That'll teach you!"

If it had not been that he still held her wrists, Eliza would have fallen. She could not fight him; she was not strong enough. He would not heed her pleading. There was nothing she could say or do that would change his mind. Nothing!

Cranwell looked at her sharply. She looked as if she was going to faint. He'd have to carry her back.

Eliza did not faint, but she was barely conscious. She was aware that Cranwell had picked her up. He was carrying her back to Montrose. He was going to tell Miss Biddy! At this last terrible thought, her senses cleared somewhat. Tears gathered beneath her closed lids. She had failed Moon. Because of her, he would be put to death. Moon! Her heart cried out to him. My darling, my love, I shall never see you again!

Her lids drooped, shutting out the sight of Cranwell's hated face. Even when Cranwell carried her into the house, Eliza still did not open her eyes. She heard a male voice protesting his entrance, and Cranwell's snarling reply. A few moments later there was a stumbling sound on the stairs, followed by Miss Biddy's raised and outraged voice. "What is the meaning of this? How dare you come into the house by the front entrance, Cranwell!"

"I tried to stop him, Miss Biddy." Jimmy's soft, frightened voice. "But he say he got to see you, ma'am."

"Be quiet, fool. How dare you speak without permission!"

Eliza heard the black man's quick sighing breath. Then Miss Biddy again. "Who is that you are carrying, Cranwell?"

"Ain't no one else but your maid, Miss Biddy." Cranwell pushed back the hood of Eliza's cloak. "Found her on the road, I did. I reckon she might have been trying to run off."

Miss Biddy's stumbling footsteps came nearer. A cold hand touched her face. "It is Harris. Trying to run off, was she? She'll pay for that!"

"But I captured her, Miss Biddy, ma'am. You won't be forgetting that, will you?"

"No, Cranwell, I won't forget. Well, man, don't stand there gaping at me like an idiot. Put the girl down."

Cranwell, grumbling beneath his breath, lowered her to the floor. Eliza felt the cold tiles of the floor against her hot cheek, but she did not move from the position in which he had placed her. Tired! Too tired, too broken in spirit to open her eyes. Let them do as they liked, say what they liked. She would be dead soon enough, and so would Moon.

"And that ain't all about Harris, Miss Biddy," Cranwell's loud voice said. "I got something else to tell you. Something shocking."

"Speak up, then. What is it?"

Cranwell's footsteps moved away. Eliza heard the buzzing of his lowered voice. Then, as it emerged clearly, "It's true, Miss Biddy. I seen 'em at it with my own eyes."

The quality of the silence that followed was terrifying. Very cautiously, Eliza opened her eyes. Miss Biddy was standing still, her cheeks scarlet and her eyes stretched wide with horror. Why the horror? Eliza thought. What a hypocrite she was! Cranwell wore a smugly triumphant expression. But Jimmy, the young black man, was gripping the back of a chair with tense fingers. Eliza's eyes stayed on him. Poor Jimmy! He looked so frightened. His skin was glistening with perspiration and his body was trembling. There was a strong bond among the blacks on the plantation, and what happened to one happened to all. There was dread in the way he was staring at Miss Biddy.

Biddy began to scream. She stood there like a statue, her mouth wide open to emit those peals of chilling sound, the cords in her throat straining.

"Christ!" Cranwell's triumphant expression had given way to fear. "Stop it!" he shouted, trying to make himself heard above the din. "Miss Biddy! For Christ's sake, stop it!"

The screaming stopped as suddenly as it had begun. Biddy's mouth snapped closed. Leaping over to the big front door, she wrenched it open. "You, Jimmy," she shouted, "ring the bell. I want all hands summoned to the front of the house."

As Jimmy rushed to obey, Biddy turned to face Cranwell. Drunk and full of venom, her eyes blazing with fury, she shrilled at him, "Go to Mindy. Tell that fat black cow that she is to come to the front of the house."

The plantation bell began to ring as Cranwell turned away. Biddy looked down at Eliza. "You filth!" she screamed above the deafening clamor of the bell. "Bed yourself with a nigger, will you, you whore!" Her foot, kicking out viciously, caught Eliza in the side, bringing a moan of pain from her. "Get up, slut. Get up!"

Panting, Biddy stood back, her glittering eyes watching the girl's feeble movements. Mindy, entering the hall, saw her mistress's expression. She did not need to be told what had happened. Poor Eliza! Poor frightened child! So her pitiful secret was out in the open. What had been so shining and beautiful to her was about to be smeared by the malice of this woman who was herself guilty. But where Eliza's misconduct, if it could be called such, had been in the name of love, Miss Biddy had acted purely from lust. There was scarcely a black man on the plantation who had not been called to Miss Biddy's bed.

Conquering her aversion to the woman, and trying not to look at Eliza, Mindy passed by Biddy and took her place outside.

Chapter 25

The hands had assembled in front of the house. It was unusual to be thus summoned from their work. Some were curious, others felt apprehension, and those who looked upon the
summons as a welcome break in their long day of labor were
lighthearted, inclined, with their smiling faces and their
cheerful head nodding, to make a holiday occasion of it. And
then there were others, those whose consciences were burdened, who felt the cold clutch of dread. But all of them, at
first, their eyes turned to the open front door, were silent.
Then, gradually, conversation broke out here and there,
punctuated by small bursts of laughter that had a nervous
ring to it. Speculation was rife, and there was even some mild
betting on the reason that they had been sent for. A small
black boy, clinging with one chubby hand to his mother's
skirt, began to giggle. The woman turned a stern look on him
and sharply bade him to hush. The child was silent for a moment, gazing about him with round and wondering eyes; then
he began to giggle again.

Justin looked at Moon. He felt a sharp anxiety as he saw
the glaze of sweat on Moon's face. The crowd, bunching up,
pushed him closer, and he felt the trembling of the big
black's body. "Easy, Moon," he said softly.

Moon's solemn eyes turned to him. "I am afraid, my
friend," he said in his deep, low voice. "Something is about to
happen. Something evil." He put his hand over his heart. "I
feel it here, inside me."

Justin too had a sense of foreboding, but he refused to give
in to it. He tried to laugh it away. "Nonsense," he said in a
cheerful voice. "You are always getting these feelings. Were I
to listen to you, I would spend my days in fear and
trembling."

"Surely I am not as bad as all that?" Moon said, forcing a smile.

"Worse." Justin laughed. "Cheer up. Perhaps we will find that we are to be given a holiday."

Moon was about to reply, but the words died in his throat as attention was once more centered on the open front door. A slim black man stepped out, carrying a glowing brazier of coals. Without looking at the assembled people, he placed the brazier down very carefully and then vanished into the house again. A moment later he returned. This time he carried a small table, which he placed beside the brazier. On the table were a large pair of scissors and a branding iron.

A wave of uneasiness swept over the watchers. A woman started to cry. "That a branding iron on that table," a man said in a loud voice. "What it for? Who going to be branded?" He glared about him challengingly, as though daring the guilty one to come forth.

"A branding iron!" Moon said. There was such horror in his voice that Justin stiffened. "We would not be assembled here to watch the branding of an animal, my friend. It therefore follows that one of us is to be branded."

Justin did not answer. A pulse pounded in his temple, and he was swept by a wave of cold anger. When he did speak, his voice was tight and controlled. "One of us, you say. I guarantee you this. If anyone attempts to lay that iron on me, I will kill him!" It occurred suddenly to Justin that Caroline was not in the crowd. His body responded before his mind could even register that fact. His heart was racing, and he felt a pang in the very pit of his stomach. Caroline was gone. He knew it.

Moon was looking toward the door. "Here comes Miss Biddy. She has Cranwell with her. Now, I wonder why? What has he to do with anything?"

From where he stood, Justin had a clear view of Biddy Markham. She looked flushed, and her eyes held a feverish glitter. She was standing very stiffly, her hands held behind her back. "It would seem that the play is about to begin," Justin murmured.

Moon's thoughtful eyes were still on Ben Cranwell. "Whatever is about to happen," he said slowly, "I feel sure that that man is involved in it."

Justin glanced at Cranwell. "Undoubtedly," he said contemptuously. "I have found, when anything dirty is going on, that that little rat usually is involved."

With a studiedly dramatic gesture, Biddy brought her hands forward. A collective gasp went through the crowd as they saw the big pistol in her right hand. "Cranwell"— Biddy's voice was harsh—"take this pistol, please."

Cranwell shrank back. The rapid beating of his heart made him feel dizzy for a moment. Why did she want him to take it? What kind of a game was she playing? He hadn't reckoned on anything like this. "Why me, Miss Biddy?" he said hoarsely. "I . . . I don't want nothing to do with no pistol."

The glare she turned on him brought the hot blood to his cheeks. "You will do as you are told, Cranwell!" Biddy snapped. She held the weapon toward him. "If you do not, you will not get the reward you crave, and further, I shall have you stripped down and flogged."

Cranwell made a strangled sound in his throat. God curse the drunken old bitch! By talking of a reward, she had made it plain that he was the cause of this gathering. The assembled people were silent, watching him, and he could feel the resentment and the hatred emanating from them. He cringed in fear, his eyes darting about him, desperately wanting to run. There was no help for; he would have to do as she said. It was essential that he get his release. Now that these people knew that he was involved, his life would not be safe. He knew of one or two murders that had been arranged to look like accidents. He had no intention of dying. He had to fulfill his dream. But a pistol! What did the bitch want from him? Was he supposed to murder somebody? He tried one last feeble protest. "Miss Biddy, please!"

"I said take it!" Biddy thrust the pistol at him. "How dare you argue with me!"

Weak tears came into Cranwell's eyes. Oh, Christ, she was up to something! She looked mad, with her hair coming down and those glittering eyes fixed on his face. Reluctantly he took the weapon from her. The butt felt cold and heavy as he hefted it in his hand. "What I got to do with it?" he muttered.

"You are to stand by. If I command you to do so, Cranwell, you are to fire on whomever I point out to you. Is that clear?"

Cranwell's teeth came together with a sharp click. He did

not want to look, but, with a horrible fascination, his eyes were drawn to the people. His stomach lurched as he saw the fierce, hating looks directed at him. His gaze traveled to the one most concerned in this affair, Moon. Standing beside Moon was Justin Lawrence. Christ help him, he thought, if he ever came up against that black giant and his friend, the tough, fierce Lawrence. They would kill him. Lawrence would for sure.

"Cranwell!" Miss Biddy's voice cut like a sharp cold blade through his dismay and fear, bringing his attention back to the present. "Did you understand what I said to you?"

"Yes, ma'am," he mumbled.

Biddy gave him a long, considering look. What was the matter with the man? He was shaking badly. She wondered if she could rely on him to do his duty. Biddy passed her tongue over her dry lips. She felt hot and unwell, and her own hands were shaking. Cranwell shook because he was a sniveling coward, but for herself there was a much simpler explanation. She needed a drink, needed one badly. The sooner she got this unsavory business over with, the sooner she could retire to her room and the much-needed drink. It was the only way to stop the shaking. Her eyes rested first on Moon, then on Justin Lawrence. She smiled faintly. The nigger and the grand m'lord, who had constituted himself the nigger's friend, had a shock coming to them.

Thinking of Tobias, Biddy frowned faintly. He, of course, would not like what she was about to do. What she was forced to do, she corrected herself. But in time he would come to see that she had upheld the law.

Dismissing thoughts of her husband, Biddy raised her hands. A child, frightened by something it sensed, set up a wailing cry. The cry was instantly muffled, as though a hand had been placed over the little mouth. Complete silence settled over the gathering.

Satisfied that she had their attention, Biddy began gravely. "I have brought you here today to witness two punishments that it is my reluctant duty to carry out. In the absence of my husband, I must not falter from my duty."

Biddy paused, her eyes going from face to face, her faint smile inviting them to understand and sympathize. Like Cranwell, she was suddenly conscious of their hatred. She was shaken for a moment; then she pulled herself together.

She was imagining things. These people would not dare to display hatred toward the mistress of Montrose. They all knew that, if she cared to do so, she could order them all to be flogged. "Some of you may have wondered what the fire and the branding iron are for," she went on in a clear, ringing voice. "I will tell you. The iron is to brand a fornicator. The letter F will be branded in the middle of a slut's forehead, so that all may know her for what she is. I know you will share in my horror and shock when I tell you that this girl, this white girl, has fornicated with a black man." She nodded toward the scissors. "Those scissors are to cut off her hair. Another way to advertise her shame."

Biddy paused to look again at Moon. His eyes were fixed on her with horror and pain in their depths. His tall form was shaken, as if with an ague, and great beads of perspiration had formed on his forehead. As she stared, she saw the perspiration pencil his cheeks and splash down onto his shirt. Justin Lawrence said something to him in a voice too low for her to hear. He placed his hand on Moon's shoulder in an attempt at comfort, or perhaps reassurance. The black man seemed to be listening, but it was evident that Justin Lawrence's words had not reassured him. He had half-closed his eyes, and his glistening forehead was puckered as if in pain. Justin Lawrence said something else to him. Moon turned his head and looked deeply into his eyes; then he slowly shook his head.

Relinquishing her private enjoyment, Biddy continued. "In indulging in this unnatural fornication, these two had flouted God's most sacred law. His law that white shall not mate with black."

A piercing scream came from the house. Shaken, Cranwell turned inquiring eyes to Biddy. "Cranwell," Biddy said in a loud voice, "bring her out." She pointed a dramatic finger. "Let my people look upon the face of one who has contemptuously broken God's law!"

That scream, that despairing scream! It struck at Moon like a savage blow over the heart. Was it his Liza who had screamed? Oh, God, God! You made me black and Liza white, but both of us are made in Your image. Protect my Liza now. Turn away from her the undeserved scorn and hatred. And forgive me, Lord. Not for loving her, but for failing to understand why I should not. Am I not Your child too? Then how can it be forbidden, this love we have for each other?

Moon's silent pleading with his God came to an end as Justin gripped his shoulder hard. While Moon's thoughts were riveted on Eliza, Justin was worrying about what Biddy had in mind for Moon. Cranwell dragged Eliza from the house. Moon's eyes filled up with tears. His Liza, with her little cap dangling down her back by its strings, her pale hair disheveled, and a look in her eyes that stabbed him with unbearable pain.

Justin watched as Eliza was forced to her knees, and he felt a terrible rage against the woman who had brought this tragedy about. Eliza's thin body was sagging, and her long unbound hair fell forward and obscured her face.

Moon stepped forward. He'd be damned if he'd let that bitch brand Eliza like an animal. He'd die first. "Don't be afraid, my love," Moon shouted. "I'm coming, I'm coming."

Eliza saw him fighting his way out of the crowd, and her colorless face was suddenly transformed. "Moon!" She rose to her feet. Her arms held out, she ran to him. "My darling! Oh, my darling!"

Moon's arms closed about her and pressed her against his body. Beneath his spread hands he could feel her bones, delicate, fragile, like the bones of a sparrow. "Liza, my little one!" Moon felt as though he were bleeding inside. Bleeding for her and for himself. His life was draining away slowly, drop by drop. He had the feeling that his declining life stream was mingling with hers, making them one in death, as they had been in life. "I love you, Liza, I love you!"

"I know." Her eyes, very wide and blue and clear, lingered on his face with love. She knew that they had reached an ending, but she was no longer afraid, for in that ending was their beginning. Why had it taken her so long to understand that? Her hand touched his face lightly in a butterfly caress. "Moon! My love!"

He had always known her thoughts, and he knew them now. She was not afraid. She would never be afraid again. His heart lifted on a great surge of joy. "Not much longer now, my Liza," he whispered. "Very soon we will be together for always. You believe that, don't you?"

"Yes, Moon, I believe it. I know it."

Very gently, Moon put her from him and turned to face Biddy.

Biddy looked wildly about her. She saw the pity in the faces turned to Moon. She saw hatred in those same faces when they looked back at her. She could not stand it, she would not stand it! Pity for that slut and that black beast, and hatred for her! She put shaking hands to her untidy hair, clutching at it, and her voice came out in a scream, "Kill them, Cranwell. Kill the unnatural and ungodly fornicators. Kill them, I say. Kill them!"

Oh, Christ, that bloody bitch! Why couldn't she shoot them down herself? Why did he have to do it? Murder! Would he ever get his land? Miss Biddy was screaming at him. She was muddling him up, giving him no time to think. His land—he must have it. There was only one way—he must act, he must shoot now. His trembling hand lifted the heavy pistol; his finger squeezed the trigger. The roaring bark of the weapon was deafening. Terrified, Cranwell staggered back. The screams of the frightened people were loud in his ears as he stared at the swaying Moon.

Moon put his hands to the hole the bullet had torn in his stomach. He felt unreal, so cold and numb that it was as if he were already dead. He looked down and saw his hands dyed red with his blood. It bubbled through his fingers and splashed in thick heavy drops to the ground. So much blood, he thought dazedly, so much! He gasped as the numbness began to lift. Now he was all pain, all fiery tearing pain, and there was no strength left in his legs. He saw Liza through a mist, a small dwindling form, going away from him, leaving him alone. Would they meet again? Was there another life, an eternity? "Liza!" His choked voice said her name in an agony of doubt. He tried to reach out to her, to touch her, but he had no strength left in him. He was falling slowly, so slowly, and it seemed to him that he fell a long, long way.

"Moon!" He turned his head toward the sound of Liza's voice. She was kneeling beside him, her hands touching him gently. She was with him. She had not left him to die alone. He fought the darkness that was pressing against his eyes, striving to see her face. Her tears were cold drops on his face as she bent forward to kiss his lips; and then he heard her voice again, "I love you so, my darling! I will love you forever!"

Forever! The word echoed in his mind. Forever. A golden word, a promise of eternity. He wanted to tell her that he would be waiting for her. He wanted to say her name, that little name that had always been so sweet on his lips, but his throat was closing, choking off words, choking off life. His lips moved into a smile. And, smiling, he died.

Justin felt a choking sensation and a cold feeling in the pit of his stomach. With the barking sound of the pistol, his fear for Caroline came back to the surface. He knew that Carrie was either dead or had run off. He rejected the thought of her death, suppressed it. And yet the other possibility filled him with an almost equal dread. Where could Carrie go except through the forest? Perspiration broke out on his forehead, and he felt sick. Carrie alone! Carrie facing all of those things she had hitherto so greatly feared!

Justin's eyes turned to Biddy. He studied her face intently. The twitching mouth, the strange look in the eyes. Fullfledged, the truth came to him. Biddy Markham was insane. He knew then that Caroline would not have escaped from Montrose unscathed. No, either she was dead or something had set her on her headlong course to destruction. Something? Someone? Biddy Markham? Crazy Biddy Markham! Carrie wounded, struggling to survive! The thought brought with it such pain that he trembled with the force of it. If she were alive, he'd find her. He loved her; there was no doubt about it. If she were dead, there would be nothing left for him. Carrie and Paul were the only two beings he had ever loved. Be alive, Carrie. For Chirst's sake, be alive! he prayed.

The only two beings he had ever loved? No, that was not quite true. He had loved and trusted Moon as he would a brother. And now Moon was dead. Murdered at the command of that insane bitch! Moon's black skin looked gray now, Justin thought. It was the color of dead ashes. Again that killing fury blazed up. He was almost grateful for the savage emotion that served momentarily to sweep away the sharp edges of his grief. Looking about him, he saw like quickly flashing portraits the fear and the horror in the faces about him. The terror in a child's eyes. The perspiration on Moon's forehead. It seemed to be frozen, for it clung to his skin like great crystal drops. His life functions dead, as he was dead. There was Eliza, the tears still sliding down her pale cheeks, her hand resting gently on Moon's hair. Biddy, trembling and wild-eyed, her mouth agape and her cheeks flushed with hectic color. Cranwell, wearing a dazed expression, his hand still clutching the smoking pistol. Mindy, standing near Biddy Markham, her skin looking almost as gray as Moon's.

It was Biddy who broke the silence that had fallen. "Give me that pistol!" she shrieked. She tore it from Cranwell's hand and leveled it at Eliza. "I'm going to kill you too, you filthy slut! You whore!"

"No!" Justin shouted. "No more killing. No more!" Frantically he began pushing his way through the crowd. "Move, Eliza! For the love of God, move!"

If Eliza heard, she did not look up. Unmoving, her eyes on Moon's face, she crouched there. Her face was ravaged with her weeping, and yet she was not unhappy. Moon was dead, but he was not gone beyond her. He would wait for her, she knew. Soon now, she would be walking by Moon's side. Her hand would be clasped tightly in his, sharing that last journey to a land where they would never again be parted.

Justin had almost reached Eliza's side when the pistol roared again. He saw Eliza's body jerk, her outflung arms, the slow seeping of blood from her mouth. In the silence that had again descended, he heard the sighing sound she made as she slumped over Moon's body.

"Eliza!" Justin fell to his knees beside her. Lifting her, he cradled her in his arms. Her pale hair spilled over his arm; her blue eyes were already glazing with approaching death. "Eliza!" he said again, the little name choking in his throat.

"Justin!" Eliza's tremulous fingers touched his face. "Find Caroline . . . gone . . . run away . . . find."

"I'll find her, Eliza." Her eyes closed. Her head felt heavy against him. She was dead. Gone far beyond malice and prejudice. Gently Justin laid her down beside Moon. "I will find Carrie, Eliza," he said again. It was a vow rather than a statement.

Mindy saw the frightened faces of the people. Nothing, she knew, could be expected of them. Miss Biddy, hysterical, crazed, had, in the absence of her husband, the power to order yet more savage punishments, and they knew it. It was man's law, not God's, that said that white must not mate with black. So for what Miss Biddy had done today, the law would applaud and uphold her. The law jealously guarded the rights of the master, who had absolute domination over slaves, indentured servants, and so-called free black men. But this thing that had happened was a nightmare. Something she would never be able to forget. Moon lying there so still, Eliza's body beside him, their blood staining the ground. Mindy clasped her trembling hands together. "Jesus God," she whispered. "Help us now!"

Mindy knew there was to be no help as yet when she saw the terrible look on Justin Lawrence's face. No, the nightmare was not yet over. He was walking toward Miss Biddy, his burning eyes fixed on her face. He was going to kill her! But he must not do it. Not for Miss Biddy's sake, but for his own! Mindy found her voice. "Go back, boy!" she screamed. "Don't do it, boy, don't!"

Justin did not even glance in her direction; his attention was all on Biddy. "Eliza is dead, you murdering bitch!" he shouted hoarsely. "Are you and Cranwell satisfied now, or is there to be more murder? Would you like to try for me?"

Biddy looked at the tall advancing figure. She could not seem to wrench her gaze from those burning dark eyes. He was going to kill her. She could see her death written there in his face. "No, no! Get back, you savage!" she screamed. The pistol trembled in her hand. "Get back, or I'll kill you!"

"You'll have to kill me to stop me now. What are you waiting for? Come on, shoot!"

Mindy put her hand over her mouth to stifle a scream. The rogue had surely gone mad. Didn't he realize how dangerous Miss Biddy was?

Biddy trembled violently. Unless she killed Lawrence on the spot, he would be a peril to her. She had the feeling that, even wounded, he would still come for her. Biddy thrust the pistol at Cranwell. "Shoot that man!" she commanded in a high, hysterical voice. "Kill him, kill him!"

Cranwell shrank back. "I've had enough. If you want Lawrence dead, you'll have to do it yourself."

"Coward!" Biddy hesitated, the struggle visible in her face. Making up her mind, she swung toward Justin again. Lifting the pistol, she aimed it at his body. Her finger tightened on the trigger.

Justin jumped to one side. He stood there for a moment; then, with a sudden spring, he was upon them. Cranwell saw

the pistol knocked from Biddy's hand. He heard her terrified
screaming as he tried to run into the house.

"No, you don't!" Justin hurled the man about to face him.
His fist exploded against Cranwell's jaw, and the force of the
blow sent him rolling down the two marble steps.

"You've killed him!" Biddy shrieked. She began to edge
away, her hands held out to ward him off. "Don't touch me!"
Her heel caught in the hem of her gown. She tried to keep
her balance, but her ankle twisted. With a despairing scream,
she fell.

"You bitch!" Justin crouched over her. His fingers touched
her throat and gripped. "I'll kill you!"

The assembled people stood there looking on. A wave of
emotion went through them at the sight of the mistress of
Montrose helpless beneath those gripping fingers. Their eyes
were on the dark, savage face bent over Biddy Markham,
and there was not one of them who did not silently applaud
his action. They all hated her. They would be glad to see her
dead.

Mindy stared at Biddy's wildly thrashing legs, and temptation came to her. It would be so easy. She had but to remain
where she was, saying nothing, doing nothing, and Justin
Lawrence would remove all the pain and grief and ugliness
from Master Toby's life. She took a deep, shuddering breath
and firmly pushed temptation from her. What had she been
thinking of? Not even for Master Toby's dear sake could she
let Justin Lawrence carry the burden of murder on his conscience.

Mindy lumbered forward, purpose in her expression.
"That's 'nough!" Seizing Justin's arm, she pulled upon it with
all her strength. "Let her go, boy," she panted, "she ain't
worth it. You kill her, and you going to be hunted down.
Ain't no place you can hide." She redoubled her efforts. "You
hear me, boy? Let go, ah say, let go!"

It was not Mindy's words as much as the urgency in her
voice that cut through Justin's murderous fury. Surrendering
to the pull on his arm, he slowly drew back. Rising shakily to
his feet, he wiped his hands on his breeches as though he
would be rid of the feel of her flesh. "Moon is dead," he said
in a dull voice. "Moon and Eliza both."

"Ah knows it, boy, ah knows. Miss Biddy, she going to suffer bad when Master Toby git back. He won't 'low murder.'"

Mindy got awkwardly to her knees. Placing her ear against Biddy's chest, she announced, "Ain't dead, boy. Heart's beating good and strong."

Justin's eyes went to the crumpled forms of Moon and Eliza. "A pity," he said in a hard voice. "She should be dead."

Mindy rose to her feet and faced him. "Well, she ain't, boy. And that's 'nough o' that crazy talk. Be thankful that you ain't got murder on you soul." Her eyes went to the silent onlookers. "Can do right well without them starers," she muttered. "Don't need 'em here nohow." She put her hands on the rail and directed a stern look at them. "Git on 'bout you work," she shouted. "Ain't nothing more for you all to see. Go on, git! Shoo!"

Still stunned by the double tragedy and a third near-murder, no one thought of disobeying Mindy's command. With a shuffle of feet, they turned to leave. There was no conversation, no laughter. They dispersed quietly, some looking at the two figures on the ground, others staring straight ahead, as if afraid to look.

As the last one disappeared, Justin stooped and picked up the pistol. Thrusting it in his belt, he looked intently at Mindy, then at the servants clustered in the doorway. "I'm leaving," he said quietly. "I'm going after Carrie. If anyone tries to stop me, I'll shoot them down. I mean it!"

Ignoring him, Mindy turned to the servants. "Jimmy, Sam, you two carry Miss Biddy to her room. The rest of you, git."

Obediently, carefully avoiding looking at Justin, the two men picked up Biddy and departed. The other servants went after them.

"How you think you go, boy?" Mindy demanded of Justin. "Ain't got no food. Ain't got no nothing. That Caroline, she teched in the head, seems like. Never thought you the same."

"I've always been teched in the head, Mindy. Anyway, I will manage. I must find Carrie, you know that. So, what now, Mindy? Do you intend to try to stop me?"

"How ah do that, boy? You got that shooting iron, ain't you? 'Sides, ah only a woman. Ain't got the strength to stop you."

"You could call somebody. You have only to ring the bell."

"Now, then, don't you go putting ideas into mah head, boy," Mindy said crossly. "Don't make me no never-mind what you do. You wanting to run, then you run. Ah cain't do nothing 'bout it. You reckon you find that Caroline?"

"I'll find her," Justin said grimly. "I must find her."

Mindy's eyes softened. "Must, boy? You loves that li'l wench, don't you?"

"You might say that."

"Then ah says it. When you finds her, you give her a right good licking, hear? Running off like she done! Ain't got no more sense than a newborn calf."

"That's not the first thing I'll do. But it might well be the second."

"Listen to me, boy. Maybe them search parties they find you, and then 'gain, maybe they don't. But me, ah ain't 'membering this conversation. Don't know nothing 'bout it."

"Thank you, Mindy." Stooping, Justin kissed her cheek.

"Ain't nothing for you to be thanking me for. Ain't done you no favor. Ah reckon they find you soon 'nough. Bring you back in chains, they will." She pointed at Cranwell's still figure. "Ain't dead, is he?"

"No. I can see him breathing. Leave him where he is. He'll come round. I'm going now, Mindy. Good-bye."

"Good-bye, boy. Ah reckon ah 'members you. You ain't easily forgot."

"Neither are you, Mindy. I hope we meet again. But not here."

"Then we won't be meeting, boy, 'less they bring you back. Ah belongs to Master Toby, even though ah ain't no slave. And ah reckons ah dies here."

Mindy watched him go, her eyes troubled and sad. God help him, she thought. When Putnam discovered that he was missing, the alarm would be raised soon enough, and the hunt would be on. Her eyes went to Eliza's body. She had spent sleepless nights worrying about Eliza and Moon. There was nothing to worry about anymore. She murmured endearingly over Eliza's body, "Don't you worry none. Ah sees to it that you gits buried with your Moon. Don't know quite how, but ah sees to it all the same. That a promise from Mindy to you, girl."

Wiping her tears away with a corner of her apron, Mindy turned and went back into the house.

Chapter 26

His eyes bright with interest and wonder, the young Indian boy stood over the unconscious woman. She lay sprawled out on the spongy ground beneath the mulberry trees. At first he had thought her dead, and then, relieved, he had seen the rapid beating of the pulse in her throat. For three days he had stalked this white woman through the forest, but on the fourth day he had lost her. Now, coming upon her unexpectedly, he felt that he could examine her at his leisure. Though she had more years than he, she was not old, he decided. He had heard many tales of these people of the white race, but never before had he seen one.

The boy frowned at this last thought. There were so many things beyond his village that he had not seen. He had been born delicate of frame and health, and when he had begun to walk, he had limped. He could not run and hunt as the other boys did, and so for all of his formative years, his elders, ashamed of him, had kept him close to the village. Then he had gained his sixteenth year and had managed partially to cure himself of his limp. His elders took counsel. It was decided that he was old enough to prove his manhood. He had been afraid of their eyes upon him when he had been sent into the forest alone, but he had not let them see his fear. He was to hunt down and kill his first animal. To make a worthy opponent, it must be strong and of a good size. After killing it, he must skin it, as he had been taught to do. Only then, bearing both meat and pelt, could he return to his village in triumph.

The hot blood of shame stung the boy's cheeks. He had seen the woman, and he had allowed himself to be distracted from his purpose. So great had been his fascination that he had spent his time stalking her. The arrows that were to be

323

turned on the animal whose killing was to prove his manhood lay still unused in their quiver.

Cautiously, closing his mind against shame, the boy went down on his knees and looked into the woman's face. Long red scratches marred her white flesh, and those same marks were on her arms and her legs. It was clear to him that she had done battle with the stunted thorn trees and had lost the fight. There were deep shadows beneath her closed eyes, and burs clung to her long golden hair.

Golden hair! The color of the sun. The boy put out a hand and touched it. Then, inspired by a feeling that he did not recognize, he gently smoothed it back from the maltreated face. Her hair was tangled and damp with sweat, but he knew how it would be when it was clean and dry. Golden hair, beautiful hair! With a tentative finger he touched the long dark lashes. It puzzled him that they should be of a different color. What of her eyes? What color would they be?

As though his mental question had penetrated through her unconsciousness, Caroline Fane's heavy lashes lifted slowly. Her eyes were brown. They were beautiful eyes. Again he put out a finger, this time touching her cheek.

Caroline stared with vague eyes at the dark face bent over her. "Justin!" Her hand reached out and touched his arm. "I knew you would come. I knew!"

As a defense against the white people, who must be considered the enemy of the Indian, the boy had been laboriously taught the English language. The elders of his village had declared solemnly, "It is well that our people should know and understand the speech of the white man. That way, whenever possible, we may listen and observe. We cannot then be caught unawares."

The boy was glad that he had been attentive at his lessons, else he would not have understood the woman's words. His enemy? His black brows drew together in a frown. Awed though he was before the wisdom of his elders, it was hard for him to think of this woman as his enemy. Wanting her to understand him in return, he spoke slowly and clearly. "I am not this one of whom you speak. I am called White Bird."

White Bird? Caroline burned with fever, and pain coursed through her body, but the boy's words managed to arrest for a moment her wandering mind. Indian! She stared at him, terror in her eyes. His features were finely cut, and his skin was of a dark coppery hue. His hair had been shaved on one side, while on the other the hair had been allowed to grow long. The hair was pulled back from his face and had been rolled into a large knot that rested just above his right ear. The knot of hair had been pierced through with three scarlet feathers. He wore fringed buckskin breeches and jerkin. Copper ornaments dangled from his ears, and chains of copper were looped about his neck. Caroline's eyes went to the tomahawk that dangled from a loop on his beaded belt. "What ... what are you going to do with me?"

The boy did not answer the question. He pointed to a red wound on her leg. "Snakebite," he said abruptly. "The venom has not yet traveled far enough to kill you."

Caroline's eyes dilated as he drew a knife from his belt. "No! Don't kill me!"

"Kill you?" White Bird said in surprise. "Why do you believe this of me?"

A whimper came from Caroline's throat. "Justin!" She clutched at White Bird's arm, as though fearing he would vanish. "I was so afraid! I thought I would never see you again."

White Bird looked at her vacant face with somber dark eyes. He understood that the white woman's mind was wandering again. Justin? Did she call for a man she had lost? He touched her hot flesh. He knew well that her spirit was striving to fly from her body and mingle with the gods. If he did not help her, she would die. Let her call for her white man, but it was he, White Bird, who would trap her restless spirit and bring it back to rest with the living. He would make her well and strong, and afterward he would take her to his secret cave, the place where he went when he wanted to be alone. He would keep her there. Then, when he had grown older and wiser, he would take this white-skin for his woman. But he would tell no one. She would remain his secret. For the elders would not approve of him taking one of the enemy into his keeping. White Bird lifted the knife.

Caroline screamed as the knife gashed her flesh. She struggled to sit up, but strong hands restrained her, forcing her to fall back again. The hands touched her leg, steadying it, and she screamed again as she felt the drawing of her flesh.

White Bird spat the venom from his mouth. Again he applied his lips to the wound and sucked. Several times he did this, until, at last, he was satisfied that he had drawn forth all

the venom. Then, speaking no word to the woman, he rose to
his feet. A little way from here grew the leaves with the
healing property. He would bind them about the wound, and
the cure would be completed. He hesitated, for he did not believe in wasting words; then he said abruptly, "I will return
shortly."

Caroline did not hear him. She was not even aware that he
had gone. She stared upward at the interlocking branches of
the great trees that shut her into a dank green gloom. Her
mouth a tight, straight line she felt her senses clearing a little.
Memory stirred, bringing a frightening recollection of the
muffled footsteps that had sounded in the distance as she made
her escape from Montrose. Terrified, feeling vulnerable, the
burden of the cloak and basket, slight though it was, had
seemed too much for her. Without thinking, she had dropped
both objects and had fled in panic into the dark all-encompass-
ing gloom of the forest. The forest! Once again she relived
her desperate fight to find her way out of that forest that had
become her prison. It had been no use, for wherever she
turned, walls of vegetation reared up to block her path.
Trailing roots tripped her, sending her sprawling and jolting
her injured body to fresh agony. Not once had she come
across another human being, but she was painfully aware of
the sinister life all about her. There were the many and varied
cries of the birds, some harsh and tuneless, some liquid and
sweet, but all strange to her ears. There was the rustle of animals slinking through the undergrowth, and once, freezing her
blood with terror, the snarl of a wildcat. Hungry and thirsty
and full of pain, she had run blindly from the sound. That
night, she had slept on a rock ledge overhung by a fountain
of greenery, and, hearing the increased sounds of the night,
she had prayed that the morning would find her still safe and
whole. She did not want to fall asleep and render herself vulnerable, but her exhaustion was too great. She awakened to
the same green gloom, for the sun could not penetrate the
close-growing trees. She heard the mumble of her own voice,
and though she tried, she could not seem to stop her tongue
from babbling. "Justin! Justin, I'm afraid! I need you. Help
me!"

Dazed and shivering, awakening occasionally to flashes of
full comprehension, she had stumbled on. Later in the morning, for she supposed it must still be morning, she had come
across a small stream. The water was clear and pure, and she

had drunk deeply. For a long time she had lain beside the stream, loath to leave it. But at last she had risen wearily to her feet. She must go on. She must find her way out of the forest. How long, she wondered, had she been struggling through this place of perpetual gloom? Had it been days? Weeks? When would she emerge into sunlight and civilization? What a fool she had been to run away. She should have waited, spoken to Justin. Together they would have worked something out. Justin! Justin, my darling. What if I should die in this forest? What if I should never see you again? Choking on the painful sobs that wracked her body, she turned. It was then that she saw the snake. Coiled and dangerous, it lay directly in her path. Another step forward and she would have trod upon it. With a cry of terror, she drew back. She was not fast enough. The flat head darted forward, and the reptile struck.

Afterward, she must have gone on, but she could remember nothing until she had opened her eyes and seen the dark face of the Indian bending over her.

Caroline's hands clenched. The Indian! What would he do with her? Was he going to kill her? Rape her? She must get up. She must run! She tried to raise herself, but almost instantly she fell back again. It was no use. She was too weak and sick.

White Bird came back through the trees. Bending over the woman, he saw that she had again lapsed into unconsciousness. It was as well, he thought. She had the appearance of one with a fighting spirit. He meant her no harm, and he did not wish to struggle with her in an attempt to prove his good intentions. To struggle with a woman was a lowering of a warrior's dignity. Crouching down, he bound the wound on her leg with the leaves he had found. Then, searching for fresh injuries, he turned her over on her stomach. He drew in his breath sharply as he saw the suppurating wounds on her back. She had been beaten, and by the look of the wounds, not so very long ago. Who had done this to her? Had the beating been administered by this man for whom she called?

Scowling, White Bird lifted her into his arms. Standing up, he reflected that his burden weighed very little. He would carry her to the stream that lay just beyond the next grove of trees. He would bathe her wounds, and he would bind them with fresh leaves, and then he would take her to his cave.

Reaching the stream, White Bird laid her down. He smiled

faintly as he turned her over on her stomach and began his task. He was wise in the ways of plants. He knew those with the juices that could be distilled to bring death, and he knew those that healed. The white woman would respond quickly to his treatment. She would be grateful to him. So grateful and so thankful for his kindness that, when at last he decided to make her his woman, she would come to him eagerly. She would be submissive and loving.

It was some time before Caroline revived sufficiently to open her eyes. She saw a patch of blue sky through a break in the trees, and a dark face bending over her. "Justin!" Her strained face broke into a radiant smile. "My darling!" Her arms reached for him; her hand found the back of his neck and drew down his face to hers.

White Bird froze in astonishment as her lips touched his and clung. He had heard that it was the custom of the invaders of his land to press their lips together as a token of their affection, but he had never seen it, and certainly he had never expected to experience it. Never before had his lips touched a woman's, and he thought that if this was their way of showing gratitude and love, then it must surely be very unhealthy.

The woman continued to hold him and kiss him, and White Bird became uncomfortably aware of the racing of his heart and the spreading warmth in his loins. He felt so strange that he told himself sternly that now was not the moment to concern himself with the question of health. Lips pressed to lips. It was really most enjoyable. It was wrong, of course, to allow a mere woman to have her way with him, but just for this once he would permit it. Later, when the light feeling left his head, he would inform her that the warrior was the master, not the squaw.

Sighing, giving in entirely to this new and pleasurable sensation, White Bird ground his lips urgently against hers. The woman belonged to him, he told himself. He had found her. He had trapped her wandering spirit and brought it back to dwell among the living. He could not yet take her fully and completely. First, before he could take her as a man took a woman, he must prove his manhood. There would be honor then in their union. White Bird thought of the man for whom she called, and he frowned fiercely. If this Justin should come looking for her, he would kill him!

Chapter 27

Biddy lay on her bed, her blurred eyes staring up at the ceiling. Her body felt heavy, as though great weights had been piled upon it. Her throat was burning from the amount of alcohol she had consumed; her mouth was so dry that her tongue kept sticking to the roof of her mouth. Swallowing hard against the dryness, she turned her head and looked at the jars on the side table. The jars had contained peach brandy, but they were empty now. She wanted another drink, wanted it badly, but there were the weights on her legs holding her down. Even were she to manage to rise from the bed, her legs were too weak and unsteady to take her down the stairs. Besides, Toby had locked her in. She was his prisoner. She was mad, Toby had said. The alcohol had rotted her brain. She was beginning to imagine things, and she was no longer to be trusted. He was forced to lock her in, not only for her own good but for the good of others. Toby had looked at her accusingly. "It is no use you calling for Eliza Harris," he had continued. "You killed her. Don't you remember that? Don't you remember anything?"

As she thought of his words, a whimper escaped Biddy's lips. He lied! If she had killed Harris, she would have remembered the deed. Toby hated her. He was trying to drive her out of her mind.

Thinking of her husband with hatred, Biddy stared toward the locked door. No matter. She would get even with him for his insults. Her face twisted as her arms began to itch. Ferociously she tore at them with her long nails, breaking the skin and raising tiny beads of blood. The itching subsided, and she rubbed her hand over the raw places, smearing the blood.

Frowning, she let her mind dwell once more upon her husband. The swine thought himself so clever. So did that fat black lump of a Mindy. But she had more intelligence than

329

either of them. She smiled to herself as she remembered the lying story Mindy had told her. She could still hear the woman's voice. "Ain't a scrap o' good you calling for Eliza, Miss Biddy. You done killed her. She been buried three days ago."

Liars! Toby and Mindy both. They were plotting against her. When Toby had locked her in her room, she had seen Harris lurking in the shadows, and that was the proof that they had lied to her. It had really been quite exciting, for Toby had not seen Harris. He had not known that his wicked scheme had been exposed. Later, she had decided then, she would confront him with the girl, but not just yet. Enjoying her secret knowledge, she had winked and smiled at Harris, and as an added admonition to silence, she had put a warning finger to her lips. Harris had obeyed her, of course, for she would not dare to do otherwise. Toby, still keeping up his wicked act, had looked at her sorrowfully. "Try to pull yourself together, Biddy," he had said in a heavy voice. "Do you think someone else is here besides me? Is that why you are smiling?"

Oh, but he was cruel and cunning! She would tell him nothing. She had scowled at him instead, and then she had deliberately spat in his face. After a while, still wearing that sorrowful expression, he had gone away. But he had not forgotten to lock the door, God curse him over and over again!

Biddy's frown deepened as she thought over Harris' strange conduct. For some reason the girl had chosen to hide from her. How dare she! Biddy thought, the hot angry blood rushing into her face. She would make that slut smart for her insolence! If she did not soon come out of hiding, she would tell Toby about Harris' filthy little secret. That dirty nigger-loving whore would be very sorry. Very sorry indeed!

"Harris," she called feebly. "Come out and attend me, you lazy slut!"

There was no answer. Conscious of a cold fear, Biddy let her eyes dart about the room. The draperies were billowing. Was it the wind that billowed them, she wondered, or were the girl and her nigger lover standing behind them? Did they intend to hurt her? "Harris!" Her voice rose to a scream. "Come out! Come out!"

There was still no answer. Biddy became aware of the ticking of the clock that Toby had brought with him from England. There was something menacing about the sound. She stared at it, her heart beginning to pound with terror. The clock! It was leaving its brass frame. It was sailing toward her. Dear God, it was going to hit her! Cowering, she tried to ward off the blow. She gasped as it caught her on the temple. The pain! A bubbling scream broke from her lips. Oh, the terrible pain! The scream turned into a long, wrenching moan as she rubbed at her forehead. It felt as though red-hot spears were being driven into her head.

Still moaning, Biddy closed her eyes. When would it be safe to open them again? she wondered. If she kept her eyes tightly closed, the clock would not be able to find her. It must not strike her again; the pain would kill her. Her eyeballs moved beneath the screen of her lids. Where was the clock now? Was it hovering over her head, was it waiting? But she could not bear this. She must know. Holding her breath, she slowly opened her eyes. The clock stood innocently in its usual place. It looked as though it had never moved at all. She stared at the clock in outrage. It had moved. It could not deceive her. She had seen it! Toby had done this to her. He had told the clock to kill her! Perhaps if she threw something at it. Smashed it? No. She rejected the notion immediately. What if she should miss? There! The clock had read her thoughts. It was angry with her. The ticking was growing louder and louder. It was filling the room with thunder. It was pounding in her head and shaking her body. "Stop!" She put her hands over her ears, trying to block out the sound. "Please stop. Please!"

Her body cold and sticky with perspiration, she lay there for a long while before she realized that the thunder had gone. Removing her hands, her fear forgotten, she grinned in triumph. She had commanded the clock to stop, and it had obeyed. That meant that she was greater than Toby. It meant that she had but to command, and all things and people would bow to her will.

The draperies were still billowing. Staring at them, Biddy knew that the girl was standing there. Never mind, let her continue to play her silly little game. She was much too tired to call to her. Later, when she finally emerged from her hiding place, she would see that Harris was severely punished for her insolence and her disobedience.

The clock was now only a soothing murmur. It was very

quiet in the room, peaceful. Biddy relaxed. She did not close
her eyes. Her newfound confidence and power were not yet
strong enough to allow her to be completely off guard. After
all, one never knew. She gazed ahead with dulled eyes, her
lips moving silently. Figures began to parade across the
screen of her mind. Upturned black faces, white faces, their
eyes watching her. So many people gathered in one place.
Why were they there? She had the sudden feeling that she
had called them together, but she could not remember why.
There was Justin Lawrence. Dark-eyed and black-browed.
With his dramatic, almost savage looks, he stood out from all
the others. Lawrence was staring at her with hatred. His lips
were moving, saying something to her. "Eliza is dead, you
murdering bitch!" She heard the words clearly, but she could
make no sense of them. "Murdering bitch! Murdering bitch!"
The words resounded in her head. Now Lawrence was coming toward her. He was stalking her, and he was still saying
those words.

"Don't!" Biddy shrieked at him. "How dare you say that to
me! Keep away. Don't you touch me!"

Lawrence was vanishing, fading into a mist. Now it was
Eliza Harris who stood there in his place. Harris moved, and
Biddy saw the hole in her back. There was blood pumping
from her mouth! Harris reached out her hands to her, and
she saw that they were red with her own blood. Biddy
screamed in wild despair as someone pushed at her. She
could not keep her feet. She was falling backward. The
waters of a scarlet sea closed over her head. Gasping, she sur-
faced. Her heart thundering, she tried to swim to safety, but
she could make no progress against that sticky tide. She was
sinking again, going down, down! It was not water in which
she battled for her life, it was blood! It was in her eyes, her
nose, the brassy taste of it in her mouth. Blood was pouring
down her throat, choking her, killing her! "Help! Somebody
help me!"

Her own loud voice pulled Biddy from her nightmare. She
came to herself with a violent start and looked wildly about
her. There was no Lawrence, no Harris, no accusing faces.
The terrible sea was gone. She must have been dreaming, and
yet she had thought herself to be awake. She was here in her
own familiar room, lying on her bed. And Harris, though still
in hiding, was here too. There! She could see Harris' pasty

face peering at her from behind the draperies. Let her stay where she was, she would not call her yet, Biddy decided. She was so very tired, and it was far too much effort to raise her voice. But tired or not, she must try to stay awake. If she fell asleep, the figures from the nightmare might come again. If they should manage to draw her back into their frightful world, they might not let her escape a second time.

Despite her determination to keep alert, she could feel her senses hazing. Finally, she fell into a half-stupor, lingering on the borderline between waking and sleeping. It was the itching attacking every part of her body that roused her to full consciousness. Cursing, crying, she staggered from the bed and pulled off her light wrapper. Naked, shivering in the wind that blew through the half-open windows, she lay down again. She tried to will the itching to stop. It was no use; she had no power over her body, her torment was increasing. She could not stand the itching. It was driving her mad. Oh, God! Oh, Christ in heaven, make it stop. Make it! Her eyes dilated with horror as she saw the spiders. Thousands of the black, hairy insects were running over her body! With one hand she began tearing frantically at herself, gouging her flesh with her long nails. With the other hand she beat frantically at the insects. Bubbling cries came from her lips as she flailed at them. She saw that she had killed some of the spiders; their obscene bodies were red and pulped against her skin. But as fast as she killed them, more came to take their place. "Mercy! Have mercy!"

Biddy's madly rolling bloodshot eyes caught sight of Eliza Harris. Harris, her face ferocious, was creeping toward the bed. With her was Moon. Following them were Justin Lawrence and Caroline Fane. Laughing, their eyes merciless as they stared at her, they ringed the bed. She wanted to beg them to help her, but her tongue seemed to be too large for her mouth; she could not manage it. She bit down on it, and tasted the brassiness of her own blood. The spiders crawled upward. They were on her chin, forcing themselves into her mouth. Oh, God, they were running down her throat! Gagging, she drew in her breath and belched violently in an effort to drive them upward. The inside of her throat began to tickle, and then gradually increased to a savage itching. Tortured, writhing madly, still flailing at her bloodied flesh, she

began to scream. Scream after scream tore from her raw
throat. Someone must come! Someone must help her!

Mindy shivered as she heard the screaming begin again.
What were they going to do about Miss Biddy? she wondered. The woman was mad, and growing steadily worse. Her
eyes heavy with worry, Mindy looked across at Tobias Markham. Slumped down in his chair like an old man, he stared
unseeingly before him. He had not even turned his head
when the screaming began.

Small wonder, Mindy thought, nervously pleating and unpleating the edge of her apron. They were all of them, master
and servant alike, growing used to the dreadful blood-chilling
sounds that came from behind Miss Biddy's locked door. The
demented howling, the screaming, had been going on for
some time now. When Miss Biddy was not screaming, she
would lie on her bed completely exhausted, her body
twitching with nerves and suppressed passions. Only a small
respite, for soon she would begin all over again. She would
go blundering crazily about the room, knocking over ornaments, throwing things, beating on the locked door with fists
that had grown raw from her constant battering, shouting
threats and curses and calling shrilly for Eliza Harris.

Mindy's legs trembled beneath her, and she sat down
abruptly. Whenever she thought of Eliza and Moon, she felt
this weakness in her limbs. Miss Biddy, since killing Eliza,
seemed haunted and obsessed by the girl. Always superstitious, Mindy wondered now if it was all in Miss Biddy's inflamed imagination, or if the pale, reproachful ghost of Eliza
Harris really did linger in that room.

Mindy's brows drew together in a frown. Was it the
thought of Eliza Harris that had finally driven Miss Biddy insane, or had it been Miss Selina's tragic death that had
toppled her over the edge? Certainly the screaming and the
raving had first started when the broken bodies of Miss Selina, Mary Messinger, Miss Selina's friend, and Robert
Messinger, Mary's brother, had been brought back to Montrose. They had been found lying beside the overturned carriage at the bottom of a deep gully. The search party that
Master Toby had sent out to track down Justin Lawrence and
Caroline Fane had come across them accidentally. The horses
were gone, no doubt stolen by the Indians who had attacked

and killed the small party. Robert Messinger was lying face downward, the back of his skull crushed in. The clothes had been stripped from Mary Messinger's body. Her neck was broken, and, judging from the blood that stained her thighs, she had been repeatedly raped. Miss Selina, her face frozen into a death mask of terror, had an arrow buried deeply in her breast.

Tobias Markham, who had arrived back at Montrose a day after his wife's murderous spree, had said little at first. Then, pulling himself together with an obvious effort, he had ordered that his sister-in-law be buried in the family graveyard. The bodies of Robert and Mary Messinger were to be taken back to their home for burial there. Later, on that same day, he had called the search party before him. Holding the arrow that had been taken from Selina's breast, he told the men that there had been rumors of several Indian uprisings. His light eyes glittering, he had gone on to add that it was for this reason and this reason alone that he was temporarily canceling the search for the two fugitives. Later, when conditions became more settled, the search would be resumed. He did not believe that either Lawrence or Fane, who knew little of the country, the customs, or the dangers that lay in wait for the ignorant and the unwary, would get very far.

Mindy also inclined to this belief. There was too much against Justin and Caroline. But still, she knew what it had cost Master Toby to abandon the search. For if Miss Biddy was obsessed by ghosts, he was obsessed by the living, and with Caroline Fane in particular. Convict though Caroline was, a woman who might or might not be guilty of the crime of which she was accused, he had nonetheless fallen deeply in love with her. He would go on searching until he found them. And because he was a just and far-thinking man, he would not punish one without punishing the other. Though it cost him his chance with her, though it would hurt him deeply, he would still punish Caroline. He was a businessman, and he ran a successful and flourishing plantation. He could not have the slaves behaving as they pleased and running off at will. An example must be made. But when the punishment was over, Mindy knew, he would still be hoping for a chance to win Caroline.

Sighing, Mindy shook her head. It was hopeless, she

thought, looking at his slumped figure. Caroline Fane was not
for him. She would never consent to a union between them.
She was obstinate, headstrong, deeply in love with Justin
Lawrence, and Master Toby's cause was hopeless.

Mindy's lips tightened. Even without Caroline Fane, Master Toby's life would be easier with that madwoman Miss
Biddy out of the way. If only it had been Miss Biddy rather
than Miss Selina who had been found with the Indian arrow
buried in her breast. If only Mindy had allowed Justin to kill
her.

Mindy glanced up at the ceiling. The screams were still
constant, but no doubt Miss Biddy was becoming exhausted,
for they were growing fainter. Perhaps Miss Biddy would not
live much longer, she thought hopefully. Certainly she was
wearing herself out. She could not sleep except for a few
minutes at a time, she ate little, she screamed and fought
with shadows, and she continued to drink heavily. Master
Toby had said that since nothing could be done to aid her
mental condition, she might just as well have the comfort of
her liquor. He had ordered that she continue to be supplied
with as much as she could drink. Mindy shivered. Sometimes
she had the thought that this was Master Toby's way of
speeding her death. Well, if it was, was that such a crime?
Had he not suffered enough?

Mindy moved uneasily in the chair. Her own fierce hatred
for Miss Biddy never ceased to trouble her. Until she had
seen for herself how unhappy the woman had made Master
Toby, she had never hated a living soul. But these days she
was always praying for Miss Biddy to die. Because of this,
she had a great fear that God would punish her. But only
Miss Biddy's death could bring Master Toby peace and happiness. He must be freed from her! Her hands clenched and
her lips folded into a grim line as a thought came to her.
They got rid of mad animals, didn't they? So why not that
woman? Yes, why not?

Tobias Markham heard the rustle of Mindy's skirt. So she
was still with him, dear, faithful Mindy. It comforted him to
have her there, even though he had not as yet addressed one
word to her. He put his fingers to his throbbing temples, mas-
saging them in a circular movement. How his head ached! If
only that mad bitch would stop screaming! He could not
think clearly; he could not seem to settle to anything. How

was it possible for anyone to scream so loudly and for so long?

His hands clenched on the arms of his chair. Biddy must die. She must! He could not endure much more. He would do anything to be rid of her. Anything at all! No one slept in this house now. It was impossible. Night and day Biddy screamed. The sound cut into one's sleep, it made tatters of the nerves, and it weighed on the mind like a stone. It was as though he carried the din about with him wherever he went. Even in the fields, with the laughter and the chatter of the workers all about him, it seemed to him that he could still hear Biddy screaming. There was only one way he could rid himself of her; he knew that now. Only one way, and he must take it. He could not banish her, for that would mean that the whole sordid story would come out, and he could not bear that. No, his way was best. After all the years of hell he had endured, he would finally be free. The thought of Caroline came into his mind, but he put the thought quickly from him. Only after he had done what he must do would he allow himself to think of her.

"Mindy." Markham rose from his chair and faced her. "Go back to your work now, please. I would like to be alone for a while. There is something I have to think out."

Mindy studied him with loving, anxious eyes. He looked strange, she thought. Almost as though he might be suffering from a fever. The brown of his complexion seemed faded, and his light eyes were overbright. Uneasy, she rose reluctantly from her chair. "Ah goes, if that what you wants, Master Toby." She took a step toward him. "But can ah ask you what all you got to think about?"

"No, Mindy, you may not ask." Markham's smile softened the words.

"Ah worried 'bout you, that why ah ask." She took another step toward him and placed her hand on his arm. "You looking purely tuckered out," she said tenderly, "and ah don't like to see that. Why don't you come to mah room tonight? Ah comfort you like ah used to do when you troubled." She looked at him wistfully. "It been a long time since you came."

"I know." His voice choked. With a sudden desperate movement he put his arms about her and held her close. "Mindy! Mindy!"

She felt the violent trembling of his body, and her love for him welled up. "Ah knows how it is, Master Toby," she soothed. "But don't you be fretting now, 'cause it going to be all right. It is, ah promise you. There, mah honey, there! Mindy make it all right."

Biddy awoke with a start from the light, restless sleep that had claimed her. Immediately conscious of the fiery stinging pain all over her body, she gave a gasping moan and began to turn her head restlessly on the pillow. It was so dark in the room, and she hated the darkness. If it were not for that patch of brightness over by the door, she wouldn't be able to see a hand before her. Where was Harris? Why didn't she light the lamps?

"Biddy! Come, Biddy, come!" A muffled voice was calling to her. Was it Harris? Had Selina come back to mock her?

"Who is it?" Biddy sat up with a jerk. "Who is calling?"

There was no answer. Her heart racing with excitement, Biddy stared through the gloom. Her gaze fell on the door and became fixed. That patch of brightness. It was caused by the light shining in from the corridor. Merciful heavens, the door was open! Someone was out there waiting for her. Who was it? She listened intently, hoping that the voice would call again. Nothing. Consideringly, she put her head on one side. Had she heard a voice, or had she been mistaken? It might be that she had imagined it. But what did it matter? The door was open. She was no longer a prisoner.

Giggling, Biddy slid from the bed. She was going to walk through the door into freedom. She would find someplace where Toby and Mindy could never find her. She would show them! She was not an animal that must be locked away. She was the mistress of Montrose Plantation, and as such, entitled to the love and respect of all.

Without bothering to put on her robe, she reeled across the room to the door. A hiccup caught her. Grimacing, she put a firm hand over her mouth. She must be quiet. She must let nothing betray her. Cautiously she peered out of the door. There was no one in sight. It would seem that the servants had forgotten or simply neglected to light the rest of the candles, for the corridor was only dimly lit. It was quite obvious to her that the household staff were becoming slovenly. Once she was herself again, freed from Toby's tyranny, she would wear out some backs for this neglect of duty. But no matter for the moment, there was sufficient light to enable her to make her way to the stairs.

She edged out of the room and began to walk along the carpeted corridor, her heavy breasts swinging. Her legs began to tremble beneath her, and fearful that she would fall, she slowed her pace. She giggled again as the thought came to her that she would like to see Toby's face and fat old Mindy's when they looked into her room and found her gone. Her giggling ceased, and her forehead creased into a frown. Her eyes were malicious as she thought of the revenge she would have upon them both. Only wait, my fine gentleman! Only wait, you nigger slut!

She stopped walking. Drawing in a deep breath, she removed her hand from her mouth. Good fortune must be with her, for the deep breath had taken the hiccups away. Pleased with herself, momentarily forgetful of the pain in her quivering body, she walked on. Her head felt so light and strange, and again she feared that she was going to fall. But she must not. Not here, not now. They would hear her. They would take her back to her room and lock her in. Suddenly she found herself remembering an old childhood trick, one that could be used to steady herself. Giggling again, the need for quiet and caution forgotten, she stretched out her arms on either side. Clever, so clever to have remembered that old trick. She would not lose her footing now; she was once again the mistress of her body.

Biddy's heart leaped and began to hammer furiously as she heard a sound behind her. Someone was following her with stealthy, shuffling footsteps. There was a dryness in her throat, and she could feel the hairs on the back of her neck prickling. Dropping her arms, she swung around sharply. "Who is it?" she demanded in a shaking voice. "Who is there?"

There was no reply. Screwing up her eyes, Biddy peered through the half-gloom. Nothing moved. There was no one there. She tightened her trembling lips. She was just nervous, she reassured herself. Nervous, and badly in need of a drink. Of course, that was all it was. She had been locked away so long, so cruelly treated, that her nerves were strung tightly and she was beginning to imagine things. All the same, just in case it had not been her imagination, it would not hurt to deliver a warning. "Is that you following me, Harris?" she said in a harsh voice. "I won't forget this game of hide-and-seek you've been playing with me. I'm going to have you flogged, you bitch!"

Harris did not answer. Biddy frowned. So she was still playing with her, was she? Harris would suffer for this. Her flogging would be very severe. Standing there, she felt the cold touch of fear again. She studied the doors lining the corridor. One door, she noticed, was standing slightly ajar. For a moment she was irresolute, and the temptation came to her to push the door wider and face the lurking Harris. No. Shaking her head, she walked on. Time enough to deal with Harris later.

Pausing at the head of the stairs, Biddy looked down into the sparsely lit cavern of the hall. Really, she thought with a touch of indignation, this was too much! First the corridor, and now the hall. How dare they be so niggardly with the candles! If she were not careful, she would lose her footing. She put her hand on the satiny wood of the banister rail, and a smile replaced her indignant expression. What fun it would be to slide down that gleaming length. About to swing her leg over the rail, she hesitated. No, better not. She would descend like a lady. If any of the servants happened to glimpse her in all her calm dignity, they would then be assured that their precious Master Toby had lied about her. Crazy? No, not she. Toby was crazy, and so was that fat bitch of a Mindy, but not she. She had never felt more cool and assured.

Biddy started as the sound of heavy breathing came to her ears. And, yes, there were the shuffling footsteps again. Her assurance left her, and she began to tremble violently. Tears came into her eyes. She was not mad, but someone was trying to frighten her into becoming so. She wanted to turn and face her tormentor, but she was afraid to do so. Whom would she see standing behind her? Everyone in this house was her enemy. They all hated her! A sob broke from her lips. "Who is it?" Her voice quavered with fear.

"Me." The grim voice was clear. The one word gave away the identity of the person who stood behind her. "You!" Biddy screamed. "You!"

Biddy was about to turn, to lash out in hate and fury, but she was given no chance. Hard, remorseless hands were on her back, pushing her, sending her hurtling downward.

Screaming wildly, she went bumping and rolling down the stairs.

There were hurrying footsteps below, raised voices. "Who that? Who doing that screaming?"

A flicker of stronger light illumined the scene. Black faces stared down at Biddy. Sprawled on her back, her head at a curious angle, the mistress of Montrose lay at the foot of the stairs. Her eyes were wide open, but she saw nothing, heard nothing. She was dead.

Someone bent over her. "She dead," a frightened voice said. "It look to me like her neck broke."

"It broke sure 'nough." A nervous titter covered fear. "I reckon she so drunk that she couldn't see them stairs nohow."

"But how she get out? Master Toby, he give orders that her door be kept locked. So how she get out?"

"How I know?" A swiftly indrawn breath came to the listener at the head of the stairs.

"And where Master Toby and that Mindy? Why ain't they here? Reckon they couldn't help hearing her when she fall."

"Don't know where Master Toby is. Ain't seen him. But Mindy, she go to her bed early. She say she tired. Don't want no one to 'sturb her."

"I reckon we 'sturb her all the same. Ain't wanting the 'sponsibility of Miss Biddy. Jed and me, we carry her to her room. Tom, you go 'long and wake Mindy. You say to her that she got to come. Ain't taking no blame for this. Ain't taking none at all."

Listening to the grumbling, frightened voices, Mindy drew farther back in the shadows. Then, as someone began to climb the stairs, she went quickly and quietly along the corridor to the back stairs.

In her room once more, Mindy seated herself and hid her face in her trembling hands. "Lord forgive me!" she moaned softly. "Ah done got murder on mah soul!" In her anguish, she rocked to and fro. "Ah hated Miss Biddy, it true. Ah hated her 'cause she bad, and she make misery for mah Master Toby. But ah done it for him, so that he be free. Forgive me, Lord, forgive me!"

Mindy did not hear the opening of the door. She did not see the frightened black man peering at her. She started violently as his soft voice said, "You got to come, Mindy, gal.

Miss Biddy, she fall down the stairs and break her neck. She dead."

Mindy stood up slowly and heavily. "Ah coming, Tom," she said as she approached the door. She brushed past him. "If Miss Biddy dead, then ah got to lay her out decent. Master Toby, he cain't see her like she is."

"She naked, and she all scratched up."

Mindy did not answer him. Shaking his head, Tom followed slowly after her. Mindy had not been surprised at the news. It was almost as though she had been expecting him. There was something here that he did not understand. Did not want to understand. To Tom's overstimulated imagination, the shadows of the corridor seemed to reach out and touch him with cold fingers. With a stifled yelp of fear, he hastened his footsteps.

Tobias Markham stared at the dead face of his wife. He was free of her at last. He could start living again, without her shadow hanging over him. Free! Thanks be to God! Across the bed, he met Mindy's anguished eyes. Thanks be to God, or thanks be to Mindy? Would he ever know? He found himself remembering words that Mindy had spoken. "Ah knows how it is, Master Toby. There, mah honey, there! Mindy make it all right." Had she made it all right? Had Biddy fallen, or had she been pushed?

Mindy's lips opened. "Master Toby, there something ah got to tell you. Ah cain't—"

"No!" He cut her off abruptly. Suspicion grew into certainty. But she must not say the words. He could not let her speak out. Dear Mindy, who might be said to love him too much. "There is nothing I want to hear," he went on. "Nothing at all that you have to tell me. Do you understand me, Mindy?"

Mindy's lips quivered. "Yes, sir. Yes, Master Toby, ah reckon ah understand."

He looked at the tears on her cheeks, and he said very gently, "Her death is a merciful release, always remember that. You know, don't you, that she would have eventually been committed to an asylum for the insane? That was what I was thinking of earlier. I was going to make the arrangements tomorrow. So you see, Mindy, it is better so. For her, for me, for all of us. You do see that, don't you?"

He knew! He was willing her not to speak out, not to bring horror into these moments of his relief. But most of all, because in his own way he loved her, he was willing her not to force him to punish her for what she had done. The burden of murder would be hers alone to carry. Her shoulders straightening, Mindy said slowly, "It a bad thing to say, when Miss Biddy, she lying here dead, but ah glad for you, Master Toby." She looked at him steadily and lovingly. "Maybe now, when you find Caroline, you git a chance at happiness." Unable to look at him any more, knowing that she didn't believe he and Caroline would ever be together, she lowered her head again. "If you find her," she mumbled.

Markham put his arm about her waist and led her over to the door. "I'll find her, Mindy. No matter how long it takes, I will find Caroline."

Chapter 28

Time and again Justin Lawrence almost collapsed, so great was his despair and his weariness of body and mind. But he continued to force himself on, his reeling gait resembling that of a drunken man. Underbrush and trailing vines whipped across his path, tearing his clothes and leaving bloody tracks on his face and arms. He scarcely felt them. "Carrie." Like a beating hammer her name kept pounding in his brain. "Carrie! I must find you."

His mouth tightened with resolution. He would find her. It seemed to him that he had been searching for her for weeks, months, and yet he knew that it was only a little over seven days. In that short time the great brooding forest had taken its toll of him. He had forced his way through dense underbrush. He had used his knife to cut away masses of trailing vines, and he had called her name until the rawness of his throat finally caused him to desist. Becoming aware of a gnawing hunger, he had filled his belly with the nuts and fruits he had found. In his weariness he had not given much thought to the possible harmful effects of the strange fruits. Some were familiar, but many of them were unknown to him. Once or twice, though, the painful cramping of his stomach had caused him to exercise a little caution. A dead man would be of little use to Carrie. At least, he had not needed to go thirsty, for streams crisscrossed the forest bed. Once, kneeling beside a stream to quench his thirst and to wash some of the sweat and grime from his face, he had almost been struck by a snake. Only just in time, he had hurled himself backward. In a sudden violent reaction, he had scrambled to his feet. Snatching his knife from his belt, he had flung it at the weaving reptile. More by luck than by judgment the knife had struck the snake in a vital spot, pinioning it to the ground and killing it instantly. At night, in the shuddering cold that descended so abruptly, he had sought what shelter he could find. Once, stumbling across a small cave, and finding it dry, and free of denizens of the forest, he had rested there. But mostly he lay down in the open. He was thankful that he had with him the means to kindle a fire. It was at least some kind of safeguard against predators. But even so, his sleep was fitful. Listening to the occasional snarling of a disturbed animal, the almost constant activity in the underbrush, and once, hearing the cracking of twigs as a heavy body slunk by quite near to where he lay, he had been very conscious of his vulnerable person. He had faced danger before, and he did not fear anything he could see in the wild green vastness. It was the hidden secret life all about him, the feeling he had that glowing ferocious eyes watched him and marked his vulnerability, the thought of the unexpected spring, which he feared. The unknown. In the daylight hours, despite his constant anxiety over Caroline, the forest was a rather exciting challenge. But at night it became something different, something deadly.

There were those other times when, lying there with his ears alert for every sound, he would find it difficult to believe that he, who had laughed and jested his way lightheartedly through life, who had mingled with London society, who had gambled and drunk and wenched, doing nothing more difficult than preparing himself for the day ahead, should now find himself hopelessly lost in the depths of a Virginia forest in the New World, and possibly marked as the prey of some prowling beast.

Justin's thoughts broke off. It was useless to dwell on all he had been through; it was what was still ahead of him that counted. His chest heaving from his exertions, he stopped before a huge tree. The mighty giant of the forest reached to an immense height. Its stout branches, thicker than his arm, were hopelessly tangled with those of its neighbor. The interlocking branches spread a dark-green canopy above him that effectively shut out the sun and invited him to rest. Surrendering, forgetful now of snakes and other perils, no longer really caring, Justin sank down on the mossy ground and leaned his aching back against the gnarled trunk. He was dirty and bearded, his body was sticky with perspiration and trembling with reaction, and the exposed parts of his flesh were lumpy and red and swollen from the bites of the insects and the swarm of bees he had encountered earlier. Something or someone had disturbed the bees, and he had become the recipient of their attack. Fortunately, when the bees swarmed about him, he had been standing by a stream. Immersing himself in the water, he had managed to deflect the worst of it.

Rubbing his scratched and tingling arms, Justin closed his heavy eyes. He was desperately tired, and the urge to sleep, if only for a few moments, was fast overcoming him. Sleep. He had had little enough of that these past few nights.

Justin smiled grimly as he thought of how he, without preparation, without thought, save only the driving necessity to find Carrie, had gone plunging headlong into the forest. Of course he was lost. What else could he expect? There were other people tracking through the forest, of that he was sure. But so far he had come across no one. It was eerie, to feel oneself to be entirely alone. He had to keep reminding himself that there were others, that it was simply that he had not yet come upon them. Yes, he was lost, but he would not remain so. There was a way out, and he would find it. He would find Carrie, too. If he did not, or if, at the end of his search, he should discover that she was dead, he would just as well die too. His tired eyes opened wide in surprise at the intensity of feeling. But why should he be so surprised? It was about time he faced his true feelings. And the truth was that without her there would be nothing left. Without Carrie by his side, life would lose its savor. He loved her. He had always loved her, and that, too, was truth. Why had he been such a blind and stubborn fool? Why had he not recognized his strong emotion for what it really was? Only now, when it might well be too late, was he acknowledging the force of his love. "Carrie!" he said aloud. "I am going to find you. I must keep on telling myself that." He raised his voice, startling the birds roosting on the branches above him. "I love you, Carrie!" he shouted. "I need you! Do you hear me? I love you!"

Only the sounds of the forest answered him. Fighting a sense of despair, he moved restlessly, his fingers tugging at the moss. "Dear Christ," he muttered, "help me. Let me find her. There is so much we can share in this great new country. So much lies ahead of us."

Amazed at this appeal he had made to a God in whom he could never quite bring himself to believe, he lapsed into silence. Either he had changed very much from the cynical man he had been, or else his brain was addled with exhaustion and anxiety. Changed, he mused. Yes, he rather thought he had. There was something about the grandeur and majesty of this America that did that to you. Here, with the clean, pure air filling one's lungs, the amazing vistas that met the eyes wherever one looked, it was inevitable that one would feel nearer to God. In this country it was possible to expand. To feel that you could achieve anything, be anything. There was a tingle in the very air. God's country, he thought. Yes, America might well be called that.

His eyes closed again. Yes, he had changed, but whether it was a change for the better remained to be seen. Rogue Lawrence he had been called. At this moment in his thinking, he believed himself to be as far from that audacious, careless ne'er-do-well as it was possible to be. If he found Carrie, he would center his thoughts, his brains, and his driving ambition on conquering his part of this country and shaping it to his desire. For somewhere, he knew, he would find a part that would be his alone. Theirs alone. A smile touched his lips. He had never thought to discover in himself an eagerness to till land and to grow crops, but so it was. He wanted to build on his own land. He wanted to leave a beautiful and lasting monument to pass on to his children. For they would have children, he and Carrie.

How young Paul would have loved to listen in on these inner thoughts of his. His brother had always prayed for the reformation of Rogue Lawrence, and it was this country that had brought about Paul's longed-for miracle. He was done with playing his way through life. He was ready to settle down and accept the challenge that America offered. Paul! If only they could have shared all this. The thought of his brother brought, as it always did, a familiar wrenching at his heart. But, surprisingly, it was not immediately followed by the surge of anger and hatred against Paul's murderers. In that, too, he had changed. But it might be, in a sense, that his brother would share in the new life. The monument he would build for his children would be for Paul, too.

Justin's attention was caught by the shrill crying of the birds above his head. Their cry had a disturbed sound. He looked up as he heard the beating of wings. Lifting from the branches, they flew away in a black cloud. He was instantly alert to possible danger. What was it that had frightened the peacefully roosting birds?

He got to his feet. They heavy silence was split by a high, eerie screaming, followed by a snarling, spitting sound. Somebody gave a wild, anguished cry. There was a crash, a frantic scuffling. Possibly an animal, Justin thought, pounding upon its prey. But no. The cry he had heard had surely been made by a human voice. The first he had heard since entering the forest.

The snarl came again. Snatching the pistol from his belt, Justin ran forward. Forcing his way through a belt of close-growing trees, he came out into a small, sunlit clearing. The sight that met his eyes momentarily froze him. A boy was lying on the ground, his struggling body pinioned by a large animal. The boy held a knife grasped in his right hand, and with this weapon he was frantically stabbing at the animal in an effort to fight his way free.

In a lightning glimpse, Justin saw the blood upon the boy's face, his expression of horror. The sunlight glinted on the creature's tawny coat, on the sharply pointed yellow teeth in the huge, snarling mouth.

Bobcat, Justin thought, lifting the pistol. His hand trembled slightly as he aimed, and he steadied it quickly. It would be a poor lookout for him and the boy if he missed.

The bobcat, sensing the presence of another, turned its head. Its ears, lying flat to its head, twitched, and the glare in its slightly crossed amber eyes intensified. It screamed as the boy's knife pierced its hide. A blow from its paw disabled the boy, and it turned on the new menace, readying itself for the spring.

Justin felt a dryness in his throat. His finger tightened on the trigger, and the pistol exploded with a deafening roar. The tawny body of the animal lifted in the air, seemed to hang suspended for a moment, then crashed down and rolled over. One of its paws struck against the boy's foot, tearing a bloody track in the flesh. The snarl was still on the ferocious face as the eyes glazed in death.

"Got him, by Christ!" Wiping his damp forehead on his arm, Justin replaced the pistol in his belt. "Are you all right?" he said, going forward to assist the boy.

The boy ignored Justin's outstretched hand. Controlling his trembling mouth, he stared with expressionless eyes at the dead animal. Then, despising the aftermath of his fear, and hoping that the man had not marked it, he pulled his bleeding foot from beneath the paw and got shakily to his feet.

While he waited for the boy to speak, Justin examined him closely. Indian! He felt a slight quiver along his nerves. How strange that he, who had given thought to all the other perils that lay in wait for him in the forest, had not once thought of the menace offered by the Indians. So perhaps, in his well-meant rescue of this boy, he had found himself a new problem. To what tribe did the boy belong? Where were his people? He had the feeling that they would not be far from here. He looked at the boy's half-shaved head, the thick knot of hair over the right ear stuck through with three feathers, the fringed and beaded buckskins, and the chains of copper about his neck. "I asked you if you were all right," he said, breaking the silence. A sudden thought came to him. "But perhaps you do not understand my language?"

The boy's intense dark eyes met Justin's. "I understand you, white man. I speak your language well."

There was a tremble in the boy's voice that Justin did not fail to notice. "Everything is all right now," he said lightly. "You must not be afraid."

The boy's finely carved copper features froze into an expression of extreme hauteur. "I am as one with the beasts of this forest," he said coldly. "I do not fear them."

"No?" Justin nodded at the dead bobcat. "It would seem that this particular beast was not as one with you."

Color mounted beneath the clear copper skin, and the dark eyes flashed angrily. "Do not mock me!" He lifted his hand as Justin opened his mouth to speak. "Wait, please. I would thank you for saving my life." He hesitated, and then gravely inclined his head. "My name is White Bird."

The thanks seemed to Justin to be rendered so grudgingly that he could not help smiling. "Since it appears to pain you so much, White Bird," he said, laughing, "you need not thank me."

A prey to confusion, White Bird stared at him. Pained him? What did he mean? It was true that he had been angered because this strange man had mocked him, had seemed to note his fear and taunt him with it. He said stiffly, "You

are mistaken. It does not pain me. I owe you a debt of gratitude. That debt must be repaid."

Justin held out his hand. "Then all is well."

White Bird looked at the outstretched hand, his brows
meeting in a puzzled frown. What did the man want of him
now?

Seeing the frown, Justin understood. "You take my hand
and shake it," he said in a soft voice. "It is a sign of friendship."

The eyes in the swarthy face were as dark as his own,
White Bird thought. With his long, unbound hair, he had the
look of those Indian brothers who dwelled beyond the waterfall at the thick fork in the river. Yet this man was no Indian. He was white. He felt as he had felt when he had found
the woman. This man could not be his enemy. Seeing the
smile in the eyes regarding him so openly, he was further
reassured. His lips moved into an answering smile as he took
the hand and shook it. "I had not thought to hear a white
man call himself a friend of the Indian."

At the smile and the tone of the voice, Justin felt a subtle
easing of his tension. "You are hearing it now. Not all white
men look upon the Indian as an enemy, you know."

White Bird, for all his gravity of demeanor and his air of
being much older than his years, was very young and uncertain. He did not have the wisdom of those brothers who met
at the campfire in solemn discussion. He had never, like the
other young braves, painted himself for mock war against the
whites. Because of his lameness and his unfortunate frailty,
he had been despised by the young braves, and so, not being
allowed to join in their games, he had been forced to keep
much to himself. But he was much stronger now, he told
himself with a surge of pride, and his limp was scarcely de-
tectable. No doubt wisdom and the keen ability to see past
treachery and deceit would come with the years. He only
knew that this man with the smiling eyes, who, despite his
weary and battered appearance, had the proud, dark look of
an eagle, had clasped his hand in warm friendship, and that
he meant him well. He would be willing to stake his life on
that, for there had been something in the handclasp that had
sent a responsive tingle through him. Dropping the hand,
White Bird stepped back a pace and said in his grave voice,
"How may I repay my debt to you?"

Adapting himself to the moment, Justin answered in a voice just as grave, "Let there be no talk of repayment between us, White Bird. You may, however, if you care to do so, aid me in my search."

"Your search?"

Justin looked into White Bird's eyes. The thought that came to him then caused his heartbeat to quicken. Was it possible that Carrie had been captured by the Indians? It might well be so. It might even be that this young boy with his grave face and the first dawning of friendship in his eyes had had a hand in it. Because he was afraid of this new and alarming thought, he answered abruptly. "Yes. I am seeking a young white woman. I have traveled through this forest for many days, but I have not as yet come upon a sign of her."

A young white woman? White Bird's mouth went dry, and he felt a heaviness in the region of his heart. Was it Caroline for whom this man searched? Caroline, who even now awaited him in the secret cave. Her wounds had healed rapidly. And now, with each day that dawned, she spoke of going on her way. He did not like to hear her speak so. How could she talk so lightly and uncaringly of leaving him? What was this feeling he had for her, and how was it possible to feel so deeply for a mere female? He, who had been taught that females were unimportant, save in those instances of giving birth and looking to the comfort of the braves. Truly the woman had bewitched him. It was a grinding pain deep inside him that she was so willing to go. There were times when he longed to strike her for the hurt she had put inside him. He thought of her when she slept, and the agony to him when her lips would form that name. "Justin! Justin!"

When he sat there at the mouth of the cave, the flames of the fire warming him, his shameful tears would trickle hotly down his ravaged face. How he despised his tears! What anger the feel of them upon his face roused! A brave did not cry over a woman. It was unmanly, it was degrading to feel as he did. It was an outrage of everything he had been taught. But even so, weak and womanly as her presence had made him, he could not let her go. She knew nothing of his feelings for her. He had not dared—indeed he did not know how—to put them into words. So she did not know how much he longed to feel again the alien but strange sweetness of her lips against his. That caress had been given to him in delirium, he told himself bitterly. It had been meant for this man, this Justin, for whom she called in her sleep. Lip-to-lip! Whenever he thought of it, his heart shuddered, and then commenced to beat so hard that he feared it would burst from his body.

Only this morning, looking at him with her big, soft brown eyes, Caroline had said to him, "White Bird, you have been very kind to me, and I shall never forget you. But I cannot stay here. There are reasons. I must be on my way."

Reasons? What reasons? He longed to ask her, but he could not bring himself to do so. She would never forget him, she had said. A lie! He was not quite a fool, and he knew better. She could not wait to leave him. If she could, she would go, leaving him alone with this painful emotion that he did not understand. Bitterness rose, tingeing his words. "You will stay, woman," he had answered her harshly. "I, White Bird, say that you are not yet fit to travel."

She had said nothing to this, but there had been a look in her eyes that had disturbed him. He had longed to put his hand on her hair, to feel its warm silky strands cling to his fingers. But because he wanted to keep that trust and friendship she had so hesitantly given to him, he had made no move toward her. He had not told her that she would never be allowed to leave him. He had not said, as he longed to say, hoping to surprise a like emotion in her eyes, "When I have proved my manhood, when I have made my kill and can come to you in all honor, I will take you for my woman."

No, he had not said it. The shameful fear had stopped his mouth. He had been afraid that she would repulse him, laugh at him. And if she did that, he would be forced to kill her. How could a brave live with himself if he allowed a woman, his inferior, to laugh and make a mockery of his deep feelings? He would never allow her to leave him; he had sworn an oath. And now this man had come, this man whom he greatly feared might be the Justin for whom she called. If he were indeed the man, then he owed him a debt. If to find the woman was his heart's desire, he could not in honor repay the one who had given him back his life by refusing to let her go.

White Bird looked at Justin, and he did not know that

there were tears in his eyes. "Your name?" he said harshly. "What is your name?"

Those tears, so unexpected in the youth's fierce black eyes, moved Justin. Whatever he had been thinking of, it must be painful to cause him to look like that. As he might have done to Paul, he put out his hand in a gesture intended to comfort, but almost immediately he let it drop to his side. The lad was not Paul, he was a young Indian brave, and intuition told him that any attempt at comfort would be an outrage to his pride. "My name is Justin Lawrence," he said gently.

White Bird had been expecting this reply, but even so it hit him with the force of a blow. Justin! He had come for the woman! The hot blood of jealousy rushed into his face, and his dimmed eyes awoke to a dangerous and flaming life. His hand hovered over the tomahawk in his belt, and the almost overpowering temptation came to him to snatch it out and bring it down on the man's head. He conquered the impulse, and it seemed to him to be the hardest thing he had ever done. Despite the surging of mingled sorrow and fury inside him, he felt a faint flicker of pride at his self-control. It was only right, of course, he assured himself, it was only just that this man should claim his woman. He had always known she belonged to another, to this Justin. Again he forced himself to remember the debt he owed to the man. Had he not been taught that debts must always be repaid? It was the way of the Indian. The only honorable way. White Bird drew in a deep shuddering breath and turned away abruptly. "I know of this woman you seek," he said. "I will take you to her. Come with me."

Justin could not move for a moment. He would take him to the woman he sought! Had he actually heard those words? He felt like shouting aloud with joy. Was it Carrie? Dear God, let it be her! On the heels of his joy, doubt came. No, he must not allow himself to hope too much. The disappointment would be the more bitter. He forced out words. "The woman I seek is called Caroline."

White Bird did not turn. A quiver went through him, and then his shoulders stiffened. He nodded his head, the feathers in his knot of hair swaying with the movement. "The woman is called so," he said in a harsh but carefully controlled voice. "Come."

Justin had heard many tales of Indian savagery, but at the

moment these were far from his mind. Had he been thinking clearly, it might have occurred to him to wonder if he was being led into a trap. But he could think only of Carrie. His Carrie! Without a word, he followed after White Bird.

Standing at the mouth of the cave, Caroline saw them coming. White Bird, the feathers in his hair vivid in the sunlight, the copper chains about his neck a bright dazzle. And another. A tall, lean, sun-browned man, with long untidy black hair that touched his broad shoulders. He staggered slightly, as though with a great weariness, but he nonetheless still managed to imbue his walk with that lithe, easy grace that could belong to only one person.

"Justin!" His name burst from Caroline's lips. She did not ask herself how he could possibly be here; she only knew that he was. The miracle for which she had prayed every night had happened. For a moment she felt too weak to move. Then, joy strengthening her, she went flying down the rough stony incline toward him. "Justin!" Her arms were outstretched. "Oh, Justin!"

White Bird saw the radiance of her face, the way her eyes looked into the night-dark eyes of the man. He saw their bodies pressed hungrily together, molded, as if they sought to become one body. Their lips met and clung with hunger.

Heartsick, White Bird looked away. Lip-to-lip. The words danced in his mind. That strange caress, which he, having once experienced, had so hungered for, she was giving to another. Savage instincts stirred. Then, as he listened to the words they spoke, the impulse toward violence died. Caroline had already forgotten him, he thought drearily. They had both forgotten him.

"Carrie, my love!" Justin's hands cradled Caroline's face. His lips touched her forehead and traced their way down to her lips.

"I love you!" Caroline said when she had recovered the breath to speak.

"And I love you. God knows I do! But I've been such a damned fool, Carrie!"

"No, no!"

His laughter had a shaken sound. "You say that now. But if I know my Carrie, when sanity returns to you, you will accuse me of that very thing."

"No, darling, never!" Putting her hands on the tangled curls of his hair, she looked at him with tender eyes. "You don't look a bit like my elegant Rogue Lawrence. You look disgraceful."

"Rogue Lawrence is dead. He will never return."

"Never?"

"Would you have that heedless, selfish fool back again?"

"You are too hard on him, my darling. He was a thief and a rogue, but he was so charming."

"You must content yourself with the charm of Justin Lawrence, reformed profligate."

"Reformed? I wonder." Laughing, she shrugged. "Oh, well, if I must, then so I will."

He hugged her close. "I love you so much, Carrie. I have, from the beginning. Only, I was too stupid to know it."

She smiled. "Yes, love, you were."

"So you are beginning to agree? I thought you would." Justin clamped her waist between his hands. Lifting her, he swung her about. "What a life we shall have together, Carrie! I will make sure that Markham never finds us."

Caroline's face sobered. "Markham! Seeing you again, I had forgotten about him. So we are to be fugitives again. Oh, Justin, will we ever be safe and free?"

"Yes, Carrie, yes. We will make our own freedom."

"Will we? I hope so! Why must we always live with a shadow over us? It was so in England. Is it to be the same here?"

He caught her fingers and squeezed them tightly. "Trust me. I won't let you down."

"I know it, love!" She said it fervently, out of the depths of her love for him, but her eyes were somber. "Where will we go?"

He laughed, caught up on a surge of excitement. "Someplace. Anywhere! Think of the choice that lies before us. Oh, Carrie, this America is in my blood. We will build, we will grow. We can become anything we want to be!"

White Bird heard her laughter join with the man's, and he heard her laughter die. Looking at her quickly, he saw that the shadow that had been in her voice was now on her face. "There are so many dangers to be faced, Justin." Caroline's voice trembled. "There is so much that we do not know."

"We will learn, never fear. Carrie, you would not let me down? Where is your spirit of adventure?"

"Let you down?" Caroline's voice was outraged. "Never! I am fully as adventurous as you."

"Bah! You are a frightened child."

"How dare you! I will show you, Rogue Lawrence. You will see!"

For a moment White Bird was puzzled by the heat in her voice, and then he saw the deep love in her eyes. Truly these white people were strange. It would seem that they said one thing but meant another. He frowned thoughtfully. Since he could not in honor claim the woman, should he help them? He knew the forest. He knew all the trails and where they led. He waited, letting the generous impulse develop and grow. Warmed by it, feeling a subtle lightening of his heart, he said abruptly, "I will help you. You need not fear."

Caroline started at the sound of his voice, and White Bird knew then that she had indeed forgotten his presence. Yet, oddly, he felt no bitterness. He was paying a debt. He had relinquished her.

"White Bird!" Caroline turned shining eyes upon him. "But what can you do? How can you help us?"

"I have heard your conversation," White Bird said gravely. "I know that you run from a danger. I know this feeling, for are not my people endangered by the white man?"

Before the bleak look in White Bird's eyes, Justin flushed. "Yes, perhaps," he said in a low voice. "But you must believe that we are not your enemies, White Bird."

"I do believe it. For if I did not, I would kill you where you stand. I would not offer you my help."

"But how can you help?" Caroline said again.

"In many ways." White Bird's head lifted proudly. "First, I will lead you from the forest, for there is no part of it that is not known to me. I know, too, the lands that lie to the north, the south, the east, and the west. You have but to follow me, and I will lead you away from this danger that you fear. Perhaps, when I have seen you safely on your way, it may be possible for you to keep this danger from entering your lives again."

"It may be so," Caroline said. "We will try to live free and proud, as you do." She took a step toward him. "Thank you!

You have been so good to me. Without your help, I would have died."

The sternness in White Bird's face made it look like a carved copper mask. Caroline sensed that in some way he had withdrawn himself from her. She hesitated, but only for a moment. He was an Indian, and alien to her, but he was also a young boy who had been kind to her. She put her arms about his neck and kissed him softly on his mouth. "I shall never forget you!"

White Bird stood very still, letting the magic of the strange caress flow through him. Without willing it, his thoughts turned to the maiden Sparkling Lake. Like himself, Sparkling Lake was looked upon as an outcast. He, because of his frailty of body, and she, because a white man had sired her. The white man had long since returned to his native land, but the mother's crime of lying with a white man had been turned upon the daughter. But Sparkling Lake walked proudly, knowing no shame, for she was proud of her white blood. She liked to call herself by the name her English father had given her, Lianne.

Standing there, unconscious of Caroline's eyes upon him, White Bird, in his mind, also called her Lianne. He remembered that she had been kind to him when others had not. She had shown him sympathy in his isolation. And even more important, she had looked at him with the soft slumberous eyes of desire. Desire! White Bird's heart began a faster beating. He would seek out Lianne. He would put his lips to hers in the way of the white man. Perhaps she would fight him, but he did not think so.

"White Bird?" Caroline said anxiously.

White Bird stepped away. "It is well," he said. He looked at Justin. "The man is wearied," he said accusingly. "Why do you stand here, woman? You must take him to the cave, for is it not the duty of a squaw to soothe her man's weariness? In two days' time I shall return. Be ready."

White Bird turned away. "Wait!" Caroline's voice halted him.

He turned back to her, his face impassive. "Yes?"

Caroline looked at the blood on his face; her eyes fell to his torn foot. "You are hurt," she said. She smiled at him. "It is my turn now to help you."

White Bird thought again of Lianne, and he was filled with

an impatience to be gone. He made a dismissing gesture. "It is nothing, woman."

"Don't say that it is nothing. You must be in pain."

"I have said it is nothing." White Bird drew himself up and looked at her arrogantly. "I have spoken, and there is no more to be said."

"But—"

"Silence! A whining woman displeases me."

Justin laughed outright at the outrage in Caroline's face. His smiling eyes met White Bird's. "Well-spoken, lad," he said softly. "You have the right idea. It has always been my contention that a woman should be kept in her place."

"But naturally." White Bird looked faintly puzzled. "What other way is there?"

"Well!" Caroline exclaimed. "We shall see about that, Rogue Lawrence!"

"All women, except mine, of course," Justin said in a low voice, smiling at her.

"Liar!" Caroline tossed her head. "You will not rule me. We will do everything together, but you shall not rule me."

White Bird waited for Justin's smile to fade. When it did not, he said in a shocked voice, "The woman has defied you. She has raised her voice in anger. You must beat her. A man must be supreme in his own lodge."

"I will think on it." Once more Justin held out his hand to White Bird. "My thanks to you," he said.

White Bird looked into the man's eyes, which, in their darkness, were so like to his own, and he felt a curious sense of kinship with him. This time there was no hesitation on his part. He took Justin's hand and gripped it strongly. "I am happy that I have repaid my debt to you, white man. Honor is satisfied. You gave me back my life. I have restored to you your woman. It is well."

He dropped Justin's hand and turned away. He did not look back as he put distance between them.

Justin lay on the spread bearskin, another skin covering his nakedness. His eyes were closed, and he looked relaxed and peaceful. He had slept for a long time, the sleep of deep exhaustion. At intervals he had awakened. In those intervals, through the fog that still held him, he would see Caroline's smiling face. Murmuring incoherently, he would hold her close to him and kiss her. But soon, the exhaustion still stalking him, he would fall asleep again.

Sitting beside him, her arms hugging her knees, Caroline waited impatiently for him to awaken. She had let him sleep, knowing how unutterably weary he was. But now, she told herself firmly, he had slept long enough. The hours were slipping by, and tomorrow morning would see the return of White Bird.

She put out a hand and touched him tenderly. In sleep he looked much younger. The harsh lines of suffering beside his mouth, put there by the death of Paul, had smoothed themselves out. Whatever he was dreaming of must be pleasant, she thought, for there was a faint smile on his lips. Staring at his lean brown face, the thick dark circles of his lashes, the crisp curling of the black hair over his slightly damp forehead, she was suddenly hot with desire.

"Justin!" Leaning over him, she kissed his lips. She saw his lashes flutter, but his eyes did not open.

"Justin!" her voice rose impatiently. "Wake up, you cursed sluggard!"

His eyes remained closed, but the smile on his lips was more pronounced. "Prettily spoken," his soft, drawling voice said. "To hear you, one might almost believe you to be a woman in love."

Caroline laughed. "Oh, you! How long have you been awake?"

"Long enough, my lass. But I thought if I said nothing that I could lie here and watch you in your frustration." His eyes opened abruptly, and she saw the smile in them as he said sternly, "Have you no decency? Must you sit there like a strumpet and ogle me so lewdly?"

"Fool! Your conceit is as big as ever." She threw herself upon him and kissed him passionately. "No, Rogue Lawrence, you have not changed. Why, damn your mangy hide, you've not changed one whit!"

He held her away from him. "And neither have you, Carrie, love. You are as romantic and as ladylike as ever in your speech." His grip tightened. "Don't struggle. White Bird has said that it is not a woman's place to struggle, but to submit. Now, then, say it quickly. What is it you want of me?"

"I won't."

"You will. Say it, woman!"

A flush rose in her face, and her eyes dropped. "You," she whispered. "Only you!"

"Then we are in accord, for I want you, love." His bantering manner dropped from him. "I give you a choice," he said unevenly. "Either undress yourself, or I will do it for you."

She looked up and stared into his eyes. She had longed for this moment, dreamed of it, but now, unaccountably, she was suddenly painfully shy. "I . . . I will do it," she stammered.

He caught her to him as she made to rise. "You are blushing like a schoolgirl, my Carrie." He touched her cheek. "Your cheeks burn my fingers with their heat."

"You . . . you said that to me once before. Do you remember?"

"I remember. Only, then you were a stranger to love. What now? Must I woo you all over again?"

"Would you?"

"Yes, if necessary. I think, after all, that I will undress you."

Caroline was very still as his cool fingers touched her flesh. She was remembering that other time when she, raw and ignorant of the tenderness that could be brought to love, hating all men because of the memory of her hated husband, had been taken by this man. This beloved man! He had forced her to become a woman, and in doing so, had led her into a new world, and the deepest and most wonderful experience of her life. And now it was to happen again.

She was trembling violently when he stripped the last of her clothing away, threw it from him, and then drew her down beside him. She closed her eyes as his hands began to caress her. His lips touched her breasts, lingering there. His lips traveled lower, kissing every part of her body, sending little shocks of hot delight through her. She began to move restlessly, longing to feel him inside her. A quivering moan escaped her lips. Her hands moved, touching him, urging him on. "I love you, Justin, so very much!"

"Carrie! Carrie!" She saw his eyes for a fleeting moment, blazing with dark fire, loving her, wanting her, matching her own hunger. "Are you ready, my love?"

She could not speak, she could only nod. For a moment he was still against her, his body crushing hers, and she welcomed the weight of him, the burn of his flesh. Then he raised himself. She felt his hands on her thighs, gently parting them, the heart-jolting shock of his entry. At first their joining was as gentle as his touch, and it was as though he feared hurting her. But she did not want gentleness. She wanted the explosive violence, the force of that first time. Her legs had been clamped about his waist, but now they moved upward to circle his neck and gripped tightly. She felt his shuddering as her body arched to meet his, jerked, urged, met his rhythm and matched it. He took her then with that blending of tenderness and sweet savagery that was so uniquely his. He lifted her to the heights, and the beating of her heart almost choked her. Then, passion spent, they went sliding down into the peace of perfect completion and momentarily appeased hunger.

Long after Justin had fallen asleep, Caroline still held him tightly to her, his dark head resting heavily against her breast. It had all been worth it, she thought, everything they had suffered, for it had led them to this moment.

Caroline's arms tightened fiercely about him. He was hers! He loved her now without reservation. They had traveled a long hard road, but they were together now, and nothing must ever part them again. Here, in America, they would make their home. They would put down roots, and their love would deepen and strengthen with the years.

She thought of Tobias Markham, and her eyes grew dark and brooding. He would not let them go easily, not if she knew him. He would continue to search for his fugitives.

Justin stirred, and she kissed his ruffled dark hair. Let him search, she thought. But I will kill him before I let him part us again!

White Bird made his way up the stony incline to the cave. The sun had already risen. It was time to go. Reaching the entrance of the cave, he stooped and looked inside. He saw that the man lay in the woman's arms, one hand touching her soft breast. They were both sleeping soundly.

White Bird looked at the bright trailing of the woman's hair, and he still thought it akin to a spill of sunlight. His eyes faintly wistful, he averted them. Straightening, he turned away. The sun grew hot. They must be roused.

White Bird picked up a handful of stones. One by one he began tossing them down the incline. The rattle of the stones would surely awaken them and alert them to his presence.

His quick ears caught a stirring in the cave, and he smiled to himself. Soon they would be on their way. The sooner the better, for he ached to be with Lianne.

He threw the last stone down the incline. Lianne, too, would be impatiently awaiting his return. Perhaps it was her white blood stirring in her veins, but she had responded passionately to the pressure of his lips on hers. Lip-to-lip. In this, at least, the white man's way was good. It created a fire in the loins. It was good. Very good. He turned his head, frowning toward the mouth of the cave. Of a certainty, he had no time to waste.

About the Author

Constance Gluyas was born in London where she served in the Women's Royal Air Force during World War II. She started her writing career in 1972 and since then has had published several novels of historical fiction. She presently lives in California where she has just finished writing a sequel to SAVAGE EDEN.

More Big Bestsellers from SIGNET.

☐ **THE OMEN** by David Seltzer. (#W7065—$1.50)

☐ **SANDITON** by Jane Austen and Another Lady.
(#J6945—$1.95)

☐ **PHOENIX ISLAND** by Charlotte Paul. (#J6827—$1.95)

☐ **ALLEGRA** by Clare Darcy. (#W6860—$1.50)

☐ **THE HUSBAND** by Catherine Cookson.
(#W6990—$1.50)

☐ **THE LONG CORRIDOR** by Catherine Cookson.
(#W6829—$1.50)

☐ **THE SAMURAI** by George Macbeth. (#J7021—$1.95)

☐ **THE PLACE OF STONES** by Constance Heaven.
(#W7046—$1.50)

☐ **PLAYING AROUND** by Linda Wolfe. (#J7024—$1.95)

☐ **DRAGONS AT THE GATE** by Robert Duncan.
(#J6984—$1.95)

☐ **WHERE HAVE YOU GONE JOE DI MAGGIO?** by Maury
Allen. (#W6986—$1.50)

☐ **KATE: The Life of Katharine Hepburn** by Charles Higham. (#J6944—$1.95)

☐ **THE WORLD FROM ROUGH STONES** by Malcolm Macdonald. (#J6981—$1.95)

☐ **TREMOR VIOLET** by David Lippincott.
(#E6947—$1.75)

☐ **THE VOICE OF ARMAGEDDON** by David Lippincott.
(#W6412—$1.50)

THE NEW AMERICAN LIBRARY, INC.,
P.O. Box 999, Bergenfield, New Jersey 07621

Please send me the SIGNET BOOKS I have checked above. I am
enclosing $_____(check or money order—no currency
or C.O.D.'s). Please include the list price plus 35¢ a copy to cover
handling and mailing costs. (Prices and numbers are subject to
change without notice.)

Name_____

Address_____

City_____State_____Zip Code_____
Allow at least 4 weeks for delivery